To Catch the Wind

BOOK ONE OF THE NW WIND SERIES

CHARLI WEST

Revised Edition

ISBN: 978-0-578-92317-8
Library of Congress Control Number: 2021910710

Charli West
To Catch the Wind
1. Oregon Trail; 2. Romance; 3. Emigration; 4. History
Book Design: Trish Karlsen
Cover Design: Rachel Wetten

Charli West
Central Oregon Coast
charliwestnw@gmail.com

Dedication

To my husband, Jeff. Through everything life throws at us, you are still the love of my life, the person I want to share everything with.

To Melisa, Spencer, and Michelle and your wonderful mates. May you always find the romance and make a rich history for yourselves.

To Trish, the wonderful friend who kept at me to finish this story. The friend who believed in me and told me to get it done because she needed to know how it ends. Thank you.

Acknowledgement

The author wishes to thank the following people
for their contributions to the novel.

Kathy Weiser-Alexander and the research she had done from the Bureau of Land Management, List Verse, Oregon-California Trail Association and Oregon History Project.

Evan Andrews and his information found online at "9 Things You May Not Know About the Oregon Trail."

Rachel Wetten for her beautiful cover work.

Melisa Cruce for my beautiful logo.

Trish Karlsen for all of her amazing technical support.

The teachers in my formative school years who taught their subject well. The names have been forgotten but their love of history was instilled in me and appreciation is still there.

Preface

My curiosity and preoccupation with the Oregon Trail began in my junior high days. It had always intrigued me that people would leave behind their families and friends to travel to a distant land—a land brimming and overflowing with opportunities, yes—but, also brimming and overflowing with dangers and with no guarantee that you and the people traveling with you would even make it there together. It was a journey full of promises and dreams, but only if you were successful in the more than 2,000-mile trek.

History is sprinkled with many names of those who took that journey with wagons. Trappers, traders, and soldiers traversed across the Continental Divide, but it was missionary Marcus Whitman and his family who are credited with opening up the possibilities of settling in the Oregon country to an ever-growing number of people who wanted what the land had to offer.

Hundreds of thousands took to the trail in hopes of something better, seeking dreams. It was no easy task by any means. It meant five to six months on the trail. Thousands and thousands died along the way. Diseases like cholera, dysentery, and smallpox were common. There there were the snake bites, just plain and simple inexperience, exhaustion, being crushed by wagon wheels, drowning in rivers, and dying from the accidental shootings that took the lives of many more. Hostile Native Americans occasionally attacked and either killed everyone or took some back as slaves or to integrate into their tribes, quite often women and children. But, it is interesting to note that more often than not, the Native Americans were helpful as opposed to being hostile. Some of the pioneers trusted unreliable guidebooks, or decided to find their own way only to end up lost. If a group waited too long in the season to start traveling, or took too many months along the trail, they risked getting caught in early snow and could freeze or starve to death, as in the case of the Donner party of 1846-1847.

The valleys, plains, rivers, and mountains all had their unique challenges and dangers. For instance, near the end of the trail at what was called Laurel Hill, Barlow Road was a descent of some 2000 feet. In order to do that with a wagon, chains and ropes would be tied off to trees along the way in order to keep the wagons from running away from them and crashing over some cliff or into trees. It was long and tedious, and any impatience or misstep could result in injury or death.

Or, if you just didn't really want to take your wagon down such a steep hill, you could disassemble your wagon and load it onto a large raft and pay to float it down the Columbia River. The Columbia River Gorge is known for strong winds and was treacherous at best. So the choices for the final leg of an already exhausting journey were only two—both being extremely dangerous.

In the midst of all of those dangers, all of those challenges, and all of those worries were all of the dreams and hopes and courage needed to forge a new life. In the middle of all of those and more I set the stage for "real" people, or at least the possibility of real people. Individuals, couples, and families who were looking for something better, perhaps escaping, maybe even running away from something, and in some cases, running to something. Men and women who had the heart and the courage, whether forced because of their circumstances or freely given, to look ahead at possibilities along with a fortitude, a lot of muscle, and a whole lot of determination. It's in this setting that I introduce men and women finding love, finding redemption, finding forgiveness, and finding, at the end of the day, peace and life—a beginning and an end.

Please join me in the Oregon Trail NW Wind Series as I introduce Book One with Lynn and Ben's story. We will find others along the way worthy of a story of their own.

—Charli West

Chapter 1

Independence, Missouri

April 26th, 1844

"Licorice"

Ben leaned his large frame against the rough-hewn log beam that divided the many-colored bolts of material from the tools. After pushing his hat further back on his head causing a thick lock of dark hair to fall across his forehead, he crossed first his arms against his broad chest and then his booted feet at the ankles. He listened patiently as the shopkeeper, Leonard Skeeley, explained once again to the plump woman standing at the counter why he was out of flour

"I'm sorry, Mrs. Adamson, but, you know that a wagon train is leaving again tomorrow. They bought up everything I have. I don't expect another shipment of supplies for two days."

Ben smiled as the woman wailed something about children to feed and she only had a couple of cups of flour left. He was about to offer her two or three pounds out of his own stock on the wagon when Leonard decided he would do the same himself.

As Leonard opened the door behind him that led to his living quarters, the door of the store opened and a young woman with three little children walked in. She had a baby in her arms while a little boy of about four years old held the hand of a curly-headed little girl, obviously just learning how to walk. As soon as the door closed behind them, the little boy let the toddler walk by herself.

Ben's dark brown eyes twinkled with amusement as he watched the wobbly steps of the little girl slowly bring her over in front of him. She was watching her feet and the floor, not really seeing where she was going. When boots suddenly appeared in front of her, she stopped and looked up. Tipping her head back to see the very large man in front of her made her lose her balance, and down she went on her diapered bottom to the heavy wooden planked floor.

Ben squatted on haunches to pick her up. When he held out hands to do so, she looked at him uncertainly for a moment, then smiled, showing off three little white teeth. He stood after picking her up, and she studied him for another long moment before shoving her hand into his shirt pocket searching around inside.

"I'm so sorry, Sophia always does that with her daddy. He usually has something in his pocket for the children when he comes home from work every day. I'm so sorry." The young mother looked horrified as Sophia continued to fish around in Ben's pocket for something interesting. She held out a hand to take the little girl.

Ben laughed as her small fist pushed the bottom of the pocket, searching into the corners. "It's quite alright, ma'am. I have a little niece who is always hoping for goodies, too. You have beautiful children, ma'am." He glanced at the other two. Someday he would have his own—someday.

Leonard had returned and was finished with the other woman. Ben walked over to him, still holding Sophia.

"Leonard, I bet that you could find two pieces of licorice back there somewhere, couldn't you?" It was a request more than a question, and Leonard smiled as he reached for a large jar behind him. Ben laid the penny on the counter. Picking up the licorice, he handed one to the little boy and stuck the other one in his pocket. Sophia looked at the top of the licorice sticking out of the pocket and giggled before pulling it out and immediately sticking one end in her mouth.

"Thank you very much, sir. You didn't have to do that." The young woman smiled thankfully even as she nudged the young boy at her side.

"Yes, sir, thank you." He nodded politely.

"Sophia, what do you tell the gentleman? Remember, say thank you." The woman pulled the hand with licorice away from the little girl's mouth for a second.

Sophia looked at her mother and then at Ben. "'Anku.'" Immediately back to the mouth went the hand with the licorice. Ben laughed at her childish talk and set her down on the floor.

"You're welcome, both of you. You be good for your mama, now, y'hear?" He tousled the boy's hair as he nodded, and Sophia noisily sucked on her candy.

"Ben, I have your order ready except for that extra rifle you wanted. I don't have it." Leonard started setting boxes on the counter for Ben to examine.

"That's alright, Leonard. I'll go down to Bert's and see if he has one. This all looks good." He grabbed a box and headed for the door to load it in the buckboard. These would be the last of the supplies he needed for the trip to Oregon.

Chapter 2

"Escape"

Lynn tilted her head back and slowly opened her eyes. It took a moment to focus on the room that shifted back and forth. Finally, she could see the bed in front of her and the dresser right beside her. When she hit the wall, she must have been knocked unconscious. She was in the corner between the bureau and the window. As she sat there for a few more seconds she became aware of a throbbing pain in her temple and sharp pains in her side. She knew instantly what the pains in her side indicated; her ribs were probably bruised again, if not cracked. It wasn't the first time he had broken ribs, so she was familiar with the pain. Her fingers shook as she gently searched her temple for the bump that was surely there. When her fingers brushed across dried blood down the right cheek, she glanced out of the window at the sun which was much lower in the sky. By the slant of dusty light that angled through the glass, she figured she must have lain there for about an hour. The shadows indicated that it was around seven o'clock.

She gasped from the sharp pain in her ribs as she struggled to grasp the edge of the bureau to pull herself up. Only getting as far as her knees, she paused for a few minutes to catch her breath. Then, with her left arm holding her side, she managed to stand up and step around to the front of the bureau to gaze into the mirror. The young woman who peered back at her was a sorry sight. Her right eye was blackening and the bump on her temple had a cut on one side that had allowed blood to trickle down her cheek then drip down onto the bodice of her pale pink dress. Her hair was tangled and wild around her shoulders. He had slapped her several times in the face before resorting to using his fist on her ribs and then her face. Her lower lip was split and swollen and had also trickled blood.

As she lifted her hand to her face again she noticed that her hand, too, was red and swollen. It was always a mistake to try to protect her face; he had hit her hands several times before pulling them down in front of her. She was not the pretty young woman of two and a half years ago who had smiled and laughed and had found humor in almost everything. Tears trickled down both cheeks as the realization of what she had become struck her so fully she was suddenly gasping for air as she sobbed. Fear had become a way of life for her—fear and trembling. She had become a mouse of a woman. A woman who feared people looking at her and feared looking at people, just knowing that if they looked very long they would see her life behind the walls. They would see the secret that held her captive to a man's cruelness and possession.

After stripping off the dress very slowly, holding her side as she did, she washed her face carefully with the cool water that was still in the basin and then undressed and climbed into the large bed. He wouldn't return for a couple of days; he never did after these incidents. Instead, he would be out gambling, drinking, and womanizing with little thought or concern whether or not she lived or died.

Sleep didn't come for quite a while because her mind was busy going over options and chances. She knew that she had to leave, having given much thought to how she could do so for several months. If she was ever to enjoy life without fear; or maybe even continue living, an escape was necessary. Jared, having made the decision to come here to Independence for a while, put another option before her. There was a wagon train leaving in two days. But, how could she take a wagon by herself? And she didn't know anyone going whom she could, perhaps, go with. To return east would be a mistake since that would be the first place Jared would go to find her. Any towns near enough he would be sure to find her in, also. The wagon train seemed to be the only choice, and yet, she had little money and wondered if she could even buy all of the things needed if she did. She knew that the people going on the wagons were buying everything in sight to take with them. New supplies came into town almost daily, but, as fast as they arrived, they disappeared. The last clear thought on her mind before she drifted slowly and painfully to sleep was that she had to get away from Jared before he killed her.

Chapter 3

"Sad goodbyes"

The sun slanted brightly through the window when she awoke the next morning. She turned over slowly and sat on the edge of the bed still grasping her side. The pain in her temple had subsided, but, the pain in her side was still sharp. With slow steps, she made her way to the bureau. A self-examination in the mirror this morning wasn't any better than last night. Instead of just black and gray, the color around the outer edges of her eye was now a deep purple. At least the cut on her temple was no longer seeping; instead, a tenuous scab had formed there as well as on her lip. However, when she tried smiling wryly at herself, the lip split afresh.

Looking at herself in the mirror was almost painful and she turned toward what little water was still left in the basin. She jumped violently when a light knock sounded on the door.

"Lynn, gal, ya in there? Please, Lynn, let me in." It was Maggie's soft voice. Maggie was the owner of the hotel and had become a good friend to Lynn in the three months that Jared and she had stayed there. Having helped with Lynn's wounds several times she was always on the lookout for Jared to warn Lynn ahead of time, if possible, of his return. Last night, she had gone to her sister's house for supper and to see her new niece. Kyle, her nephew by her older brother, had probably told her about the commotion last night that told a sad story.

"Yes, Maggie, just a moment." Lynn started towards the door and then realized that she had gone to bed last night and hadn't even locked it. "Come in, the door isn't locked." She stood for a moment holding her arm firmly against her side as she waited for Maggie to come in. Pain and a measure of embarrassment lined her eyes as she watched the tall, stocky woman enter, look at Lynn's condition, and then put her hand over her mouth in disbelief.

"Oh, honey, I'm so sorry." She gasped as she shook her head. "You've got to get away from that man before he kills ya." Maggie returned to the door to talk to someone just outside. "Quickly bring some water, Kyle, for Lynn's bath." After closing the door softly behind her, she spun around to survey the room and then gaze worriedly at Lynn.

Lynn sighed heavily, slowly shaking her head. "I know, Maggie. I have been thinking that for a long time, but I have few options. The only choice I really have is to go on the wagon train leaving soon, either tomorrow or the next day I believe. I don't have much money and I don't have any idea how I would get everything together that quickly, anyway." Lynn rubbed a hand across her eyes and sat down on the bed with her head back looking up at the ceiling. "I do have a necklace and brooch that had been my mother's, but I really hate to sell it. It is the only thing I have left because Jared has taken everything else and sold it. He doesn't know I have these. I always wanted to pass them on to my own daughter someday. Plus, the other day I overheard a couple of men saying that the wagon train is buying everything in town—it's hard even to buy flour or molasses. Besides, I seriously doubt the jewelry would bring enough money to buy everything needed for such a trip." Her eyes saddened at the thought of her mother and the husband who had loved her so dearly. Anna Helton died of rheumatic fever when Lynn was only seven years old. Her father, Matthew, had died a few months later. Her grandmother had said it was from a broken heart. He had adored his lovely wife and even the love of his young daughter could not make up for the loss of his beloved wife. Lynn's grandmother and grandfather had raised her on their little farm. Her grandfather was a doctor, and when Lynn got older she would accompany him on house calls at times. Those opportunities resulted in her learning empathy and kindness, and people enjoyed having her ready smile and helping hand.

"Why don't you let me see if I can get anything for the jewelry, honey? I think your mama would want ya to live and have a chance of having a daughter someday. The way you're living right now, ya may not see another month, let alone a daughter." Maggie picked up the torn dress and was taking the basin of water with her to the door. "I'll be back in a minute and I'll bring the tub so that ya can wash up proper like." Quietly opening the door, she left the room quickly and left Lynn alone to think.

By the time she returned a few minutes later with a washtub in tow and Kyle following closely behind with hot water, Lynn had retrieved the jewelry from its hiding place and held it out to Maggie with tears in her eyes.

Kyle took one look at her face and flushed angrily. He was a tall, young man of seventeen and came to live with his Aunt three years ago when his folks had died in a wagon accident. He was a great help to her and was usually very talkative. Lynn was aware that he had a boyish crush on her and was always kind and friendly towards him. He had blue eyes that danced when he laughed and unruly blonde hair. His body was at that gangly stage that made him at times appear awkward, but he had a man's large hands and feet already and his shoulders had started to widen holding the promise of strength.

Lynn turned away from Kyle's angry face, shame warming her cheeks that he was seeing her like this. Maggie set the tub down in the middle of the room and now Kyle poured the hot water into it. He left only to return a couple of minutes later with two more buckets of hot water. One more trip downstairs and he now returned with one bucket of hot water and one bucket of cold.

"Kyle is going to go see about getting things for a wagon ready. I'm afraid you may be right about trying to find anything at this late date, but I figure it is certainly worth a try. I'll go and see if I can get some money for these." Maggie held up the necklace and brooch. "Oh, I was thinking that a woman going alone on the train would be impossible, especially with you looking like that. People would talk, and word would get back to Jared quickly. I'll bring ya some men's clothing. Ya'll have to disguise yourself somehow." Maggie frowned slightly at the thought of Lynn trying to pass herself off as a man, but there really was no other way. People would ask questions and Jared would find her before they were even out of town.

"I agree. I've been thinking the same thing." Lynn was pulling off her stockings since Kyle had left the room and was anxious to sink her sore body into that hot water. Maggie stopped at the door for a moment to gaze at Lynn one more time before she left.

"Ah, honey, I'd like to kill that man myself." Lynn looked up to meet Maggie's angry brown eyes and worried face, but said nothing. What was there to say? When Maggie left and closed the door behind her, Lynn stood and walked over to the bureau.

She squinted at the reflection in the mirror; changes were needed. There was hesitation for a moment, but then she made a decision. Pulling open the third drawer of the bureau and crying quietly, she pulled the scissors out and cut her hair short. Her hair had once been so beautiful. She would brush the long, wavy tresses until they shone like burnished copper. It was dark, but, in the summer, she would spend hours out in the sun and it would turn a dark, rich auburn. It was only a little past her shoulders right now because several months ago Jared had become angry when some man commented on her beautiful hair, and so he had brought her back to their hotel room and had cut her hair shoulder length. He didn't want men looking too much at his lovely wife and yet he loved to show her off. He was a center of contradictions, and unfortunately, the contradictions usually resulted in Lynn's getting the angry slap of a hand or fist. Even a couple of times the razor strap or belt and once, a horsewhip.

When she was done, she looked with teary eyes at the hair on the bureau and floor and then slowly pulled off Jared's dressing robe and her chemise. She again turned to look in the mirror. Her body had always been slender and willowy, the envy of many young women of her acquaintance. Her breasts were small above a small waist, and she had slender hips and long legs. But, over the past two years, she had lost a lot of weight being always worried about Jared's mood for the day and her meals were not always regular. Jared would at times leave her to her own devices for two or three days at a time in a hotel room, for he would forbid her to leave it, and would not think of giving her money to buy food. There had been a few times when the owner of whatever hotel they were staying at would allow her to do a little mending or cleaning to earn a few cents to buy a meal. That is how she first became acquainted with Maggie.

Her wandering thoughts were brought back to the present when she heard the sound of a fight outside on the street. Hurriedly getting into the tub, she let the steaming water work wonders on her aching body. Reaching for the rose scented soap that Maggie had brought her, she hesitated, and grabbed instead the rough soap that Jared used when he bathed. It wouldn't do for her to smell like a woman while being dressed like a man. She would have trouble enough pulling this off if she could even get her hands on a wagon in the first place which the more she thought about it, the less likely it became. She tried to think of other options, but none came to mind.

Maggie knocked lightly a few minutes later bringing with her men's breeches, shirts, and some heavy socks. She showed Lynn the jacket, long underwear, and boots she had found somewhere. Then, she held an old oversized hat up in the air for Lynn's inspection.

"This should work perfect to help hide your face." Elation at finding such a prize made Maggie smile even though the circumstances surrounding the need for the hat were not a reason to be happy.

Lynn couldn't help but smile a little back, even though the movement caused her lower lip to hurt. Maggie spotted the hair on the floor and bureau and returned a moment later with a broom. After sweeping it up she turned to inspect the short hair now framing Lynn's poor bruised face. Sighing heavily, she tried to think positive.

Maggie frowned as she watched Lynn put a finger to her lip. "I'm sorry, honey. I'll just go now so's ya can get dressed. I'll return in a few minutes to see how you're faring. Besides, just as I was coming upstairs, I heard Kyle return. I want to go see what he found out about a wagon." Maggie hurried out of the room with a last worried glance behind her. She didn't want to tell Lynn, but the chances of finding a wagon and enough supplies were very slim although she knew that Lynn was already aware of that. As she left the room she was saying a prayer and trying to figure out another option should the need arise.

Lynn slowly rose from the water. It was starting to cool, and she knew she must finish quickly before she lost her nerve to continue in the direction she was headed, if indeed this direction was even going to work anyway. She dried off and then cut some strips of cloth that Maggie had brought to bind her ribs. It was a slow and painful process, but she had done this before and so knew what she was doing, all the while saying a prayer of thanks under her breath for the skills she had learned from her grandfather. She extended the bindings across her bosom also, being thankful for small breasts since they would be much easier to bind and hide than if she was well endowed.

The long underwear were scratchy, but the nights especially were still chilly and she knew that on the wagon she would want to stay warm. She pulled the heavy socks and then the breeches on, carefully tucking in the flannel shirt. Examining the hat for a moment before setting it upon her head, she pulled it low across her forehead. Looking at her appearance in the mirror, although she wasn't a very manly man, she certainly didn't look much like a woman, either. Being taller than the average woman, though, would certainly be a plus in favor of this disguise. Although, because her cheeks were smooth as a baby's bottom, they would probably think she was just a very young man and had just barely started adolescence. That would be a good thing; it would help explain her awkwardness and perhaps quietness.

Maggie knocked on the door and then entered again. Her voice bespoke her excitement. "Kyle said that when he went to Eb Price's store, he overheard him telling the smithy's wife that there was a family that decided that they wouldn't be able to go with the train and that they would sell all of the supplies—lock, stock, and barrel.

So, Kyle told Eb that he wanted to look over what was there and although he wouldn't want it all, that he definitely wanted the wagon, oxen, and supplies."

Lynn tipped her head to one side as she thought about what Maggie said. "I don't know how much the necklace and brooch will fetch yet and although I did find almost six hundred dollars that Jared hid in his chest, I know that can't be enough." Lynn's voice was quiet and cautious; how could she tell Maggie that she could go ahead and buy it when she didn't know how much it was going to cost her?

"Well, Eb said that he would take the jewelry in trade for it with an additional one hundred and twenty-five dollars. So, I gave the money to Kyle to give to him and so ya now have a wagon. I talked to the wagon master, Benjamin Alenson, and he wasn't none too happy having just you by yourself taking a wagon to Oregon. But, I told him that ya was goin' to live with your sister and her family. He seems a fair man but try to avoid him. I wouldn't want him angry with ya. He's a large man, kinda quiet spoken, but he makes his presence known."

Avoiding the wagon master would be a top priority as far as she was concerned. She would avoid him like the plague since the last thing she wanted was another man to contend with. She had seen him across the street a couple of weeks ago, and the only reason she knew who he was, is because Jared was cussing him. It seems that he had lost fifteen dollars to the big man a couple of evenings previous. The day she saw him he had been in deep conversation with a man about sawmill parts. He had glanced at her briefly, giving her a direct look up and down, smiled in appreciation, and then had turned his attention back to the conversation. Thank goodness Jared had not noticed the look he had given her; his attention had been elsewhere. Nope, not a problem, she would mind her own business and avoid him at all costs. Retrieving the money that she had found of Jared's she held it out to Maggie.

"Here, Maggie, I'll still owe you a lot, but I'll pay you back as soon as I can." Her voice was soft and low as she wondered how she was ever going to repay this woman for her kindnesses.

Maggie snorted and shook her head, "I don't want that. 'Sides, you're goin' to need that. Ya can't go on the train without money. There'll be things you'll have need of long before ya get to the Oregon country." She turned toward the door. "I'm going to send Kyle back up in a few minutes to get your trunk, so pack up whatever ya want. Ya need to eat something."

At the mention of food, Lynn suddenly realized how hungry

she was. As if reinforcing the thought, her stomach growled causing Maggie to turn back with a guilty expression.

"I'm so sorry, honey, I shoulda thought a long time ago that ya needed somethin' to eat. I was just so busy thinking how to get ya outta here before Jared comes back that I wasn't thinking about how hungry ya must be."

Lynn shook her head. "Don't worry about it because I wasn't thinking about food either, Maggie. I, too, have been thinking about how to leave by this afternoon or this evening at the latest." Worry creased her brow as the weight of this decision rested heavy upon her. She was taking her life in a direction that would change it forever and it scared her. There was also the reality that if Jared caught her, he would surely kill her this time. It also terrified her how she was ever going to manage a wagon and oxen all by herself. It would be difficult under normal circumstances but with her being injured how was she ever going to manage? But, her choices were almost zero, and this was probably going to be the only opportunity to escape for a long time. She said a brief prayer of thanks before she turned back to Maggie.

"I'll be ready in a few moments." A quick survey of the room was made to decide what to take with her. She couldn't very well leave the dresses here where Jared would see them when he returned, and yet the trunk only held so much. By the time she put the remainder of the men's clothes in it, there wasn't much room. Finally, she decided to take the pale blue dress and her favorite green one. After packing her stockings, chemise, and a few undergarments, her brush, and her shoes she closed the trunk. She looked at the hand mirror laying on top of the dresser. Picking it up she looked at herself in the glass. Frowning at the young woman who gazed back at her, she tossed it on the bed and decided she didn't want to see that reflection ever again. The next time she looked in a mirror, she wanted to see a reflection that would remind her of the young woman of two and a half years ago. She folded the other two dresses in her possession, the other old chemise, and two pairs of stockings, and then turned to go to the door just as a knock sounded. She would give them to Maggie to pass on to somebody who would be able to use them.

"Lynn? I'm here to get your trunk." It was Kyle trying to keep his strong, young voice low.

Upon entering, his eyes immediately went to her black eye and the bruise on her temple. She pulled the hat a little lower on her forehead. It almost covered her eyes when she tucked her chin just a little. Lynn smiled slightly, pointing to the trunk.

"I guess I'm ready, Kyle. Thank you for getting that for me." She walked out of the door as he grabbed the trunk, and then followed her after she quietly shut the door without so much as a backward glance. Walking slowly and carefully down the stairs while holding her side as she went, she caught the delicious smell of beefsteak and fried potatoes. Her stomach growled again, reminding her of how long it had been since she had eaten. Yesterday morning she and Jared had eaten bacon and eggs with bread and honey, but that had been the only food she ate all day. Jared had left for a few hours and then returned about three o'clock. Being in a good mood, he wanted to go out and eat at the restaurant down the street from the hotel. They hadn't gotten very far when he got angry at a couple of young men who had looked at her, and one of them drunkenly brushed against her. Jared blamed her because he said they wouldn't have done that if she didn't look so nice that afternoon. How do you explain that kind of reasoning? Lynn had never figured it out, but that was reason enough for the pain she was now experiencing.

Her thoughts came back to the present as she stepped into the kitchen and looked at the wonderful food that Maggie was just setting on the table. Lynn sat down at Maggie's urging to a thick beefsteak with fried potatoes, fresh bread slathered with butter, cherry preserves, and a cool cup of milk. Maggie set another plate down for Kyle and then finally sat down herself. She pushed back a few strands of hair from her face that had come loose from the neat bun at the nape of her neck. Her eyes took on a speculative gleam as she watched first Lynn, then Kyle, busy eating.

"I don't see how you're going to take a wagon by yourself. Now I know that ya have experience with buckboards and harnessing up horses and the like from your life on your grandparent's farm, but this is very different. So, I've been doing some thinking and Kyle should go with ya." Kyle paused briefly in chewing the bite of meat he had just put into his mouth, looking up with astonishment. He had been wanting to go west since the first time he saw a wagon train four years ago. Now hearing his aunt's words, disbelief and excitement filled his eyes. Lynn's hand stopped midway to her lips with the cup of milk as she turned to look at Maggie with disbelief in her dark eyes.

"I couldn't take Kyle from you, Maggie. I know the great help he is to you." She smiled slightly, set her cup back onto the table, and swung her hand in Kyle's direction. "How could you manage without him?" Just because she was unsure how she was going to manage, when you don't have a choice, you do what you have to do. Taking Kyle with her would be the answer to a prayer and yet how could she take away Maggie's help like that? It didn't seem fair. She already owed more than she would probably ever repay to this woman!

"I can manage just fine. I used to do fine without him before and although I will miss him greatly, ya need him far more than I do." She turned to Kyle, her mind already made up. "You go pack another trunk with your things." Turning back to Lynn, "I would go with ya myself, but, Jared would then figure out where ya went. Too many people know me and if I went on the train, they would tell Jared and he would know that ya were with me. But, if Kyle were to go, well..." She tapped her fingers against the table for a moment and then continued. "Jared barely knows that he exists, so he wouldn't think anything about it. And, if he did notice he was gone, I could always tell him that Kyle went to visit some relatives in New York for a couple months. My other brother lives there." Excitement lit her features, her mind was rushing ahead. "I'll come out next year after I sell this place and find the two of you and set up another hotel or something." Her face was getting more and more animated with each step of a plan.

Kyle had jumped out of his chair quickly and came back into the kitchen a few minutes later with another trunk loaded. With a rifle in his hand, he hurried around the small room grabbing this and that to add to the stash in the trunk. He stuffed the rest of the steak in his mouth and then disappeared out of the door to load it into the buckboard. After they ate, he would take their things down to the wagon. They would spend the night in the wagon because Ben Alenson, the wagon master, wanted to leave bright and early the next morning.

To all of Lynn's mild protests, Maggie had simply argued that Lynn needed Kyle much more than she did right now and that was that. Lynn finally conceded that it was truly wonderful to have Kyle's company and help, but she still felt bad about leaving Maggie without his assistance.

While he was gone, Lynn stayed busy helping Maggie, since she was confident that Jared wouldn't show up for at least another day. She felt nervous about not going out to the train earlier, but at the same time, it wouldn't be smart to be there too soon either. What if someone started asking questions? So, for now, staying out of sight in the hotel also kept her thoughts preoccupied, even though her insides felt ready to explode at any time just from the suspense. They did the dishes, then Lynn peeled apples for a pie. She and Maggie talked about the dangers of the trail and the people going to Oregon or California for a new way of life. Another box was packed with medicinal things that may be needed on the way. They talked about the kind of people who may be on the train and Maggie mentioned the possibility of Lynn finding a good man someday, but she shook her head at that thought. She had enough of men for a long time. Jared had put her through hell and she didn't even want to think about another man. Maggie tried to assure her that not all men were like Jared, but that thought did nothing to comfort Lynn. There were other things about marriage that she hated. The intimate part of marriage did nothing for her except bring discomfort and fear, making her dread it when Jared made those demands upon her. No, she definitely didn't want any man! Her biggest regret, however, would be not having children.

They ate supper of richly flavored beef stew and dumplings and hot tea. Kyle had great difficulty sitting still during the meal. Finally, after eating two pieces of apple pie, he jumped up, ready to go to the wagon.

"Let's go, Lynn. We gotta settle in." His thin cheeks were flushed with anticipation.

Lynn looked up at him, her dark eyes smiling patiently. "In a few minutes, Kyle. I want to help Maggie with the dishes." Lynn rose slowly from the chair to take the dishes to the wash pan, but Maggie stopped her by taking her plate.

"Actually, I think Kyle is right, honey. Ya need to go and get settled in. It's already almost seven o'clock and those wagons are leaving very bright and early tomorrow. Ya need to get a good night's rest."

Indecision was apparent as she looked first at one and then the other. She knew they were right; the trail was going to be long and hard and the more sleep she got tonight the better she would be tomorrow. Her side still ached terribly, and her head hurt when she turned too quickly. Actually her whole body ached, reminding her that she was beginning this with a strike against her already. And now, on top of everything else, she hated to go and leave the woman who had become such a dear friend.

Finally, she nodded her head slowly and walked over to Maggie. After putting her arms around the older woman and giving her a hug, tears welled up in Lynn's eyes. "Thank you for all you have done for me. I will pay you back somehow. Maybe I can get a job teaching. We will be waiting to see you next year and will have a place for you." Maggie returned the hug and then turned back towards the dishes and started scrubbing them furiously. Lynn walked towards the door away from the woman who had done so much for her in the past few months. She saw Maggie lift the apron and touch the corner of her eye. Maggie's hand stilled for a moment when she heard the door open. Then Lynn shrugged into her coat, turned back to the door, and closed it gently behind her.

Chapter 4

"The wagon master"

Lynn was mildly surprised when she stepped out into the evening air. The sun had been shining brightly all day, but she actually shivered from the cold air that hit her in the face. She was glad for the coat that Maggie had found. The weather had been beautiful for the past week; warmer days and cool nights, causing the snow to melt which meant there was mud everywhere around town. Out of town a little way, there was still a light smattering of snow on the ground, but, it was quickly disappearing.

Lynn tried to keep up with Kyle, whose long legs and excitement were carrying him along the boardwalk at an alarming pace. Finally, extending an arm in his direction, she called to him with as deep a voice as she could muster, but had to speak twice before he realized it was her. He turned around to look at her with a question in his expression. Seeing her flushed face and heaving chest, his gaze turned guilty.

"Ah, Lynn, I'm sorry. I plum forgot your condition." Hurrying back beside her, he lightly grasped her arm to help her along. She gently, but quickly pulled away from his hand.

"Kyle, you can't treat me like a woman or this farce will be done before it even gets started. Just let me catch my breath for a moment." She whispered at him, her face thoughtful for a moment. "I need a man's name." Kyle's eyebrows shot up, his blue eyes widening at the suggestion, but then realized that it really couldn't be helped. It was true; she could hardly be dressed as a man but have a woman's name. He had simply been too preoccupied about the chance to go on this wagon train that he had forgotten why they were going in the first place. His face flushed once again with guilt.

"How about Kenneth Adams?" She glanced up at him to see what he thought. He hesitated only a second before letting her know.

"Please, not Kenneth. When I was little there was a smithy in town that used to yell at me whenever me and my Maw went by there. He hated little kids, my Maw said, boys especially, but he was just plain mean to everyone." The disgusted expression on his face made Lynn want to laugh although as soon as she started to, her lip split again, causing Kyle to frown slightly. As she brought a finger to her lip Kyle suggested another name.

"How 'bout Larry? Larry Clark was the name of the man who owned the general store where we lived, and he would always give me a piece of candy whenever me and my Maw would go in there." His eyes took on a hopeful gleam and after Lynn thought about it for a moment, she conceded that Larry would be alright.

"Okay, Larry Adams it will be!" Lynn cast a furtive glance around them and decided that they had better keep moving. There were a lot of people milling around and she was afraid that maybe, just maybe, Jared would return sooner than usual.

"We'd better get going." Kyle walked beside her this time, trying to squelch the desire to run as fast as he could for the wagon.

They had gone about half the distance. when suddenly Kyle grabbed her arm and pulled her to the other side of the street. He hurried her so quickly that when they reached the other side and were back on the boardwalk, she jerked her arm out of his grasp, grabbing her side at the same time.

"What are you doing?" she gasped.

"Didn't ya see him? Jared was walking down the walk just ahead of us. He went into the saloon." Panic fringed his voice as thoughts of what would happen if Jared had seen Lynn went through his mind.

Lynn's face paled as she fought to catch her breath, and those same thoughts went flying through her mind, making her legs momentarily weak. "Thank you, Kyle. No, I didn't see him. I was busy trying to keep my head down and watch the walk. I wasn't really watching ahead for fear of having someone recognize me." They walked quickly on even though Lynn still hadn't gotten her breath back. She was shaking by the time they made it to the edge of town and turned the corner to see the wagon train come into full view.

Lynn's attention was immediately captured. Oh, she had seen other wagon trains from a distance, but Jared had never allowed her to go near them, saying that they were full of lecherous men who couldn't be successful where they were so were heading somewhere else. She knew better than that, of course, because she knew of a couple of families from her hometown who decided to go west. The opportunities there were drawing people of all kinds and from many different circumstances, but Jared had mocked anyone wanting to leave the east.

As they walked closer, she saw the people who were busily attending to tasks around and in the wagons. There were families, many of them by the looks of it, and they looked anything but lecherous. She studied their faces as they walked by several of them and the eagerness that was clear upon them. The thought suddenly struck her that these people were heading west for many different reasons but all for the same purpose: they wanted another chance; a second chance or maybe a third or fourth chance. For her, it would be a second chance, and she hoped that it would turn out to be a successful one.

Two young boys about sixteen or so waved at Kyle as they walked by. She glanced at the animation on his face and couldn't help but feel some of it starting to build within her chest. She had undertaken this enormous task, this decision, for the sole reason of survival. But now, seeing all the faces gleaming with anticipation, she could feel the beginnings of that same feeling within her belly.

They reached their wagon and Kyle quickly showed her around it and then climbed inside to show her all of the provisions in the various barrels and boxes and trunks. They had just climbed back out of the wagon when a deep, quiet voice reached Lynn's ears from behind them.

"So, you must be the cousin. You going to introduce us, Kyle?" Lynn spun on her heel to see one of the biggest men she had ever seen. Instantly, she knew who this was, but he was even bigger standing in front of her as opposed to across the street than she had thought possible. She was taller than the average woman. However, standing so close to this man she felt anything but tall. It was Benjamin Alenson, the wagon master, that Kyle had talked about during supper. She tipped her head back briefly to look into piercing brown eyes and was immediately aware of dark wavy hair, broad shoulders and chest, and large hands with long fingers that flexed slightly as they adjusted the well-worn hat on his head. Maggie was right, a person definitely felt this man's presence.

Kyle nervously introduced Lynn. "This is my cousin, Ly...Larry Adams. Larry, this is Mr. Benjamin Alenson." Kyle swallowed hard at his near mistake.

"Please call me Ben. We're going to spend a long time together and I would rather be on a first-name basis right away." Ben watched with interest as the color drained from Larry's face, making the bruise and black eye stand out. Kyle seemed nervous, or maybe it was just excitement, and yet, he shifted back and forth from one foot to the other as he introduced them. Ben's gaze returned to Larry. The young man was looking down at his boots and kept his hands behind his back instead of holding one out to shake Ben's hand. He looked weak and sickly, his stature slender, and the top of his hat came to just below Ben's shoulder. His height didn't really matter, Ben was used to being taller than most men. But, his shoulders were narrow, and as Ben's gaze lingered he seemed agitated as well.

"What did you do before deciding to go west, Larry Adams?" Ben watched curiously as Larry jumped slightly and then coughed briefly before answering.

"Well, I, uh...I helped my grandparents out on their farm, sir." Lynn struggled to compose herself and willed herself to look briefly up at the large man in front of her before turning to Kyle. "Well, Kyle, I think I'll go take a look at that harness." Nodding slightly in Ben's direction, she added, "Nice to meet you, sir. Goodnight." She tried to swagger a little as she walked toward the front of the wagon. Not daring to turn around, she felt the wagon master's eyes bore into her back. She walked around the side of the wagon and when she disappeared from his sight, leaned against it when her legs threatened to drop her to the ground. That man was huge! One slap from his large hand or fist into her face and it would be all over. Maybe this was a mistake! Maybe she should go back and try to come up with another idea! There had to be another way! She leaned her head back against the heavy canvas and closed her eyes, all the while knowing that there were no other ideas, no other choices. This choice had been made, this decision, and now she would have to live or die with it. Opening her eyes, she realized she had caught the attention of the two families in the wagons nearest her and Kyle's. Four children and two women with red hair were watching intently to see if she was alright. She lifted a hand to wave slightly and then straightened to go look at the harness.

Ben watched her walk away and was suddenly aware that something was different about this young man. He was too soft, too weak, too...too something. He didn't know what, but he felt like they were hiding something from him and he didn't like it. The bruise and the black eye on Larry's face suggested that he liked to fight or maybe didn't like to fight but definitely looked like he couldn't defend himself well. At the least, he obviously didn't know how to get out of bad situations. Ben also noticed the hand holding his side a couple of times, especially climbing out of the wagon, suggesting maybe a sore rib or two. Larry didn't seem to be in very good condition to be on a trip like this one. Ben stood thoughtful for a moment, and then bidding Kyle goodnight walked back towards the Aames wagon.

Bud Aames was a short, stocky man with a kind face and gentle eyes. He was married to Rachel, who like her sister Leah, had very bright red hair. Leah was married to Willy Emerson. Between the two families, they had eight children, six of whom had the same bright, red hair. Bud and Willy were loading two barrels into the back of the wagon while the rest of the family was watching something up towards the wagon he had just left. At his approach, Rachel turned to smile and greet him.

"Hey, Ben, is everything pulling together alright? How are those two young fellas going to do? That shorter one doesn't look too well." Her brown eyes were warm and friendly and her smile genuine. He had liked both families from the first meeting.

Ben pushed his hat back from his forehead a little and rubbed his eyes briefly before answering, "Well,...I really don't know about those two. I agree with you about the shorter one. His name is Larry Adams, and he sure don't look like he can do much. But, you never know. Time will tell." Willy and Bud had the barrels loaded by now and walked over to join the conversation.

"Kyle seems like a decent young man. Me and a couple of the boys were talking to him earlier this afternoon. He is one excited boy. Said that his Aunt is going to come out next year and join him and his cousin." Willy put his hat back on that had fallen off while they were loading. He was actually a man of about forty, but looked, at first glance, like a kid. His boyish face always had a ready smile and his tall, thin body gave him a teenage gangly appearance.

"Have to agree with that." Bud pointed toward Kyle, "My boy, Adam, said that Kyle helped him load some supplies into the wagon when I sent him and his brother to the livery a while back. He's a helpful sort."

Ben was thoughtful for a moment. "You fellas help keep an eye on them for me would ya? I have a feeling about them. Can't explain it, just do." Ben shook hands with them before walking further down the line to talk to more of the men on the train.

Lynn watched Ben out of the corner of her eye and became aware that she and Kyle were the center of the conversation when one of them gestured toward Kyle. When she realized that, she moved quickly out of his line of vision. Although there was still some light out, she decided it was time to retire for the night. She beckoned to Kyle and told him she was going to bed. About half an hour later, Kyle came into the wagon also and bedded down on the other end. Most of the travelers would sleep under their wagon or in small tents erected each night. But since Lynn and Kyle had only basic supplies needed for survival, their wagon was not packed as tightly as most, which enabled them to sleep within its confines. Both dreamed. Kyle dreamed that he had killed a buffalo and was proudly skinning it out. Lynn's dreams, however, were not that pleasant. She kept having the same dream over and over; Jared found out where she was, and he came and pulled her out of the wagon. But, instead of just leaving with her, he stripped her down to her chemise and then horsewhipped her in front of everyone. And nobody came to her rescue. She thought Ben would, but he just laughed and then rode away on his horse.

Chapter 5

"Jared!"

The next day dawned as beautiful as the days before, and the air was crisp but held the promise of later warmth. Lynn awoke to coffee pots banging, men yelling orders, and women laughing. She sat upright with a start as she suddenly realized where she was, causing her to grab her side as she did so with a gasp of pain.

"Kyle?" Lynn looked around the wagon. Kyle must already be up and doing chores. She eased her still sore body off of the makeshift bed that would be hers for the next few months. Pulling her coat and hat on, she climbed out of the wagon, looking around as she did so. People were busy everywhere, putting harnesses on the oxen, loading last-minute items, checking out wagons, saying goodbyes to others who had come to see them off. All of them busily attending to things as the wonderful smells of breakfast wafted gently through the cool morning air. Kyle had started a campfire and laid out a skillet, plates, and some eating utensils. The coffee pot was nowhere to be seen, so she figured that he must be doing something about making coffee. Lynn just put bacon in the skillet and started mixing up biscuit dough. Turning around to grab a spoon, she saw Benjamin watching her. She almost dropped the bowl that she held in the crook of her arm.

"Oh! I... I'm sorry, I didn't see you there." Lynn's eyes widened in surprise and dismay. Her hope of not dealing with him today obviously didn't happen, so she dropped her eyes to the bowl and continued mixing the dough. Had her voice been deep enough? She certainly hoped so but had doubts when she saw the puzzled look he gave her before turning her attention to the task at hand.

"Sorry. I came by to tell you that we're leaving in half an hour. Be ready. Don't see how you're going to get all that done and eat before we leave." He looked pointedly at the bowl.

"I'll just have to hurry." Lynn turned her back on him and spooned some of the dough into the hot skillet to make hard biscuits that would serve them for lunch, too. That's why she had made a double batch. They could eat them with cold ham and maybe some pemmican. As she turned them in the skillet, she realized that maybe a man wouldn't have thought about that. It was going to be hard to think the way a man would. This disguise was going to be even more difficult than she had imagined.

Kyle returned and rescued her from further conversation. "Good morning, Ben. How are things goin' this morning?" Kyle nervously eyed Lynn and then Ben. Ben caught the look that passed between them, and it made him uneasy. These two were hiding something from him. He had the feeling that it should be obvious what it was. Whatever it was, it escaped him, which made him irritated since he was generally very observant.

"Fine, Kyle, fine. I just stopped by to tell the two of you that we're leaving in half an hour. So please be ready." He gave them a curt nod and started to walk off, but only got about fifteen feet when he stopped and turned around, tilting his hat back on his head as he looked at them.

"There is something about the two of you. I don't know what it is, but just to let you know, I'll be keeping an eye on you. And you, young man," pointing a long finger at Lynn, "I don't know what it was that you did or how you got into the fight that earned you that black eye and bruise and whatever is wrong with your ribs, but let me tell you this: I don't tolerate any fighting on my wagon train, you understand? You start any fights, and I will throw you off of this train, you got it? We don't need problems of that sort. Problems will find us all by themselves without bringing any with us."

His voice was quiet yet firm, making them both realize in that moment that this was a man to be reckoned with. Lynn shuddered slightly as again she recognized that this man could kill her with little effort. Kyle suddenly obtained an incredible amount of respect for this big man. He heard him to be an honest and honorable man. He now knew that he would never want to be this man's enemy. They both nodded their heads and then watched as his long strides took him quickly back in the direction of his wagon.

Kyle harnessed up the oxen and put the last few things in order as Lynn finished making the hard biscuits. They would eat after they were on the trail.

They didn't leave quite when Ben wanted to, and that slightly irritated him. But finally, the last goodbyes were said, final items were packed away, and all the harnesses were hitched. He kept a close eye on the two young men whose behavior made him uneasy and curious. But he knew that sooner or later, all things would be revealed. It was hard to keep a secret on a wagon train. This would be the third and final train that he would lead. The money was good, but the months on the trail took a toll on a person. Tempers tended to rise and nerves would be frayed within a couple of months at most, and there were a handful of people on this train who already had short fuses and were edgy. There were others whom he already liked very much. If they settled close enough to him and his family, they would always be friends. It was always a mix, an interesting mix most of the time, but it always included some people that were not good. Regardless of that mix, it was his responsibility to get these people safely to the Oregon country.

He no sooner turned his horse towards the front of the train to canter up to his wagon when the sound of galloping and a man yelling came from behind him. Shifting in the saddle, he saw mud kicking up behind a horseman coming from the direction of town. He caught a movement out of the corner of his eye from Larry and Kyle's wagon, so now turned slightly to look in their direction. Larry's eyes were huge, and his face looked like he had seen a ghost. Ben watched as Larry glanced back at the horseman, and then faced the front of the wagon as he pulled the overlarge hat down further, if that was possible, on his forehead. Kyle, too, looked ashen and quickly faced the front of the wagon after glancing back.

Ben's attention once again focused on the rider. As he got closer, he recognized Jared Malen from a few nights ago at Mallory's Saloon. Ben and two other men had been playing poker when Jared walked in and demanded to play. Jud and Allan, the other men in the game, hadn't been too enthused about letting him play, which Ben took as a sign and became very guarded when Jared sat down. Ben ended up winning a few more dollars off of the three men. However, only Jared got angry. Ben finally had enough of the cursing and swearing. When he decided to leave the game and got a mug of ale from the bar, there were a couple of men and one of the saloon ladies who had given him an earful about Jared Malen. It turned out that Jared had a reputation for being an excellent boxer with a mean temper. He had no friends and seemed to make his livelihood from gambling. Somewhere, he kept a wife pretty well hidden because no one could really remember seeing her. Supposedly, there was some woman whom he claimed was his sister, a tall pretty woman but very quiet. No one saw much of her either, and since Jared didn't talk about his family, everyone came up with their own stories and theories if they wanted something to talk about. Other than that, no one really cared.

After Ben left the game it only took about half an hour and a fight broke out. Jared had accused one of the men of cheating. Ben was told correctly, Jared Malen was an excellent boxer. He delivered blow after blow to his opponent, and before anyone could step in and break it up had Jud Stevens out cold on the floor.

Now Benjamin faced him across the top of his big bay's head. Eyeing him closely, he watched as Jared sent a scathing search toward the train and then turned with an angry face back to Ben. His eyes were angry slits as he looked at the big wagon master.

"Is there a Lynn Malen with these wagons." His eyes darted once again toward the wagons, searching. The horse he was on fidgeted nervously and he reined it tightly so that its head swung to one side trying to relieve the pressure of the bit in its mouth.

"No."

Jared's attention jerked back to Ben at the simple, short answer, his glare accusing him of whatever Jared seemed to think he should be guilty of.

"Let me reword the question. Do you have a slightly built, brown-haired, brown-eyed young woman about five foot nine inches tall; very mousy and timid that has joined your train?" Jared's voice lowered slightly as he challenged Ben.

"No." Ben watched as the glare turned to pure hatred and undisguised fury. "Sorry I can't be of help. There are several women with this train; however, none fit the description or the name you gave. There are only two young men who seem to want to get as far away from you as they can get. It looks like you worked them over pretty good a couple of nights ago or so. Now, if you're finished, I really need to get this train on its way. We have a long ways to go, and the sooner we start the sooner we get to where we are going. Sorry, you've lost your wife, but I can't help you on that." His eyes narrowed as he watched Jared closely, waiting to see what kind of reaction he would get.

Jared's eyes blazed and he fairly spat out the words, "Who said it was my wife?! I'm looking for my sister. She has the tendency to take off without consulting me first!"

Ben studied Jared's face as it turned red with fury. He felt sorry for whoever the woman was, wife or sister. He hoped that wherever she was at, she was successful in getting far away from this man.

"Well, sorry I can't help you out." Ben purposely made his voice bland; he wasn't in the mood to waste any more time with this obnoxious man. "But I have a wagon train to get going so I'm going to have to say goodbye." He turned the big horse around gently and kicked him up to send him back to the front of the train.

Jared thought for a moment about the comment referring to two young men, then remembered the two that had jostled Lynn. Yes indeed, he had worked them over good. So, they decided to go west, huh? Good riddance to garbage! The sooner the town was free from that kind, the sooner he would be happier. He wheeled his horse around savagely, spurring the poor animal angrily as he headed back to town. Sooner or later he would figure out where she went and when he did, he would make her pay dearly. The little trollop, she had probably run off with some other man. Men always looked her direction with admiration. He could always see the desire in their eyes. Hell and damnation but she would pay!!

Chapter 6

"And so it begins"

Ben glanced briefly at Larry and Kyle. Although Larry's gaze remained fixed ahead, Kyle met Ben's stare, however, and the anxious look on his face made him wonder why they would still be so scared. Surely they didn't think Jared would actually hunt them down and beat them again, did they? Well, he couldn't think about that right now, there was a wagon train to get moving. He tied his horse to the side of his wagon, climbed up onto the seat, and slapped the leather on the backs of the oxen.

"Wagons Ho!" Swinging his arm and standing, Ben finally yelled the words that would take him in the direction of home.

Kyle put his arm briefly around Lynn's shoulders, the relief showing in his face when the wagons started to move. Jared had disappeared from sight, and they were finally leaving. He glanced down to look at Lynn as he felt her tremble.

"You okay?"

"I think so." She paused for a moment as she unclenched the fists in her lap. "I was so scared, Kyle. I just couldn't believe it that he would figure it out so soon". When she realized that Jared had left and was returning to town, she almost passed out with relief. When she first realized who was yelling earlier, the sides of her throat had stuck together, and she couldn't swallow. The blood had drained from her face, she knew because she felt every last drop leave. As she watched the wagon in front of them, she made a pact with herself that she would become strong enough to never let another man scare her like that again. She never, ever wanted to be that scared again, and once she became strong, she would never run again.

As she stayed lost in her thoughts for a moment the sound of

'Wagons Ho' started at the front of the train. The excited yells and whoops were like a wave that suddenly, briefly, hit them and then passed over and onto the next wagon. Lynn didn't much feel like yelling anything, but Kyle joined in the cry as it went by them. She felt scared, excited, nervous, and more than anything else, she could feel the barest, tiniest beginnings of hope. The adventure, the journey that would change lives—indeed, take lives—had begun.

Chapter 7

"Suzanne"

June 10th, 1844

The smoke from the fires wafted slowly through the camp, bringing with it various wonderful smells of bacon, biscuits, stew, beans, and even a skillet made cake. Lynn leaned up against the wagon wheel as she watched small groups gathered here and there around the camp as people did various chores after supper was finished. She enjoyed watching everyone, especially since she had slowly put names to all the faces. Six weeks on the trail, a lot is learned about those who had become their fellow travelers. Kyle told her everything that he learned from the interactions he had with everyone, since obviously, Lynn herself couldn't talk much with anyone and that frustrated her terribly. But, she couldn't fit in with the men and didn't really want to try. She was fearful that sooner or later, the closer she got to people they would figure out that she was not who she claimed to be. So, the men were off-limits and, of course, so were the women since no one would be very comfortable with a man over talking to the women all of the time. Besides, she would end up giving herself away there, too. Everyone pretty much avoided her, too, since Larry avoided them and wasn't very friendly. If Larry wanted to be left alone, they would leave him alone.

A sudden burst of laughter made her turn in Kyle's direction. He was talking with the Aames' and Emerson's boys. There were two Aames boys, Adam, who was seventeen, and Jacob, who was ten. They had a sister, Sarah, who was almost sixteen, and who had caught Kyle's eye from the first time he saw her. There were four

Emerson boys; Matthew, seventeen; Samuel, sixteen; Luke, fourteen; and finally, John, twelve. They had one sister, Mary, who was only eighteen months old.

Lynn watched them for a moment, smiling to herself as she caught bits and pieces of the boys' conversation. Slowly, her gaze moved around the circle of wagons. Ben was talking with a large group of men on the other side of the circle. She and Kyle had been pretty successful in avoiding much contact with him. Obviously, they would have to talk occasionally, although Lynn let Kyle do most of that. For the most part, when the train wasn't moving there were always many chores to do and everyone stayed pretty busy. After a long day on the trail, everyone was also very tired, so most people retired early.

They often felt his gaze upon them, but he kept his distance unless there were directions that he wanted them to know from him in person. Otherwise, he usually had Bud or Will pass on information to them, which was fine with them. The big man's eyes didn't miss much, and Lynn was afraid that sooner or later he would figure her out. Actually, it amazed her that her cover hadn't been blown weeks ago. To travel for this long and still have everyone think of her as a man was surprising. She almost felt insulted. She had once felt she was a very feminine woman, but this whole experience was making her doubt that.

Now she watched as Ben laughed with the group of men, the corners of his dark eyes crinkling with amusement. Lynn had to concede that he was a handsome man in a rough sort of way. She watched him covertly from under the brim of her hat. He had the habit of throwing his head back when he laughed. With his hat pushed back on his head, she could see dark hair peeking from underneath. His square jawline bespoke strength not only physically, but in character, also. His beard had grown out, same as the other men, and his teeth showed white against the dark whiskers and tan skin. A good sense of humor meant that he got along well with almost everyone on the train.

Bud Aames and Will Emerson were among the group talking. But, others she knew now, too. There were Stanley and Jake Emmons who were brothers going west to start their own cattle ranch. Stanley was the eldest and was married, although his wife was not with him. She would have a baby in a couple of months and so would come out next year with another Emmons brother and his family. Jake was not married and had quickly sought out any and all eligible young women among the families. He wanted to settle down with a family of his own when they got to Oregon. Unfortunately for him, there weren't any single women even close to his age other than Lynn, and obviously he didn't know about her. Both brothers were fairly good-looking men with thick, dark hair and beards and strong bodies.

Then there was Jeremiah Seckers. He was a friendly young man who often spoke briefly to Lynn, or rather, Larry. He and his wife, Leann, were happy and excited about the thought of a new life. Leann was a pretty little thing with blonde hair and blue eyes. Her handsome husband adored her and was thrilled when the news broke that she was about four months with child. Leann had laughing eyes with a ready smile, and Lynn longed to be able to talk with her, knowing that they would easily become friends.

Abraham Johnson was talking rapidly at the moment and had everyone's full attention. Lynn caught an occasional word here and there, something about buffalo and hunting, making pemmican, and this being a good place to dry meat and hides. Then someone else commented. About that time another peal of laughter came from the group of young people, so Lynn failed to catch any more of the conversation at the moment. She turned with a smile once again to the boys and their raucous laughter. Her eye caught the movement of Suzanne Smith and the smile froze on Lynn's face.

Suzanne was an enigma, Lynn couldn't figure her out and neither could anyone else. No matter how friendly the women tried to be with her, she constantly rebuffed them. When asked a question, she would give a minimal answer and then disappear from sight. Her duties were done perfectly and with an orderliness, yet with no joy or obvious pleasure. Lynn recognized a sadness within her, and something else she felt she should know, and yet couldn't put her finger on it. Suzanne was small with brown hair with streaks of gray, and dull brown eyes. Her shoulders were often slumped with weariness. Although now a woman of about forty, Lynn had the feeling that at one time Suzanne was probably fairly attractive.

Suzanne glanced up from the duties she was performing and then suddenly turned and quickly disappeared behind the wagon. Lynn's gaze followed the direction of Suzanne's glance and understood why she disappeared so quickly. It took about three weeks, but most everyone finally figured out that not all was well with Suzanne and her husband, Nathan. He was built low to the ground with short legs, a barrel chest, and broad, powerful shoulders. His hands made Lynn think of meaty hams and his fat face was round with dark, squinty eyes that sent shudders down Lynn's spine whenever she felt his glance on her.

He darted a heavy scowl at her and then disappeared around the wagon, also. A moment later Lynn could hear his angry voice raised slightly to his wife. The sound of flesh hitting flesh resounded in Lynn's head and caused her to stand upright quickly with her full attention in the direction of the Smith wagon. Her face paled as memories came flooding back, and she suddenly realized what it was that she couldn't put her finger on all this time. Suzanne had a husband like Jared! Nathan had never hit her so that other people could hear it before. Lynn glanced around quickly, but no one seemed to have heard now, either. It was only her close proximity at the moment that allowed her to even know the truth. When she glanced around again, her gaze caught Ben's. His eyebrows were raised slightly as if contemplating her and then lowered his eyes to her hands. She realized that she had automatically clenched her hands into fists like she was ready to do something in Suzanne's defense. What a fool! What could she do? She was another Suzanne, just a younger version, and the realization made her shrink in horror against the wagon. Was that what she would have looked like had she stayed with Jared? Bile filled her throat as she pushed away from the wheel to escape to the other side, away from prying eyes.

Ben glanced up from his conversation with the men just in time to see Larry suddenly stand up straight from the wagon he was leaning on, his hands forming fists at his side. His face had taken on a stricken, yet, angry look. Ben's glance encircled all of the wagons and then had rested on the Smith's. Benjamin suspected what Larry had either seen or heard. For some time now, Ben was suspicious of Nathan Smith and how he treated his wife. Yet, he could do nothing about suspicions. He watched as Larry turned and walked around the wagon. He was a strange young man, and after talking with the men about hunting buffalo tomorrow, he suddenly made a decision. They decided to stop here for a couple of days. They hadn't stopped for more than a day in the six or so weeks that they had been on the trail. Everyone needed two or three days rest to catch up on chores that could be done by the river. So far, they were fortunate, no major problems had found them yet. Two tipped but rescued wagons crossing the last couple of rivers and a snake bite had been the only problems. He considered the wagon train very fortunate, but they still needed a break or exhaustion would start affecting them.

As the conversation around him got more animated about the agreed hunting expedition tomorrow, he excused himself and went to the boys first to tell them about the plans and then went in search of Larry. He needed to go hunting and learn to become a man. In the past weeks, Ben had watched Larry. He seems to have healed from his wounds nicely, no longer holding his side as much and the bruises were completely gone from his face now. Yet, he still wasn't a very strong young man. He had trouble lifting anything that weighed more than about thirty pounds, and Ben still got the feeling that he was missing something about Larry, which irritated him immensely. But, he didn't have a lot of time to dwell on the matter. Being a wagon master, he was constantly dealing with decisions and minor problems of one kind or another.

As Ben walked around the side of the wagon, Lynn couldn't believe her misfortune. She straightened quickly from leaning over the wagon wheel, the need to vomit having passed, but still feeling queasy. She was still shaky, but stretched to her full height to look Ben in the face briefly before glancing away.

That irritated Ben. He liked to look a man in the eye, not seeing the side of his face all of the time. The annoyance made him get right to the point. "We're going on a hunt tomorrow. I would like you to come. It would be good for you I believe." As he watched Larry's reaction, he fingered his beard, a habit when he was in deep thought. He wondered why Larry didn't have more facial hair to show for his age, realizing that some men don't have much of a beard until they are well into their twenties, but Larry didn't seem to have any. Yes, this young man definitely needed to toughen up, start looking and acting like a man, with or without a beard.

Lynn shot a look of surprise at him. That was the last thing she expected to hear. She figured that he would be wondering what had happened earlier. She could see the curiosity in his eyes and looked away again.

"I fear that I am not a good shot. I don't use a rifle very well at all." It took all of her willpower to keep her voice as deep and steady as possible.

"I figured as much. However, you can come along anyway. You can help carry the meat back if you're good at nothing else. We can always use extra hands to do that. I expect you and Kyle to be ready at six in the morning." He watched her for a moment longer then offered another suggestion if it could be called that. "I think you might use a good bath sometime soon." Lynn's face flamed as she watched him turn away. She knew that she needed more of a bath than the spit baths she had been giving herself for the last few weeks. Yet, how could she do it? Every river they stopped at for a couple of hours the women had taken baths together and then the men had. She couldn't very well bathe with either one, now could she? It was very frustrating. She had never thought about the little things that would be involved in dressing like a man. Now that they were going to be here for two or three days she had already figured out how she could finally take a bath. She would take one at night when everyone else was sleeping. Tomorrow night she would finally have her bath.

Kyle came over a few minutes later, talking excitedly about the hunting expedition the next day. He was finally going to have an opportunity to shoot a buffalo. He had been eagerly anticipating it for weeks and mentioned it to Lynn almost every day. Lynn told him what Ben expected of her. Kyle frowned slightly then his boyish face broke into a grin.

"That's alright. You won't have to hunt. Just help carry back, like he said. You'll be fine." He ran his fingers through his hair and climbed into the wagon. "I'm going to retire a little early tonight, so I can make sure that I'm rested for the hunt tomorrow."

Kyle's reassurances helped ease her mind so she decided to retire early, also. She rested easier these days, but with tomorrow to look forward to she didn't know how she would sleep tonight. The days and nights were so much more wonderful when you didn't have to live in fear. It had taken about three weeks, but suddenly she started to relax, just a little more every day. She was growing tired of being a 'man,' however, and tried to figure out how she could break the news. Should she just show up in the morning as herself? She didn't know how everyone would react to that, especially Ben. Would he be angry, having been deceived since his own reputation for honesty was so good? What about everyone else; wouldn't they also be upset at having been deceived? And then last but far from least, she feared the reaction of Jake Emmons. How would she deal with a man who was on the lookout for a wife should he decide he liked her? Confusion and indecision was her daily quandary. But on the good side of things, she was also growing stronger every day. The sun, rain, and the wind felt so good on her face; she soaked it into her soul. As she lay there thinking about the past weeks, she smiled to herself and then drifted into a deep sleep.

Chapter 8

"I want to catch the wind"

June 11, 1844

The day dawned bright with no clouds in the sky. A light prairie breeze felt good as it held the promise of a good day. Everyone was up early with the excitement of the coming hunt. The buffalo had been spotted late yesterday afternoon about a mile and a half from the camp just to the east and over a rise in the prairie. They had seen many signs of buffalo in the past week, but this was the first time the huge beasts themselves were seen and the men were anxious to be on their way. Breakfast was done in a hurry, and the women were getting out tools to be used to dry the meat and skin and tan the hides when the men brought their prizes back.

Ben was talking to a group of men gathered around him when Lynn walked in their direction, but stopped a short distance away while hoping not to be noticed. She was ready to carry meat or whatever else the men needed help with since she had been unable to come up with an excuse to get out of this ugly chore. When her grandfather had butchered, she always helped him and her grandmother but had never liked it. She had little choice in the matter now either, it seemed, so decided to just do it and get it over with.

Ben noticed her, however, and excusing himself from the group after giving last-minute directions, approached her.

"I'm glad to see that you're ready to go this beautiful morning. Let's get started. You follow closely behind the rest of us. When we get to the hunting site, stay back so that you don't disturb anything until we're ready. We want to make sure that when they stampede they go the opposite direction from the wagons." His dark eyes were bright with excitement just like Kyle's had been with their conversation at breakfast. He turned away from her then and she was able to breathe a sigh of relief. He always made her nervous. She just knew that someday he would figure her out.

Her gaze followed him as he joined the other men and they all started walking toward the buffalo. His long confident strides brought her attention to muscled thighs that were fitted tightly with his brown breeches. The blue shirt he had on this morning also fit snugly across broad shoulders. Physically, he was a formidable man, his sheer size making him intimidating. However, from watching him and hearing things from others the past few weeks, he had a gentle, kind side, also. Most of the children seemed to be drawn to him and he almost always took time for them, often laughing, telling jokes, and sometimes playing games with them when he could do so. His big hands gently holding little Mary Emerson reminded Lynn of her father. Her thoughts then turned to Jared for a moment. He didn't like children, having no patience for them, and had always told Lynn that she had better never get with child because he "didn't want no brats". She shook herself mentally, noticing that she was too far behind the men, and ran to catch up.

Lynn loved the beauty of the prairie as they traveled through the wide-open spaces and she didn't think she had ever seen anything more beautiful than the sunrises and sunsets over the rolling hills of the grasslands. A few moments later, she knew that she was wrong. As she reached the top of the hill that the men stopped briefly upon and then slowly crept over, the most awesome sight she had ever seen greeted her eyes. Hundreds of buffalo were spread out before them on softly rolling prairie hills, grazing peacefully on the succulent grass. With the blue sky above them and the green and golden grasses all around them, their dark bodies stood out in sharp contrast. There were many calves either lying sleepily on the ground or nursing from their patient mothers. There were three to the left that were running like they were playing tag with each other. Her jaw dropped in sheer amazement for a moment, as she soaked in the beauty before her.

A light breeze lifted the hair at the nape of her neck and she suddenly felt alive; alive in a way that she hadn't felt in almost three years. The prairie and its wonders were breathing life back into her very soul and she felt laughter building up in her throat. She wanted to laugh for the sheer pleasure of life and all that it held at this moment in time. Realizing that no one was looking at her since their attention was on the buffalo, on impulse she tossed her hat to the ground and flung her arms open wide, throwing her head back to feel the full warmth of the sun. She closed her eyes and took a deep breath, filling her lungs with the sweet fragrance of the grasslands that came to her on the light wind. Drawing her arms around herself for a brief second, she flung them wide once again, as if trying to catch the wind and hold it to her breast; wanting to capture the freedom of where it had been and where it was going. She wanted to fly upon it, to let it carry her hither and thither across the prairie, allowing the beauty below and around her breathe new life into her, making her the girl of yesteryear.

Ben chose that moment to glance back to see who was behind him and out of the corner of his eye caught the movement on the hill. He was captured immediately by the spectacle before him. Larry had tossed his hat aside and was standing with his arms open wide, his head back and it looked like his eyes closed. Was he really seeing what he thought he was seeing? What man did something like that? In that moment Larry looked like a woman! Ben felt the sudden rush of blood from his face. He realized with a start what he had been missing all this time. He knew something wasn't right about Larry! Now he knew what it was! The young man wasn't a man at all! He no sooner took a step toward "Larry," than the crack of a rifle jerked his attention back around. His sharp eyes caught the smoke still left from the shot that Jeremiah Seckers fired. The buffalo were immediately on the move, quickly running away from the men who had come up on their sides unnoticed. Ben ventured one last glance back before pursuing the big beasts. "Larry" had put his hat back on and his full attention was on the scene below.

Lynn's rapt attention was captured again by the beautiful animals below her on the wide-open prairie. But this time she was marveling at how swiftly the huge animals moved and shifted, as if caught in a wave that swept across the prairie at a speed that amazed her. The men were aiming and sending shots into the herd as it swept by and away from them. She saw two go down and then one more fell before they were completely out of firing range. The men were elated at their fine kill and they fell upon the downed animals immediately and started to butcher them out. This was the part Lynn hated, and she stayed away until they had done most of the worst part and then slowly made her way down to them to help out.

She went to the one that Kyle was helping out with and lent a hand doing what she knew how to do. She was uncomfortably aware of someone's gaze on her. When she glanced around, she discovered that Ben was watching her with a speculative gleam that she failed to understand, so she turned away quickly and went back to work.

Supper was late that night. It had taken all day to work up the three buffalo, prepare their hides, and cut up the meat into small strips to salt them so that they would dry quickly in the hot sun. The whole camp had taken part, and the meat would be split among the families. After cleaning up dishes, she washed up as good as she could and then retired to the wagon trying to sleep for a while. She was exhausted and sweaty and really wanted a hot bath, but knew the best she was going to get would be a bath in the river. After the rest of the camp had gone to sleep she planned on getting just that. It would be wonderful to feel clean and get the last traces of blood and animal smell off of her. She laid out the drying cloth and the heavy bar of soap and then laid down to wait.

The moon was full and bright when she climbed out of the wagon two hours later. Coyotes howling had awakened her. She hadn't meant to sleep for quite so long, but that was alright for the camp was completely quiet. No one would be up this time of night. She grabbed the drying cloth close to her side, her clean clothes, and the heavy bar of soap and walked towards the river.

For Ben, as tired as he was, sleep was not coming to him. Oh, he certainly had tried, but instead, laid there thinking about Larry Adams. Was Larry really a woman? Or were his eyes just playing tricks on him when he saw a woman dressed as a man today on that hill? Why would a woman dress as a man? That question took his thoughts to Jared Malen. Was this the sister that he was looking for? He had been unable to find a way to talk to Larry today because of the enormous amount of work that went into the preparation of the buffalo. The whole camp had been busy until almost ten that night. But tomorrow, he would make sure he made the time and opportunity to talk with Larry or Kyle. Although, he had the feeling that Kyle wouldn't tell him anything. Well, one way or the other he would get to the bottom of it all.

Leaning against a tree in the small wooded area that followed the river for a ways, he now straightened to return to his wagon, but his attention was caught with light splashing in the river just down from where he stood. He inclined his head to one side trying to hear any other noises that would indicate what was making the splashing this time of night. When he heard nothing else he decided to go and investigate. He didn't want to be surprised by Indians or a wild animal coming this near the camp. So far, they had been very fortunate and without any catastrophes. He wanted it to stay that way.

As he edged quietly closer to the splashing, he saw a dark form standing near the water's edge. He stood for a moment and realized it was a person but couldn't tell whether or not it was someone from the camp or perhaps an Indian checking out the camp surroundings. He carefully crept closer until he was within about forty feet. It was not an Indian. Suddenly, the form stepped out into deeper water where there were no shadows from the trees. The full moonlight revealed the bare back of a woman. Ben started to turn away, having no desire to watch a woman bathing who belonged to another man. But, it suddenly struck him that this woman didn't look familiar to him. The hair was short, no woman on the train had short hair. She was also rather tall with a slender back and slim hips. The water and shadows were dark against her backside. As she stepped further into the deeper water, she soaped up her hair and then her face. He watched for a moment trying to figure out what was so familiar about her, and yet couldn't figure out why at the same time she wasn't familiar at all. No woman on the train was this tall and slender with short hair.

She stood still for a moment when the howling of coyotes caught her attention. She turned her head in the direction of their howling, and when he saw her moonlit profile it suddenly hit him who it was. It was Larry! His jaw dropped in surprise at the lovely sight before him. Larry was a very attractive woman. So, his eyes hadn't played tricks on him today after all! He knew they hadn't. He had watched Larry off and on all day and saw how at times he seemed weak when the typical man wouldn't be. Then again, at other times he had seemed like the typical young boy with boyish tendencies but wanting badly to show himself a man. Ben thought maybe he was just too tired from the weeks on the trail and had imagined the whole "catching the wind" thing after all. But now thinking again back over the day's events, how could he have missed it?! His thoughts went flying back over the past few weeks. He saw Larry struggling to pick up a heavy barrel, Larry trying to help fix a broken wheel, Larry trying to use a gun. Then he also saw Larry cooking, and he remembered all the wonderful smells that often came from their campfire. He remembered seeing Larry mending a shirt and the neat small stitches that were made. No man that he ever met could cook or mend that well.

She had turned back to her bathing, and now that she was all soaped up, she scrubbed herself and then dunked under the water to rinse off. She came up spewing the cold water and shaking her head, spraying water all around her. The slight breeze moved the trees, causing the shadows and moonlight to play hide and seek across her back and hips. When she started to turn to come back up to the bank where her clothes and drying cloth lay, he caught a glimpse of a small, firm breast, a flat belly, and curved thighs. He turned quickly away from this ethereal sight for fear of what it would do to him. Now was not the time to think about a woman, since they were still a long way from Oregon. His breath caught in his throat at the sight of this one, but he knew when it was time to move on. Moving quickly back through the woods, he went to his wagon but didn't climb inside. Instead, he waited in the darkness of the shadows surrounding him and watched until he saw Larry return. Her hair was shining in the moonlight without the hat that was constantly on her head and a small smile lit her face as once again she turned to listen for a moment to the coyotes before climbing into the wagon.

Lynn felt wonderful as her body still tingled from the cold water. She was clean, and her hair and body smelled good. The moon was huge and yellow and with the coyotes howling, it seemed like she was in a different world far away from everyone else. She had loved the sheer freedom of the bath and wished that she could have one like that every night. Sleep came quickly, and she dreamed sweet dreams of wide-open prairies, cold rivers, and the howling of coyotes.

Chapter 9

"It's a woman?!"

June 12, 1844

Lynn awoke with a smile on her face and was up even before Kyle. She hadn't felt this good in a long time. The sun was barely peeking up over the east prairie hills and the sky was beautiful. As she watched the muted oranges, reds, and pinks splattered against the blue of the sky, she caught sight of a coyote trotting over the nearest hill, which was still far enough off so as not to pose any threat to the camp. She sauntered jauntily toward the little woods to take care of morning business, breathing deeply of the cool prairie air with the feeling that nothing could possibly ruin this day.

When she got into the trees, she thought she heard a cry of some sort and stopped for just a moment, trying to ascertain where it came from. Not hearing anything else, she continued on while watching the morning shadows dancing with sunlight that was slowly filtering upwards through the trees. As she sidled around some bushes, a movement in the trees just ahead and to the left caught her attention. She stopped abruptly, recognizing Nathan Smith. She would wait until he disappeared, having no desire to run into him this morning, or any other morning for that matter. When he disappeared back toward the wagons, she continued on her way. Again, she thought she heard a muffled cry. The sound was barely audible, but as she listened, she realized it was coming from the bank just above where she had taken her bath the night before. She stepped carefully and quickly through the rest of the underbrush that lay just before the path that led to the river. Peering stealthily around a tree, she spotted her.

Suzanne Smith lay on her side with her head in her arms on the bank by the water's edge. As Lynn approached, her foot stepped on a stick making it snap. Suzanne quieted for a moment and then started moving her body away from Lynn without even looking up. Obviously, she thought that Nathan had returned. Lynn squatted beside her and she held out her hand as she spoke quietly.

"Suzanne? It's alright. It's just me." Lynn, in her anxiousness, used her own normal, soft voice. Suzanne lifted her head to look at her and immediately Lynn realized what she had done. Confusion overlapped fear in Suzanne's eyes when Lynn took off her hat.

"Don't tell anyone, okay? I'm sorry to scare you. But, I heard you crying and had to come over. Let me wipe your face off for you." Lynn dipped a rag into the cool water and started to wipe the blood off of Suzanne's face. Her cheek was starting to purple, her lip was cut deeply on one side, and her left eye was blackening already as well. The knuckles on her right hand were bleeding where she must have scraped them on the rocks that were along the river edge, or perhaps when she had tried to protect herself from Nathan's blows, just as Lynn had always tried to do with Jared. As soon as Lynn touched her eye she cried out in pain. The swelling indicated that Nathan had severely bruised the bone. Suzanne tried to swallow her pain, but she cried out softly one more time as Lynn gently wiped the blood off her lip and jaw.

Both women heard a noise through the trees, someone was walking quickly towards them. They were the quick, noisy steps of someone not caring who heard them coming through the underbrush. Lynn stood quickly and slammed the hat back onto her head just as Nathan appeared out of the trees. Suzanne cast a fearful glance at him and hid her face back in her arms. Nathan surveyed the scene before him for just a moment with an ugly scowl deepening the lines on his broad forehead. His hands formed fists at his side and the beady eyes shot venom in Lynn's direction.

Lynn was a battlefield of emotions. One part of her wanted to run from this man and from this ugly scene. Another part of her wanted to lash out at his cruelty. Nathan made the decision for her. She stood stunned, blinking back shock for a moment at his accusation.

"What did you do to my wife, boy? You gettin' your thrills out o' beatin' women? Suzanne, what did he do to ya?" Nathan took a step towards his wife as he uttered the words in a tone that Lynn had heard so many times. The tone that said that Suzanne had better not disagree with him or she would regret it. If she spoke against what he said, he would make her pay dearly later. Lynn was dismayed to feel herself jump slightly at the familiar threat. How well she knew it. How dearly she had paid more than a few times until she learned what it meant. She shuddered as memories came flooding back. Suddenly, she was enraged. She was shaking, not only from fear but from anger, anger so deep and immense that it threatened to explode within her chest. Her temples pulsated with pressure, and it was all she could do to control the tremor in her voice.

"How dare you claim I did that to her, Mr. Smith." Lynn's voice was steady as she spoke to him, remembering to deepen her voice this time. She sounded braver than she felt, but her intense anger made the words come. By this time about a dozen other people had gathered. They heard Nathan's angry voice and they came to see what was going on. They listened to the exchange with interest. Larry was a strange young man, but he didn't seem the type to do this. As for Nathan, most people knew him to be a cruel and bitter man. So they watched and listened to see what would come of this. Someone was sent to fetch Benjamin who, amazingly enough, had not arrived yet.

"I don't have any interest in beating women, Mr. Smith. I believe that is your line of business." Lynn was playing with fire and she knew it. But she couldn't just walk away as people had done with her. People who must've known that something wasn't right, that the bruises and the pains weren't just accidents. People who were too scared to stand up and say something. She couldn't be like those people.

Nathan's face turned red at the accusation as his thick, beefy hands clenched at his side. "Young man, you don't really want to be sayin' things like that, now do ya? That would be a mistake on your part." His eyes bulged slightly as he waited, and Lynn recognized the raw hunger in them. Jared's eyes always had that same raw hunger when he wanted to hurt someone.

"Actually, I do want to say what I just did. Don't you think you have beaten this poor woman long enough?" She pointed to Suzanne who still lay on the ground with her face hidden from view from the others. Lynn's heart pounded wildly in her chest until she thought everyone must see it through her shirt. She was a fool to infuriate this man, and yet she couldn't just walk away.

Nathan's temper simply couldn't take any more of this impertinent young man. His face looked as though it would explode as he bellowed, swinging towards Lynn with fists raised and spittle spraying from his mouth as his rage reached a boiling point. Lynn saw it coming and sidestepped the first hit he thrust towards her. However, she tripped over a rock and was fighting to regain her balance as he swung back around, hitting her full force in the side of the head. She reeled back from the blow, shaking her head slightly and trying frantically to gain her balance once again. Hands in front of her face didn't prevent him from striking her again, this time to the jaw. The tenuous hold she had on solid footing was lost, making her fall first to her knees and then to her side, hitting her head on a rock. The last coherent thought she had before darkness overcame her was that Ben had told her that if she got into any fights she would be thrown off this wagon train. What would she do now with no one to help her get to Oregon?

The first thing Ben saw when he ran down to the river was Bud and Jeremiah pulling Nathan away from an inert Larry. People were gathering around the slender form on the ground pointing to her with questioning looks on their faces. Larry's hat had come off in the fray and without the hat, her face was fully visible for the first time in the six weeks they were traveling. The shirt that had always been very loose now clung to her chest. It was obviously not a man's form, which made them question who this really was.

"What in thunderation happened here?" Ben pushed aside the group around Larry. Kyle had pushed into the crowd just seconds before him and was wiping the blood from a gash on Larry's head. He had tears in his eyes, fearing the worst. Ben shot him a curious look, but then turned to Larry. She looked so frail. Her pale face, with blood running from her head wound, looked terrible. There was also a bruise forming on the side of her head and her jaw was swelling. He put his ear to her chest realizing that she was still alive, but she was going to have to be moved to a more comfortable place as soon as possible. Laying on the rocks at the river's edge couldn't be easy on her back. He easily picked her up and started barking orders as he looked around. He saw the battered Suzanne also on the ground, closely watching him and Larry.

"Bud, you and Jeremiah please take Suzanne to your wagon. Rachel, you can clean her up. Willy, you and Stanley, and Jake go find Nathan. I want him now! Leann and Leah, follow me with cold water and rags to help me clean up...." he hesitated for a second and his frown deepened as he glanced briefly down at the inert form in his arms, "Larry." At the command in his tone, everyone jumped into action. As he started walking towards the wagons, Jake stopped him for just a moment.

"You realize that Larry is a woman, don't you?" Ben could almost laugh at the expression on Jake's face. There was another woman on this train after all and by the looks of it, probably around Jake's age. But, she was in men's clothes, was bleeding from a bad head wound, a bruise was forming on the side of her head, and she possibly had a broken jaw.

"Yes, I came to that realization yesterday."

"Yesterday? You mean you really didn't know all this time? How did you find out yesterday?" Jake was surprised. He thought nothing escaped the wagon master's notice.

"I'll tell you about it some other time, alright? Right now, you have something I need you to do, and I have to get this young woman to the wagon before she bleeds to death while I stand here and talk to you." Jake had the decency to turn color as he turned away to follow orders, but not before he took one last look at the slender young woman in Ben's arms.

Ben had never been as furious as he was at this moment. His thoughts had centered on Larry long after he should have been asleep last night, going through all kinds of reasons why a woman would want to dress up as a man; none of them making sense except one. She must be running away from someone. That line of thought immediately took him in Jared Malen's direction. This must be the sister he had spoken of. As he looked down at her pale face in the warm morning sun, he was angry with himself for not figuring out sooner that this was a woman. Now that he knew, it was so obvious that it was a slap to his manhood that he had been so blind. Her heart-shaped face with long lashes and full lips were so clearly feminine. Even thinking back to watching Larry walk, there was a feminine grace to the steps. Oh, there was an attempt at a swagger in there, but Ben had chalked that up to a young man trying to prove himself. He glanced down at the slender hands with long fingers. The fingernails were blunt from the hard work on the trail, but he could imagine them tapered and clean as she held a cup of tea in her hand entertaining other ladies in a fine parlor. Again he chided himself for being so blind.

His thoughts were pulled away abruptly. Leann had a questioning look on her face. She must have asked him something and he hadn't heard her being so deep in his own thoughts.

"Pardon me, I didn't hear what you said, Leann."

"I wanted to know if you think I should get a needle and thread. That gash on her head looks bad and I'm thinkin' it will need stitchin'." She glanced worriedly at the wound.

Leah nodded her head, "I'm thinkin' the same thing, Ben. The girl's gonna need that taken care of proper like. It looks pretty bad to me, too." Leah stopped beside Ben as they reached the wagon. He climbed inside laying Larry on the bed nearest the back of the wagon.

"Please get whatever it is that you think that you may need. I'm going to get a bucket of cold water and I'll be right back."

Leah stayed with Larry as Ben and Leann quickly went in different directions. As she looked a little closer at the wound on the unconscious woman's head, she wondered why no one on the whole train had figured out that this was a woman. Her big hat and her loose shirts had hidden her face and figure very well so no one ever really got a good look at her. And of course, she had stayed away from everybody and they had thought that rather odd. Most people on the train were very friendly and even if they weren't particularly talkative, they still would gather with the others at times just to listen to them if nothing else. But Larry had stayed away. Now they knew why.

Ben and Leann returned and they started the process of cleaning the wound and then Leann closed it up with small, neat stitches. Larry moaned a couple of times and moved slightly while Leann was busy, but Ben gently held her until Leann was finished. Afterward, while the women cleaned up, Ben went to find out how Suzanne was faring. Rachel had done an excellent job cleaning her up and putting salve on her cuts. Lenore Johnson had helped and the two women were busy talking since they had made Suzanne lay down and rest in the Aames' wagon. They asked about Larry.

"How is she doing?" Rachel's face was anxious. "That cut on her head looked really bad, Ben. Is she going to be alright?"

"I think so. Leann put seven stitches in and...," again, the slight hesitation, "Larry... moved around a little, although she didn't wake up. Time will tell." Ben's tongue felt thick when he called her Larry. That name was now hard to say, but not knowing her real name, what else could he call her? "I'm going to talk to the men and find Nathan. Let me know if anything happens with either of them, alright?" Both women nodded in agreement and then quickly walked in the direction of Larry and Kyle's wagon to get a better look at this young woman.

Chapter 10

"A wife found"

Nathan was not hard to find. The men had simply formed a circle around him, and he was sitting with an angry red face on a rock a little ways off from the wagons and close to the river. The men were talking among themselves, and Ben heard snatches of conversations as he drew closer to them.

"Ought to hang him." "Naw, hangin's too good fer him. Tie 'im up and leave 'im fer the coyotes." "There any Indians around? We could prob'ly get some good trade fer 'im".

The circle fell quiet, however, when they saw Ben walk into the center and face Nathan. Ben stood with arms crossed against his chest and contemplated Nathan for a few moments. When he finally spoke, his words were clipped and angry. The anger on his face warned anyone who may have a different opinion than his to lose it quickly.

"I'm not interested in your reasons. No man hits a woman on my wagon train. I also warned all of you about starting fights on this train. I told you that I do not tolerate them and that anyone who engages in them will be thrown off. I will draw you a general map of what lies ahead and where to find the next couple of water holes. You are on your own. You will unload any of your wife's belongings and then you will leave immediately." Ben stood with his legs spread slightly as though ready to take a charge from the furious Nathan. Ben's eyes had taken on a hard gleam, and Nathan knew in that instant that he wouldn't stand a chance against this man. He couldn't resist one thing, however.

"I don't see any need to unload my wife's things. I'll take what's mine and that includes my wife." His face had gotten redder at Ben's order to unload Suzanne's things. Who did this man think he was?! Suzanne belonged to him, and no filthy wagon master was going to take her away from him.

Ben cocked an eyebrow as he assessed the man who stood before him. Was Nathan really that stupid?

"Do you think that I am going to let her go with you after what you've done to her? The poor woman deserves to have a rest." He paused for a moment thinking.

"I want to see your dust within fifteen minutes. Do you understand?" Nathan heard the steel in Ben's voice and made a decision that went against what he wanted to do. Maybe he should thank the wagon master for taking the stupid, simpering woman off of his hands, but it still made him angry. He shook himself a little, trying to compose himself, and then shoved his way through the circle and headed for his wagon.

Ben jerked a thumb in his direction but addressed Jeremiah, Bud, and Willy. "Can you keep an eye on him for me? I need to talk with young Kyle, there." Kyle heard his name and looked up, knowing what Ben was going to ask, and he knew that only Larry could give him the information he desired. He waited silently, his arms hanging at his side helplessly as he watched Ben walk over and stand in front of him. Ben waited until the other men had dispersed and then asked the question that had burned in him for the past two days.

"Who are you and who is the young woman with you?" The question was quietly spoken and he waited patiently as he watched the emotions and turmoil play across the younger man's face. Kyle looked pained and remained silent for a moment, clearly indecisive as to what to say. He looked at Ben with pleading eyes until at last, he answered.

"I am who I said. My name is Kyle Parish. Larry is not my cousin. She is someone my Aunt and I knew back in Independence." He almost whispered the words, his eyes on his feet as he spoke. When he would volunteer no more information, Ben prodded him gently.

"What is the young woman's name and who is she if she is not a relative?"

"I'm sorry, but I can't tell ya that. I promised her that I wouldn't tell anyone anything 'bout her. If I told ya now, she would be very upset with me. I don't want her mad at me." His boyish manner reminded Ben that although Kyle had been doing a man's work for the last few weeks, he wasn't a man yet. He was still young and he obviously loved Larry very much and wanted to protect her. He had figured as much and now was suddenly impatient to know who she was. At least a name would be helpful.

"Couldn't you at least tell me her name, Kyle?"

Kyle was silent again for a moment and Ben saw the hesitation in his face. After thinking about it for a moment he decided against saying any more.

"Naw, I better let her tell ya when she's ready." He started to turn away from the older man and then turned back for just a moment. "She is going to be alright, isn't she? She didn't deserve this, ya know. She deserves a lot better than this happenin' again. I promised my Aunt that I would take care of her." His voice broke and suddenly his face was in his hands, his back and shoulders shaking with fear and guilt. Ben's heart went out to him, and he placed an arm around his shoulders.

"She seems like a tough young woman. I think she'll be alright. Why don't we go check on her and see if she is awake yet?" He eyed Kyle speculatively and stood there thinking about Kyle's comment about "this happenin' again". What did he mean "again"? Kyle finally got control of himself and they silently walked back to the wagon.

Several of the women and a handful of men had gathered around Kyle and Larry's wagon. Among them was Jake Emmons. Leah and Rachel had dropped the wagon cover over the back to afford some privacy as they took off the men's clothes and had replaced them with a shift and an older dress that one of the other women had located and would let her use for now. They had also untied the strips of cloth that she used to bind down her breasts. So, although the dress was a little big on her slender frame, it made her a woman, and an attractive one at that.

Now as they climbed out of the wagon, the men wanted a glimpse of Larry. Leah pulled back the wagon cover again to allow a slight breeze to go through the wagon, being worried about a fever forming now which meant keeping a close watch on her. Jake was at the front of the small crowd that had gathered and realized that they had all been made fools of. Larry's hair was shiny and damp from cool water being wiped across her forehead in case of fever. As it dried, it framed her pale face with small curls around her ears and jaw. Her lips were slightly parted like she was ready to be kissed, and a tinge of color framed the high cheekbones. How on earth had they ever believed that this was a man? What idiots! This was definitely a woman—a very pretty woman!

Ben and Kyle made their way through the crowd to the back of the wagon. Ben felt a tremor of irritation when he saw Jake standing nearest to the back of the wagon as he looked in at Larry. It was a quick feeling that he just as quickly pushed down. Everyone knew that Jake was looking for a wife. Why should Ben be annoyed that maybe Jake finally found himself one? The irritation rose again in his chest at that thought and he frowned as he walked up beside the other man to look inside the wagon. What he saw surprised him. Larry had a dress on. It was a little large on her, but it still managed to make her look very much the woman. She no longer had a flat chest, and although not heavily breasted, there were definitely some curves there. Ben had a flashback to the night before down at the river. Looking at the lovely face and pink lips, he had the sudden urge to wrap his arms around her and pull her close. He knew almost nothing about her, but just the barest pieces of her past he was catching glimpses of, made a wave of protectiveness swell inside him. And now seeing her pretty face, he realized why everyone had gathered around and why Jake continued to stare. Again, the irritation flared. Abruptly he spun around.

"Alright, folks. Let's return to your own wagons and chores. Larry needs to rest and hopefully regain her strength. We'll all know soon enough what we're all curious about." He pulled the wagon cover down so that Larry was hidden from view and everyone slowly went their way. Except for Jake, that is.

"I'll stay and help keep watch on her for now, I think." Jake crossed his arms and leaned back against the wagon.

Ben frowned at him. "Leah, Rachel, and Leann can keep better care of her right now than you are able to do. I'm sure your brother will need your help with things, anyway. We're going to be here a couple more days at least. We just as well do repairs and other things that need done while we're here."

Jake knew when he was being told to leave and, standing arrogantly for a moment looking at Ben, finally decided that he would go for now. But he would be back and check on Larry often. Little did he know that Ben had the same idea, as he too, walked toward his wagon after seeing Jake leave for his.

Leah caught up with Ben, touching him lightly on the shoulder as he walked deep in thought.

"I must tell you something, Ben." Her voice was low and secretive and immediately caught his attention. He stopped and looked down at her.

"When we changed Larry's clothes we noticed something." When she hesitated, Ben nodded his head urging her to continue.

"Well, she has several scars on her back and upper arms. Many of them are rather faded looking. But some are still a little on the pink side, more recent." She wrung her hands and tears came to her eyes. "She has been beaten many times by someone awful."

Ben didn't know what to say at first. Although suspicions were forming, he hadn't expected it to be that bad. His thoughts went back to a few minutes ago when Kyle had made the comment about her 'not deserving this again'. There was quite the mystery surrounding Larry, and he could hardly wait to have answers to the questions. In the meantime, he wished silently to himself that he knew the person who left those scars on that slender body so that he could kill the man who did it. His mind flickered briefly to Jared Malen, but why would he beat his own sister? His chest heaved with anger for a moment and then, getting control of himself, he turned to Leah.

"Thank you, Leah. I'm going to ask you to not repeat this to everyone else. The whole train does not need to know what you just told me, alright?" He placed a hand on her shoulder reassuring her before she nodded and turned away to return to her family.

It was two days before Lynn regained consciousness. It was late in the morning, the sun almost at its zenith when she slowly moved and her eyelids fluttered open. A pounding headache was the first thing she felt. As she gently probed her head, her fingers found the stitches. She moaned as she tried to sit up and fell back onto the bed, feeling her jaw move slightly and painfully as she did so. Rachel appeared seemingly out of nowhere, placing a hand on her shoulder and talking quietly.

"Don't try to sit up, dear. You have stitches on your head where you hit a rock when you fell. Leann Seckers stitched it up for you. And Ben doesn't think that your jaw is broken, but it is badly bruised. We've been very worried about you. You've been unconscious for two days and you had a slight fever for about a day and a half." Rachel continued to talk quietly, hoping that the words would keep Larry awake for a while. She needed to drink some water as they had been able to get very little down her. "Ben has been very undecided as what to do. He didn't want to move you yet. But we need to get back on the trail. We're behind schedule and he's becoming impatient. I'm so glad you are coming back around, dear." Relief showed in her eyes when Lynn could finally focus on her. At the mention of the wagon master's name and his impatience, Lynn became worried, remembering once again his warning about fighting and subsequent consequences.

"Move me? Move me where?" Becoming gradually more aware of things, she realized that she was in a dress and not men's clothes anymore. They finally knew that she was a woman. Now Ben would really be angry! "Where did this dress come from? Is he very angry with me? I don't know if I could take a wagon by myself. When do I have to leave the train?" Her voice was slurry and talking made her wince as her jaw had a sudden twinge of pain. A panicked look settled in her face as she started to rise again from the bed.

Rachel was confused, "Leave the train? I don't know what you are talking about, dear. Ben wouldn't make you leave the train." She tried to make her voice soothing, but Larry continued to look panicked, and she placed a hand once again on her shoulder to push her back down.

"Yes, yes he will. He told Kyle and me that if we got into fights we would be thrown off the wagon train. And I got into a fight with Nathan Smith." Suddenly remembering why, she asked, "Is Suzanne alright?" Her brow furrowing, she turned worried eyes to look questioningly into Rachel's confused ones.

Before Rachel could say anything, however, another voice answered for her, having heard the last little bit of the conversation. "Yes, she is fine. Rachel and Lenore did a nice job nursing her wounds. To answer your other question, I'm not making you leave the wagon train. I'm not an unfair man. Nathan has left, however. He left the same day of the fight. I consider the surrounding circumstances before I pass a judgment." He saw the panic in her eyes slowly disappear as she comprehended what he said. He thought once again how big a fool he was to miss the obvious. The past two days had not been good to her. Her face was still pale, the fever had caused dark circles under her eyes, and her hair was uncombed. The lower side of her face was purple and swollen where her jaw had been hit so hard. Even with all of that, she was still an attractive woman. He cast a sideways look at Rachel.

"Do you have some soup or something that" he hesitated, "Larry can eat? I am going to go fetch Kyle. He was down by the river a few minutes ago fishing with your two boys. I'm sure he'll want to talk with," again a hesitation, "Larry." He turned to look at her with eyebrows raised. "Do you have another name perhaps? I really dislike calling you Larry."

Lynn had been scared to death when Ben first approached. She was so sure that he would make her leave right then and there. But after he started to talk in that deep, calm voice of his, she relaxed slightly. When she realized that he wasn't going to make her leave, her relief was great, like a large boulder rolling off her chest allowing her to breathe again. Now, when he asked her for her name, she was thankful to Kyle for keeping his promise to her. She wouldn't be able to carry a man's name anymore, but did she want to go back to her own? She thought for a moment and noted Ben's quiet patience as he waited for her answer. His arms were crossed against that muscular chest of his, and with his head cocked to one side he gazed directly into her eyes making her blush. Dropping her gaze to her sleeve hem, she fingered it as she thought for a moment. Maybe she would use her own first name, but certainly not her last one. Finally looking up again, she knew she needed to give him an answer sooner or later and it just as well be sooner.

"Lynn... Adams." Ben barely heard her whisper. His patience had paid off; he could at least call her by a woman's name now. He had doubts, however, about it being her real name. The way she hesitated suggested that it probably wasn't. But at least they could get rid of "Larry". His smile and eyes were warm as he studied her face for just a split second, thanked her, and then turned towards the river to go in search of Kyle.

Lynn was surprised at Ben's smile and glanced at Rachel, who had been sitting and quietly listening to the exchange. Rachel simply smiled back and her brown eyes sparkled with happiness that they finally had a proper name for her. Lynn laid her head back onto the pillow again and closed her eyes. She thought about his brief study of her face and had the idea that he didn't believe her about the name she offered him. The brief conversation had tired her, and she dozed off after Rachel went in search of some food for her.

Rachel smiled to herself as she walked quickly back to her wagon. Leah and Leann met her as she came around the outside of the wagon carrying a plate of stew and half of a biscuit a couple of minutes later and she explained that 'Larry' had awakened and she needed to get some food into her. She also told them that "Larry" was now Lynn. They decided to accompany her back to Lynn.

By the time they made it to the wagon, Kyle and Ben had returned. Kyle was talking to Lynn, holding her hand and apologizing to her that he hadn't protected her better. Lynn, seeing the women coming, struggled to sit up explaining to Kyle at the same time that it wasn't his fault and that he should stop blaming himself. Ben stood with ankles and arms crossed, leaning his back up against the side of the wagon with his usual relaxed and yet somehow vigil stance. He was so intent on Lynn that he failed to notice the women walking toward him until he saw Lynn look their way. Leah smiled slightly and winked at her younger sister. Ben's interest was obvious. He had told them briefly one night a couple of weeks ago that there was a young woman at home who imagined herself in love with him, and since women weren't exactly in abundance in the west, he was thinking he would probably settle down with her and start a family. When Leah had asked him if he was in love with her, he had thought for a moment and then replied that no, love wasn't the most important part of a marriage and that the young lady was likable enough. Leah had been ready to argue that statement but Will had frowned at her. But now watching him, both sisters knew that Ben was having second thoughts about the young woman back home.

Rachel spoke up first, "We've brought some stew and a biscuit for you, Lynn. Eat what you can and don't worry about it if you don't eat it all. It will take a while to get all of your strength back." Her smile warmed Lynn's heart in a way that nothing else could right now. She gazed at the three women and was so relieved that her charade was over. How she had longed to be able to talk to these women! Jared hadn't allowed her to get close to any woman. And with them moving all of the time, by the time she finally did become acquainted with one, she was never able to become friends with them. Maggie had been the first. Now, maybe she could have women friends once again. Her heart had ached for so long and needed the nurturing that friendship offered.

"I'll try to eat as much as possible. It smells wonderful. Thank you very much." Her eyes were moist with sudden emotion and she smiled as she took the plate offered her. The three women and Kyle started talking among themselves about things and people around the wagons, and she listened with interest. After she ate four or five mouthfuls, she became aware of being watched and glanced around. She caught Ben's intent gaze resting on her, and she was suddenly alarmed. There was keen interest in his eyes, and when her eyes met his, a smile warmed his face. She had never noticed before now, but he had a small dimple in his left cheek. That naked look of interest in his eyes unnerved her. She must look a sight! But then, men had always glanced her way. There were some men who were insolent in their looks—looks that showed raw hunger in their eyes. Then there were others who were simply appreciating a pretty woman when they saw one. It never made her egotistical, her grandparents had always told her that 'pretty was what pretty did'. It took her a while to figure that one out, but she had finally understood.

Ben noted the blush and how she looked quickly away when she realized that he was staring at her. He wondered again at his own blindness. He was suddenly aware of other people around them. They had noticed the gathering around the wagon and correctly guessed the reason behind it. A small crowd was gathering and everybody was talking at once. Lynn was becoming self-conscious with all of this attention and after a couple more small spoonfuls of stew, pushed the bowl away. She had drunk two glasses of water and Rachel kept trying to give her more.

"Wa'll aren't you a sight for sore eyes!" Jake Emmons walked up to the back of the wagon and peered inside at Lynn. He looked her boldly in the eye as he thrust a small bouquet of wildflowers in front of her. Lynn looked into piercing brown eyes and was startled at the realization that he was already courting her. She was suddenly fearful of what was happening. Her face, which had begun to get the littlest bit of color in the last fifteen minutes, paled quickly and Leah, noticing the panic on her face, suggested that everyone leave now and let the poor girl rest.

"I'm agoin', I'm agoin', Mrs. Emerson, but I'll be back." Jake had turned to talk to Leah but directed his next comment back to Lynn. "Yessir, I'll be back later to talk to this pretty young lady." With that promise he sauntered off, seemingly happy with himself that finally there was a proper woman on this train and he'd found his wife.

Ben had straightened at Jake's approach and quietly watched the short exchange with a heavy frown, his smile disappearing quickly at Jake's bold overtures to Lynn.

Leann noticed the frown he wore and nudged Rachel who smiled. "The rest of this trip should be very interesting, don't you think?" Rachel whispered. Leann smiled in return, her eyes sparkling with humor as she nodded in agreement.

Chapter 11

"A little intervention"

June 28th, 1844

The next couple of weeks were very emotionally and physically wearing on Lynn. Her body had healed once again, and the bruises were gone along with the aches of sore muscles and bones. Emotionally she was trying to heal as well, but that was a little more difficult. She was now trying to rethink everything not just as a woman, but as a supposedly free woman; one who didn't have the shackles of a domineering and cruel husband. She wasn't used to thinking that way and it presented its challenges in many forms, which meant that the simplest decision would be made and then she would wonder if Jared wouldn't like it that way. Then she would remember that it didn't matter what he thought, he wasn't there. That would bring a small smile to her face, uplifting her spirits for the rest of the day.

Ben had pushed them hard to make up for the lost time, but she enjoyed the beautiful plains with their wildlife and the rivers that ran through them here and there. The river crossings were often treacherous, and more than one wagon had tipped over losing many of the contents therein. But, nobody had died or gotten seriously hurt yet, although Ben held his breath waiting for what he knew would come sooner or later. There were no problems with anyone on the train; all the families got along well and worked together as a strong unit. The only problem from Ben's perspective was Jake.

Jake was relentless in his pursuit of Lynn making it obvious that as far as he was concerned, he had finally found himself a wife. Every day he brought her something; flowers, if they could be found, fresh water when they were near any, a slab of deer or antelope backstrap when he shot one, or just a few minutes here and there when he would run back to their wagon to check on her. Lynn would smile softly and quietly say "thank you" for the gifts, but the whole time would be in emotional turmoil within. Whenever Ben happened upon the gifts or Jake conversing with Lynn, his eyes would darken with irritation and he would stalk off. Rachel, Leah, and Leann watched the exchanges with amusement, sometimes feeling sorry for Ben, who just stood back instead of doing his own courting. Rachel finally got tired of seeing him just turn the other way and could no longer resist encouraging him to do something about his feelings.

The evening was warm, and the moon was a beautiful crescent. Ben was looking up at the night sky a little ways from the camp. He sat on his haunches, his arms resting on his strong thighs when Rachel quietly approached him. She, too, looked at the moon for a moment before turning to him with resolve on her face.

"It is truly lovely tonight, isn't it?" Ben glanced up at her, waiting. He recognized that tone in her voice and look on her face. She had something to say, and he smiled wryly to himself as he thought about her and her sister. Bud and Willy had bold, fiery women. His patience paid off when she finally spoke what was on her mind.

"Surely a night to share with someone, isn't it?" She raised an eyebrow as she looked first at him and then pointedly in Lynn's direction. Suzanne had started traveling with them, and the two women often walked together as they traveled during the day. Right now she and Lynn were doing some sewing around the campfire. Lynn was sitting with her back to Ben. Kyle sat opposite her with Sarah just an arm's length away. They were talking and laughing as Lynn showed Sarah something about the shirt she held in her hand. Kyle frowned slightly making it obvious that the two women were teasing him. Then, suddenly, he laughed loudly and leaning forward, playfully tugged on the shirt in her hand.

Glancing in the direction Rachel indicated and then back at her, Ben frowned and said nothing.

Rachel's voice was insistent, "Don't you think that you should ask her to go for a walk and enjoy talking with her without any interruptions?" Ben's frown turned into an outright scowl as he studied the ground.

He was almost growling when he finally answered, "I'm sure that Jake will ask her the same thing any time now. I'm surprised that he hasn't already."

"Well," she chuckled softly, "I'm sure he probably will as soon as

Bud and Willy get done talking with him. Leah and our men are, uh, kinda keeping him busy for a few moments." She smiled mischievously when Ben jerked his head up in surprise.

"What makes you think that she would want to go for a walk with me?" He asked quietly, and yet Rachel could hear the hopefulness in his voice.

"What makes you think she won't want to? Just because Jake is always around her doesn't mean that she wants him to be. I've seen her gaze follow you more than they follow Jake. He seems to frighten her or at the very least make her skittish." Her face took on an innocent air and she waited for the words to sink in. He shot her another look of surprise.

Rachel had linked her hands behind her back as they talked, but now she held one out to Ben as she took one step back. Ben studied her for a moment as doubt and then hope took turns passing over his face. He pulled his large frame up to tower over the fiery-haired woman, shook her hand briefly, and then walked toward the small group by the wagon. Rachel watched for a moment when he reached them, and they raised their heads to look up at him. Ben spoke to them all for a moment and then turned his attention to Lynn who sat perfectly still as if not believing what she had just heard. Then, she set her mending aside and slowly got to her feet. Ben offered his hand, but she had declined to take it. Rachel smiled to herself as she walked back to her wagon and winked at Leah. Jake hadn't yet seen what had transpired behind his back and when he did, he wasn't going to be happy. But, "oh well", the two women thought, and they continued to keep his attention for a while longer. It wasn't that they didn't like Jake, they did. He was a good man and would make some woman a fine husband someday. However, they didn't see Lynn with Jake. Not knowing her past except for bits and pieces, they still surmised abuse had taken place, and probably at the hands of a man, which meant Jake wasn't what she needed. Not that he would be abusive, but he was too overbearing. Lynn needed the quiet strength of someone like Ben, a man with strong character, but with a gentle side to him. Yep, the two sisters had already made the decision, Ben was the one for Lynn, whether either one of them was aware of it or not!

Chapter 12

"An evening walk"

Lynn was more than surprised when Ben came over to ask her to go for a walk with him in the evening air. She hesitated for a few seconds, then decided that maybe it would be alright. Jake practically smothered her. He was certainly a good man, and an attractive one too, but he was not really what she would want in a husband even if she could marry again. She had no doubt that he would make some woman a good husband someday, but she was not the one. He had dreams and plans laid out in his head with such precision that he could relate the smallest details of everything his life would hold from here on. While she didn't think he would be harsh with his wife, he would be demanding. After having heard some of the things he wanted his wife to be able to accomplish in a short period of time, she knew that he would be asking an awful lot out of a woman. While not being afraid of hard work and enjoying the feeling of success that came with a job well done, she certainly didn't feel she would ever be able to live up to what he would be expecting. Hopefully, all of his plans went well, but she already knew from harsh experience that life is seldom what you plan it to be. She was learning quickly to take pleasure in small moments and maybe make plans for the future, but not carving them in stone.

Lynn felt rather than saw the glance that Ben gave her as they walked around the perimeter of the large spring where they had stopped for an extra day to catch up on chores and rest the livestock. With Jake constantly hovering around her, Ben seemed to avoid her most of the time. When he did look her way, it was usually with a frown. Now, she wondered what she had done that he needed to speak to her about. Her thoughts went flying back over the last few days and couldn't think of what it could be. She patiently waited for him to speak.

"Nice night isn't it?" His comments took her by surprise, and he saw her glance up at him before she replied.

"Yes, it is. I love the openness of this country. I could almost stop here and settle."

It was his turn to be surprised, even though he was aware that she was one of the few who enjoyed the open country they were traveling through right now. Most others complained of the constant dust that covered everything and made it hard to use anything without first washing it. The women were constantly washing and shaking things out, trying to stay as clean as possible. Seeing its beauty was one thing, wanting to settle here was entirely a different matter, however, and he was intrigued by her comment. He thought of home and his family waiting there for him to return. His brother, Jad, would be anxious for him to get back so they could break more ground this fall before the rain and maybe snow fell. His niece, Cathleen, he missed very much. She was three and a beautiful copy of his younger sister, Shaline. She and her husband, Allen Colton, lived in the farmhouse with Ben's brother and mother, Grace, who still ruled her family with an iron hand. Or so they let her think, anyway. Thoughts of home warmed him and brought a smile. His thoughts made him start to talk as they walked slowly through the tall prairie grass. Lynn clasped her hands behind her back as she gazed straight ahead.

"If you think this is pretty country, wait until you see the Oregon country. My family's spread is about three miles outside of Oregon City. The land is rich with timber and water. There is a large river not far from our house and my brother and I often go and fish there." Lynn glanced up as his voice changed from his usual low tone to one with excitement. He had a faint smile hovering around his mouth and his expression was animated with his description. When she stopped to listen to him, he turned sideways towards her, looking down at the warm interest showing in her face.

As she stood there and listened to him talk, she breathed deeply the warm night air and the smells it brought her of the country around them. It was edged with the faint smell of gun powder and coffee on the man beside her.

"Have you ever tasted smoked salmon?" She shook her head. "Then that is one of the first things you shall taste when we arrive. Jad always has salmon in the smokehouse curing."

"Jad?" The question was softly spoken, and he glanced down at her mouth, but caught himself when he noticed her cheeks slightly color. A couple of tendrils of hair blew across her face and eyes, catching some of the light from the fires behind them, causing it to glow red and orange. When he continued to stare at her, she turned away to look at the horizon from embarrassment, he mentally shook himself and answered the question.

"Oh, uh, Jad is my younger brother." Her face held other questions that she was shy to ask, so he went ahead and answered them for her. "I also have a sister, Shaline, her husband is Allen Colton. A good man. Hardworking, honest, and adores the ground my sister walks on." He rolled his eyes as he said that, and Lynn laughed at the exaggerated expression on his face. The laughter caught his immediate attention and he looked at her once more. Her soft laughter always got his attention. It sounded almost musical. He thought that sounded silly even in his head, but he thought it anyway. It had a carefree sound to it, and he suddenly realized that he wanted to hear it more often.

He went on, "My sister has a daughter, Cathleen, who is a mischievous three-year-old, actually almost four years old now. And then there is my mother, Grace, who thinks she still rules the family." Lynn noticed how his voice softened with affection at the mention of his niece's and mother's names. His head tipped with curiosity. "What about you, what kind of family do you have?"

His question caught her off guard, and for a moment all she could do was stare into his face. Her hands had moved from her back to them being clasped together in front and now back again. Nervousness was obvious, but he waited with patience and interest as she stood deciding what to tell him. Then she composed herself and answered with as little information as possible.

"I have an Uncle in New York. The rest are all dead." Just before she turned away to walk a little further on, Ben saw the hurt and sadness in her eyes. Although he wanted to know more, now was obviously not going to be the time. He studied her straight back and gentle curve of her hips as she walked. He decided that she had one of the most graceful walks he had ever seen. Her strides were long and smooth, almost athletic. He couldn't explain why he felt that way, other than her body seemed to move in one fluid motion, well-coordinated. Cocking his head slightly to one side for just a brief moment, he decided he would certainly enjoy watching her walk for the rest of his life. He changed the subject.

"How are your supplies holding up?" Lynn was grateful for his thoughtfulness and it briefly brought back memories of a couple of days before when Jake had asked the same question about her family.

When she had made a brief comment to him, he kept pressing her for more information until she had left with the excuse of needing to talk to Rachel about something very important. She could gladly answer the question that Ben posed now, though.

"Very well, thank you. Kyle's hunting skills are getting better all of the time and he keeps a steady supply of meat coming." So does Jake, she thought to herself. She realized that Jake irritated Ben for some reason unknown to her, and she didn't want to spoil the quiet conversation of the moment. Walking and conversing with this big man was turning into a pleasant experience, and she decided to encourage him to tell her more about his family, whom he obviously loved very much. Over the past few weeks she had come to realize that although when he needed to be heard around the train he could make his voice carry very well, he was usually quiet spoken. It was a pleasant surprise and welcome change from what she was used to.

"So, how big a place do you have in Oregon?" She stopped beside a small tree and stood looking up at the crescent moon. Leaning her back on the tree, her hands behind her flattened against the rough bark. The million stars that sparkled down upon her seemed to quietly encourage her to keep the conversation going with this gentle man.

Ben glanced down into her uplifted face and suddenly felt an urge to kiss the lips that were slightly parted as she stood looking up into the night sky. He took a step towards her, but when she glanced towards him with a questioning look on her face, he shook himself mentally and answered the question with a slightly husky edge to his voice.

"Well, we,... uh, we have almost twelve hundred acres between the three families."

"Three families?" Lynn didn't understand.

"Yes, me, my brother, and then my sister and her husband, also. We combined the properties and are working the land together. Jad and Allen were going to start putting a sawmill together when I was getting ready to leave. They should be putting out some lumber by the time we return." He swung his hands behind his back and held them there by sheer force. He wanted to put them around her small waist so bad that it hurt. He remembered the night when he had seen her form in the moonlight, and he ached with the thought of the lovely creature of that night. Even prayers to God asking Him to remove those memories from him hadn't been entirely successful—he fought them constantly. She was lovely now, too. Her voice was soft and sweet.

There was the slightest breeze and it caught the short hair around her face, making it flit across her eyes. She brushed it back with long, slender fingers. How he wanted to hold those fingers in his own! But, he dared not do anything that may scare her. She seemed tough and yet fragile at the same time. Perhaps it was the memory of the scars that Leah had told him about that instinctively told him not to move fast with this woman or she would bolt like an unbroken horse.

"That is a lot of land! It must be hard to know where you start and where you end." She paused for a moment but seemed to want to say something else. Ben was a patient man, he stood quietly to give her time. She looked down at her hands, and then she looked up at him as if she got the sudden courage to say whatever it was.

"Is there a need for a teacher where we're heading? I taught school for a couple of years, and I was hoping that there would be a teaching position open somewhere in Oregon." Her eyes were hopeful but hesitant, her chin lifting with determination.

He was taken aback by her question. He didn't really know what he was expecting her to say, but it certainly wasn't that. "Well, I don't know for sure, but the people around there want to have a teacher. We've had a couple, but they up and got married and when I left there wasn't a teacher. That was several months ago, and they may have filled the position by now. The closest school to us only had about fourteen children. Of course, that changes quickly, especially with more and more people moving in." His expression was thoughtful for a moment and then he went on. "As soon as we get there, I'll find out for you about a teaching position." He smiled down at her and was ready to suggest they head back around towards the camp when a voice reached them, making Ben frown heavily and causing Lynn to jump with dismay.

"Why in tarnation would you want to get her a teaching position? Married women don't teach, Ben, you know that!" Jake had finally spied them, and he made it clear that he wasn't happy to find them together. Ben had wondered how long it would take. Jake walked up quickly beside Lynn and taking her elbow, began to walk back toward the camp. Ben quickly followed closely behind.

"She's single and she asked me about the possibility of a teaching position, that's why!" Lynn could hear the irritation in Ben's voice and wondered how Jake could not. She also wondered why Jake annoyed Ben so much. She made a mental note to ask Rachel and Leah about that. They seemed to know Ben pretty well.

"Well, she won't be for long, not if I have anything to say about it." He grinned at Lynn and started walking faster toward the light of the fires. Lynn tried pulling her arm out of his grasp. He wasn't hurting her, but his grip was too strong. Ben noticed the movement she made trying to free her arm and had to hold himself back to keep from grabbing Jake by the shoulder and swinging him around to give him a fist in the face. He tried a different tactic instead.

"Jake, you'll have to excuse us for a moment, I was having a private conversation with Lynn. If you'll be patient for a few minutes, I'll give her to you shortly." Ben placed one large hand gently on Lynn's shoulder and stopped. Jake couldn't believe his ears.

"Wa-a-all anything you have to say to her, you can certainly say to me." He glared at Ben without taking his hand off of Lynn's elbow.

"Since you haven't married her yet, I can still talk with her in private. I haven't heard of any engagement or the like, so I figure I can speak to this woman without you being here." Ben glared back.

Lynn listened to this exchange with growing impatience and irritation. She made sure they both understood that this behavior was not acceptable!

"I don't belong to either one of you and can, therefore, speak to whomever I want, whenever I want." She looked pointedly at Jake. "I am not a piece of meat to manhandle or pull back and forth, and therefore, you will both unhand me this instant." She looked at one, then the other. First Ben, then Jake pulled their hands away and dropped them to their side. "I am tired and am going to bed, gentlemen. Goodnight!" She straightened her back and walking quickly to her wagon, said something to the small group still around the fire, then climbed into the wagon.

As Lynn laid down she still felt the warmth of Ben's hand on her shoulder. When Jake had grabbed her elbow, she hadn't felt anything but annoyance, although she was sure that his hand had been warm, also. Where Ben had touched her was different somehow. Her shoulder felt like it was on fire, the same way she had felt whenever Jared had touched her when he was courting her. He had been more demanding, like Jake in his touches, but at the time, they had felt like fire, too. After they were married, and she realized how cruel he was, his touch had made her skin chill instead of heat up. Now Ben's touch had that same fiery effect on her and it frightened her. How could she make the same mistake again? She wouldn't, she refused to go in that direction!

With confused thoughts and bad dreams, Lynn slept very little that night.

Chapter 13

"Worth fighting for"

After Lynn left the two men, they simply stood there for a moment in surprise that this usually mild-tempered young woman had put them in their place, quietly of course, but put them in their place nonetheless. Jake stood there for a moment, glaring angrily at Ben who returned the look with narrowed eyes for just a moment. Without saying anything, Jake abruptly turned and walked quickly to his wagon for the night. He could be heard for several minutes angrily bouncing things around in the wagon before finally making up his bed beneath.

Ben, however, declined bed in favor of walking back to where Lynn had stood looking up into the night sky. Leaning his back against the same small tree, he thought about what it was he wanted. He had seen another small piece tonight of what he concluded was a very private and complicated woman. The past few weeks had told him little about her past. Watching her for the past two weeks or so he was learning that she was kind, helpful, usually soft-spoken. She loved all of the children on the wagons, and they all loved her. She would often take Baby Mary, as she was called by her big brothers, the Emerson boys, with her for a while as the women walked alongside the wagons. Or when they had stopped for the night and chores were done, she would rock her and sing to her softly. He had noticed one time when Leah, Rachel, Leann Seckers, who was almost five months pregnant now, and Lynn were talking about babies, that Lynn suddenly started to cry and quickly left the small group. When Leah had followed to offer comfort, Lynn had declined help and then hurried away on the excuse of having work to do.

Had she been married, perhaps, had a baby and it died? Maybe she had a little brother or sister who had died as a baby. Or maybe her mother had died in childbirth. She had said that all of her family was dead. Ben didn't know, and it frustrated him to no end that he knew so little about her. He didn't know how to reach out and comfort her. He longed for his mother's advice with this young woman. She always seemed to know what to do in situations like this. The one thing he did know for sure was that this woman was worth fighting for, and if Jake didn't like it, too bad. He was glad that Rachel had given him a little push tonight. When he thought of Carrie, the young woman in Oregon who wanted to marry him, he suddenly realized that he couldn't settle for anything less than loving the woman whom he married. He had come to realize, too, that this woman who had gone through a lot of some kind of hell, was starting to mean an awful lot to him. Jake could find himself another wife for all Ben cared, he wasn't going to get this woman.

With a heavy sigh and a last glance toward Lynn's wagon, he walked back to his own, made up his bedroll beneath it, and slept just as fitfully as Lynn and Jake.

Chapter 14

"It's all her fault"

July 29, 1844

Jared slapped his hat against his thigh trying to get a layer of dust off of it. A cloud rose on his leg, caught the air, and curled silently up and around him. He cursed under his breath and not feeling appeased with that, started cursing out loud as rage filled him for the thousandth time since he had left with this blasted wagon train a month and a half ago. His chest tightened with anger as the reason why he was with these cursed people and now driving a wagon crossed his mind. When he found her, he would choke the life out of her with his bare hands. His fingers fairly itched to try them out on somebody now.

Johansen was yelling something about moving out now that they had the last three people buried. Jared scowled heavily and with a few last words to whoever may or may not be listening, climbed back onto the wagon and slapped the reins on the backs of the oxen. He hated Johansen Tull, the wagon master. He wasn't a very tall man, but he was built solid to the ground with a huge chest and long arms. He reminded Jared of a gorilla he saw in a picture once. Tull's dark hair was long and shaggy, and he always smelled like rotten fish. He chewed tobacco, so he had a constant line of dark slime dripping down one side of his chin, and when he spit, he didn't care where it landed. More than once it had landed on someone's shoe or person. If they protested, he would just look at them with those dark, glaring eyes and nobody ever carried it further than a mild protest. Jared knew with an uneasiness that this man would kill you if the thought crossed his mind and he wouldn't even bother to tell you why he did it. How he had become elected as the wagon master was something Jared still hadn't figured out. All Jared knew was that he wanted to get to Oregon as soon as possible to find that wench who had dared walk out on him!

When he had returned to the hotel and found out that Lynn was nowhere to be found he had gone mad! He had raged through the whole town and finally went to the coach office to find out if she had taken a stage out of town. He was told that she had bought a ticket, but she had never gotten on. The man at the coach office remembered it well because the driver had waited for several minutes for her to show. When she didn't, he was very angry, because some "durn woman had slowed down progress," and he had left in a fury.

So, then he went to all of the nearest towns. He sent telegraphs everywhere to find out if she had somehow taken a stage elsewhere. All the telegraphs came back negative.

He finally remembered that the old woman at the hotel had befriended Lynn, and he went back there. She, of course, denied knowing anything. When he noticed that the young man who was always helping her was no longer around, he asked where he was. She had replied that he had gone to visit an uncle in the East. Her nervousness, however, prompted him to pursue that line a little more. After asking around town, he found a young man about the same age as Maggie's helper and after a lot of questioning and a little bit of bribery, found out that Kyle, as he turned out to be named, had gone to Oregon City and with a cousin. After hearing the description of the cousin, Jared realized who it really was. His persistence had paid off. But now, he was going to have to go on a wagon train with a bunch of people who, in his estimate, were no good, low-down nothings.

It took him several nights at the tables to win enough money to get the supplies to join a wagon train. He hadn't planned on driving a wagon. Instead, he had convinced a young man named Joseph Mathis to drive it for him. Jared would supply everything if Joseph would do all the work. Jared wasn't about to get his hands dirty doing menial labor! However, after two weeks on the trail, his horse died from exhaustion and he had no choice but to ride with Joseph. That was bad enough, but then there was an outbreak of cholera, and Joseph died along with four others. Now, Jared not only had to drive the wagon, but he also had to cook and wash his clothes, too. He had tried to hire some of the women to do it, but they either were too busy taking care of their own families or their husbands wouldn't let them. No one on the train liked him and he couldn't tolerate any of them, either. Well, there was one pretty little thing that caught his eye, but her parents kept a close eye on her and never let him get within ten feet of her. Bloody heathens! What was a man supposed to do out here with no woman for months on end?!

And all of this was her fault! His fists ached with the hunger to slap her until her teeth rattled for doing this to him. After all he had done for her. He had taken her away from that stupid little farm with those old relatives of hers and had shown her the world. They had traveled to New York and she had seen amazing things that her grandparents would have never shown her. They ate at restaurants; she didn't have to cook. He brought her books to read while he was gone for a few days doing his own thing. She was so ungrateful. Just because he had disciplined her a few times for her silliness she had done this to him!

The dust billowed around them as the forty-some wagons moved out into the prairie. The sky was blue, and the air was hot and dry. As Jared pulled the bandana up around his nose to help protect his face from the dust, his fingers curled into his dirty palm as the thoughts of choking her came into his mind and formed a dam against his skull that allowed nothing else to matter, nothing else to be seen, nothing else to be thought about. Discipline would be sweet!

Chapter 15

"Fishing diversions"

August 12th, 1844

The evening air was still and hot. Lynn was as thankful as the next person when Ben had announced that they would stop here to rest. The river was low and would be wonderful to wash clothes and take baths in. Their livestock also needed the rest; the two days prior had seen three oxen die which meant that weight had to be lessened within the wagons. Lynn watched with pity as heirlooms and dreams were left behind on the side of the trail.

Lynn glanced into the night sky as she helped Rachel do dishes. The two families had taken up the habit of eating together most nights.

"When are you going to walk with him again?" Rachel washed the plate in her hand and handed it to Lynn with a smile on her face.

Lynn tried to appear as if she didn't know whom Rachel was talking about. With that mischievous little smile on Rachel's face, Lynn knew she wouldn't get away with that. She glanced in Ben's direction as he talked with some of the men, all the while casting glances in their direction. She had been fairly successful in turning down both Ben and Jake in their requests to walk with her since the incident of a little over two months ago, which she thought was very impressive since they were around each other constantly. She told them she had mending or she was tired, or some other trivial excuse that had valid enough truth to it. The real truth was, that she needed to avoid them because they both frightened her, although each in a different way.

"I don't think it would be a very wise idea."

"Why not? If you don't do something soon, Jake will be over here asking for a walk, you know it. You know you want to, and Ben most certainly does. It's been weeks, why do you keep avoiding it?" Rachel's brown eyes went in another direction where Jake and his brother, Stanley, were busy fixing a wagon wheel that had broken and had caused them to stop earlier than usual tonight, not that anyone had minded. On the contrary, everyone was very pleased to stop early. The last week had not been a good one and everyone was thankful for the extra rest. Cholera had taken two lives and a rattlesnake bite had caused another. People were getting tired and cranky from the constant dust, walking, jostling, and break downs on the wagons. Lynn hadn't known the three people who had died very well, but she was still sad for the loss. It had especially affected Ben, who had been proud of the fact that after so long on the trail there had been no deaths. He was also very disappointed that she kept refusing to walk with him. Lynn glanced in the direction that Rachel had looked, and she sighed. Jake, although trying to be patient, was becoming more and more irritated with her lack of appreciation for his persistence.

Lynn sighed wearily. After thinking about the probability of Rachel being right about Jake asking her for a walk as soon as he was done, she decided to disappear for a walk on her own. Not that she needed to walk, she did that all day. But a little private time would be good. She didn't feel in the mood for his company tonight, even if only for a moment.

"I'm tired of walking since that's all we do." A grimace marked her features. "I saw a pretty place I could sit by the river when I was getting water earlier." She handed the drying cloth back to Rachel and, smiling to herself, turned around and walked toward the river. She glanced out of the corner of her eye and saw that Jake was much too preoccupied to notice where she was heading. It only took a moment to reach the place she had seen a couple of hours ago. It was rather hidden from view from most of the camp and even though it wasn't completely dark yet, she would be able to remain well hidden for as long as she liked. She had some thinking to do anyway. It was almost impossible to do serious thinking while in the company of the other women all day. When she traded places with Kyle and let him walk, the jostling of the wagon made it miserable to do much serious thinking either. And then there was the dust and heat. The dust had been miserable and the heat almost unbearable the last few days.

Ben watched Lynn walk quickly toward the creek and after waiting for a moment, followed her. He had been waiting for several days now for another opportunity to speak with her, to be close to her.

Jake, however, seemed to see to it that there never was an opportunity open for him. Lynn had successfully avoided both of them when at all possible and he did at least feel gratified that she refused to walk with Jake, also. Then, with all of the disasters of the past week, Ben hadn't been in the best of moods, anyway.

Now he approached the creek quietly, looking for where she could have disappeared to. After searching the shadows for a couple of minutes and failing to see anything, he started to turn around, wondering perhaps if she had decided to return to her wagon and he hadn't noticed somehow. Then, almost out of his line of vision, he saw a flash of white and recognized the blouse she wore with the plain brown skirt. She had moved or otherwise he wouldn't have seen her.

He watched as she sat down behind some small bushes. He hesitated for a moment trying to decide whether or not to disturb her solitude. She must have felt his eyes upon her, because just when he decided not to break in on her thoughts, he realized that she was watching him. Another moment went by, but when he heard Jake somewhere behind him saying something to Rachel, he walked quickly toward Lynn's hiding place.

At first, Lynn was dismayed that Ben found her so quickly. She thought her spot a little harder to find than that. Because now the way she sat, she couldn't even see the camp. She could see the glow that fires cast into the darkening evening air, but she couldn't see the fires themselves.

As Ben reached her and sat down beside her, she felt her heart pound against her ribs and she expelled a breath. A sudden lightheadedness made her realize she had been holding her breath. Deep inside she admitted that she was glad to have Ben's company. The more she watched him, the more she realized that this man was so different from Jared. His gentle, easy nature is what drew her to him the most. Her grandfather had a similar disposition and her father. She had known them to be the best sort of men. She knew deep down that not all men were like Jared or Nathan.

"Another beautiful evening isn't it?" After settling down on the grass with his long legs stretched out in front of him, he leaned back on his hands. Ben looked down into her face, watching the emotions that played across it. He recognized alarm, then pleasure, embarrassment, then to his surprise he thought he saw fear. Was she afraid of him? Why? His thoughts went flying backward over the past two and a half months. There was nothing there that would frighten her, was there? Memories came back of Rachel and Leah telling him about Lynn's scars. He had so many questions. Would they never be answered?

"Yes, it is. I wanted to sit for a few moments just breathing in the slightly cooler air here around the water. It smells so good without dust billowing around."

Ben smiled. "I have to agree with you about that one. The constant dust gets to you after a while, doesn't it?" When she nodded and smiled in agreement, he was encouraged to say what had been weighing on his mind for weeks.

"What happened a few weeks ago, you know, I didn't mean to upset you." Ben cleared his throat and then continued when Lynn looked up at him but remained silent. "Jake seems to bring out the worst in me." Lynn turned away to lean forward and watch the water.

Lynn had asked Rachel about Ben's feelings toward Jake and she had just smiled saying that it was probably some "man thing".

Ben drew his legs up until his knees were bent. Then he leaned forward, putting his forearms on his knees and letting his hands hang down over the tops of his boots. From the corner of his eye, he saw Lynn study his hands for a brief moment then return her gaze to the water. He sat patiently waiting for her to speak.

What could she say to this man who seemed capable of tying her insides into knots? She was angry with herself for even feeling this way whenever he was near. She always felt so confused. Hadn't she learned that men can't be trusted? Somehow she knew this one could be. A desire for him to touch her and set her skin on fire lingered like a dream. Yet she was scared, as memories of Jared slapping her crowded into her mind as well, making her catch her breath. And the worst part of all was that she was still married anyway, although the first thing she was going to do was obtain a divorce when she got a job. Now, however, she could sense Ben waiting for her to say something, anything. She knew she needed to say something, anything, but what was she supposed to say? This subject was not a good one so she decided to avoid it.

"Do you think there are any fish in here?" Her question caught Ben completely off guard, and for a moment he just sat there staring at her profile. This diversion made it clear that she didn't want to talk about the past, whether it was two months ago or two years ago. He didn't know why, and it frustrated him because that was exactly what he wanted to talk about, but he respected her feelings and answered the question.

"I'm sure there are plenty of fish in here. I saw downstream just a little ways what looked like a pretty good fishing hole." He hesitated just a second, "Would you like to join me there tomorrow afternoon and we'll see if I'm right?" It surprised him how much he wanted her to say yes, that she would spend an hour with him fishing along the river.

She recognized it for what it was. Thankful that he didn't pursue the other subject, she gave him a warm smile and a nod. He unknowingly endeared himself to her by respecting her feelings and having patience. She knew what he really wanted to know, and yet he wouldn't push her like Jake had tried on numerous occasions. Everyone wanted to know, and she did want to tell someone. Just not Ben, and not now.

"Well, I hope to get all caught up with washing in the morning, so yes, I would like that very much." She felt like he was already fishing; he had thrown out the hook and she was caught and only barely putting up a fight. His eyes now gleamed with happiness. Her heart did a strange dance making her breathless for the briefest moment.

"Well, I think that I had better retire. I have so many things to do tomorrow if I am going to go fishing with you in the afternoon." Her lips curved upwards slightly as she made a move to get up, but before she could, Ben leaped to his feet and, extending a hand, helped her up. He held her hand for a few seconds longer than necessary. She glanced at his hand still holding hers and then up into his face. Afraid of what she saw there, she pulled her hand out of his, turning quickly to walk away. Ben placed a hand at her elbow to help her up the small bank even though it was obvious that she didn't need his assistance. Just before turning toward the camp, he leaned forward so quickly that before she realized his intention, he just barely brushed his lips across her forehead. Then stepping away just as quickly, he walked toward his wagon.

Lynn stood there for a moment with her mouth agape. Her fingers and elbow still burned from his touch and her forehead tingled where his lips had touched her. She saw Jake on the other side of the camp circle looking for her, so she hurried to her wagon. Glancing one more time in Jake's direction, she climbed quickly inside. He had turned around and spied her just as she reached the wagon. When she saw out of the corner of her eye the move he made in her direction, she moved quickly to avoid any contact with him tonight.

Ben watched from the corner of his wagon as Jake saw Lynn. Lynn disappeared with haste and Ben smiled to himself, well pleased with the evening. Even with the dust and sweat of the trail, Lynn had still smelled good, like a woman. He took a huge chance when he kissed her lightly and he knew it. But, it was all he could do to hold himself back from taking her in his arms and kissing her properly. Memories of her midnight bath came flooding back to his mind. He wanted to feel the length of her body against his own and to taste her sweet lips. He wanted— never mind what he wanted. It would only make him frustrated because he couldn't have what he wanted right now. Besides, it wasn't proper anyway. He shook his head to clear his thoughts and then decided to go to bed.

There was only a handful of people still up and it looked like they were heading toward their beds also. Ben smiled to himself once again as he saw Jake scowl in the direction of Lynn's wagon. Then he, too, retired for the night.

Chapter 16

"Laughter and tears"

By mid-morning most of the women had breakfast done and had stripped their wagons of easily movable contents. They had gathered everything that was washable and were busy washing, bathing, and chattering at the river. There was not the slightest breeze stirring the air that was already hot, so the women embraced the cool water of the river. They knew all of their cleaning wouldn't last for very long, but the temporary reprieve was enjoyed nonetheless.

Kyle and Willy had strung up rope between a couple of trees and also between their wagons so that as their women finished washing they could hang the items up to dry. Most of the men disappeared to go hunting, leaving the river for the women so that they would also have the chance to bathe. The men would take to the river tonight while the women made supper.

Suzanne and Lynn worked side by side scrubbing a blanket and Kyle's breeches. They already had their own clothes done and hung up to dry. The talk and laughter along the river made them happy. Lynn and Suzanne worked silently for a while enjoying the snatches of conversation around them. Leah and Rachel were down from them just a little ways and Leann Seckers and Rachel's daughter, Sarah, were on the other side of them laughing.

"Kyle promised to make me some moccasins if he shot himself a deer. I would love to have some." Sarah was leaning forward in the river with a shirt in her hands, but not doing anything about washing it. Her mother had a mock frown on her face.

"I'll wear them if you don't get busy, young lady. Besides, I really don't think Kyle even knows how to make moccasins." Rachel winked at Lynn.

Sarah was indignant. "Yes, he does. He said that his Aunt had shown him how to make a pair one time. And he would have brought them, but he's outgrown them." She started scrubbing furiously on the shirt while casting her mother an impatient look.

"The trouble with my daughter is that she thinks that the sun rises and sets in your young Kyle, my dear." Rachel was laughing and looking at Lynn. The other women around them were laughing also as Sarah's face flushed pink.

"All we have heard for two months is 'Kyle this' and 'Kyle that'. I swear I hear about Kyle in my sleep." She rolled her eyes with pretended disgust.

"Mother!" Sarah's cheeks brightened even more when the very young man whom they were talking about appeared, walking quickly toward Lynn. He hadn't heard any of the conversation, but he got suspicious when suddenly everyone was quiet, and all the women had large smiles upon their faces. He looked at Sarah's embarrassed cheeks, and when she wouldn't look up at him, a broad smile covered his face.

"I must've been the center of conversation, huh? Waaa'll, I guess women just have to talk about the most handsome, eligible man on the train, don't they?" He was well pleased with himself when that brought hoots of more laughter and succeeded in having Sarah's head jerk up to look at him. She was quiet for a second before she, too, started laughing.

Getting the response he wanted, he now turned toward Lynn. "I came down here to tell you, Lynn, that I laid the fishing pole on the seat of the wagon. I sure hope you and Ben catch something. I'm getting tired of venison and rabbit." His gaze went to Sarah, so he failed to notice that it was now Lynn's face that turned pink. Tipping his hat in Sarah's direction, he turned and walked away.

"Well, you ladies have fun now and don't forget to talk about me some more." That comment brought more smiles, but not laughter this time because they were thinking more about his earlier comment, including Sarah, who just had to say something.

"You goin' fishing with Ben?" Her eyes were large and questioning. Lynn, who had worked very hard at avoiding the two men on this train who seemed hell-bent on pursuing her, was going fishing with Ben? She couldn't believe it!

At first, Lynn hesitated, not particularly wanting to share anything. Looking down at the blanket in her hands she sighed, knowing she would have to say something.

"Yes, he asked me last night. Since I'm getting tired of venison, too, I decided to take him up on his offer to show me a good fishing hole. I used to love to go fishing with my dad when I was little and then later with my grandpa." She tried to brush it off lightly as if it was just a fishing trip with her grandpa, but without success because none of the women were going to go for it.

Leann spoke up with suppressed laughter in her throat. "Well you might like to fish, but somehow I don't see how Ben Alenson could possibly remind you of your father or grandpa. He's far too handsome and too much a man for you to think of him in that way." Laughter bubbled up with her comment and the others joined in with comments of their own about how manly Ben was—not in the least grandfatherly. Lynn couldn't help but smile at the thought of trying to imagine Ben as her grandfather. Ben did remind her of her grandfather because of some of his qualities. But that was where the comparison stopped. Her grandfather hadn't been any taller than herself, with graying blonde hair and gray eyes. She had gotten her soft voice from him. He could sit for hours at a fishing hole and not say more than ten words the whole time. Her grandmother would often complain that she had no one to talk to except the cat. Lynn laughed at the memories, wrapping them tightly within her heart.

No, Ben certainly didn't look anything like her grandfather. Ben had a commanding presence even when he wasn't talking. His large frame and dark inquisitive eyes were startling and searching. And she loved his dimple that appeared when he smiled. She did know one thing though. Her grandfather would approve of Ben. He never had liked Jared.

"You are right about that one. If I was a single woman, I would give Ben a run for his money. Watch out, honey, if I ever lose my Willy." Leah laughed as she pointed a finger in Lynn's direction.

Lynn pretended to be horrified, "Why Leah Emerson, I thought you adored the ground that Willy walked on!"

Leah shook her head, playing the game that they had started, pretending to be shocked. "Whatever gave you that idea? I don't adore the ground he walks on, just the sky above his head!" Laughter burst out once again and Lynn reveled in it. Her life had been too long without it and now, out here, that seemed like a lifetime ago. She would never see that painful part of her life again. It was gone, and she wanted to bury it forever, especially once she had her divorce.

"Amen, sister!" Rachel raised her hands above her head towards the sky, laughing the whole time.

"You're a fine one to make comments, sis, since you do adore the ground your man walks on." Leah placed her hands on her hips looking at her sister with pretended indignation.

"Yes, I do, but at least not the sky above his head." More hoots of laughter.

"Be glad that you have good men. There are some out there not worth a penny and sometimes they show up more often than we like to think." Suzanne rarely said much, although she loved the company of her new-found friends. She mostly sat and listened to their conversation, rarely offering her own thoughts. So now, they turned to look at her with quiet faces, the laughter gone. Finally, Lynn spoke.

"That is true. Sometimes what we think we have turns out to be just a show they put on for those around them. It's what they want others to think, and sometimes they fool even us into thinking that we have something good, when really it's not." What on earth made her say that? Lynn's heart lurched painfully. She needed to share with someone else the load that weighed her down. It was heavy to carry by herself. Maybe it was time to share. Her voice was very soft, the words barely audible.

"There are men out there who can convince you that you can't do anything right even when deep down, you know that you've done nothing wrong. Men, who have to have absolute power over everything you do, you think, you feel, you wish, you dream. Men who are cruel and laugh at your pain and at the blood that trickles from your lip or down your back. Men who take their pleasure and can make you cry. Men, who.... men that...." Lynn was appalled at the tears that ran down her face and that she had said far more than she had intended. It was as if once she started to speak, she couldn't stop; the words just kept coming. Putting a hand over her mouth, she leaned forward over the water wishing, willing it—no, demanding—that the water's flow would wash the words away. Not only the words, but the pain and memories that caused them in the first place. But she had spoken and, although these women wouldn't hold it against her, she hadn't meant to share quite so many details. It was too embarrassing, too awful, too painful.

Now, she just sat there on her haunches, leaning over the river with tears dripping down into the water at her feet. Everyone just sat there for a moment dazed, trying to digest what she had said. Full realization of the implications hit them hard. She had been another Suzanne! They looked at Suzanne who was watching Lynn with eyes brimming with tears as well. Rachel, Leah, Leann, and Sarah suddenly surrounded both women and gathered them into their arms, offering comfort. Some of the other women further up and down the river looked their way but stayed where they were. They would find out soon enough what was happening, and they knew that everyone has their secrets and their past. And when you decided to tell it, you didn't necessarily want the whole world to know.

Lynn wept hard and deep. She hadn't allowed herself the luxury of crying to empty out the pain. She had wanted to keep it inside so that she wouldn't make the same mistake again. Now she clung to Rachel's shoulder and cried tears of bitterness and hate and pain. It was several moments before she raised her head to talk about the life that had come before, as the friends who had become so dear to her sat and listened with hearing ears and tender hearts.

Chapter 17

"A slip on the rocks"

It was an interesting scene that greeted Ben when he walked down the small incline to where Kyle said the women were gathered near the river. He hadn't been very successful with hunting, so he came back to camp hoping that maybe Lynn would be able to fish a little earlier than had been planned. Thinking about fishing with Lynn had been part of the cause for his lack of successful hunting. His thoughts were on her instead of being on game, and he missed a young buck a while ago and hadn't seen anything else. He saw Jake with a doe and a couple of the other men with rabbits and grouse. Even Kyle had a grouse under one arm a moment ago.

Now looking down upon the women gathered around Lynn and Suzanne, he was alarmed that something had happened. Maybe Lynn had gotten hurt somehow. He started to walk faster, then saw Lynn raise her head from Rachel's shoulder and was talking. Leah looked up and saw him coming. She shook her head slightly at him and frowned heavily, telling him to stop. No one else had seen him yet, so he turned around and walked slowly back the other way.

His perception told him that Lynn wasn't hurt. She had finally decided to talk about her past and by the looks of the faces surrounding her, it was not a pretty one. He could hardly wait to talk to Rachel or Leah. His insides were eaten up with the impatience that gnawed at him and curled itself around inside him making him restless. He walked over to where some of the men were gathered, taking care of the game they had brought down.

"Nice looking doe." He commented to Jake as he walked by on his way to Kyle.

"Thank you. I guess the women must still be down at the river, huh? Have you seen Lynn?" Jake's attitude was a bold one since he directed the question to Ben. He knew when he asked it he would receive a frown. Sure enough, Ben was frowning when he turned around to answer.

"Yes, they are still at the river. They looked pretty busy."

Jake was annoyed at Ben's implication to leave the women alone, referring to Lynn, of course. "Well, I'm almost done here and then I think I'll go for a walk with Lynn. Nice day for a walk along the river, don't you think?" He smiled boldly at Ben, who scowled in return but made no comment, instead turning to continue his walk over to Kyle.

"You just have to irritate him, don't you?" Stanley looked at his younger brother and grinned. He realized how badly Jake wanted a wife. Lynn was a very nice, young woman. A very pretty one, also. When her hair grew and was long like a woman's hair should be, she would be beautiful. It was also obvious that Ben was enraptured by her. He sure hoped Jake knew what he was doing. Lynn seemed almost afraid of his brother, and Stanley didn't think that Jake realized that.

Jake looked over at his brother as he wiped his hands on a cloth. "I don't want to irritate him. He just needs to know that she is already spoken for and he just as well give it up. Besides, he has a woman in Oregon who wants to marry him when he returns. He doesn't need this one, too."

Stanley was thoughtful for a moment. "I think that she is a little bit afraid of you, Jake. I see it in her eyes every time you approach her."

Jake turned around with a frown creasing his brow. "What? Afraid of me? Why would she be afraid of me? I've never hurt a woman in my life!" He rested his arms on his thighs, thinking. "You think maybe she's been talking too much to that Suzanne?" The frown turned into a heavy scowl. Just because she had a bad one didn't mean they were all bad, especially him. He would have to talk with Suzanne about this.

He finished the butchering quickly and then went in search of Suzanne and then Lynn. It didn't take him long to find them. They were still gathered at the river. The Aames, Secker, and Emerson women were gathered around Lynn and Suzanne. Rachel had her arm around Lynn's shoulders and at first, he thought maybe she was hurt. Then he saw her talking. Enough of this woman talk; he needed to talk to Suzanne for a moment and it wouldn't wait. Leah saw him first and said something to the group because they all looked up at him and their conversation fell quiet.

"Good morning, ladies. Looks like you've been busy this morning. That's good." He looked at all of them then centered in on Suzanne. "I need to speak with you for a moment." The women looked at each other, and then back at him in surprise. Suzanne hesitated for a second, looked at Lynn who barely shrugged her shoulders with a questioning look on her face, too. Suzanne rose slowly from the group of women and followed Jake downstream where they were not within hearing distance of anyone.

"You've been telling Lynn not to have anything to do with me, haven't you." It wasn't really a question. "Just because you had a man who was no good, doesn't mean that there aren't good ones out there. I'm one of 'em." He stood with his arms crossed and squinted at Suzanne with a frown.

Suzanne trembled slightly at his angry face. Her eyes widened at his accusation. She had suspected for a long time that Lynn's past was similar to her own; today proved it. Lynn already knew what she needed to beware of. She certainly didn't need any advice or help from Suzanne on the subject of men. Her voice was very quiet when she finally replied.

"I have never said anything to Lynn about you or anyone else, Mr. Emmons. Lynn's choices are her own and have nothing to do with me."

"Then why is she afraid of me? My brother thinks that she's afraid of me. Now, I've never done nothing that would harm her. So, now why's she afraid? You answer me that." He jabbed a finger in her direction.

"Maybe you should ask Lynn about that yourself. She has good reasons to be wary of men. Especially those who are demanding."

"What are you talkin' about?"

Suzanne turned to walk back toward the group still gathered at the river. "You need to talk to Lynn about that. I'm not one to give away confidences." She walked quickly back to the women.

Jake stood there for a moment trying to figure out what she was talking about. Then, as determined as ever to prove his worth, he disappeared towards the wagons for a few moments before coming back down the small incline to the river.

In the meantime, Suzanne had related what was said to the curious group. Lynn was dismayed, for this meant that she would have to tell him something when she didn't want to tell him anything. Closing her eyes, she rubbed her temple from the headache that suddenly pulsed there. Maybe she would go lay down for a while. She finished up the blanket she had been washing and walked toward the wagon.

Jake, coming down to the river, saw her and turned in her direction, almost running to catch up. She was starting to hang the blanket across the rope when he caught up to her and spoke, at the same time holding out his hand.

"Lynn, I need to speak with you for a moment."

She jumped slightly at his voice, not hearing him come up behind her. Finishing with the blanket, she turned towards him, and then her eye went in the direction of his outstretched hand. The beautiful gold chain flashed in the sunlight, making her breath catch in her throat at its loveliness. A small heart with a rose etched on the front swung gently from Jakes's hand. As Jake turned it over she saw a large 'E' etched in very fine script on the back. Her eyes widened in surprise, and she took a step back at the implications of Jake's actions.

He talked fast, trying to say everything he needed to say before she could stop him. "I don't want you to be afraid of me. My brother is convinced that you are. I want you to marry me. I can wait until we get to Oregon if you want, but I'd just as soon do it now. I bought this before I left the east so's I could give it to the woman I was gonna marry. I figure now's good a time as ever." He waited with his hand outstretched and eyes that watched her reaction with hopefulness in his anxious gaze.

Lynn searched his face and realized that his actions were sincere, but she wondered if he was talking from his heart. She didn't think he was an impulsive man. Knowing that he was fond of her or he wouldn't ask, was a nice thought. But she also knew that he would be thinking about the practical side of having a capable wife to help out on a farm and, of course, Jake knew that she had grown up on a farm. She sighed heavily, knowing he wouldn't like what she was going to tell him. Her heart ached slightly; she never liked to see people hurt. When he saw her hesitate, he spoke again.

"I don't know your past. Suzanne said you have good reason to be afraid of men. But, I'm not like her husband. I've never hit a woman in my life. So, if that's the problem, I promise I'd never hurt you. A woman needs a strong man like me to protect her and give her a home. I need a wife for a farm and I want a passel of kids around someday. I figure you'd be a good choice for those things. You work hard and all the kids on this here train seem to like you real well. And besides all of that, you're pretty." He stopped, obviously well pleased with himself for giving her good reasons why she should marry him.

A wan smile lit her features. She was right. Her thoughts about him wanting a practical wife were true. He didn't really love her although he liked her. She hesitated, then finally and carefully put her thoughts into words that would be gentle and yet firm at the same time.

"Mr. Emmons, I know without a doubt that you are a good man. I've seen your dealings and heard about your honesty and hard work for about three months and am aware that you are truly good. I am not, however, a good woman for you." When he started to protest, she raised her hand to him, frowned slightly, and then continued. "I do not desire to tell you about my past. It's painful and it's now behind me, where I plan on leaving it. But, because of it, I know that I am not the woman to fill your needs. There is, I believe, a woman in Oregon someplace that is the perfect one for you and I wish you all the happiness that you truly deserve." Her eyes and smile were warm and as she held out her hand to shake his in friendship; it was his turn to hesitate. When he continued to hesitate, she added what she hoped would be taken as a true token of friendship.

"I want to always be a friend of yours and someday, your wife's, too."

He suddenly smiled broadly and grasped her hand. It was obvious that he hadn't expected the rejection and didn't welcome it, but, he knew her well enough to comprehend that no amount of arguing would change her mind, or at least not yet. Maybe before they arrived in the Oregon country she could be convinced to think otherwise. For now, he would wait. And if she still refused, well then he would have to wait until Oregon to find himself a wife.

"You always have my friendship and I still hope that someday I can convince you of more. Until then." Turning abruptly on his heel, he walked quickly away.

Lynn watched him go, blinking in surprise. She thought she would have a fight on her hands. He had started out forceful and so sure of himself. When he gave up without a fight, she was shocked. Through the whole conversation her nerves had made her pulse quicken, she could feel it jump in her neck. Knowing that he was a good man didn't change the fact that she was still a little afraid of him.

After heaving a huge sigh of relief, she stared into nothing for a moment, just letting her thoughts catch up with her heart. After a moment, she became aware that she was being watched.

Ben had been watching the whole scene and, although he didn't hear the words, he knew by the actions that Jake had just asked Lynn to marry him. He had stood with a great deal of apprehension while waiting to see Lynn's reaction to the question. Jake didn't look happy, and yet didn't look upset either as he had walked away. Ben could only wonder at her comments. He hesitated for just a moment and then seeing Lynn look in his direction, decided to go ahead and ask her about fishing.

She stood waiting while his long strides brought him over quickly to stand in front of her, forcing her to tip her head back slightly to look into his face when he stood close. She saw the curiosity in his eyes as he studied her face. The desire to ask about her conversation with Jake was written all over his face. His eyes showed the struggle that was going on inside his head. He wanted to ask, but at the same time knew he shouldn't.

Finally, he asked quietly, "Did you still want to go catch a fish for supper?"

Lynn welcomed the calm, clear voice of this man. It sent her nerves scattering, but in a different direction from where they had been a few minutes ago.

She swallowed nervously, her headache now forgotten. "Yes, just a moment, I need to get the fishing pole that Kyle left over there." She pointed briefly to the front of the wagon as she walked to get the pole. Ben followed her, watching the gentle sway of the plain brown skirt on her slim hips. Her tall figure was naturally slender, and it made him long to place his hands upon the soft flare of her hips. When she stopped to grab the pole, he looked up quickly before she could see where his eyes had strayed.

"I guess I'm ready now." She turned around with a smile.

"Well then, let's go and see if we can catch us something to eat other than venison or rabbit." He led the way downstream about eight hundred feet. As they topped a little hill and walked down to the river, glancing back, Lynn realized that they couldn't see the camp anymore.

Now looking where Ben pointed, there was indeed what looked like a wonderful fishing hole. Her grandfather would have called it grand. That's what he always called a good fishing hole. He never called anything else grand, just good fishing holes. She chuckled softly to herself now, thinking about it.

Ben turned when he heard her quiet laughter, raising his brows in question. Lynn smiled and answered the unspoken question.

"My grandfather would have liked this fishing hole. He used to call a good fishing hole grand. Was the only time he ever used the word." Ben smiled as she told him about the memory. They set bait upon their hooks. After casting them into the water, Ben asked more about her grandfather.

"So, tell me more about your grandfather. He sounds very likable." Ben saw a variety of emotions race across her face it.

She stared out into the water for a moment and then turned, smiling, to look at him, musing briefly before she finally spoke.

"He was very likable. Everyone knew him because he was a doctor. And he would doctor anything from people to dogs. I remember one time, the Hanson's had this pig that was supposed to be raised for the sole purpose of getting butchered, but had become a pet instead. Well, a couple of coyotes got a hold of it and before the kids could scare them off, the pig had been pretty badly chewed. Grandfather stitched up a couple of wounds and spent all of one-night taking care of it. It got well, and the Hanson's were very happy that they didn't lose Frank." She shook her as she laughed. "A lot of people thought he was crazy, but those who really knew him knew that Grandfather just cared a lot about animals and about people. He knew that the Hanson kids would be sad if Frank died, so he saved him."

Turning toward him, she rolled her eyes as she laughed. "Want to know a really crazy thing?" She didn't wait for an answer. "He even once saved a young coyote pup. There were a few people mad at him for that one. She lived with our dogs for about two and a half years before someone shot her. I'll never forget Daisy." She grinned with eyebrows raised waiting for the response she knew would come.

"Daisy! What a name for a coyote!" He laughed loudly at the silly name.

She watched him, liking the way his laugh made the corners of his eyes crinkle slightly and his cheek dimple.

"Gramma named her. She always said that with all the people mad at Grandfather for saving a worthless coyote, that someday soon the pup would be pushing up daisies. Gramma was surprised that she lived as long as she did and didn't get shot sooner." Lynn laughed quietly, her thoughts buried in the memories that the funny little story invoked.

Ben was still laughing when suddenly Lynn's pole jerked. She had been busy talking and not paying attention to her fishing. Her attention was immediately brought back to her pole now, however, since it was being pulled out of her hands. She tried jerking it back to set the hook, but whatever was on her line wasn't going to give up that easy. As she struggled with the pole, her feet slipped, and she landed on her bottom, the rocks along the bank of the river gouging into the soft flesh of her buttocks.

Ben put his pole aside and was reaching out to help when she had slipped. At first, he was concerned but then was surprised to hear her laugh. Most women would have been crying to have landed that hard on the rocks. Yet, Lynn was seeing the humorous side of her situation. He smiled then started to chuckle also as he grabbed hold of her pole. She gladly relinquished it to his stronger arms. She continued to sit there covertly rubbing her sore bottom, however, and watched as he pulled in the biggest fish she had ever seen.

"That is the biggest fish I've ever seen. What is it?" She was slightly breathless from awe and also from struggling to pull her skirts up, while at the same time trying to get gracefully to her feet. She didn't succeed very well because her left foot caught the edge of her skirt, causing her right foot to slip on a wet rock. Not being able to keep her balance, she fell forward.

Ben saw her falling out of the corner of his eye and caught her with one arm while trying to control the fish with the other. When Lynn finally regained her balance, she had one palm spread against a hard chest, the other having been flung out to the side in an attempt to break her fall. Ben's shirt was warm against her cheek and his arm was around her waist, his fingers firmly on her side helping her balance. Now her balance was threatened from something else entirely.

Her hand and cheek burned from the touch of him and where he still held her waist. She looked up into eyes that were warm and tender and suddenly smoldering with something she readily recognized. It was the same one her father used to give her mother. A shiver went through her at the memory, making her stare at him in consternation.

"Did you hurt yourself when you fell? Your ankles, they okay?" Ben dropped the pole with the fish and bending slightly, picked her up as though she were a feather pillow.

Another nervous tremor went through her as her body tensed with the fear and sudden realization that she was falling in love with this man. Knowing that he had deep feelings for her as well, her heart beat painfully against her ribs. She couldn't do anything but hurt him. If, when, she did obtain a divorce, did she want to marry again? Yes, she may love this big, gentle-hearted man, but she remembered the nights of hurt and fear anytime Jared had come to her wanting his husbandly dues. She didn't want to do that ever again. At the same time, she wanted to stay here in this moment forever.

Ben's arms were wrapped around her; one around her back with his fingers curled up around her ribs. The other arm was under her knees. His breath was warm and the spicy smell of cloves wafted against her cheek as he looked down at her. Her thoughts went twenty different directions and as bad as she wanted to stay where she was, she also wanted to run away just as fast as she could. Finally, she looked away, not being able to meet his gaze any longer.

"No, I'm fine, really. You can put me down." She sounded breathless even to herself, as if she had just climbed a mountain.

"Are you sure? You're trembling." The concern showed in his eyes as his gaze darted to where her ankles peeked from under her skirt.

"No, really, I'm okay." When he continued to hold her, she repeated her former request. "You can put me down now."

Ben didn't want to put her down. He liked her right where she was, in his arms. He wanted to marry her and then carry her, just like this, to the house they would design and build together. He wanted to take her into their bedroom, lay her on a big bed with warm quilts and large feather pillows, and make love to her. He had never dreamed of loving someone like this. There had been a couple of young women whom he had kind of liked, but never with the depth of emotion that this woman evoked from within his heart and soul.

He suddenly realized that she was looking back at him with fear in those beautiful brown eyes. It was difficult to focus in on the emotions that shifted with lightning speed in her face. One thing was clear, however, fear. Why was she afraid of him? Maybe it wasn't him, maybe it was something or somebody else. His question was gently asked.

"Lynn are you afraid of me?"

She hesitated, her chest tight within his embrace. She struggled to find the right words.

"I'm sorry, Ben. I'm not afraid of you. Just," she let her voice trail off. When he patiently waited for her to speak she closed her eyes for a moment before finishing. "I'm just afraid of what you are." Heat rushed to her face. Puzzlement flashed in his eyes and she turned away. How could she explain? It was hard for her to understand it herself. It seemed simple and complicated at the same time. She could feel his eyes on her, trying to understand what she meant.

"I don't understand." A simple statement, but full of doubt and questioning. "What am I?"

"A man." It was spoken so quietly that he barely heard the words. She looked down at the hand that lay in her lap and bit her lip. He finally set her down gently and slowly to her feet. His hands were on either side of her waist while she let hers drop to her side.

He gazed down at her for a moment and then before he could stop himself, his mouth lowered slowly to touch hers ever so slightly. The shock in her expression should have warned him to stop, but her breath was warm and sweet and when she didn't move away, he kissed her again. It was still a gentle kiss placed on the corner of her mouth, but he applied a little more pressure, making her catch her breath. She let out a strangled cry and pushing him back, she wheeled around and ran toward the wagon train, disappearing over the little hill quickly.

What a fool! Why did he do that? He covered his face with his hand, rubbing his eyes. He knew why. Because she was the sweetest, prettiest, and the most frightened young woman he had ever seen. She was also one of the strongest and yet most strangely fragile women he had ever known. He wished that they were already in Oregon so that he could talk to his mother about what Lynn had told him just before he kissed her. She would know what to think because he didn't have the slightest idea. He decided then and there that he would drive this train just as hard as he dared. He needed to understand this woman and at the same time knew he would need another woman's, his mother and maybe his sister's, help to do so.

Chapter 18

"A slow down"

August 19th, 1844

Jared didn't like the man at all. His beady eyes reminded him of a rat, and the constant sneer he wore irritated him immensely. However, after only a few moments in the man's company, he had learned enough to reassure himself of finding Lynn. Nathan told his version of the story to everyone who would listen the two weeks he had been with the train. No one particularly liked him, but, he was a good shot and had shared some game with a couple of families who needed it.

Jared wiped the sweat from his brow and turned toward the river. They lost two wagons there this morning and three people had drowned. Two of them were little children and the other was their father. Their mother, a young woman of about twenty-four or five was sitting on the far side of his wagon seat staring into the open prairie stretched out before them. She had been pretty enough before they started on this journey, but now her blonde hair was stringy around her sunburned face as she kept wringing her work-worn hands. Her husband had not treated her well, so there was no great loss to her on his account. But she mourned the loss of her two young children.

Jared offered to let her ride with him in his wagon. Every other wagon was full to capacity, especially since wagons had been lost and whole families now walked or took turns riding with others. Since hers was no longer useable and no one else had so far offered, she accepted. He had gone long enough without a woman and he figured that with a little bit of cleaning up, this one would do nicely for a while. Clara wasn't as pretty as Lynn, but she was attractive enough. She wasn't very tall, only coming up to the middle of Jared's chest. With a little care and washing, her face would be pretty. She had generous curves in the right places. He stood watching her for a few moments and then moved toward Johansen Tull. His nose wrinkled in distaste as the pungent odor of stale sweat and tobacco wafted towards him on the heavy afternoon air. If Tull ever bathed it was beyond Jared's knowledge as to when it was.

"Well, we certainly lost plenty of time today. Do you think we can push it a little harder for the next few days, Johansen?" Jared challenged the wagon master for a moment before turning sideways. Jared was well aware of just how far he could push the man.

Johansen's gaze narrowed as he sent a stream of tobacco juice toward Jared's boots. It missed, but barely. He heartily disliked Jared Malen, but at the same time respected the man. Jared knew how far to push, and would push to the limit, and yet seemed to know exactly where that limit was. He knew Jared was a gambler, obviously knowing when to call and when to fold. And with Tull, he knew when to shut his mouth.

"I plan on traveling very hard and fast after we've had a break for two days. These people need a rest. Our livestock need a rest. We all need to hunt. Any questions, Malen?"

His voice grated on Jared's ears and he scowled angrily. Jared jerked his head in answer and then moved toward his wagon and Clara. He wanted to go faster, travel harder. Now they were going to slow down. He wanted to get these next two days over with as quickly as possible and get his hands on Lynn, his palms itching from the mere thought.

Chapter 19

"Whiskey breath and memories"

August 28th, 1844

Lynn watched Ben out of the corner of her eye as he reigned in the big horse and stood talking to some of the men. He had driven them hard and fast since that time at the river when he had kissed her. At the memory of that tender kiss, she touched her fingers to her lips as she had done a hundred times in the last two weeks. Ben turned just at that moment to look in her direction. He had seen her do that many times in the past days. She quickly turned the other way with a pink face, pushing a curl that had fallen forward in her eyes. Ben smiled to himself and then continued talking to the men.

"The trail up the Blue Mountains is very steep. We want to make sure that all ropes and chains are in good order. We're going to stop here for an extra day. There's good water just over there and it will give the animals a day to rest before starting the ascent. We need to watch our wagons closely and make sure that we take no chances. It's going to be very slow-moving."

"How about double-teaming? That should work pretty good, don't ya think, Ben? Worked doggone good that last big hill we went up." Bud spoke up and the others nodded in agreement.

"We can give it a try. That's one reason we're going to stay here an extra day to give the animals a rest. I've been driving everyone pretty hard and fast and we all need a break."

"I agree with that one." Kyle grinned wearily. Ben had almost been a slave driver the last couple of weeks. They were leaving at the first sign of daylight and traveled until the last ray of sun. They were all anxious to get to the Oregon country but they wanted to make it there alive. Everyone was exhausted and cranky. The women hadn't had any time to do any substantial washing so everyone smelled of sweat and had dirty, dusty clothes. People were also getting low on meat because there had been no time to hunt. They really needed this break for a day, and were glad that Ben had decided to stop here. The mountains surrounding them were beautiful but were going to be a lot of work to climb and no one was looking forward to it. Tempers were short, food and water were low, and animals were exhausted.

After the wagons formed their circle, the children and men went to the river to gather water while the women got out cooking utensils and started fires with the little bits of firewood they could collect. Soon the smell of beans and biscuits was in the evening air. Kyle went back to the river to retrieve two more buckets of water.

Lynn started cooking when Suzanne decided to wash them some clothes. The air was still warm, and they would probably be dry by the time supper was done. They had stopped about four hours earlier than usual because they were at the base of a mountain and there was a good water source. She wanted a bath so bad. Several of the women agreed that after supper was over and the dishes were finished, they would all head to the spring on the far side of a thicket of trees. Lynn could hardly wait. She stirred the beans and then turned the fry bread over to brown on the other side. She was deep in her thoughts when Ben's voice made her jump.

"Smells very good. You make the best fry bread I've ever eaten, Lynn." Ben handed her a jar of cherry preserves. "I've had these hidden away because I only had one jar. Thought I would get them out tonight. That alright with you?"

She glanced up at him and then continued with the bread, "Yes, of course. Mmmmmm...cherry."

"Kyle told me the other day that they are your favorite. I wish I had known that sooner. I would have brought them over a long time ago." After squatting on haunches near her, he watched as she deftly laid another chunk of dough in the skillet. Her hair had a light layer of dust from the trail on it, as did her clothes, and yet he still wanted to reach out and touch her.

He sighed as he let his hands drop over his knees. He had taken to eating with them most nights and decided now would be as good a time as any to apologize to her. The apology was long overdue, and he wondered at how it seemed like he was always needing to apologize for something stupid he said or did.

"Lynn, I've wanted to say that I'm sorry, but I haven't had the opportunity." He waited for a moment, folding his fingers together in front of him in nervous action. When she didn't say anything, he continued. "I shouldn't have kissed you when I know that you're afraid of me. You just seem to cast a spell over me whenever I'm around you." He watched as her fingertips went to barely touch her mouth at the mention of the kiss. It seemed to be an automatic gesture now. She stared into the flames for a moment before she spoke, her voice barely audible.

"I'm not afraid of you, Ben. It's what you are that makes me nervous."

Ben sat on the ground and placed his hands on his knees in a gesture of resignation. After studying her face for a moment, he repeated the same words he had uttered the other time she told him that.

"I know, a man. I still don't understand."

"I know you don't and I'm sorry I can't explain it to you right now. Maybe someday." She turned to look at him with a sadness hovering around her eyes. The fire reflected in his gaze, the flames dancing with the confusion she saw there. A slight breeze caught the dark hair at his temples and blew it forward into his eyes. She watched as he brushed it back with a large hand. A hand that she had come to learn could be gentle and kind like her father's and grandfather's had been. She eyed his mouth, heat tingling her cheeks as she remembered that mouth on hers. His kiss wasn't like Jared's had always been. Jared was bruising and demanding with his kisses, using his mouth to punish her. For some reason, she was confident that Ben's kisses would never be like that. That thought brought another rush of heat, and oddly enough, comfort. Hastily she turned her attention back to the fry bread.

"Is that supper about ready? I'm starving." Kyle saved her from any more embarrassment as he joined them. A moment later, Suzanne, had the clean clothes hung and was taking a plate to eat with them also.

The two women sat and listened to Ben and Kyle talk about the next few days and the mountains they were going to have to climb. It would be very difficult and would be hard on the oxen. Ben said that these were some of the steepest with the exception of Laurel Hill just before Oregon City. That hill had caused many deaths and lost many a wagon.

Leann and Jeremiah came over to listen in on the conversation. A few minutes later so did Willy and Leah and their family along with Bud and Rachel. Sarah sat down beside Kyle who grinned and put an arm around her shoulders. Kyle had won the Aames approval, and they had said that when Sarah turned sixteen next April they would be allowed to marry. Kyle would turn eighteen in January, and he was a hard-working young man with potential.

The women took care of supper dishes and then headed off to have their much-needed baths. Some of the men had already bathed. The others who wanted to take one would do so after the women were done. There were two nice springs and some of the other women decided to go to the other one nearer the camp.

Although they were all so tired, the women talked with animation about being able to stop for a day. Being able to bathe made them all feel wonderful again. As they were getting dressed, Lynn decided to stay behind for a few more minutes.

"I want to enjoy the peace and quiet for a few more minutes before I go to bed."

Rachel and Leah were skeptical about leaving her out here by herself for very long. "Well, as long as you don't stay very long. Ben said that there were mountain lions and bears in these mountains. So, please don't stay out here long." Leah showed her motherly concern by warning her about the possibility of wolves, too.

"I won't be long, I promise." Lynn smiled patiently and was warmed by their concern.

As her friends left, she found a big boulder a short way from the spring and decided to sit there and watch the final rays of the sunset. The moon was lifting full and high in the darkening sky. As she was climbing up the rock, she heard the howl of what must have been wolves in the distance somewhere. Then all was quiet again and she enjoyed the solitude of the moment.

She was so lost in her thoughts that she failed to see or hear his approach until he spoke to her.

"Well, aren't you a pretty sight for sore and tired eyes. You look just like a queen sitting up there."

She turned quickly to see Jake at the base of her rock. He was looking up at her with his hands on his hips. He had been friendly to her for the past few weeks but had stopped trying to court her. She noticed that whenever he was around Ben, there seemed to be some underlying tension, but no arguments or anything had happened between the two men. Jake had continued to make her uncomfortable with his presence because although he was no longer courting her, she could tell he was still hoping she would change her mind. Now, she wondered if this was an accidental meeting or if he had purposely searched for her.

The slight breeze drifting to her caught the smell of whiskey, and suddenly she was alarmed. Memories of Jared and whiskey made her breath catch in her throat. He was always meaner after he had been drinking. Alarm rang loud, like a roar in her ears, and she almost didn't hear him as he answered the unspoken question.

"The women said you had stayed behind to watch the sunset and look at the night sky. I thought I might join you for a while."

Not waiting for her to answer, he climbed up beside her and sat so close their thighs were touching. She couldn't move away because the only way off the rock was either over him or off the other side. On that side, the rock sheared off so that she would have to drop about fifteen feet. Her body tensed as she watched him warily.

He was watching her with a strange and new glint in his eyes, one that made her heart skip a beat against her ribs. The pungent blend of whiskey and tobacco on his breath was nauseating when he leaned toward her.

"I came to talk with you about that proposal I gave you a few weeks back. I've been thinking that maybe I let you go a little too easily. I know that Ben's been trying to win your favor, too. It seems that you must not want him either. You could do a lot worse than me in the Oregon country, ya know. A lot of desperate men gonna be there waitin' for a woman to show up and marry them." The words were slightly slurry and the whiskey fumes smothered her, making her cringe slightly and try to lean away from him. This was the first time she heard of him drinking anything on the trip. He hadn't seemed the drinking sort and she was shocked. She wondered how much he had imbibed in.

He paused, seeing the alarm in her face. "I saw you run off from Ben that same day that I had proposed when you two were fishing." He scratched his beard as though contemplating what to say next. Seeing embarrassment redden her cheeks didn't phase him.

Lynn couldn't believe her ears! He had seen the kiss that Ben had given her? She was horrified. Her face felt icy as the blood drained from it.

"I think that even though you told me that you're not the woman I need, that maybe I'm the man that you need. I wouldn't pussyfoot around like Ben has been. He didn't really kiss you. Why it looked to me like he just barely touched you. I bet you've never been properly kissed."

No longer being able to breathe, her fingers dug into the rock beneath them. When he stared at her mouth and then leaned closer into her face, her head spun with dizziness as she started to shake.

She blinked several times, trying to stay focused on what he was doing. When his arm went around her shoulders to pull her to him, she placed hands on his chest to push him away. His strength overwhelmed her as she felt that old familiar weakness hit her in the middle of the chest. Her eyes clenched shut when suddenly, memories of Jared taunted her.

Jake was far stronger than her, and when he took her hands in one of his and held them, she panicked. His hold was not cruel or hard like Jared's had been, but, it was firm, and it brought all the old fears and pains crashing back into her with a physical force that was nauseating. Sweat broke out on her forehead. She had thought herself free from all of this! What was happening to her!?

His lips came down on hers with a commanding force that was choking. His whiskey breath took her own away and she struggled to breathe. Trying to turn her head did nothing. He worked his mouth against hers until she thought she would faint. Vomit rose in her throat and she made a retching sound. With an enormous effort, she wrenched her face away and cried out.

"Jared stop, please stop. No, Jared, please! Stop!" She was sobbing, not realizing what name she spoke until suddenly she was pushed away with such force that she almost fell from her already precarious position.

"Jared? Who the heck is Jared?" Jake glowered at her.

She was saved from answering, however, as Ben's furious voice reached them.

"Get down off that rock Jake Emmons so that I can beat the hell out of you!" Lynn could see his eyes blazing even in the near dark. Jake jumped down off of the rock and stood before Ben.

"I don't want her. You can have her. I want a woman who hasn't been touched before. I don't know who Jared is, but he obviously has had his way with her, whoever he is." Jake spat the words out with disdain, making Lynn sound cheap.

"It isn't going to be quite that easy." Ben swung at Jake, hitting him square in the jaw with a blow that knocked him backward. Jake shook his head trying to regain his balance and then came up swinging, landing a blow on the side of Ben's head. Lynn climbed down off of the rock and ran between the two men to stop them, her hands against both of their chests as she sobbed.

"I'm not worth fighting over! Stop it! Stop it now!" The noise brought several other men running to where the three of them stood. The two men glared at each other. Jake stood with one hand rubbing his jaw. Ben's solid stance with fists at his side made the men look anxiously from one to the other. Lynn stood between them with her arms stretched out toward each man. Her eyes were wild with shame and humiliation.

Bud and Kyle came running up first. "What's wrong? What's happening here?" All eyes were first on Lynn's tear-stained face, then Ben and finally Jake. No one spoke for a moment. Then Ben relaxed his stand and told the group that everything was alright.

"It was just a little misunderstanding. Everything is alright now." Jake relaxed some and then turned and stalked to the wagons, but not before sending Lynn a look of distaste.

Lynn, turning abruptly on her heel, ran through the trees behind them that went deeper into the woods.

"Lynn, wait. Where are you going?" Kyle started to follow her but was stopped by Ben.

"I'll find her. Go ahead and go back to the wagons." He looked at the rest of the men. "All of you now, go back to the wagons. It's getting late and we all need the rest." With that, he turned and went quickly in the direction Lynn had taken.

Lynn just couldn't handle any more. She had been fighting an enormous emotional battle within herself for the last several weeks, especially the last two. Ever since she realized that she had allowed herself to fall in love with Ben, she came up with all kinds of excuses why she shouldn't be. Of course, none of them made her heart feel any better. And now Jake's assault brought back the worst memories of her life. Then, when she saw the two men fighting, she felt her whole world collapse around her. She knew Jake to be a good man. He hadn't really hurt her but it brought back a pain so deep that she was afraid she would never be completely rid of it. She wasn't worth fighting over. She couldn't marry. She couldn't bear children—two and a half years with Jared had proven that. She hated the intimacies of marriage. She wasn't marriage material. However, just because the past was always on her mind, so was Ben. How could she blend the two together into a future? She didn't know.

She ran until her breath was coming in gasps and her chest heaved painfully. When she finally stopped, she could see from the moonlight that she was near the edge of a cliff that dropped into a small ravine full of rocks. Near her, there were a couple of large rocks she could climb onto. She climbed up onto the smaller of the two and looked over it into the ravine below her.

Her thoughts went back over the last months. She had made new friends, saw the beauty of new places, and was slowly becoming strong again. Even if she never remarried, even without love in her life she could still enjoy the small pleasures that made life worth living. At the same time, she craved family, someone to love and hopefully love her in return. Her fingers rubbed at her eyes as the woven web of raw emotional confusion made tears trickle slowly down her cheeks.

The sight that greeted Ben's eyes when he finally found her made his blood chill. She was standing on a rock looking down into a ravine. Her arms were wrapped tightly around her waist as her body swayed gently in the night air. He wanted to yell at her to get down but knew that it may startle her, causing the very thing he wanted to prevent. So, with great effort, he kept his voice calm, soothing.

"Lynn, you don't want to do that."

She turned his way. "I don't want to do what?" She glanced down into the dark ravine. "Don't worry. I'm not going to kill myself." She stared at him, sighing heavily, "But, it is foolish to fight over me."

His chest tightened in alarm. Her words were firm, resolute as if a decision had been made and she was ending any possibility of discussion. His heart pounded within his chest. "How can you say that? You're a beautiful, kind, gentle, caring woman."

She struggled to talk through her tears. "No, you're wrong. You see, you don't really know me. I have a past that is terrible. Sometimes life changes us in ways that we would never welcome. That's what the past has done to me. I try to run from it and it catches me. I try to hide from it and it finds me. No matter where I go, it's always there. And because of it, I can't be the woman Jake wants me to be and I can't be the woman you want me to be. I can't even be the woman I want to be." Shame marked her face when she looked down at him before staring down into the ravine.

Ben could see tears glistening on her cheeks. A slow step at a time and he edged closer until he could almost touch her. He watched as she shifted her vision from the ravine to tip her head back and look up into the night sky at the beautiful moon. When she closed her eyes, Ben sensed her losing her balance rather than seeing it. He lunged forward just as she swayed, her arms suddenly thrown out to try to catch herself. A frightened gasp escaped her just as Ben caught her skirt and used his superior weight to swing her around so that she fell sideways down onto him instead of down the side of the ravine.

Her weight landed on his shoulder and chest, causing him to lose his balance and fall backward with her light form landing on top of him. The fall knocked the air out of him, and he fought to catch his breath. A few seconds later he felt her hair against his cheek and her body shaking. He lay perfectly still for a moment listening to her cry into his shoulder. A rock gouged his lower back, so he shifted his body while carefully moving hers with him. His arms tightened around her as his own body shook from the rush of concern that consumed him. He talked to her in low, calming tones.

"It's alright now. Go ahead and cry it out. You are worth everything to me. I love you. I want to marry you when we reach Oregon City. It's okay." He murmured softly for a few more seconds until she raised her head. She didn't say anything as she watched him, her eyes flickering with something he didn't understand. He smoothed her hair back from her face with one hand. The other was still around her shoulders. Becoming intensely aware of her body's softness against his chest and thighs, his gaze went to her mouth. He lifted his mouth to place a soft kiss against hers.

Lynn's thoughts were muddled with emotion. A good man was right in front of her, she was sure of it. And yet, the last two years had taken a deep toll on her. Trust no longer came easily. Knowing something to be true and giving yourself over to that knowledge were two entirely different things. She felt the biggest wave of unhappiness and frustration she had ever felt. She wanted to feel love again, and the possibility of that was in the big wagon master. But how do you give yourself over to something you're still afraid of?

Things happen that later, we look back and wonder about the feelings and questions that are raised. Right now she found herself laying on top of Ben as he talked quietly in her ear. His strong fingers were splayed across the back of her head and gently pulled her face down closer to his. When his lips touched hers, she still didn't move. She wanted this and at the same time, she was terrified of it. She held her breath as she waited to see if he would turn into a Jared or Jake, but somehow knowing that he wouldn't. Again, the past raising its ugly head to influence her. When Lynn didn't move from his touch, Ben kissed her again, this time pulling her face down to his. His lips left a trail of small, feathery kisses from one side of her mouth to the other and then up one side of her face to her temple and back down again. She stared down at him, and he watched with interest at the emotions that caused a slight frown, but then disappeared with a soft sigh. His hand left the back of her head and went down her back, softly massaging her shoulders and ribs. The other arm moved down her back to her waist and stayed there. Still, her eyes remained open, and still he watched. At the first hint of fear, he would stop.

He pressed his lips against her mouth, applying a little more pressure, but remaining undemanding. Her lips quivered slightly, and he waited patiently to see what she would do. Her mouth moved against his again, but he decided that enough was enough. A slight tremor ran the length of her frame with his last kiss. Not sure if fear was a factor, it was time to stop.

He shifted his weight once again so that he could sit up and help her do the same. He pulled her up beside him and kept his arm around her waist until he could see that she was steady. She cast him a puzzled look and he felt uncomfortable beneath her steady gaze. She finally looked at her hands that lay in her lap and quietly asked two surprising questions.

"After what I told you, you don't seem to be afraid. Why? Why would you pursue a woman who has been ruined?

Ben's eyebrows shot up as his eyes widened in shock. What had happened to this woman? Maybe it was a good time to find out a few things after all. Just who was Jared, anyway? Did he have anything to do with her? Was she the sister he claimed to have lost? Or was there someone else who had damaged this woman? He took her hand gently in his own and asked the questions he had wanted to know for so long.

"Who are you? What has happened to you in the past that you feel so bad about yourself? And who is Jared?"

A pained expression crossed her features. Tears started to well up in her eyes once again. She was silent for a moment and then decided that maybe it was time to tell him everything. He deserved the truth. Maybe it was time to get all of it out in the open; after he knew, he wouldn't want her anymore, anyway. Who would want such a soiled woman?!

"Jared Malen was—is my husband. I ran away from him in Independence because I couldn't take any more of his beatings. Now you know why I can't marry Jake or you or even be the type of woman I want to be, let alone be the type of woman some other man wants me to be." The depth of shame in her eyes and heart was overwhelming.

Jared Malen. Looking for his sister, indeed! Ben had been right when he had asked him about his wife. No wonder Jared had been so angry. He didn't know what to think now. Lynn was still a married woman. And he was in love with her. He had kissed this woman several times, thinking that it was just a matter of a few more weeks and he would marry her. But now what? Now where was his life going? In disbelief and frustration, he stood up, shoved his hands in his pockets, and stood for a few minutes staring into the dark. He glanced at the woman sitting on the ground, her hands laying quietly in her lap with a look of defeat upon her lovely face.

His heart went out to her. He felt guilty at his own selfishness. He was thinking about his future, but what kind of future did she have? Jared would eventually come looking for her out here. He would surely figure out where she went. He may even now be on a wagon train coming this way. He would probably want to kill her when he found her. That type of man would want to heal the pride that had been seared when she left him.

Ben wanted to protect her from Jared when he came looking for her, no matter how long it took. A million thoughts went flying through his head all at once. He wondered if it was possible for her to get a divorce, although pretty sure it would be fairly easily obtained if they had a lawyer in town finally when he returned. Marrying a divorced woman was almost scandalous, but he wanted to marry this woman. This gentle, kind, and patient woman who liked everyone and whom everyone liked. This woman, who until now, had been strong, facing challenges with resilience and fortitude and beautiful smiles that reminded him of his mother.

Lynn continued to sit where she was, her eyes gazing unfocused into the night. She didn't want to think about anything. Everything was too painful to think about. Everything was in ruins. She knew that here was a man she could trust. He hadn't forced himself on her. His kisses and his touch had love in them, not demands. He must surely hate her now. She hadn't told him the truth all these months and he must be thinking about what a deceitful person she was. The truth was she had unwittingly fallen in love with this man. But, she couldn't have him. Right now, thinking was painful.

Ben held out his hand to help her to her feet. She stared at his hand for a few seconds before accepting, allowing him to help her up. When she stood and was steady on her feet, she pulled her hand free and started walking back toward the wagons. He trailed behind her. When they reached the wagons, there were still a few people milling around waiting for them to return. No one said anything to either one of them, but they noticed Ben and Lynn's sad expressions. Lynn turned briefly to Ben and looking up at him, told him goodnight before climbing into her wagon.

Ben hadn't known what to say on the way back to the wagons. What was he supposed to say? He was confused and angry. At the same time, he wanted to reach out and hold and caress away all of her pain. He knew, though, that if he reached out and touched her that he wouldn't be able to stop at just holding her for a few minutes. That obviously was not a good idea, so he spoke nothing and kept his hands to himself. He retired and fell asleep quickly because of the exhaustion on the trail, but not before he thought briefly about how his bright future had just turned to ashes in his hands. If he couldn't have her, then he wouldn't marry at all. It would be up to Jad to keep the family name going.

Lynn fell asleep quicker than she usually did when she was in turmoil. On the walk back to the wagon, she had decided that feelings were not a good thing. She would be better off without them. Ben not speaking to her, but just walking quietly behind her, had finished off any hope within her. She could feel his bitterness and disappointment, and guilt lay heavy in her heart. She resolved to feel nothing from now on. It would make life much easier from here on out. She curled herself into a tight ball and fell asleep, her tears gone and her heart beating painfully against her breast.

Chapter 20

"A place to go"

Sept 26th, 1844

The last month had taken its toll on everyone. The exhaustion of the animals and people had caused severe problems. The men were too tired to do much hunting, so the meat was gone and most of the other supplies were running extremely low. Tempers were short, nerves frayed, and patience gone. Six wagons tipped over on Laurel Hill. Two were lost entirely, and three people had died.

Four people suffered broken bones when the wagons went over. Kyle was one of them. He had been helping another family with their wagon when it tipped, catching his arm in one of the wheels, wrenching his shoulder out, and breaking his arm. He was still in a lot of pain and it made extra work for Suzanne and Lynn, who were already exhausted. The two women took turns driving the wagon and walking with Kyle. He preferred to walk instead of dealing with the jerking and jostling of the wagon.

Ben worried about Lynn. Like the rest of the women, she went through all of her chores in a routine manner. Where she would have a few weeks ago seen beauty and adventure, now she seemed to care less about their surroundings. There was something different about her, even though her gentle nature was still intact. When Ben glanced her way there was a determined thrust to her chin, a stubbornness in her gaze, and a focus on the trail that had not been there earlier.

Ben stood in the stirrups and surveyed the wagons behind him. Tired smiles were on the faces of some this afternoon because they would see Oregon City within the next two or three hours. People were starting to get excited as the realization hit them that they had finally made it. They were at the trail's end.

He trotted up next to Lynn who was walking. Suzanne had just taken over the wagon, giving Lynn a chance to stretch her aching back.

"Lynn, I was wondering if you would ride with me for a little while on my wagon. I would like to talk with you." He jerked a thumb toward his waiting wagon. "Please, come with me for just a little while." After a moment's hesitation, she barely nodded in agreement. He dismounted and walked beside her to his wagon. After tying the horse to the wagon, he assisted her up to the wagon seat. After climbing up beside her, he lifted the reins, slapping the leather against the backs of the oxen.

He contemplated the leather in his hands for a moment before speaking. He had been thinking for a long time about that fateful night from a few weeks past and what to do about Lynn. He knew that Kyle would be able to homestead. Although, with a broken arm he would need a lot of extra help, Bud and Willy had already formed a plan to have Kyle help them for now and stay with their families for the winter. Suzanne already stated that she would be fine, she had a cousin she was sure she could stay with for the winter who had come out the year before.

But, what about Lynn? She, of course, had spoken about a teaching position. He felt that she needed time to recover not only from the trail, but also her life of the past couple of years. Rachel and Leah had both offered to have her stay with them for a while. But they had their own hands full for now with large families that needed their care. No, Lynn needed nurturing and he knew the two women in the world capable of doing that. He wanted to take her to his families' home but needed to convince her of that. He was also more determined than ever to find a way to marry this woman someday. The information she had given him that night required a lot of thinking, a lot of deciding. There was little interest on her part in talking with anyone other than Kyle and the women she had become good friends with.

Darting her a sideways look, he finally spoke. "I know that you are hoping for a teaching job as soon as possible, right?" He studied her face.

That was certainly not what she expected him to talk about. "Yes, I'm hoping for that if possible." She flicked a glance up at him and then studied the road ahead.

"Well, I was thinking that it may be a good idea to take you somewhere so that you can gain your strength back and get well before you take on a bunch of young'uns. I would like to take you to my families' home for a few weeks until you are able to teach, if there is a teaching position even open." He fiddled with the leather in his hands.

Her eyes widened and she shifted to look at him again. "Oh. Hmmm, well I don't think that's a good idea. There must be a boarding house or hotel or something, right?"

He needed to do some convincing about right now. "My mother and sister can always use the extra help. My sister has her hands full with Cathleen and she was hoping to be with child again soon. I've been gone a little over a year. She may have already had another baby for all I know. But, even if that's not the case, you would still be a big help to them. Please consider that you would earn your keep if that's what you're worried about." He didn't really want her to do any work for a while, but if it made her feel better to think she would be earning her keep, then all the better.

She was thinking about what he said. She was tired, no she was beyond tired. She felt like she could sleep for a month. Her muscles ached, and her bones felt weak. She must look a sight if she looked anywhere near how she felt. She would love to meet his family, but she didn't know if that was a good idea; she would just become more attached to this man.

"I'll have to think about it. I just don't know if that is such a good idea." She repeated her thoughts of a moment before.

Ben knew what she was referring to, and he was thinking of how to convince her that it would be alright. She turned to him suddenly, her eyes puzzled, and asked him a question.

"Why would you want me to live with your family for a while? After all you know about me and how I failed to tell you the truth, why would you want me near the people you love?"

Ben's eyebrows shot up as his hands tightened on the reins. What kind of love did she think he had for her? Did she think it was some fleeting thing? Of course, in the last weeks he guessed he hadn't really done a whole lot to convince her, now had he? He studied her face for a moment and then reached out and brushed her cheek with the back of his hand.

"Because Lynn, I love you and I will marry you someday and show you that I can make you happy instead of living in fear. I want you to be happy again. I want you to feel safe again. And I want you close to me so that I can protect you." Leaning toward her, he placed a small kiss against her temple. "The past weeks I've had time to do a lot of thinking, thinking about what I want, who I want. That's you."

For a moment she studied the depth of his stare. What she found there were tenderness and love. It surprised her that even though he knew some of her worst secrets he still loved her, wanted her. "That amazes me." She flashed him a small smile before looking ahead of them once more.

That smile was all the assurance he needed right now. Putting an arm around her shoulders, he pulled her against his side. The occasional glance down told him that her eyes were heavy even though she fought to stay awake. Ben kept his arm around her, supporting her head until finally, she drifted into sleep. He studied the fragile structure of her beautiful face. Right now, she looked tired and dusty from the trail. But he imagined what she would look like with just a couple of handfuls of weight on her, after a bath with her hair shiny and her soft lips parted and waiting for his kiss. He found himself daydreaming about a wedding night, a night of happiness and passion. A night of education for Lynn. He wanted to be the one to awaken a passion within her, to show her what it really meant to love someone and to share the physical part of a man and woman with her. He growled at himself at the daydreaming that accomplished nothing but make him anxious. God was going to strike him for the way his thoughts wandered if he didn't get them under control. He tried to divert his attention to other things along the trail with only limited success.

Chapter 21

"Destination"

Lynn awoke with a violent start. She heard a rifle being fired several times and men were yelling. She jerked upright and looked up at Ben who was smiling and laughing and then started yelling back. As she faced forward, she realized that there were several buildings coming up on their left and an actual street in front of them. It took a few more seconds to realize what that meant. Three men on horses rode up beside Ben.

"Hey, Ben, glad to have ya back."

"Yore Mama gonna be happy yore home, boy!"

"Jes' seen yore brother over there at Chapman's store. Him and Allen in town to buy some goods fer that young'un what jes' arrived a few days ago."

Ben's face lit up as he asked eagerly, "A young'un you said? My sister had another baby? What did she have, Sam?" He had been gone too long. At least he had come home to great news.

"Wa'll now, I don' know if'n I should say nothin'. Better ya ask yore brother-in-law." The tall, lanky man looked over his shoulder just as Allen Colton walked out of the door. He thrust a thumb in that direction. "Ya can ask the man hisself, right thar." All three men stopped their horses and waited alongside the wagon.

Allen and Jad looked up the street at the same time that Ben looked in their direction. Jad let out a loud, whooping yell and set down the box in his arms. Allen took a second longer to do the same, and then both men came running across the street toward them. Ben jumped down and the three men grabbed each other in turns, slapping backs, and shaking hands with big grins on their faces. They were all talking at once when finally, Ben held up his hand to Lynn and gestured for her to come to the edge of the seat so that he could lift her down.

"This is Lynn, boys. I would like you to meet her."

Jad and Allen noticed the way Ben's eyes softened when he looked at Lynn. They exchanged a look with each other and then curiously watched Ben. Jad was the first to speak, his eyes amused at some secret joke as he faced Lynn, took her hand, and kissed the back of it.

"I'm very glad to meet you, ma'am. You must be quite the woman to catch my brother and I can hardly wait to get to know you." Mischief hovered around the wide grin he flashed her.

"Likewise." Lynn murmured quietly smiling in return, but her eyes turned to Ben, wanting him to correct his brother. She had realized, of course, right away that they were brothers. The younger man had the same dark hair, strong build, chiseled good looks, and dark eyes. When he smiled he also had the same small dimple in his left cheek. His eyes were laughing, and Lynn got the impression that they were very often that way.

Ben finally commented on his brother's remark, but it wasn't what Lynn expected him to say.

"Yes, she is quite the woman, brother, and you just remember who found her first." That earned an even bigger grin, if possible, from Jad. Lynn had to clench her teeth to keep her jaw from dropping.

Allen saved them from further comments. "Ma'am, I'm Allen Colton. I'm related to these two clowns because I married their sister, the better of the three of them." His eyes twinkled as he held out a hand. He was as tall as the two brothers but not as heavily built. His frame was a little more on the slender wiry side. But his hand had the same calluses as Ben and Jad, and there was a quiet strength about his manner. She could see the affection for the two brothers in his eyes and in the smile he gave her. His comment earned him a cuff upside the back of the head from Jad, who had mock sadness written on his face. Lynn liked them both immediately, thinking how good it must feel to belong to such a family.

Ben introduced the other three men on the horses who stood waiting patiently to meet this woman who rode with Ben. "This here is Sam Clarke, Micah Wallace, and Slip Evans." He pointed at each of them in turn and they touched the brim of their hats to acknowledge the introduction. They could hardly wait to pass on the interesting news that Carrie Owens was finally going to have some competition in this town. It was obvious that this here young woman was going to be beautiful once she got cleaned up and rested up. Her eyes were dark, with a heavy fringe of dark lashes that accented her narrow lovely face. They could hardly wait for the fur to start flying. There hadn't been a good cat-fight in town since Carrie and that young school teacher had one about a year ago at the fall dance.

Ben finally turned to his brother-in-law with a note of impatience in his voice and excitement in his eyes. "Is it a girl or boy, Allen? What did Shaline have?" Impatience and excitement were heard in his voice. "How is Shaline? Is she doing alright? How old is the baby?"

Allen laughed as he raised a hand. "Whoa, whoa, one at a time. Yes, Shaline is fine. Very tired, of course, but very well. The baby is almost two weeks old and is also fine. Another strong healthy girl. She's a whole pound more than Cathleen was." Allen was as proud a father as Lynn had ever seen. He obviously didn't care that he didn't have a boy; his proud grin showed that he adored the new girl as much as it showed that he adored his older daughter.

"What's her name?" Ben was more excited than Lynn had ever seen him, and she was wishing for some of the energy that flowed off of him right now.

"Wa'll, that's been the only problem. We can't agree on names. Shaline wants to name her Margaret Hazel. I want to name her Katrina Laura. And as for Mama, well, of course, she has her ideas of what she should be called. So, for right now, she's just been 'sweetie' which is what Cathleen is calling her." His eyes were smiling as he watched Lynn.

Jad kept glancing back and forth between her and Ben. Ben stayed close to Lynn's side with a protective hand upon her shoulder. Jad finally had to make the comment that was on his mind the moment he saw Lynn on Ben's wagon.

"You know who's going to be mad when she sees Lynn, don't ya?" He glanced pointedly down the street at some building that Lynn couldn't decipher.

Ben followed his glance and merely shrugged. "I made no promises. Anything that she thinks was going to happen, was all in her own head and you know that."

"Yeah, well, she's been waiting for you to return so you can pick a date and decide who's gonna be in the wedding." Jad ignored the glare that Ben was sending him. He knew Ben wanted him to shut up, but how could he resist seeing his older brother squirm just a little? And Ben knew it.

Ben was uncomfortable. He knew that Jad was doing this on purpose. If Jad could stir something up he would do it. He loved to get reactions out of people even if the reaction was to smack him upside the head. Lynn was looking up at him with pink cheeks of confusion.

When he didn't say anything right away, she turned to walk to her wagon. Ben caught her elbow before she got more than a couple of steps.

"I'll explain later, Lynn. It is not what you think, I promise." He helped her back up on the wagon.

Ben sent another glare at Jad and then made a request of him out loud. "Jad, I would like you to take Lynn home to Mama with my wagon and horse. I need to give people on this train some general directions of where to find the land office, bank, and general store and where they can camp tonight. It's getting late and these people are just as tired of traveling as I am. Allen, can you come with me? I want to introduce you to some good friends. And then, I'll ride with you in the buckboard for home." Jad and Allen gave him quick, affirmative nods and followed him as he walked back toward the other wagons, talking as they went. But, they were now out of Lynn's earshot.

"Jad, Lynn is not an ordinary woman and I want you to tell Mama to take good care of her until I get there. She'll need a hot bath, some warm food, and a soft bed. She's been through a lot. I'll tell you what I know later. Right now, however, I'm gonna entrust her into your care while I take care of the last of my responsibilities here then I'll be home for the same hot bath, warm food, and soft bed." Ben's orders were spoken with the firmness of an older brother in charge, but also with trust that his brother would carry them out.

Lynn cast a wary eye as Jad climbed into the seat beside her. Jad was cheery, though, and it didn't take long to have her smiling at something he said. Her exhaustion didn't allow for much conversation, but Jad didn't seem to mind as he sang silly little songs along the way and pointed out things that he thought she would find interesting.

It took about twenty minutes before they reached a large log house sitting in a small opening nestled in among large fir trees. A creek ran alongside the far end of the clearing and there was a milled barn standing nearby. Smoke curled up out of the chimney giving Lynn immediate thoughts of how cozy a warm fire would feel. It had been too long since she had felt the warmth of a fireplace or woodstove warming her. She almost shivered in anticipation. Although still having serious doubts about this being a good idea, she was looking forward to meeting the rest of Ben's family, having real food in her stomach, and a fire to cozy up to.

As they drew alongside the house, a little girl came running out of the house screaming. "Uncle Ben, Uncle Ben!" Her face was comical as she suddenly realized that it wasn't Uncle Ben, after all, it was just

Uncle Jad. She stood with her hands on her hips and pouted, making her long dark braids bounce.

"It's just Uncle Jad! Where's Uncle Ben? Who's the pretty lady? Why isn't Uncle Ben on the wagon?" Then, turning on her heel quickly, she ran back into the house, leaving the door open without waiting for any answers to her questions. "Gramma! Gramma! Uncle Jad is here with the wagon and a pretty lady, but Uncle Ben is not here." Jad was still laughing as he stopped the oxen and helped Lynn to the ground.

"Jad? Where is Ben?" Lynn looked around to see a small, petite woman standing on the porch wiping her hands on an apron. Her hair was dark with silver threading through it, and Lynn could see from where she stood, she had the same dark eyes as her sons. The woman looked at Lynn and then back at Jad with an anxious stare.

"He had to take care of things with the people on the train. Show them the land claim office and bank and whatnot. So he sent me ahead with the wagon and Lynn." He turned to Lynn. "I'm sorry, I didn't catch your last name."

"Malen." Lynn answered softly.

"Mama this is Lynn Malen. Lynn, this is mine and Ben's Mama, Grace Alenson. She's the fireball of the family and still thinks that she tells us what to do." They had reached Grace by that time and he grabbed her around the waist as he swung her around the porch while she protested even though she smiled at the same time.

"Jad! Jad Alenson put me down this instant! I have work to do and you're leaving this poor woman standing on this porch. She obviously is bone tired and looks half-starved. Now draw up some water for a bath while I get some supper warmed up." Jad laughed at his mother as he put her down and winked at Lynn, who smiled wearily back at the warmth and welcome of this family.

Jad knew that Mama would take right good care of Lynn and Ben had known that, too. Lynn was a pretty lady, as Cathleen had called her, and he bet that when she was cleaned up, was rested, and had a few more pounds on her, the word used to describe her would be beautiful. Leave it to his brother to find one like this. Whew, boy! Was Carrie gonna be mad when she found out about this! Lynn was going to give ol' Carrie a run for her money.

He whistled as he cheerfully stomped into the house, grabbing up Cathleen who squealed in delight as he tossed her into the air. He was thinking how a hundred wild horses couldn't drag him away from this place for the next few weeks. It was gonna be interesting!

Chapter 22

"Scars"

Lynn was sleeping peacefully in a large bed in the loft. Unbeknownst to her, it was Ben's bed. There were only two bedrooms downstairs. One belonged to Grace and the other belonged to Shaline, Allen, and the girls. By the time Ben arrived home, Lynn had eaten some elk roast with potatoes, carrots, spinach greens, large fluffy biscuits with honey, and two glasses of fresh milk. The supper was delicious, and although Lynn would have loved to eat more, she simply didn't have the energy.

By the time she was done eating, Jad had gotten the tub filled on the other side of the kitchen so Lynn was able to have a bath. Sinking down into the hot water was pure heaven, and she soaked within its embrace for several minutes.

When Grace brought in more water to rinse her hair, Lynn declined help, insisting that she was perfectly capable of doing it herself. She didn't want the older woman to see the scars. Just leaving the pitcher of water beside the tub was probably enough to catch sight of some of them.

By seven o'clock Lynn was snuggling down into a huge, warm bed. Her head barely hit the pillow before she was sound asleep.

Grace stood in the doorway, staring at her contemplatively as she wondered about the scars on her back. She was such an attractive young woman, even with her shoulder-length hair. Grace wondered about that, too, but it wasn't what concerned her the most. When she saw the scars, she realized why Lynn hadn't wanted any help.

Heaving a heavy sigh, she returned downstairs just in time to have Ben and Allen come through the door. Then the process repeated itself, except for the going to bed. Ben was eager to talk and see his new niece. Cathleen wouldn't budge from his lap until she finally fell asleep and had to be carried to bed by her father. Shaline had ventured into the living room to sit in the rocking chair near the fire. The family spent the next two hours trying to catch up on what had happened in the months since they had last seen Ben.

Grace finally spoke up about Lynn. "Who is she, Ben? I ask, of course, because I am curious about her background, but also for another reason." She was quiet for a moment, then continued when she got curious looks from her children and a gesture from Ben to continue.

"She's certainly a quiet young woman. Is that from exhaustion from the trail?" Grace grimaced. "I well remember those months and how tired I was. After eating and having a bath, I could tell that she relaxed a little bit. I lent her one of my nightgowns, although it is very small on her. She was quiet, talking little although very polite and very, very thankful." A frown creased her brow as she stared at Ben. "She has a great many scars across her shoulders, Ben. I'm guessing they go down her back, but I didn't get a good look. Most of them look old, but she does have a couple that are still quite pink. What do you know of that?"

Shaline gasped sharply and looked wide-eyed at her older brother. Jad and Allen straightened in their chairs as their gazes went to Ben as well.

Ben rubbed a hand across his now clean-shaven face except for a heavy but well-trimmed mustache. After rubbing his eyes with his forefinger and thumb he told them what he knew, which was limited. He had spoken to Rachel and Leah, gleaning a little information out of them after the river ordeal. But they had felt like they were betraying a confidence and so had told him very little. He had put two and two together, however, and had come to the realization that a man had beaten her even before that night when Lynn had finally told him that it was Jared who had done so. As he talked with his family there were a few things he left out, like the midnight bath when he found out that "Larry" was a woman. He told them most other things but also failed to say how many times he had kissed her and held her. They all sat quietly, trying to soak in this information when Jad suddenly erupted out of the chair.

"I'd like to kill that man! I'd kill any man who dared touch my sister or mother that way. I can't believe that a man would do that! How did you keep from turning around and going back to find him and kill him?!" His hands were fists at his side as he walked around the room with aggravated movements.

"By the time I found out, Jad, we were three or more months on the trail. I couldn't very well turn around then." Ben sighed and stretched his long legs out towards the fireplace. "Believe me, I've thought about how I would like to torture the man if I ever see him, and I'm sure I will."

"What do you mean, Ben?"

Ben turned to look affectionately at his sister. "Because a man like that won't let her go without wanting revenge for her leaving him. He'll come looking for her and he'll find her, I can feel it. And I'll be here to protect her this time." His family looked at him with surprise at the fierceness and fire in his voice.

Ben stood up, stretching his tall frame, and decided it was time to retire for the evening, but only after looking in on Lynn. He climbed the stairs to the loft where he and Jad ordinarily slept. They each had their own bed up there. Tonight, however, their mother would sleep up here while he and Jad would share her big bed downstairs.

He stood looking at the dark lashes that lay against her cheek. A couple of curls had fallen forward over her eye, and he gently slid them behind her ear. It was amazing how fast her hair had grown in the past five months. His thumb followed the outline of her cheekbone then down to her mouth where he just barely brushed across them. He leaned over and gave her a kiss above her brow and then on that soft mouth. When she moved slightly in her sleep, murmuring something, he stared at her as she curled a hand up under the pillow.

As he turned around, he realized with a start that his mother and Jad were standing in the doorway watching him. He grinned sheepishly as he started down the stairs until Grace's voice stopped him.

"She seems like a nice little thing, son, but be careful falling in love with her. It may be very hard to convince her that you won't treat her the same as her husband did. She may be afraid of you. And too, getting a divorce may be quite the challenge." Her voice was soft with concern.

He sighed heavily, "I'm sorry, Mama, but I've already fallen in love with her. I loved her the moment I saw her on that hill with her arms spread wide trying to catch the wind. Something told me then that she would be my woman someday." His smile was tired and slow as he looked first at his mother's worried face, and then at Jad's amused one. He knew what Jad was thinking; he couldn't wait for the fireworks that were bound to come within the next day or two. If he wasn't so doggone tired, he may have seen the humor in this situation and would have grinned back at Jad's devious mind. As it was, it was about all he could do to walk instead of roll down the stairs.

"Goodnight, Mama. 'Night Jad." He walked wearily down the stairs and without a moment's hesitation headed into his mother's room, jerked off his pants, and collapsed into bed. It only took five minutes to be fast asleep.

Jad was still smiling as he climbed into bed with his older brother. Yes indeed, it was going to be fun around here. He smiled because he was happy to see his brother finally find a woman whom he could love. Jad had been afraid that Ben was so realistic that maybe he didn't believe in love. But, tonight he saw evidence that he did indeed, and that it was going to be an interesting mess to figure out. Ben would have to fall for a woman with a lot of problems! Folding his arms under his neck, he figured if any man could win a woman's trust, it would definitely be his brother.

Chapter 23

"The nightmare"

It took a few seconds to realize that the crying was indeed real, not just in a dream. Ben jerked upright in bed, throwing back the covers. Jad bolted out of bed behind his older brother. As Ben pulled the door open, he realized that the crying came from upstairs. He ran to the stairs, taking them two at a time with Jad and then Allen right behind him.

Grace waved them back as she saw them appear on the top of the stairs. She sat on the bed holding Lynn against her breast while rocking back and forth, smoothing Lynn's hair back from her face. Lynn wept with her arms wrapped around the older woman. With Grace's soothing voice, she had slowly quieted and was now crying softly as she tried to catch her breath from her earlier fright.

Ben refused to be waved back and came to kneel down in front of Lynn, who wasn't aware that anyone else was even present. She just knew someone motherly was talking to her and holding her. Tears still streamed down her face, but her eyes were closed tight as she clung desperately to Grace.

"Lynn? Lynn, it's alright." Ben took one of her hands in his and caressed the back of it with his thumb. She opened her eyes at Ben's voice then, and after a few seconds, she fully realized where she was. She let go of Grace and flung herself into Ben's embrace. Ben, surprised, gathered her up into his arms, and sat on the bed beside Grace.

"Lynn? Tell me what happened. Talk to me. Mama always says that talking about it helps. Tell me about your dream." Ben's voice was soothing. As she calmed down she gradually released her tight hold around his neck, dropped one hand into her lap, and turned teary eyes up at him. Lynn focused on the one person she knew to be the strength and stability she needed. After a quick glance at Grace, she shifted back to Ben. The two men behind her on the stairs stood quietly waiting with concern on their faces. Unaware of anyone besides Ben and Grace, she wiped fingers across her eyes, trying to muddle through the fog that encompassed her.

Why she would have this dream now she didn't know. Was it because she wanted something good and wonderful so desperately that her subconscious mind refused to accept the possibilities? She used to have nightmares like this all of the time. After they were on the trail, however, she had one only three or four times, and certainly none this horrible. A shiver ran down her back as the dream came to her as clearly as if she were living it.

They had to strain to hear her, she spoke so low. "Jared found me. And...and he was,....he had a horsewhip and he was hitting me with it. I didn't care because he had killed you and,... I just didn't want to live anymore. So, I let him beat me and didn't try to stop him anymore. I just didn't care...I didn't care anymore." Her eyes squeezed painfully shut again as she leaned against his chest crying softly.

Ben's hand gently rubbed her back. "Well, I'm not dead, sweetheart, I'm right here and I won't let him hurt you anymore." He paused for a moment, then asked a question that made him angry to ask because he was sure of the answer. "Has Jared used a horsewhip on you before, Lynn?" He glanced up to see Allen and Jad clenching their fists at their sides, anger flashing up in their eyes.

How do you admit to cruelty? How do you confess that your life has been hell? Never before had she spoken of this to anyone, not to this extent. Maggie certainly knew some things because she saw the after-effects. But even with her Lynn had never told the details of her misery. But this was different, this was a safe place, Ben was her safe place. Somehow she knew that Grace was as well.

Finally, she murmured into his chest, "Just once. He usually used his fists and sometimes his belt."

It was hard to ask the question, anger made Ben's throat constrict. "Why did he use the whip, Lynn? How long ago was it?"

"I, uh...I was talking to a man at the general store. Jared said I was flirting with him. I was just talking with him about his little girl. He had the cutest little girl. But, but I should not have done that. I knew he would be mad. I should not have talked with Zach about his little girl. I was wrong. But, I was just talking about his little girl, that was all. It was just about his pretty little girl." She started crying again in earnest as her body shuddered with the memory of Jared's cruelty.

Ben wrapped his arms around even more tightly. "No honey, you weren't wrong to be friendly with someone and talk with them about their little girl. It's alright now, Jared isn't here. He's not going to horsewhip you anymore. He's not going to hit you anymore. I'm here to protect you." Ben continued talking to her as he heard noises downstairs.

Jad and Allen had both gone back downstairs. Jad's angry voice could barely be heard. He must have hit something because Ben and Grace heard something fall over and hit the floor. Allen encouraged him to go outside. Shaline was calling for Allen, so telling Jad he would be out in a moment, he went into the bedroom to tell Shaline what was happening. He needed to help her with the baby, who was by then, crying.

Lynn was oblivious to all the commotion below, the memories had flooded back with a ferocity that overwhelmed her. The fear that enveloped her right now made her angry. She had thrust this all aside after a few weeks on the trail. This was to be left behind her. A new life was hers and she wanted happiness. This nightmare made her aware of how weak she felt. Strength had certainly been gained in these last few months. Obviously not enough, though. Her hands clenched with frustration as she resolved to flip this around, to turn it into a path of self-reliance. Tears continued down her cheeks, but they were tears from anger now as much as from fear. She would rise above this one way or the other.

Ben shifted on the bed which caused the too-small nightgown to rise up on her legs. Grace drew a small quilt off of the chair beside the bed to cover her with. Ben realized why. The material was taut across her breasts and a hasty glance gave him good view of her feet and lower legs. Her calves were slender, which he knew already from seeing her bathing that night so long ago. He thought briefly how that night seemed just like yesterday and at the same time like a lifetime ago. So many things had happened in such a short time. He waited patiently for Grace to arrange the quilt around Lynn.

Ben sat quietly until Lynn gradually stopped crying, falling back to sleep with her cheek pressed into his chest. Grace inclined her head toward the pillow, encouraging him to lay her back within the covers. He didn't want to, though. He was so tired and yet his body was very aware of the soft bottom that lay on his thighs. Earlier, he had felt that same softness when she had clung to him and her breasts were against his bare chest. It was difficult to control the rage that filled him as he studied the sweet face pressed against him. He failed to understand the cruelty that destroyed her happiness. Her laughter and smiles were a bright part of any day. Those dark eyes should sparkle with amusement and love. It would happen again, he would make sure it happened again. He wanted it as he had never wanted anything in his whole life. It was an all-consuming fire within the depths of his heart and soul. Never again would she experience pain, misery, and fear.

Ben hesitated a moment longer, trying to find an excuse to hold her a little longer.

"Do we have a judge yet? Or did old Judge Perkins come back into town?" Ben looked questioningly at his mother.

Grace grimaced. "Yes, he is. And just as cranky as ever."

He smiled at that but was relieved to hear it. He didn't really want to make a trip clear to Stumptown. There were so many things to be done before winter set in. It wouldn't be fair to expect Allen and Jad to do it all. They had already carried the load all these months. He was here now and wouldn't be leaving again. While he was eating earlier they had told him about how the sawmill was up and running and starting to produce some good lumber. It would work even better now with another set of hands and they were all anxious to make it run more efficiently.

Grace eyed her son thoughtfully for a moment. "Why don't you just go in tomorrow and find out what needs to be done?"

Ben looked up. "Well, I thank you for the offer, but I've been gone long enough for a while. I need to stay here for a few days and help out. Besides, I want to be here in case she needs me again. Jared could show up on any of the wagon trains coming in for the next two months or so. And, I don't want her facing Carrie without me here. I'm sure she knows by now that I'm back, and knowing Carrie, it wouldn't surprise me if she showed up tomorrow. I'll go into town in a couple of days and look up Judge Perkins and see what he can tell me."

Finally Ben stood and Grace pulled back the covers. Gently pulling the smaller quilt off also pulled the nightgown askew once more. Ben inhaled sharply at the glimpse of Lynn's knees but looked away as his mother quickly pulled the blankets up over her. When he looked back around a second later, Lynn was turning over onto her side with an arm curled beneath her head.

Grace raised an eyebrow at her son. "I hope you haven't done anything to compromise this woman, son." The softly spoken statement was more of a question.

He looked around at his mother. "No Mama, I haven't. But, I must admit, a thousand times I have wanted to take her to my bed. I respect her and love her too much to cheapen her. And I love and respect God enough too. I won't make love to her until she is my wife."

Grace nodded, a small smile hovering as she patted his hand. After giving Lynn a light kiss on the forehead, he followed his mother downstairs.

The rest of the family had gathered in front of the fireplace, sipping tea.

Ben settled into a chair, rested his forearms on his thighs, and frowned. His thoughts went back to something Jad said earlier.

"Jad, why are you so convinced that Carrie will be mad about this? Hasn't she found anyone else to harass? Surely by now some other man must have moved into town that has caught her eye."

Sitting back abruptly, he thought about the blonde woman. That he was actually thinking about marrying her and settling down when he returned made him cringe! His family hadn't been real enthused, but she was a decent enough young woman. She had never been married, which he used to think was absolutely necessary. That was before Lynn, however. Now he wondered at his selfishness and why that had been so important.

Jad laughed, "You kiddin'? She's been counting the days since you left. There have been a couple of fellas that wanted her. But, they weren't good enough for her. Nope, she wants a man who she figures is going places. One who's gonna have something someday. She's used to livin' high on the hog." Jad sneered. He never had cared much for Carrie Owen. As far as he was concerned, she was just a spoiled banker's brat.

Shaline yawned, "Well from where I'm sitting, I think that who she wants and who she's going to get may just be two different things. And with that conclusion, I'm going back to bed." Shaline kissed her older brother on the temple, tousled Jad's hair, kissed Grace, and then tugged at Allen's hand. "Come on, dear, I need you to keep me warm."

Ben stood and stretched. After a quick peck on his mother's cheek, he returned to bed as well. Jad followed on his heels, the usual mischief flickering in his glance. Ben ignored him, although knowing that it would do little good. Jad lay on his back with his arms folded up under his head, a smug look plastered on his face. "So what ya gonna do when Carrie comes calling today?"

"Today?" Ben yawned deeply as he pulled the covers up to his bare chest, "What do you mean today?"

"Well, considering what time it is, I think it would be safe to say today. Do you really think she's going to let you have any peace when she hears you're home? Besides, you can bet that a whole lot of people beat a path to her door, not only telling her that you're home, but that you have a pretty young woman with you as well."

Ben didn't need a light from a candle to know there was a smirk on Jad's face. He could tell by the tone of his voice that he was loving every second of this. "She's gonna be madder than a hornet. She's gonna be here with her claws out, for sure." He was quiet for a second before adding, "I sure wouldn't want to be you, brother. But, I sure can't wait to see what you're gonna do about it."

Ben grimaced at his brother in the dark. "Thank you, brother, just what I wanted to hear. Well, if I've got to face that wildcat tomorrow or should I say today, I need some more sleep. Goodnight!"

Jad's grin just deepened at Ben's obvious annoyance.

Chapter 24

"If I had a baby"

Lynn awoke to the wonderful smells of bacon, eggs, and coffee. Sunlight slanted through the single window as she turned over to look around the small space. Seeing men's clothes hanging on the hooks and the guns in the corner, she felt guilty for displacing the brothers from their beds.

Grace had delayed making breakfast as early as she usually did because she knew that Ben and Lynn would both sleep late. She had been correct in her assumption. Although she, Jad, and Allen had been up for a couple of hours, Ben didn't rise until almost seven-thirty and Lynn shortly after. When Ben started stirring around, then she decided to make breakfast. She asked Jad to watch over things while she went upstairs to give Lynn something clean to wear.

Lynn was looking out of the small window after making the bed. She didn't know what to do about her clothes. The nightgown she had on was way too small, and she couldn't remember where she had put her dress from last night. She turned when she heard Grace's warm words.

"Good morning, dear. Oh, you look so much better this morning. Your face doesn't look quite so tired. A couple more nights of good sleep and you will feel so much better." Grace handed Lynn a large mug of steaming coffee. "Do you need sugar or cream in that, dear?"

Lynn gratefully accepted the coffee and shook her head. "No, thank you, Mrs. Alenson. This smells wonderful." She inhaled deeply the rich fragrant aroma of the dark coffee. After taking a sip she sighed with appreciation.

Grace laid out one of Lynn's dresses from her chest that had been in the wagon. "Jad brought your trunk in, and I took the liberty of going through it and finding you something to put on that would fit." She smiled and looked pointedly at the nightgown.

Lynn chuckled. "Thank you so much. It is a little tight in some places, isn't it?" She looked at her breasts. "It's a good thing that no one else saw me in this, isn't it?" Grace smiled in return, nodding her head and deciding not to tell her about last night. If she didn't remember, what good would it do to remind her? Grace laid her pale blue dress on the bed, some underclothes, and after handing her a brush and a mirror walked to the top of the stairs.

"When you're done, breakfast is down here. I'd better get back down there before Jad has it ruined." She smiled and winked at Lynn as she cocked an ear toward the stairs waiting for the retort that soon followed.

"I heard that Mama." Jad's jovial voice rang out from the kitchen.

All the family had gathered in the kitchen to eat breakfast together as usual. Shaline was covertly nursing the new baby. Cathleen was sitting on Uncle Ben's lap teasing him as she tugged gently on the mustache that curled above his laughing upper lip. Ben was happy to hear Lynn's soft voice a few minutes earlier. He was anxious for her to come down, hoping that she looked more herself from earlier months. When Grace entered the room, Ben looked her way. Her smile was encouraging as she caught his questioning gaze and nodded slightly.

Lynn studied the reflection in the mirror. A different woman stared back at her since the last time she had looked at herself in her hand mirror at Maggie's hotel in Independence. This young woman had skin that had darkened from the sun. Her eyes looked different, they held experience and adventure in them now. There were hints of independence, sadness, and regret. Sadness that she was in love and that scared her. Regret that she had caused him to fall in love with her when all she had done so far was to bring him pain. And regret that she hadn't met him first, before Jared. How different her life would be now.

Her eyes didn't have the same glow that they had almost three years ago, but they were no longer nervous and terrified, either. But now, even in just this short time, she began to feel some warmth return to her soul and she rightly attributed it to this family she hadn't even gotten to know yet but knew in her heart that she would love them all soon.

Resolve stared back at her as well. The nightmare last night was a turning point. There was a determined thrust to her jaw, a resolute stubbornness that her life was changing. It would be good from now on, she would make it good from now on. Jared was far, far away and she would do whatever was needed to be free from him completely.

She marveled at how a different woman stood there. Someone vastly different from the girl who had married Jared, but also vastly different from the woman who left Independence just a few months ago. A sense of wonder filled her that she had made it to the Oregon country, wonder that the long trail had ended, and a new life could begin.

A wave of something else lifted her spirits now, too. The decision she had made in Independence had led her here, to freedom. The shackles would be completely thrown once she had a divorce.

Hearing laughter below, catching Ben's deep voice teasing his niece, she reveled in the warmth emanating from this family. She didn't know how to explain it, but she just felt like she had already been embraced within them.

She brushed her hair until it shone and curled slightly around her face. It had grown a lot in the last five months, barely touching her shoulders. She pulled it back from her face with two combs that Grace had shown her last night and then laid on the nightstand beside the bed. She gave a last look in the mirror and then turning abruptly, went down the stairs.

The family was gathered around the table passing breakfast when she entered the kitchen with her coffee mug in hand. She hesitated at the doorway, soaking in the scene of this happy, united family laughing and eating together. It was something she had never fully experienced. A small, dark-haired young woman with laughing eyes spotted her standing in the doorway. After putting down her fork, she extended a hand toward Lynn with a warm smile on her pretty face. She had the same dark brown eyes as her brothers.

"You must be Lynn. I'm Shaline. I'm so sorry I didn't get to meet you yesterday. I was not feeling well. Come on in here and join us."

Shaline's smile caused the others to turn to look in Lynn's direction. Ben and Jad both jumped to their feet to pull out a chair for her. Ben, however, having Cathleen on his lap, was slower and so Jad pulled out the chair next to him. Ben scowled at his younger brother who just grinned back, fully amused at the look his brother gave him.

Lynn failed to catch the looks between the brothers; she was too busy watching the baby nursing at Shaline's breast. Shaline was modest and had thrown a dishtowel over herself, but the babies' feet and little arm moving immediately caught her attention. She was instantly enraptured. Having been with her grandfather at several births, she had seen newborns before, but it had been a long time. Whenever she saw a baby when she was with Jared, he would get very angry if she so much as smiled at it or the mother.

Ben was gratified to see that she looked much more rested this morning. It was amazing what a hot bath and comfortable bed could do even in just one night. The pale blue dress she wore complimented her tall slender figure, although it hung a little loosely around her frame. She would gain back the few pounds that had been lost on the trail from the lack of substantial food and so much hard work and walking. But even now, her face had more color in it and her eyes shone brightly as she gazed at the baby in his sister's arms. His eyes followed her as she sat down next to Jad and across from him.

Ben saw the hunger in her eyes as she watched Shaline with the baby. Leaning forward, he asked Lynn what she would like for breakfast.

"Lynn, what would you like? Some good fresh eggs here. Haven't had them for a while. How about some milk? Nice fresh milk, too." Lynn turned in his direction and nodded at both. He slid two eggs, a couple of pieces of bacon along with a fluffy biscuit on her plate. As he poured a glass of milk for her, he suddenly thought of something. "Mama, don't we have some cherry preserves? Lynn especially favors them." He rose from his chair, handed Cathleen to Allen, and went in search of some, surprising his family.

Jad looked her over as she slowly ate. "Wa'll, I'll say one thing for sure, if you keep improving at this rate every morning, you'll have all the women in Oregon City keeping their husbands away from you."

Heat tinged Lynn's cheeks. "They have nothing to worry about from me."

"Jad Alenson, leave Lynn alone. She needs to eat and not be distracted with the likes of you." Grace chided her son as she waved a knife at him from across the table. Jad just gave his usual grin and poured more milk into Lynn's glass.

Ben came back into the room with a jar of cherry preserves in his hand. Taking Lynn's biscuit, he cut it in half, spreading some of the preserves over half of it.

"Mama and Shaline make the best preserves around." Smiling, he handed it back to her.

She watched as he did this small thing for her while thinking about Jared. He had never done anything so simple, yet kind, for her all of her time with him. He had always thought only of himself.

Flashing Ben a smile, she took a bite and turned to Grace.

"It is very good, Mrs. Alenson. Thank you for a wonderful breakfast."

"Please, dear, don't call me that. Please call me Grace. Maybe someday you can call me Mama if Ben has his way." Grace looked affectionately at her older son so she failed to notice that Lynn's face once again colored slightly.

About that time, Shaline spoke up. She, too, had noticed the look of hunger and envy that Lynn had given her and the baby a moment before. "Would you like to hold 'sweetie' for me? I would like to finish eating now, too."

"I would love to!" Lynn dropped everything, and with shining eyes turned quickly to take the baby from Shaline's arms. As she gathered the infant into her arms, she sighed with delight. The rest of the family exchanged looks. Lynn's attention was entirely wrapped up in the small bundle in her arms and so failed to notice anything else.

"You know, we really need to name that baby, Sis. Sweetie just doesn't sound very becoming." Jad, putting his hands behind his head, had leaned back in his chair watching Lynn and the baby with interest. Lynn wasn't paying the least attention to the conversation around her. She was too busy playing with the tiny fingers.

"Well, maybe the pretty lady could name her," Cathleen spoke up then. She had been watching the whole affair and now decided it was time to get into this conversation.

"I'm sorry, muffin. I never introduced you to the pretty lady, did I?" Ben pointed at Lynn. "That pretty lady is Lynn." Lynn looked up with a warm smile for Cathleen. "And Lynn, this pretty girl is Cathleen."

"How do you do?" Cathleen showed her manners well.

"Very well, thank you. I've heard a lot about you from your Uncle Ben. I think that you must be very special." Cathleen flashed first a smile at her and then turned to Uncle Ben.

"I like her, and I think that she should name my little sister." Cathleen turned her attention back to Lynn, waiting expectantly.

When Lynn started to protest, Shaline agreed that Cathleen may be right to at least get some ideas for names since the family was at a standstill. They hadn't come up with any that they could agree upon. "What would you name her, Lynn?" The whole family waited.

"I,... I don't know. I hadn't thought about it. I shouldn't be the one to name her. She's not my baby." She looked down at the tiny face in her arms. The baby wiggled slightly and yawned. Then pursing her little lips, she blinked her eyes up at Lynn. Lynn's eyes glowed, as silently she wished it was her baby, and she was able to choose the name.

Allen encouraged her gently. "Why don't you suggest some and we'll see if we like any of them." When he got a slight nod from Shaline, he prodded her a little more. "If we don't like any of them, we won't be any worse off than now."

Lynn looked down into that sweet, innocent face thinking about what she would want to name her if the baby was hers. Her mother's middle name was Helen. She would want to name her after the mother she had lost.

The family watched as Lynn was lost in a world of her own for a moment. Ben saw the tenderness as Lynn caressed the tiny face and soft, downy head. His heart ached for her, knowing that she wanted a baby more than anything else. Rachel and Leah had told him months ago when they had been talking about Lynn that she wanted a baby very badly.

"I would name her after my mother who died when I was seven. Her name was Anna Helen. And my best friend when I was growing up was Mary. So, I would name my baby Helen Maryann."

"Helen Maryann." The family tried out the name seeing how it sounded on their tongues. Allen and Shaline smiled at each other, Shaline nodding her head.

"What a beautiful name. Just in case you have a little girl someday it would be wrong to take that name from you." Shaline pondered Lynn's suggestion for a moment, "But what about Maryanna Grace? I always have liked your name, Mama." Shaline smiled when Lynn's face lit up with delight. "I think it has a nice sound to it. Maryanna Grace Colton." She looked at her husband questioningly. When he repeated it a couple of times to himself, he nodded his head in agreement. Rising from the table, she started to clear away breakfast dishes until her brothers, husband, and mother demanded that she sit right back down saying that they would do it.

Lynn looked guilty and started to rise to hand Maryanna back to Shaline. "I should do them. I have done nothing to help." Again more protests, with Ben being the loudest as he rose from his chair grabbing dishes as he did so.

"Certainly not. You will please finish your breakfast. Then you and Shaline go in the living room to rest while we help Mama with these." Lynn finished her breakfast quickly while the rest of the family visited as they cleared the table.

The two younger women retired to the other room at Ben and Allen's insistence and visited while the other members of the family cleaned up the kitchen. Shaline had given her back Maryanna to rock, and they talked about babies. Shaline explained that birthing Maryanna had been difficult and she still wasn't feeling herself. A few minutes later, Ben joined them.

"Lynn, would you like to go for a walk with me? I would like to show you around the place." Ben saw the hesitation in her eyes to give up the baby. But, she rose and handed Maryanna to Shaline and after Ben put a light jacket around her shoulders, she followed him outside. Jad had already gone out. Allen followed shortly. She was glad for the light jacket Ben had given her to use because the fall air was cooler now. The leaves were turning their beautiful golden yellows and reds and she breathed deeply while smiling to herself.

Ben was obviously very proud of the homestead. He showed her the barn that they had built out of milled lumber instead of logs. The chicken house was also milled. The pride in his voice as he explained different parts of the farm impressed upon her the value of hard work and a family.

She had learned hard work when she lived with her grandparents, but she had missed having brothers and sisters. Being raised alone was very different from being raised with siblings, and she was envious of the affection that freely flowed between the two brothers, sister, and brother-in-law. The few minutes with Shaline this morning made her wish for a sister. Shaline had Jad's sense of humor, but it was tempered with Ben's seriousness. She wanted to be part of this family so bad that it hurt. She hoped that somehow, she would be able to.

She cast a glance up at the big man walking beside her, not really hearing at the moment what he was saying; she was lost in her own thoughts. Somehow, she trusted this man, she knew in her heart that he would never hurt her, although the thought of intimacy with him still made her very nervous. But, if he loved her and didn't hurt her, she decided that she could tolerate it.

Ben felt her eyes upon him and looked down at her upturned face. Her eyes were thoughtful as they contemplated him, and curiosity surged within him as he wondered at her thoughts. Learning from past experience, however, he knew she would talk when she was ready and not before.

Her pulse quickened when he smiled down at her. On impulse, she reached up to gently touch the dimple in his cheek with her fingertip. When his smile broadened at her touch, she dropped her arm swiftly to her side, feeling heat spread across her chest. He put his arm around her shoulders and they continued down the path toward the sawmill. She didn't protest or try to pull away, but instead, enjoyed the warmth and protection of his arm.

It was very short-lived, however, due to the noise of a buckboard coming up the road to the house. Jad and Allen were walking ahead of them and at the noise turned to see who it was. When Ben saw Jad's eyebrows shoot up and a wicked grin on his face, even before turning around, he knew who it was. Carrie had arrived.

Chapter 25

"Carrie"

Carrie had been excited to hear that Ben had finally returned from that infernal trip he insisted upon taking back east. Why he wanted to guide another wagon train out here had been beyond her understanding. She couldn't remember all the details, probably because she had cared so little about the reasons. She had been worried for a year that he wouldn't make it back and she would have to try to find another man who would have the same credentials as Ben Alenson. She knew that was about impossible. The only one who came close was Jad, but Jad irritated her. He never seemed the slightest impressed with her charms. If anything, he was always totally oblivious! No Jad wouldn't do for her at all! Only Ben would. Her great relief that he had made it safely home had been short-lived, however.

Ben and that blasted sawmill! She had tried to convince him, of course, that he didn't have to work that thing; there was always a job waiting for him at the bank, which he still balked at. After they were married, she would convince him one way or the other, though. He had a good business head on him and was wonderful at numbers. Her father had tried to talk him into working with him several times, too, for all the good it did him. She would use her womanly charms on him once they were married to convince him where he really belonged.

Now, however, she had other things to worry about. She had three people tell her yesterday that Ben had a woman on his wagon when he came into town. He wasn't married to her, she had gathered that much, but she didn't know why there was this woman. According to Sam Clarke, the woman was very attractive, also. Blast! Another complication. Well, Carrie Owen was one very attractive woman, too, and she knew it. This woman, whoever she was, was not going to stand in Carrie's way of getting the only eligible man worth anything in Oregon City. Ben's younger brother, Jad, was the only other man who was going to amount to anything, but she couldn't stand that stupid grin he always had on his face. She always felt like he could see right through her and it drove her mad! She ignored him to the best of her ability, which sometimes was very difficult because Jad was very good at making sure he couldn't be ignored.

Ben frowned at Jad, closed his eyes, and sighed heavily. Annoyance flickered across his face.

Lynn was puzzled at his expression. She turned with him to see who was coming up the road. Her eyes widened at the lovely sight before them. The young woman on the buckboard was a small, petite blonde with lovely eyes. Her hair had been pulled to one side and part of it hung in large curls over her left shoulder. Her green gingham dress pronounced her figure in the best possible manner. It was obvious that she wasn't afraid of showing off her remarkable figure because the buttons and lace drew a person's attention to her bosom. She stopped before the house and after looking around for a moment, spotted them by the edge of the trees.

"Ben! Oh Ben, how glad I am to see you!" Her slightly husky voice carried to them on the light breeze that flowed through the clearing. She stood up in the buckboard, waving her arm while waiting impatiently for Ben to help her down.

Ben didn't have much choice because he could tell that neither his brother nor Allen were going to offer any help. Much to his irritation, they were leaving that "honor" to him. After sending a heavy scowl over his shoulder at them, and narrowing his eyes at Jad's pretended innocent shrug, he took Lynn's elbow to direct her toward the other young woman. He was not looking forward to this confrontation, but knew it couldn't be avoided. Just as well get it over with; the sooner the better he supposed.

As they walked toward her, Carrie eyed the other woman. This woman would be no competition at all. What was Sam talking about? She was tall and thin. Her breasts were small, barely a hand full, not at all eye-catching like her own. Her own was overflowing and were exactly what men wanted, the thought of which made her cringe slightly. This tall woman's hair, although shiny and pretty, was only shoulder length. She did have a pretty face, Carrie had to concede, but all in all, how could Ben possibly want such a tall, skinny thing when he could have herself? No, she decided, this woman didn't scare her any after all.

Ben reached the side of the buckboard and held out his arms to her. She fairly fell into them, flinging her arms around his neck while pressing herself against his chest and, for just the briefest moment, pressing her mouth to his. She had every intention of using her body to her advantage. She would show this woman who had this man!

Lynn watched as the attractive blonde threw her arms around Ben and gave him a kiss on the mouth while pressing herself against him. Then she pretended innocence by dropping her eyes demurely to the ground.

"Oh Ben, I'm sorry. I know I shouldn't have done that, but I'm just so happy to see you. Why didn't you come see me last night when you got back in town? When I found out you were back I went all over town looking for you, but you were already gone. Father wouldn't let me come out here last night." She pouted prettily. Jad snickered behind Ben, winning a quick glare from her blue eyes.

"It was late, Carrie. I had been on the trail for about five months. I was tired and anxious to come home to a hot supper, hot bath, and a warm, soft bed. I showed the people on the wagons places they needed to know about, then Allen and I came home." Ben was irritated at such a silly question. Wasn't it obvious why he would come home as soon as possible? Lynn would never ask such a ridiculous question. In his mind, he was doing a lightning speed comparison of the two women and Carrie was coming up way short.

Carrie was very attractive with an ample bosom and curvy hips and at one time he had thought that he liked how small she was standing next to him. That was before Lynn and her tall, slender build. Lynn had curves too, gentle ones that his hands could easily flow over with unhurried ease. Carrie was frivolous and flighty, spoiled and she liked to pout when things didn't go her way. He couldn't picture Lynn being any of those. Lynn was steady and serious with an easy smile and sense of humor. She was kind and loving and thought of other people instead of herself. She would make sacrifices for those she loved, Carrie would never do that. She thought only of herself and what would benefit her.

As he contemplated the two women standing in front of him for just a moment, he was so thankful that he had gone east because he had met the woman he needed and wanted. Lynn would make him a good partner. He suddenly shivered as the thought of coming home to Carrie every night passed before his eyes and he was horrified at what his life would have become.

Jad poked him in the ribs with his forefinger. "Are you cold, brother, or are you having visions?" The remark earned him an elbow in his own ribs as Ben jerked his arm back. Jad only laughed loudly which meant another glare from Carrie.

Ben could only wonder at the insight that Jad had sometimes. It was almost as if he could read his thoughts. Guessing what the shiver was about probably wasn't too difficult since it wasn't cold out. But Jad was too smart for his own good sometimes.

Carrie frowned briefly at the antics of the two brothers, not understanding what Jad could have meant by such a comment. It sounded ridiculous to her since it was obvious that Ben wasn't cold in the least. When they were married she would make sure that Jad didn't come to the house very often. His influence was bad on Ben. The two of them wrestled and argued often, albeit good-naturedly. But she didn't feel the need to put up with such antics. Their relationship with each other as brothers would change drastically very soon. Her thoughts scurried to a halt when Ben introduced her to the tall woman by his side.

"Carrie, I would like you to meet Lynn Malen. Lynn, this is Carrie Owen. Her father, Jonah, owns the bank in town." Ben watched the reaction not only in Carrie's eyes but also Lynn's.

Lynn smiled and held out her hand to Carrie, who ignored it. The blonde simply looked at the taller woman, gave a quick, fake smile, and returned her attention to Ben, who was appalled at her rude behavior.

Lynn dropped her hand, feeling silly and suddenly tired, decided that she had walked far enough for one day. She wanted to return to the house to soak up some more of the warmth that was there not only from the fire but more importantly from the people within its walls. She turned to Ben as she touched his arm.

"I think I will return to the house and help Grace and Shaline. I would love to see the mill perhaps later if that is alright."

He shifted his gaze back to Lynn. "Of course. I probably shouldn't have taken you for such a long walk already. You need to get all your strength back and I was probably pushing you too far today, anyway. I'm sorry." He started toward the house with one hand on Lynn's elbow again, but Carrie put a hand on his arm, stopping him.

Fury hit her chest when Carrie saw Lynn touch Ben. How dare she? Did this woman think she had a chance? Carrie glared at her, but she seemed oblivious. She needed to divert Ben's attention back to herself. Placing her hand on Ben's arm, she used her sweet voice, the one that got her the attention she wanted.

"Ben I would love to see the mill. You never have shown it to me." Again, the pretty pout.

"You have never wanted to see it before, Carrie. Why would you want to now?" Ben's eyebrows shot up at Carrie's request. Jad covered his mouth trying not to laugh while Allen simply turned his head the other way, so no one would see the smile on his face.

Carrie did have the decency to turn slightly pink, but she was not to be swayed.

"Well, I know I haven't given the mill much thought in the past, but I was thinking that if I'm going to be married to a mill owner, I probably should get used to the idea." She was gratified to see Lynn's eyes widen and her face turn bright with color.

Lynn had heard enough. Pulling her arm out of Ben's grasp, Lynn walked quickly toward the house. Jad ran a couple of steps to catch up with her. Allen followed a little slower. That left Ben with Carrie pulling on his shirt sleeve to take her down to the mill. He had little choice in the matter, and his frown deepened when Jad turned around to look at them with a big grin on his face. He was the one now walking beside Lynn. Ben's scowl just made Jad throw back his head, laughing loudly.

Jad shook his head slightly when Lynn, startled at his laughter, looked up at him.

"I'm sorry Lynn. I don't mean to laugh. And you don't have to be scared of Carrie. She just thinks she's got ol' Ben wrapped around her little finger. She don't. It's always been her idea to marry Ben. Ain't never been Ben's idea to marry her." Jad smiled down at her. Nope, Jad thought to himself, Ben wasn't so dumb to marry that empty-headed woman who was just a bunch of fluff when there was this 'looker' walking beside him. This one seemed to have some senses anyway. If he ever married someday, he didn't want just a piece of fluff. He wanted a woman with a brain in her head. This one obviously did.

When they entered the house, Grace had just come into the kitchen with a basket of apples in her arms from the cold cellar.

"Now what you making, Mama. Pies?" Jad pulled up a chair and gently pushed Lynn into it. Grace had a questioning look on her face as she looked from one to the other.

"Yes, and what are you boys doing back here? I thought you were headed for the mill."

"Wa'll we were, but, Ben's favorite city woman stopped by." Jad waggled his brows.

"Oh no, Carrie is here already this morning? That means we'll have to invite her to stay for lunch." She frowned slightly as she looked at Lynn who sat quietly listening to the exchange. "So, you've met Carrie Owen. Well, don't worry none about her and Ben. I may not know you very well yet, but I've watched you long enough to know that you're more woman than Carrie Owen will ever be. And Ben knows that, too." She sat down to start peeling and slicing apples.

"Is Shaline taking a nap, Mama?" Allen asked his mother-in-law.

"Yes, she was so tired. Birthing takes a lot out of a woman and I told her to go take a nap."

Lynn watched for a moment as Grace worked on the apples and then decided that she couldn't very well just sit there. She wanted to help. She loved to cook and bake. Her grandmother had taught her well.

"Do you have another apron? I would love to help you make pies," Lynn asked quietly.

"Why yes, I do." After retrieving another apron from the other side of the kitchen, she handed it to Lynn. Lynn took an apple and started peeling, then handed them to Grace to slice. The two men decided that they weren't up to listening to woman talk so disappeared outside to cut firewood.

The two women worked at the apples for a while in silence before Grace asked Lynn about her life.

"Where did you grow up, Lynn? Do you have any brothers or sisters? Did you grow up in the country or in town? Tell me about your childhood, dear."

Grace's kind voice was all Lynn needed to talk. She missed the friends she had made on the wagon train. So now she was very happy to have another woman to talk to. She told Grace about growing up with her grandparents on their little farm. Grace was particularly intrigued about the visits she made with her grandfather and so learned some doctoring. When she was seventeen she decided to get her teacher's certificate and taught at a small school for a year near their town.

After hesitating for a moment, she figured Ben would eventually tell his mother about her being married, anyway, so decided to talk of that part of her life a little. She talked of how no man had caught her eye until Jared had charmed his way into her life. She spoke little of the way Jared had treated her, but Grace could read between the lines when Lynn's eyes and tone of voice spoke volumes even though her words didn't.

The pies were baking, the kitchen floor had been scrubbed and a pot of baked beans had been put on by the time Ben and Carrie came to the house.

Ben's chest was tight with irritation by the time they entered the house, but Carrie seemed totally oblivious to it. She had clung to his arm the whole way down the path to the mill. When he tried to explain some of the things about the mill in simple terms that even she should have been able to understand, she still asked ridiculous questions. She wasn't paying the least attention to anything he was showing her, anyway.

So, he decided enough was enough and suggested they return to the house. That prompted Carrie to fling herself at him again, trying to press herself against him and emphasizing how happy she was that he was back. When she tried again to kiss him but failed, she pouted, having to satisfy herself for now with pressing her breast against his arm as they walked. All it succeeded in doing for Ben was to make him frown with irritation. Her breast pressed against him did nothing for him. At one time it would have heated his blood. But now his thoughts went back in time to a river and a woman's moonlight kissed skin that had been glistening with water. It seemed like a lifetime ago; another world, another time.

The scene that greeted them when they walked into the house warmed Ben's heart but irritated Carrie immensely. Shaline had risen from her nap and had come into the kitchen with Maryanna, who was wide awake and happy since she had just been nursed. Cathleen was sitting on Gramma's lap, playing with a little bit of dough that had been left over from the pies. Lynn had the baby and was rocking her near the cookstove, singing to her a childhood ditty. Shaline was crocheting a baby sweater while sipping hot coffee. The women Ben loved most were enjoying each other's company, and it brought a smile to his face.

Ben immediately left Carrie's side, walking to Lynn to lean over and look at Maryanna. The baby turned her little face to look at him as he spoke to her. Squatting beside the rocker, he had one hand on Lynn's shoulder as the other smoothed the baby's soft, downy head.

Carrie's stomach knotted in frustration when she saw Ben's hand on Lynn's shoulder. How dare he just turn his back on her after their little walk! She was about to say something when Shaline spoke, breaking the silence.

"How is your mother, Carrie? I haven't seen her since she was sick with that terrible cold a couple of weeks ago. I hope she is better." Shaline glanced at Carrie but kept a more interested eye on Ben. He stayed close to Lynn, using the baby as an excuse to linger near her.

Carrie's gaze flickered to Shaline for just a moment. "Oh, she's fine now. Dr. Barclay gave her some elixir to help with her coughing." She edged closer to Ben and Lynn, craning her neck to see the baby in Lynn's arms. Ben laughed suddenly at her yawn and the funny face she made afterward. Lynn laughed, too, and she looked up into Ben's warm eyes. For just a split second it was as if they were in a world all their own. This was their baby girl and they were happily married and deeply in love.

When he asked to hold the baby for a moment, Lynn kissed the soft cheeks before handing her over to her uncle. He picked her up from Lynn's arms, cradling her close to his chest while talking to her. Maryanna stared at the big man with the gentle voice while still making funny little baby faces.

"Have you named her yet, Shaline?" Carrie looked at Shaline.

"Yes, we have. Or should I say, Lynn has? Well, kind of anyway." Carrie's eyebrows raised at that. She turned back toward Lynn, her anger glaring at the woman who sat quietly watching Ben with his niece.

"Lynn named her? Isn't she a little new here to be naming babies? It's not like she's part of your family or anything." Jealousy laced the words. How could they let her name this baby when she just got here? Ben may have known her for a few months now, but this family certainly didn't. How ridiculous was that! She wasn't pleased with the idea that Ben had spent a lot of time in this woman's company for several months.

Ben spoke up then, "Yes, her name is Maryanna Grace. Anna was Lynn's mother's name. Shaline attached Mary to it and then wanted to name her after Mama also. It seems to fit her well." He kissed the baby on the cheek and then handed her to Lynn, who eagerly took her back.

Carrie cringed at the thought of having babies. It was bad enough to have to deal with little kids. But babies? They were too much work and ruined your figure. She knew that Ben wanted children; he loved children. But, she would do all she could to keep from getting pregnant once they were married. She would probably have to give him one child, but there certainly wouldn't be any more after that. She was going to risk her life only once.

"Are you going to stay for lunch, Carrie? You just as well. I've got stew on the stove and biscuits to warm up." Grace may not want her to stay for lunch, but she wouldn't forget her manners and fail to ask her to.

"Why, thank you Mrs. Alenson. I think I will. I left the house so early this morning I didn't eat much breakfast. I was just in such a hurry to see Ben." She laid her hand on Ben's arm to pull his attention back to her. Ben walked away on the pretense of getting a cup of coffee. Carrie pouted, deciding to take Ben's rejection out on Lynn.

"So, tell me, Lynn, what are you doing here? Are you a friend of the family from back east?" Her stare bore a hole into Lynn, trying to figure out why she would be here at the Alenson homestead. She was positive that she wasn't related, but no other good reason came to her. It couldn't possibly be that Ben wanted that woman over her! That would be preposterous!

"I didn't know Ben until I joined the wagon train." Lynn's eyes were clear and direct as she answered, her usual soft voice remaining calm. Carrie had embarrassed her earlier, and she felt irritation come up into her chest. Her life with Jared was in the past along with the abuse that went with it. No more would she just take whatever people dished out to her.

"So, you joined the wagon train all by yourself? You must be pretty manly to drive a wagon alone." Carrie leaned back, looking satisfied with the little dig directed at Lynn's femininity or lack thereof as far as she was concerned. The taller woman wasn't nearly as feminine as she was with her ample curves and long blonde curls.

Inside she was fuming, but her voice was steady when she answered. "Not at all, a very good friend of mine, Kyle Parish, was with me and later another woman on the train, Suzanne, joined our wagon. There's nothing manly about driving a wagon. Driving oxen is pretty easy, actually."

Carrie jumped on Lynn's mention of a man. "How close a friend is this Kyle? You engaged to marry perhaps and you're here just until he gets everything settled? You're very fortunate to make friends with Ben. He always feels sorry for those less fortunate than the rest of us." Carrie smiled smugly, ignoring the flash of warning in Ben's eyes when he spun around to face her. She knew there had to be an explanation for Lynn's presence here.

Lynn saw the anger in Ben's face and answered quickly. "No. Kyle is quite a bit younger than myself. He's only seventeen and has plans to marry a young woman he became fond of on the wagon train. I have a good friend in his aunt back in Independence. He had always wanted to come west, and so came with me to help me out." Lynn saw the disappointed look on Carrie's face and almost felt sorry for her. But not quite, especially after her next remark.

"Well, one thing I've found out about most people coming west is that they are either looking for opportunity or they're running from something. Which is it for you? The only opportunity out here for women is marriage. I'm sure that you'll find someone desperate for a wife. Heaven knows I've had enough offers." She tossed her head slightly at the remark, making her hair bounce. "But I don't want just anybody."

She smiled at Ben who just about choked on a swallow of coffee. Things were going from bad to worse and he wanted to choke her. But he was pleasantly surprised and pleased with Lynn. She was sparring with Carrie and coming out on top every time, much to Carrie's irritation and Ben's mirth. Especially after Lynn's retort back at her, Ben chanced a quick glance at his mother and sister. Grace was trying to hide a smile behind a cup of coffee, and Shaline had her head bent low over her knitting, her shoulders shaking in quiet laughter.

"Everyone is running from something at some time in their life whether they know it or not, Miss Owen. I have teaching credentials, if I choose to use it. And like you, I won't settle for just anybody if I choose to marry. However, I look for different qualities in a man than I believe you probably do." As Lynn rose she handed Maryanna to Shaline and, turning abruptly on her heel, went to the door. "Now if you'll excuse me, Miss Owen, it is very warm in here. I need some air."

Carrie blinked and remained where she was in the chair beside the rocker. Grace and Shaline smiled at each other with satisfaction that this spoiled child had finally met her match. Ben, after digesting that Lynn had just put Carrie in her place, followed her outside.

He stood for a moment on the porch searching for her. He finally saw a glimpse of her blue dress through the edge of trees by the path that led to the barn. She was walking swiftly and before he could catch up with her, had disappeared into the barn.

Lynn was shaking from a mass of confusing emotions. It had been a long time since she had to deal with a jealous woman. She always found it distasteful to have to defend herself against such petty jealousy. She disliked it even more now. She sat down on a stool that was probably used for milking. After putting her face in her hands, she sighed heavily and fought back tears. Why was happiness so fleeting for her? It was there for a moment and then gone again. She didn't understand the relationship between Ben and Carrie.

To believe Jad would mean that it was only in Carrie's head that she and Ben had made promises for each other. And it was pretty obvious to her that Carrie annoyed Ben immensely. He seemed to go to great lengths to ignore her although he had taken her to see the mill after she requested and pouted for him to do so. But even Lynn had to admit it would have been rude for him not to at that point. There was so much confusion again. Her brain was having difficulties trying to muddle through it all and come up with any real conclusions.

When Ben entered the barn he saw her sitting at the far end with her face in her hands. She hadn't heard him enter so when he walked up to her and spoke, she jumped, dashing her hands quickly across her eyes to wipe the tears that had come despite her best efforts.

"Lynn?... I'm sorry, I didn't mean to startle you." He squatted on his haunches in front of her, taking her hands in his. "Don't cry, sweetheart. Carrie is,... I don't know what she is. Jad says she's a spoiled banker's brat. I think that about sums it up." Her cheeks were wet from tears and he wiped them away with his thumb.

"I never used to be like this when someone said mean things. I'm just tired of hiding who I am. I'm sorry. I'm such a mess." She looked at him with tear-filled eyes. "Why are you so good to me? What do you see in me? I've been here one day, and I feel like your family has taken me in completely and is there to protect me. Why? Why would they do that?" Her brown eyes searched his dark ones.

"I am good to you, as you call it, because I love you. My family has taken to you because they see what I see; a good woman who has not been appreciated in the past. They also trust my judgment. I've never found a woman I wanted to marry until you, so they know that you must be someone very special." As his arms went around her, he pulled her to her feet and against his chest. He laid his chin on the top of her head, breathing deeply the sweet scent of her hair.

"You do things to me that no other woman ever has. I can't explain it. I just know that you are what I need and want. I'll do anything to have you for my wife as soon as possible and always be here for you." When he paused for a moment, she decided it was time to make a couple more truths known to him, as painful as that would be.

He inclined his head to listen closely. Her soft voice was even more so whenever it seemed to be a painful or embarrassing subject, "Ben, I don't think you will want me for your wife. Remember, I told you once before that I can't have children. I see how you look at Maryanna and Cathleen. You want children and I won't be able to give them to you. What then?" Her voice was slightly muffled as she spoke into his shirt. Her arms were tucked in between her breasts and his chest.

Ben's chest tightened. No children? He looked forward to being a father, he wanted kids. He exhaled a long breath. But he only wanted children with one woman. "What then? Yes, I would like to have children. But, I don't want children with anyone but you. If we don't have children, then I'll be happy just spoiling my nieces and hopefully someday, nephews. No, sweetheart, I don't care if we don't have children as long as I have you beside me."

"There's another thing Ben." She hesitated. "I,... I don't really like, um, I mean,... you know,... the things that husbands and wives do, I,..." She let her voice trail off. Squeezing her eyes closed, she turned hot cheeks into her hands. She refused to look up at him, instead, fighting tears of embarrassment.

His reply was gentle. "I know that already." Her eyes flew up to look at him in surprise. "I figured that out the first time I kissed your lips. There was fear in your eyes." He looked down at her with understanding, "That's because Jared hurt you, didn't he?" When she barely nodded, he continued, "But, I've noticed that now when I kiss you, the fear in your eyes has disappeared. I will never hurt you, Lynn."

As if to reinforce his statement, he cupped her chin and tipped her head back. After wiping the tears from her eyes, he kissed her very gently. Then, he left a trail of slow, feathery kisses across the side of her face and down one side of her neck. By the time he came up the other side, her eyes had closed again, but this time she felt something else entirely. She shivered. He left a kiss on either eyelid and then whispered in her ear.

"I want to give to you, not just take from you like Jared. Remember, I'm not Jared." His left hand dropped from her shoulder to her waist while his right hand gently pulled her arms from between them. She wrapped her arms around his waist. His arms pulled her even closer as he held her for a moment, laying his cheek on the top of her head. He had told his mother that he wouldn't cheapen this woman. But right now, it was all he could do to keep that promise.

The door of the barn creaked open as Jad walked in. "Well, it's about time I found you two. Mama says that lunch is about to get served. So if you're hungry, now's the time to return to the house. By the way, Lynn, I'm sure glad to see another woman put that wench in her place. Carrie sure was mad when she left."

Jad had his usual grin as he leaned against the barn door with his arms crossed over his chest, watching them trying to separate quickly, but with dignity, as he talked. Ben shot him a glare that Jad figured, if looks could kill, he would be dead about right now. But since looks didn't kill, he waggled his brows at his brother and winked. Lynn's face went several shades of pink in about two seconds flat. He didn't think he had ever seen anyone color that quickly, and for just a moment, he was almost fascinated. At the fist that Ben shook at him though, he figured his fascination was better left for another time. Instead, he just grinned at his brother. Shaline had told him and Allen what had happened when they came into the house after seeing first Lynn run across the yard and then Ben in hot pursuit after her.

Ben put a warm hand against the small of Lynn's back as they walked toward the door. The three of them walked back to the house in silence. Carrie had left under the pretense of a forgotten chore, making Lynn thankful for the reprieve.

Chapter 26

"Kisses all around"

After lunch, the men left for the sawmill while Lynn helped Grace clean up from the meal. Lynn and Shaline were then both told by Grace to go take a nap along with Cathleen. Both the women were very willing to do so, although Cathleen protested until Lynn, after asking Grace's permission to do so, promised her that she could help Lynn make blackberry tarts for supper. Cathleen jumped up and down, clapping her hands with delight at such a proposition. She loved to help in the kitchen, though most of the time, her help was usually closer to being a hindrance. But Grace had patience with her grandchild and loved to have her in the kitchen.

Lynn was still sleeping when Ben came in a couple of hours later for a break. Grace smiled at his excuse; Ben rarely took breaks. Shaline was awake and in the kitchen nursing Maryanna.

"I think she is still sleeping, Ben. Your conniving niece convinced Lynn to let her take her nap with Lynn in Mama's bed. Go check on them. I know you want to." Shaline smiled wickedly at her brother, earning an affectionate squeeze on the shoulder and a smile in return.

Ben was still smiling when he slowly pushed open the door to his mother's room. The sight that greeted his eyes made his heart pound. Cathleen lay on her side with her back to Lynn and her rag doll in her arms. Lynn lay curled against her with one arm around her waist and the other arm bent under Cathleen's head. Ben went to the side of the bed watching them for a moment. He traced the curve of Lynn's jaw lightly with his thumb, then kissed them both on the temple before quietly leaving the room.

Lynn waited until he left before opening her eyes. She had

awakened shortly before Ben had entered the room. Wanting to see what he was going to do, she had pretended she was still asleep. That actually hadn't been hard to do, she was still at that stage of not being fully coherent, anyway. When Ben had kissed first Cathleen then her, nerves tingled immediately, and she was wide awake. Laying there for a few minutes, she contemplated her situation.

She wanted to marry this man and be part of this incredible family. At the same time, she was scared; scared of the feelings that welled within her whenever he was near, scared a little bit of the thought of intimacy with him yet, and scared of what her future was. He had also awakened a longing in her that she thought had disappeared. His touch was always so gentle, so full of tenderness. In the final stages of courting with Jared, they held hands and he kissed her, and her insides had heated with a desire for something more. Of course, after their marriage, those feelings soon disappeared with Jared's cruelty and selfishness.

Now, however, she was starting to get them back. Not much, just a little. This afternoon in the barn when Ben kissed her, she felt a slight stirring of excitement, a slight warmth in her belly. Once again she was longing for something, not knowing what it was. Maybe, just maybe, with Ben she would find out what that longing meant.

She finally stretched, deciding to wake Cathleen if they were going to make tarts. Those took time and she wanted to serve them with whipped cream.

When supper was almost ready, Grace had Cathleen go to the porch to ring the bell that they used. If the men didn't respond shortly, then Cathleen would have to go to the mill. But, tonight they were already on their way to the house when they heard the bell. Cathleen waited on the porch for the men and was rewarded for her patience when Allen came up the steps, swinging her up to sit her on his broad shoulders. She giggled with delight while hugging her Papa hard around the neck, almost choking him as she chattered.

"Guess what Lynn and me made. We made blackberry tarts and Lynn said she'll help me make cherry pie and teach me how to make good biscuits like Gramma and then we're gonna use the cream from Lucy's milk to make whipped cream for the tarts. Did you know that it takes a long time to make blackberry tarts? But Lynn said that I'm a good helper and I can help again tomorrow if it's alright with Mama." Her lively chatter made them all salivate in anticipation at the thought of fresh tarts with whipped cream.

Jad has his usual grin as he came in the door, kissing first Mama and then Shaline on the head. He started for Lynn, but Ben was already beside her giving her a kiss on the temple. Lynn turned wide eyes on Ben, and a shade of pink, from the loving attention. Obviously, this was a usual custom. When Ben didn't move from her side, Jad couldn't help himself.

"Waa'll Mama, looks like you don't get a kiss from Ben anymore at dinner time. Lynn's gonna get 'em all." His drawl made Grace smile, Shaline and Allen laugh, and Ben give him a mock scowl. Then suddenly, Ben surged in his direction. Jad backed away with his hand in the air, giving the impression that he didn't want a fight.

"You can have her brother. I'll steal a kiss later when you're not lookin'!" Jad's laughter rang through the kitchen as he ducked under Ben's left arm, but got caught from behind as his older brother wrapped him in a bear hug while trapping his arms to his sides. Ben lifted his feet off the floor and started for the door.

"Open the door, Cathleen! We're throwing this rascal out of here." Cathleen giggled and running for the door, flung it open. However, just before getting to the door Jad wiggled out of Ben's loose hold and went for Cathleen, making her scream in delight. He called her a traitor as he flung her up into the air, catching her, and then turned her upside down, making her dress and petticoat drop toward her head. Grace was aghast.

"Jad Alenson! Turn that child back around correctly. We're trying to teach her modesty, and then you come in here and within just a few minutes you have her bloomers showing!" The older woman was standing by the stove with her hands on her hips ready to serve up supper, but laughter hovered around her lips. "Now, get washed for supper. Let's eat before this gets cold." She served up mashed potatoes and gravy, fried chicken, and warm cornbread. Jad set Cathleen down while laughing at his mother and cuffing Cathleen lightly on the head. Lynn stood near the table setting plates and smiled contentedly as she watched the scene before her.

Chapter 27

"I have to find me"

The blackberry tarts with whipped cream were wonderful. Ben and Jad both ate two, with Jad expounding greatly on Lynn's abilities in the kitchen and telling Ben that if he decided he didn't want Lynn, that he, Jad, would gladly marry any woman who could cook like that. That earned him a bop on the head from his older brother, much to everyone's laughter with the exception of Lynn, whose face turned pink while trying to ignore the comments although smiling at the same time. After the kitchen was cleaned up, everyone retired to the living room for a couple of hours to enjoy the warmth of the fireplace. Grace and Shaline were both knitting. Since Lynn didn't really have anything to do, she read to Cathleen, holding her in her lap in the rocking chair. Cathleen finally fell asleep and Allen carried her to bed.

"I'm tired, too. I think I will retire. I just can't seem to get enough sleep yet." Lynn yawned and rose from the rocker.

"Oh, I remember that. It seems like it took forever before I felt truly rested again," Shaline agreed.

"Well, probably because you were also with child at the time, remember dear?" Allen put his hand on his wife's shoulder. "I think it's time for us to go to bed. I don't want you getting overtired now, either."

Shaline put away her knitting and followed her husband after kissing everyone in the family including Lynn. Lynn looked at her with surprise seeing the smile and affection in Shaline's face. Lynn smiled back, giving her hand a squeeze in return.

Ben followed Lynn to the bottom of the stairs, giving her a kiss on the temple once again.

Everyone fell asleep quickly with the exception of Ben. He lay there for a long time trying to figure out how to get away soon, so he could go talk to the old judge and see about Lynn's divorce. He couldn't come up with any solutions except to try to get the necessary work done as quickly as possible. He finally fell asleep after nudging Jad back over on his side of the bed.

Lynn awoke trembling around two-thirty. She had been dreaming about Jared again, and so was soaked with perspiration. Why, after all of the months on the trail, would she now have these nightmares? She needed some fresh air.

Creeping quietly down the stairs, she went out on the porch to sit for a while in the swing. She had her own nightgown on now, a pale green flannel. Because she was still so warm, she decided against putting on a shawl. Her toes pushed against the wooden planks of the porch floor as she pushed the swing into motion. She pulled her feet up onto the swing, wrapped her arms around her knees, and looked up at the beautiful night sky. The clouds had disappeared and there were a million stars brightly shining.

Ben heard the familiar creak on the second stair from the bottom, waking him up. When he heard the door open, he figured that it must be Lynn. His mother wouldn't have any reason to go outside. He slipped a shirt and pair of pants on quickly and stepped out onto the porch to see Lynn sitting in the swing gazing out across the yard and up at the night sky.

Lynn turned in surprise at the sound of the door opening. "Oh, I'm sorry. I didn't mean to wake anyone." Feeling self-conscious without a wrapper on, her grip tightened on her legs, pulling her knees even tighter against her breasts.

"Well, looking at those stars I think I'm glad you did. I'm happy to see a clear sky. We need to get the rest of the firewood in. A couple of nice days will sure help out." Ben leaned against the doorpost, looking at the stars for a moment before turning his attention to her.

"You alright? What are you doing out here?"

"Oh, I just couldn't sleep." She avoided looking at those piercing eyes, instead, turning her attention back to the night sky. Telling him about another nightmare wasn't what she wanted to do. And she had a feeling that he wasn't going to like what she was planning, either.

"Did you have another nightmare about Jared?" That jerked her head around to him immediately just as he expected, and he saw the surprise in her eyes.

"What do you mean, another dream about Jared?"

He hesitated for a second, "Well, after the one you had last night, I thought maybe that's what woke you up tonight also." A sudden thought crossed his mind. His mother had made a comment to him about maybe Lynn not remembering that nightmare. He shifted his feet uncomfortably. "Um, you do remember, right?"

She sighed heavily as she nodded. "Yes, I remember. And yes, that's what woke me up tonight." Her eyes shifted back to the night sky, quiet for several moments. She looked sideways at Ben. This was one of the things she appreciated about him, his patience. He simply stood there, watching her and waiting.

"I've been doing lots of thinking, Ben. I need to go. I need to find a job, either teaching, if there is an opening for a teacher. Or, something else." She stood, folding her arms across her breasts, wishing again she had grabbed her wrap. "I appreciate, more than you can know, the warmth and love from this family. I have already fallen in love with your family, Ben. But I am not a free woman, yet, in more ways than one. I need to make myself whole again. I need to find the person I was because she was lost somewhere along the way in the last three years."

Her toes pushed against the curve of the rocker that sat next to the swing. "It's hard to explain, Ben. I know that the old me, the girl who existed before Jared, isn't there anymore because of all of my experiences since marrying him. But there are pieces of that girl I liked, I want those pieces back again, the happy pieces. I can't find those here. I have to find them within myself. I need to find myself."

She lifted a hand when he opened his mouth. "I know you want to help with that, but you can't. You see, I think we need space between us for a while. Space and time so that you can truly examine what you want in your life, how you want your life. We both need time to think, Ben."

She didn't want to leave, but she needed to. Lynn dashed at her eyes trying to dry the tears that threatened to flow. How she wanted to throw her arms around him and soak up the warmth from his broad chest. She wanted that comfort so bad she ached inside. But she was afraid. What if she was never free of Jared? What if Ben's love for her was forever unsatisfied? Worst of all, what if he just thought he loved her, but it was all based on pity? They had been around each other constantly for months. He didn't know what it would be like to see her from a distance; to see her in normal circumstances the way a man and a woman should see each other. If he had that opportunity, would he still love her? Or would he instead turn to Carrie, the beautiful blonde?

She was right in telling him that they needed space and time. It would be for the best.

What she was saying made Ben catch his breath. He didn't want her to go. He needed her here, close by, to protect her and show her how much he loved her. And yet, as much as he didn't want to admit it, he could also see the wisdom and reasoning in her words. Reasonable or not, his chest beat against his ribs painfully.

"Lynn, I don't want you to go. I'll leave you alone. You can stay and work as a teacher if there's a job for that. But here, I can protect you if you're here. I may not be able to do so if you're in town."

"Protect me? From what?"

"Jared will figure it out eventually, and if he doesn't die on the trail, he will come looking for you. I'll give you space, I promise. And plenty of time to think and figure things out. But I don't want you to leave here."

She reached out and placed a palm against his cheek. His hand immediately covered it. "Ben, I have made the mistake of depending too much on you. I've been so scared and wasn't used to making decisions for myself for so long that it was easy to let you make them for me. But, I can't take advantage of your family's generosity and love. I also don't want to hurt you. I can't marry you, not until I am free from Jared. Who knows how long that will take. Plus, I have a feeling that once I'm away from you for a while, you will decide that I'm not really what you want in a wife. Right now, maybe you feel sorry for me, and so maybe you're just mistaking those feelings for love."

She paused for just a second before rushing on, sensing that he wanted to interrupt her, "And maybe the feelings I have for you aren't real either. Maybe I have them because you have been my knight. Maybe once I stand on my own two feet we won't want each other at all. There's a lot of maybes in there, I know. But, I can't live with maybes anymore and I wouldn't want to ask you to do so either."

The look in her eyes scared Ben as he had never been scared in his life. He suddenly felt cold as the blood rushed from his face. The import of what she was saying almost knocked the air out of him. As he fumbled trying to make words she continued.

"I would like you to take me into Oregon City tomorrow, so I can find either a teacher's position or work somewhere else. I have a little money left, so if I can find work, I can stay at one of the hotels in town, also." Her voice was calm, determined. "Please, please, I know this is the right thing to do. We both need to think with clear heads. I need to become whole again. I need to learn to think for myself again and have confidence in who I am, or I will never be any good to anyone. Do you understand, Ben? We both need to learn who I am now."

What could he say? She had her mind made up, and he knew she was right in most of what she said. Right in everything but one—he didn't just feel sorry for her. He loved her with a depth of heart and soul like he had never loved anything or anyone in his life. Yes, he would take her into town tomorrow and help find her a position somewhere, but, he would also make sure that he reminded her constantly how much he truly loved her. If she didn't really love him now, he would do everything in his power to see to it that she fell in love with him soon.

He nodded his head sadly in agreement with her request. "Okay. I'll take you into town tomorrow, or should I say today? But one thing you do need to know, I love you, Lynn. It has nothing to do with feeling sorry or anything else. I've never loved any woman before now, and I know without a doubt that I'll never love another woman other than you." The slight tremor in his voice made Lynn search his face as he looked down at her.

Suddenly, standing on tiptoe, she threw her arms around his neck, giving him a kiss. It was so brief that if his lips didn't still tingle from the warmth of her kiss, he would have sworn it was just a dream.

His arms went around her waist and back automatically when she threw her arms around his neck. They tightened as he stared at her.

"You need to know that I love you for the person I've seen you to be for several months. I know the reasons I have deep feelings for you. Although my heart goes out to you for the pain that you have suffered through parts of your life, those are not the reasons I love you. I love you from the depth of my heart and soul. Believe that, sweetheart, with all your heart. And I'm going to do everything I can to make you love me in return."

She saw the moisture in his eyes and was quiet for just a moment before answering. "Well, you have already succeeded, Ben. Because I love you in return even though that scares me to death. But I can't help it and I don't know why, but I don't want to stop loving you even if that kills me someday. But we need space between us until I truly am a free woman in every respect. You know that's true." After giving him a teary smile, she pressed another kiss to him. Breaking free from his embrace, she turned and ran into the house.

Ben leaned against the porch post looking out at the stars, although not really seeing them. His heart melted within him when she told him she loved him, too. But she was still going into town tomorrow, that didn't change. Closing his eyes briefly against the fear in his heart, he turned to go into the house.

He didn't get very far when his mother's voice reached him. She sat in the dark in the rocker near the stove.

"She's not only a lovely young woman, but she's also a very smart one. You do realize that, don't you?" Grace smiled softly at her son as she pointed to another chair for him to sit down for a moment. He hesitated and then did so, leaning forward with his forearms resting in his thighs.

His eyebrows drew together, "How long were you in here, Mama?" Ben wondered how much she had heard.

"I heard her go outside. I thought maybe she had another bad dream, so I was getting out of bed when I heard you go out also." She hesitated for a moment, looking down at her hands. "I have to admit, I sat here waiting to see what would happen. I know what young men think about, son. I was married to one once, remember." When Ben sat back abruptly with a frown and was about to speak, she put up her hand to stop him. "No, no. Your father was a patient man and always showed me proper respect. I wanted to make sure that you do the same for her."

Ben leaned forward again, putting his elbows on his knees and his face in his hands. He rubbed both eyes with forefingers that slightly shook from the emotional turmoil of the last few minutes. "Mama, I promised you that I would not cheapen Lynn. I'll keep that promise. But mostly because I love her like I've never loved anyone in my life." He stood abruptly, suddenly irritated.

"I need sleep since I'll be taking Lynn into town tomorrow morning right after breakfast." Stopping at the doorway, he turned around, returning to his mother to give her a kiss on the top of her head. The longing in his voice when he spoke went straight to his mother's heart.

"I love you, Mama. I need your and Shaline's help with this one. I can't lose her. I just can't." After looking earnestly into his mother's face, he turned again, going to bed and drifted into a restless sleep.

Grace sat thoughtfully as she rocked for a long time, contemplating her son's future. Her heart went out to him. She knew what it was like to love deeply. She missed her husband terribly and longed for the times that had once been. Death can come so quickly, and she was thankful that John had never wondered how much she loved him. And she was a very fortunate woman because she was loved deeply in return. She wanted her children to feel that same security. Shaline had a wonderful man in Allen. He adored his wife. She knew that Jad someday would find someone to love. But Ben,... Ben had always worried her a little. His heart was big, and yet he seemed to build a wall around it for protection. When he had shown up with a woman on his wagon and had even brought her to the house, Grace had been surprised. Lynn was a remarkable young woman. It didn't take but a short time in her company to see why Ben had fallen in love with her. Now his happiness seemed threatened. Yet, Lynn was right in what she needed to do. Grace knew that Lynn loved Ben, she could tell from the way her eyes softened whenever she looked at him and her cheeks would flush. But first, she needed to learn to love herself again.

Stretching her tired limbs, she sighed deeply before climbing the stairs back to bed. It didn't take long for her to find sleep. She would make sure that Lynn was always welcome in this house. She was thinking that having Lynn come every week for Sunday lunch and dinner after church would help.

Chapter 28

"Town"

Lynn fell asleep immediately after going back to bed. Now that there was some kind of plan to work with, to make her a life again, she felt sure of herself. Although the thought of leaving this family made her cringe, she knew that she could find herself again only by being by herself. She needed to become whole again. The only way for her to accomplish that would be for her to depend on her own decisions and ideas. She hated to hurt Ben tonight, but he knew she spoke the truth.

Lynn packed her few belongings back into her trunk after breakfast dishes were cleaned up. The air outside was crisp, although it promised to be a beautiful day because the sun was shining brightly as she stepped out onto the porch.

Ben went to the barn to fetch the wagon. Jad came out to stand beside her, his hands pushed into the pockets of his pants and the usual grin was gone. He was quiet for a moment, looking out over the yard with a contemplative look before finally speaking.

"You know, Lynn, the family really wants you to stay here with us. Ben plans on going to talk to the old judge right away and find out about gettin' a divorce for you. Then, when he gets that done you two could get married." Pity welled up in Lynn's heart as she watched his eyes plead with her.

She laid a hand briefly on his arm. "I'm sorry, Jad. I would love to stay here with your family. In the very short time I've been here, I have come to love them already. I wish I could explain it all to you, but you'll just have to trust me when I say, that for now anyway, it's for the best. Ben actually knows me very little. He doesn't know me in normal life. I think he needs to see me for who I am the rest of the time. Do you know what I mean? It's good to see people through the rough and crazy patches we all go through, and we've certainly seen each other go through some of those. But, we don't know each other through just the normal routines of life. Maybe after Ben sees those, he won't be so impressed with how he looks at me. Does any of that make sense?" She folded her hands together in front of her as she talked, begging him to understand.

After studying the boards on the porch for a moment, he nodded his head in agreement.

"Maybe you're right about part of it. But I know my brother. He don't fall in love just because. And that man is in love with you. I hope I love a woman someday like he loves you. And unless you love him that much in return, don't disappoint him by marrying him. He's a good man and deserves to be loved in return the way a woman should love a husband."

She felt the moisture start to build in her eyes and turned away quickly for fear that he also would see it. "I know he is, Jad. I promise you that I will."

Cathleen came running out the door. She stopped with her hands on her hips, looking up at Lynn with her mouth set in a resentful pout.

"Mama says that you aren't gonna stay with us no more. Why not? Don't you love us no more?" The dark Alenson eyes glistened with unshed tears as she suddenly clung to Lynn's legs. "You can't go. I don' wan' you go!" Her childish voice wailed in the morning air as Ben came around with the wagon.

Lynn gently pulled Cathleen's arms from around her legs. "Come sit down with me for a moment." Lynn walked the four steps to the swing while holding the little girl's hand. When she had sat down, she picked Cathleen up, sitting her on her lap and wrapping her arms tightly around the sobbing girl. Her words were very gentle as she tried to reason with her.

"Cathleen, I'm only going into town. I'm not going to be very far away. Your Gramma has made me promise to come out here for dinner every Sunday and you will have to talk your Mama and Papa into coming to visit me, okay?" Lynn's voice was soothing as she spoke to the sobbing child. She hesitated for just a moment before continuing, "I need to do some things that are very important for me. Sometimes adults have to do things that they really don't want to do, but they need to do them anyway. I'll miss all of you very much, but these things that I need to do are very important to me and I can't do them here with you, love." Lynn wiped the tears off of Cathleen's pink cheeks. Just before setting her down, she gave her a big hug and a kiss on the top of the head. "Be a big girl now and you help your Mama with Maryanna, okay?" Lynn smiled through her tears.

After handing Jad his niece, she walked into the house. Shaline, Grace, and Allen were gathered in the kitchen. They looked up as she entered the room. First, she went to Shaline and Maryanna, who was asleep in her mother's arms.

"Thank you very much for being a friend and, I think, a sister. I shall miss you very much. I would have never thought it possible to feel so close to people in such a very short time. But—" her voice broke. "But, I have never felt more welcome anywhere than here. I truly, deeply want to return here someday and I truly, deeply want to call this family my own someday." After giving her a hug, she turned to Allen and held out a hand for him to shake. Allen looked at her hand then grinned.

"We don't shake very well in this house." He grabbed her, wrapping his arms around her in a huge hug. "I'll make sure that I bring Shaline and Mama into town to visit with you often. And we'll be seein' you on Sundays."

Surprised, Lynn returned the hug, then when he released her she turned to Grace. Grace, too, wrapped Lynn in a warm, motherly embrace. "You are always welcome here, dear. I understand why you feel you need to go. It is a wise decision, but know that you have a family here for you whenever you need one. And there is a man outside who loves you more than life itself."

At Lynn's look of surprise, Grace just nodded gently. Lynn couldn't help but tighten her embrace on the smaller woman as she fought back tears for the third time that morning. Jad swept her up in a big hug also when she returned to the front porch, but he said nothing. She felt like she was leaving for the east instead of just four or five miles away.

As Ben handed her up into the buckboard, he caught the sweet smell of her rose-scented hair and he closed his eyes briefly at the thought of waking in the morning and her not being there. He had seen her every day for over five months. The thought of not having her near him made him catch his breath for an instant of time, and he hesitated before he climbed up into the seat and eased his big frame down on the seat beside her. She glanced sideways at him, offering a tremulous smile before turning her attention to the people on the porch. She waved a gloved hand and then gave the road before them her rapt attention.

They rode for several minutes before Ben finally broke the silence.

"I'll take you to The Falls Hotel. When we arrived in town, Marsha Townsend told me that they could use some help. If anyone knows about a teaching position, it would be her. That way, if there isn't one, then maybe you can get work with her and Ivan. They may have already found someone, I don't know. You'll like her and her husband, Ivan. She makes the best apple dumplings in town." He glanced down at her face.

Feeling his eyes upon her, she looked up at him. She saw raw emotion gleaming in his eyes, and suddenly remembered what his mother had told her in the kitchen. Did he really love her more than life itself? Mothers usually knew more about their children than children knew about themselves. If only it were simple!

The divorce wasn't much of a question anymore. The more she thought about it, she was sure that it would be fairly easy to get. But, she wasn't sure about the cost. She certainly didn't want Ben paying for it, although he had already said that he would and gladly. It wasn't his responsibility and she didn't feel that it was the right thing for him to have to do. She would save every penny she could so that she would be able to pay for it herself.

As they neared the sheer rock bluffs above the town, he stopped the buckboard. Lynn caught her breath at the beauty of the falls far below them. When she had passed this way with Jad just a few days earlier, she had been too weary to notice much. Now she realized that someone had felled some of the huge trees along the bluff, making a hole in the forest that otherwise surrounded them. They couldn't see far in either direction, but what could be seen caught Lynn's full attention. The scene below her was breathtaking. The river flowed quickly to falls that dropped fifty some feet before rushing down around a bend between the rock bluffs that rose sharply on both sides. On this side of the river, however, the bluffs rose higher than the other side and the city spread out below them following the river. Smoke came out of numerous chimneys and was picked up by the fall air that drifted down the river, taking it away and around the curve further down. The sky was as blue as a robin's egg and the rays from the sun hit the rocks on the other side of the river, casting an orange glow in the crisp, morning air.

"It's beautiful!" Lynn exhaled softly, her eyes wide as she drank in the scene. Finally, feeling Ben's eyes on her, she turned to him.

His expression was warm, a small smile showing as he studied her face. His eyes traced the outline of her face, first on her cheeks, then her mouth where her lips were slightly parted in awe. His hand raised, and he followed the same trail that his eyes had taken, with a finger gently touching her face. Lynn's eyes widened even more as he leaned forward, placed a hand behind her head, and kissed her, gently at first and then with more urgency. When she didn't protest, he gathered her in his arms, pulling her so close to him she was felt molded against the rock hardness of his thighs and chest. He didn't want to scare her, but oh how he wanted her! He was pleased to feel her arms going slowly around his neck. He deepened his kiss, wanting to taste her lips as she responded slowly to the pressure of his mouth. He felt her hesitate for a second, but he continued, testing gently how far she would let him go. The sweetness of her lips made his senses reel. He finally tore his mouth away from hers, catching his breath with difficulty. Placing his chin on top of her head, he continued to hold her close as she leaned her head against his chest, her arms still around his neck.

Heat rushed across Lynn's chest and up her neck. Warmth pooled in her belly in response to Ben's gentle persistence. When he first reached for her, she was surprised given the circumstances. But she welcomed his kiss, his arms, the love in his embrace. She was feeling things she had long ago forgotten. The warmth from his lips lingered on hers and she could still taste the cloves from his tongue. Taking a deep breath, she fought to steady her nerves.

Ben sighed deeply as he straightened, pushing her gently away from him. "We need to go before I'm unable to keep a promise I made." At her puzzled look, he answered the unspoken question. "I promised my mother and God that I would not touch you before we were married. It's the hardest promise I've ever kept." The intensity of his eyes made her blush a deep pink and she turned away, choosing to look down at her hands that she had placed back in her lap. A large hand cupped her chin and brought her face up to meet his steady gaze once more. "I won't cheapen you, Lynn. You'll be my wife legally before I make you my wife physically." Placing a light kiss on her lips and then tucking her left hand into his right one, he picked up the reins with the other and they continued their journey into town.

There were people everywhere, but none that she recognized until they got close to a general store in the middle of the street. She saw Leann Seckers about the same time that Leann spotted her. Leann broke into a large smile and walked quickly in their direction dragging Jeremiah with her as soon as he walked out of the door. He had a small bundle in his arms wrapped in blankets and Lynn knew immediately what that meant. Before Ben could stop the buckboard, she was calling out to Leann.

"You had the baby! When did you have the baby? What did you have?" Ben knew she was anxious to see the new baby and so placed his hands around her waist and swung her down in front of him. He left a hand on her shoulder as they walked the few steps to the Secker family. He was aware of several men on the street staring in Lynn's direction. He wanted it known right now that Lynn was his and they had better stay away from her. She hadn't noticed anything or anybody. Her total attention was wrapped in the small bundle that now lay in her arms. It was obvious that she was immediately enthralled with the baby. Ben felt a pain in his chest at the thought of her never having children. She would make a wonderful mother. And yes, it pained him a little that when they married he would never hold a son or daughter of his own. But, he would rather have Lynn by his side than have another woman who could give him children.

When he finally focused on what was happening around him, he realized that others they knew had gathered and the women were talking a mile a minute.

"His name is Samuel Casey Seckers. He was born very late the night we arrived. This is the first day that I have been up and around much. But, I had such an easy delivery."

"Leann had the easiest delivery I've ever seen!"

"What are you two doing in town? Are you married yet?"

"Lynn! how good to see you!"

"I've missed you and your family so much!"

"Isn't he beautiful?!" That came from Rachel, who stood with one arm around Lynn's waist. Sarah stood beside her quietly, with Kyle standing beside her with an arm possessively around her waist. Ben smiled at Kyle's possessive attitude. He had obviously noticed young men looking at Sarah. More and more families moved in all of the time, but single women, especially attractive ones, were still scarce.

About that time, Bud and Willy walked out of the store, pausing to engage in conversation with the group that had steadily gathered. Lynn was smiling and hugging people who had become good friends. She truly missed their company.

After spending close to an hour catching up on everything, Ben touched Lynn's shoulder, making her turn to look up at him.

"It's getting close to lunch. We really should be going." He smiled gently down at her as she glanced at the pocket watch he held. Lynn gasped at how the time had just flown. She gave last hugs and goodbyes and then apologized to Ben.

"I'm so sorry. I know that you need to get back soon to your own work and here I've kept you late." Creases formed slightly on her forehead as a frown crossed her face.

"Actually, I'm not in any hurry to go. I enjoyed catching up with friends, too. Besides, I'm not particularly looking forward to leaving your company any time soon. However, my belly is telling me that it is time for some lunch." His stomach rumbled, emphasizing his words.

Lynn chuckled softly. "You need to get home for lunch, Ben."

"I have a better idea. How about we go on down to the Falls Hotel? Marsha serves a good lunch. That would be a good way to meet her and see if she still needs help, alright?"

"Okay. That sounds fine. How far is it? Can we walk? It's such a lovely day, it seems a shame to waste it riding when we could walk if it's not too far." She searched the street looking for a sign to the Falls Hotel. When she finally found it, she realized that she had asked the wrong thing; it was way down the street and on the opposite side. A short walk would have been fine to ask for, but it seemed unreasonable to ask Ben to walk that far since it would mean the buckboard was back here.

"Of course. I agree it is a beautiful day for a walk." Ben held out his arm for her. When she hesitated, he thought maybe she didn't want to be seen holding his arm in public. Her next comment put to rest any doubts there.

"I must apologize again. I didn't realize it was that far. We don't have to walk that far if you don't want to."

"You worry too much. No, it's not too far. As you said, it's a nice day for a walk. Besides, this way you can familiarize yourself with the shops along the boardwalk." Pausing for a second as he continued to look down at her face, he held out his arm once more. He felt the warmth in her fingers as she laid them on his arm and they started down the walk. His chest swelled as he saw several men stop and look at the newest, attractive woman in town. Pride welled up in him that this pretty woman was on his arm and was in his company. Nothing would be able to remove the smile on his face.

Lynn's awareness of Ben's warmth and solid manliness left her feeling somewhat dazed as she laid her fingers upon his arm. Her fingers trembled slightly, and she hoped he didn't notice it. She was thinking about the kiss from earlier in the buckboard and it made her catch her breath. A shiver shimmied down her back despite the warmth of the fall air. Her awareness of this man's sensuality was growing in leaps and bounds. It scared her, and yet made her feel like a woman again. A woman who was truly attractive and desired, not just a possession to show around and then use behind closed doors.

It was a strange feeling, but she reveled in it, enjoying the feeling of happiness that brought a smile to her face.

Ben thought nothing could wipe the smile off of his face. He was wrong. They hadn't gotten very far when Ben heard a voice that was all too familiar. He wasn't at all pleased to have to turn around and acknowledge Carrie with a brief nod of his head.

"Ben! Ben, I wondered when you were going to come into town to see me!" Carrie quickly overtook them as she stepped out of the mercantile with a package in her arms. "Oh, I am so glad you finally came in. I was beginning to wonder what had happened to you. Here, be a dear, and take this parcel for me, would you? It weighs just too much for little ol' me. I asked Mr. Dale to have that boy of his carry it home for me, but he just wouldn't do it."

While thrusting the package into Ben's hands, she managed to push Lynn aside and take Ben's arm herself. Ben frowned as he realized what Carrie had done. He didn't want to be rude, but he was not about to walk down the boardwalk with Carrie on his arm. The woman he wanted hanging on his arm now stood aside with a slightly bemused look flickering across her lovely features. A light breeze caught the hair at her temples and blew it across her cheek. The urge to lift a hand and gently push it away was powerful and it took him a great deal of effort to not follow through. Finally gathering his thoughts, he turned his attention back to the little blonde who continued to talk.

"Ben? Ben! I was asking you a question. Where are you going now?" Her voice was reproachful at his lack of attention, her lips pouting slightly as she looked at him through thick blonde lashes. "I'm famished. Why don't we go get a bite of lunch?" She pressed her ample bosom against his arm.

"Actually, I'm taking Lynn down to the Falls Hotel for lunch. She needs to get acquainted with the town." Ben's frown deepened as he watched Lynn turn and walk slowly down the boardwalk, gazing into the windows of shops as she went. He realized that she had seen Carrie press herself against his arm. What she didn't realize was that Carrie's ample figure didn't do anything for him. At one time he had thought marrying Carrie would be alright although he certainly never had felt love for her. But the thought of having an attractive woman on his arm and having a family had made him think Carrie would be fine to take as a wife. Now, however, all he wanted was Lynn. He didn't want fine, he wanted love; he wanted contentment, he wanted spark and humor—he wanted Lynn. He wanted her by his side.

Glancing down at the woman clinging to his arm, he realized that he had never experienced those feelings with Carrie. Carrie had simply been an attractive woman who would make a decent wife and give him the children he wanted. How ironic, he thought, that the woman he now wanted with all his heart, wouldn't even be able to give him the children he had always wanted.

Turning back to the problem at hand, however, he gently pulled his arm out of Carrie's grasp.

"You may come with us to lunch if you like, Carrie. I will carry your package for you down to the Falls. However, we were going to walk. Do you want to walk that far?" Ben couldn't help a small smile at her reaction.

"Walk? Clear down there? Why on earth would you want to do that? Your wagon is just right over there. And I have mine right here. If Lynn wants to walk, let her. But, you come with me. She shouldn't tire you out like that. Doesn't she know that you have a lot to do at home?" A look of pretended horror crossed her face and a tone of disgust edged her voice. Rolling her eyes in Lynn's direction, she smiled beautifully up at Ben. "I would always be more thoughtful than that."

Ben scowled. "It's a beautiful day and we both decided that a walk would be nice. Besides, this way, Lynn can become more familiar with the shops." Seeing where Carrie had pointed to her wagon, he walked over and set her package inside. "If you would like to meet us there, I can help you up." He pointed to the seat. He didn't particularly want Carrie to come to lunch with them, but he didn't have a choice; he couldn't very well tell her that she couldn't come with them. That would be very rude.

For once, Carrie was at a loss for words and was torn as to what to do. She didn't want to walk any further than she thought was absolutely necessary. She also wanted to be with Ben, and in the process, keep Lynn away from him. But, the thought of walking that far when it wasn't necessary was horrifying, so she allowed Ben to help her up into the wagon. However, she couldn't let the opportunity pass without one more dig at Lynn. Glancing pointedly in Lynn's direction, she turned back toward Ben with a satisfied air.

"Well, at least I won't be sweaty from that kind of exercise." She wrinkled her nose and then paused for a moment. "I'll save us a table." After smiling brightly, she slapped the reins on the horse's rump, sitting proudly without a further glance in Lynn's direction.

It only took a few strides to catch up with Lynn. She was gazing through the window of the mercantile. She glanced up into Ben's frowning face, hoping that it wasn't meant for her. She doubted it, but he didn't speak for several minutes. After taking her hand and placing it back on his arm, they continued their walk. They walked in silence for a few moments, with Ben struggling with words to explain about the situation with Carrie. He needed to make her understand that Carrie was not who he wanted. Not the woman he wanted by his side for the rest of his life.

Finally, he spoke, but quietly so others around them wouldn't overhear.

"I need to explain to you about Carrie." He paused for a moment trying to put the words in the right order.

Sensing his hesitation, she felt the need to ease the uncomfortable silence. "You don't need to explain, Ben. I think I already know what the situation was before you left for Independence. Your mother and sister told me. Jad also mentioned, that although Carrie had her sights centered in on you, you hadn't really set your sights on her." She gazed down the walk, smiling at another woman who passed them on her way to the mercantile.

Ben looked a little surprised. His family had told her? He should have known they would. They never really cared much for Carrie. They had taken a strong liking to Lynn, however. He felt a slight twinge of irritation at them for telling her things that he should have been the one to tell. But, at the same time, was relieved. It would make it a lot easier to tell what little bit was left to tell.

"Well, they're right." He brushed his left hand down his face before continuing. "Carrie took a liking to me. She is a pretty woman and I decided it was about time to settle down and have a family. I had never told her that I was going to marry her when I returned, she just figured that's the way it would be. I just never disagreed with her. She's a decent young woman. At the time I had figured I could do much worse and so, I guess, I went along with her idea." His eyes darkened with emotion once again as he smiled. "But, that was before I met you. Now I realize I can do so much better. We were never engaged, and I have no obligations towards her. I need you to know that, okay?"

A wan smile touched Lynn's lips before she finally spoke. "You may have made a terrible mistake, considering my circumstances."

Covering her hand that rested on his arm with his much larger one, he stopped. Her upraised eyes were questioning as they searched his face. Ben's voice was firm when he finally spoke.

"I will be talking to Judge Perkins this afternoon after we get you settled into someplace. Hopefully, within a few weeks at the most, your circumstances will be very greatly changed." A rueful smile passed over his lips. "I'll wait forever, if that's what it takes, Lynn." His glance stole over the fullness of her mouth and the smooth line of her jaw and neck. It took a lot of strength to not kiss her soundly right there on the walk. He realized she must have guessed where his thoughts went because she suddenly blushed and turned away, looking ahead of them instead. Smiling again, he continued down the walk with Lynn staying in easy step beside him.

They walked in silence until they reached the hotel. Marsha greeted Ben and had to have a hug from the big man. She grinned from ear to ear as he explained that he just couldn't stay away from those apple dumplings of hers any longer. After introducing Lynn, he explained that Lynn would be interested in a teaching position if there was one open. If not, then she was interested in working with Marsha if the job was still open.

Marsha eyed the tall, attractive woman standing beside Ben with curiosity. She heard about her from the locals who had seen her ride in the first day with the wagon train. All the gossips had repeated the same thing: when she got rested, she would be turning heads all over town. Well, she must have gotten rested, because out of the corner of her eyes, Marsha could already see heads turning. The younger woman's erect carriage, slender figure, warm and friendly eyes, and smooth skin would be enough to catch every man's eye, whether young or old. Marsha had also been told that Ben was quite taken with her. As she watched for just those few seconds, she realized that there was truth in that piece of gossip, too. Ben's expression was intense and warm when he looked at the dark-haired, dark-eyed woman beside him. The arm around her waist and glance around the room challenged any man there to come closer to what he claimed as his.

Finally, she spoke, "Well, we got a teacher last winter who seems to sticking to the job. So can't help you there. But we'll give you a try. You get room and board and four dollars a week. You work Monday through Friday, breakfast, lunch, and supper. And Saturday breakfast and lunch. I don't serve supper on Saturdays and we take Sunday off for the Lord. Any questions?"

The relief on Lynn's face was obvious. She had some work to support herself. Four dollars a week was pretty good wages and having room and board meant that she would be able to save some money. Shaking her head about any questions, she explained that her things were in the wagon and they would retrieve them after they had lunch. Marsha returned to the kitchen after taking their orders and Lynn turned to the slight pressure from Ben's hand on the small of her back. Ben saw the table at the far end where Carrie sat waiting with a frown on her face.

They only walked a few steps when suddenly Lynn stopped and looked up at Ben. He patiently waited for her to speak.

"When I asked you if we could walk down here, I had forgotten all about my things in the wagon. Now we'll have to walk back to the wagon, so we can bring it down here anyway. I'm so sorry." He could see from the corner of his eye the frown on Carrie's face deepen as he lifted his hand and smoothed the lines from Lynn's forehead.

"I've told you before, you worry too much. After we eat, I'll have Marsha show you to your room and I'll go fetch the wagon with your things." As she started to open her mouth in protest, his thumb touched her lower lip. "It's fine, I like to walk and remember, it is a beautiful day." Placing a large hand on her shoulder, he turned her so that once again they were headed toward the table.

Carrie's eyes narrowed as Ben held out Lynn's chair for her and then sat down between the two women. His sharp eyes took in the friendly smile that Lynn tried to bestow upon the now scowling younger woman. Carrie's smile in return was meant for bare politeness because Ben could see the ice coating it. Her eyes narrowed for just the barest of seconds before turning her attention to Ben. How the woman could have a glowing smile and a pout at the same time never ceased to amaze him. As he searched his memory briefly, he realized that she was always pouting about something. He finally answered the question she put to him as she placed a hand upon his arm.

"The family is fine, thank you. Lynn needed to come into town and get acquainted with it, so I offered to bring her in."

Lynn interrupted, "Actually, I just took a job with Marsha. She needs some help here at the hotel and I need a job. So, perhaps I'll see you often." The latter part was half question, half statement. Lynn was trying to make polite conversation, but Carrie didn't want conversation with her, she wanted conversation with Ben.

"I doubt it. I don't come in here unless Ben decides to come into town and treat me to supper." She turned glittery eyes back to Ben's face. "When will we be coming here for supper, Ben? I want to know ahead of time that way I can look my best. I would hate for you to see me in some old dress I keep for housework."

Ben seriously doubted two things. One, that Carrie had any old dresses, and two, that she did any housework. It was all he could do not to be sarcastic when he replied. But, his mother had taught him well that rarely was there a good reason for rudeness and he had a hard time breaking that rule even now.

"I have a lot to do before the rains come, Carrie. I don't think we'll be doing dinner anytime soon. I've been gone a long time, and Jad and Allen need help getting things done." He leaned back from the table as Marsha placed steaming plates of hot roast beef with mashed potatoes and gravy in front of them. After setting bread, butter, and steaming cups of coffee in front of them, she went back to the kitchen.

Carrie wasn't happy with Ben's pronouncements of being too busy to take her out. She knew the real reason, and it infuriated her. How dare he just forget her like this! She had plans for them. She had even designed a house for them while he was gone on that infernal trip! The design had taken her several weeks. She loved the bedroom design the best. Having placed a dressing room in between her room and Ben's, she would have the privacy she wanted without having to worry about sharing a bedroom with him all of the time. She had heard of that being done with wealthy people back east when they built their big homes. Ben may not be wealthy yet, but she was certain he would be by the time she convinced him to leave that stupid sawmill and go to work for her father. Although, the sawmill would come in handy long enough to build the house she wanted.

Now she saw all of her dreams going up in smoke in front of her very face. All because of this woman sitting across the table from her. She wouldn't let this woman take the only good man in this stinking town away from her! She would fight for him with all the feminine wiles that she possessed. It should be easy to win Ben back. In her eyes, this Lynn woman lacked a lot when it came to feminine wiles. My goodness, her own bosom was twice as ample as Lynn's. Yes, she would use what she had to win this man back. Men all wanted the same thing, after all. When she was done with Ben Alenson, he would gladly want her back; she would have him panting after her. Before he left she was sure that she almost had him to that point, anyway. He was such a hard man to know his thoughts, but she had been so certain that he had wanted her.

Carrie suddenly had a new look about her as she started to eat. A look of determination came to her eyes as she looked speculatively in Lynn's direction. If she could find some man who Lynn would be interested in, then maybe, just maybe, Ben would see that Lynn wasn't for him after all.

"So, Lynn, what type of plans do you have now? You plan on settling down in town with some nice man and raise a family?"

Ben saw through Carrie's sugar-coated question for what it was and he cast a frown her way. Besides, the thought of Lynn marrying another man made his belly twist painfully.

Lynn looked up from the plate of food and set down the glass of water she had been in the process of bringing to her lips. "No, not at all." Pausing for a moment, she then decided to turn the tables. Her voice lacked the sarcastic sweetness of Carrie's, however. "What about you? What are your plans?"

The sugary smile Carrie gave Ben only made him scowl more as she looked up at him with shining eyes. "My plans center around whatever Ben wants to do. You probably already know, but we had plans to marry this fall when Ben returned, didn't we, dear?" Leaning toward Ben, she laid her hand on his forearm. She tipped her head victoriously when Lynn's attention returned to her plate. Yes, this woman needed to be put in her place. She would talk to Ben very soon about bringing her into town again by himself. It just didn't look good. Jad should have brought her into town. Or better yet, Allen and Shaline could have done it.

Lynn contemplated her answer for a moment before replying. "Well, I've discovered that it's always good to have more than one option because things don't always go as planned." When Carrie glared at her, she merely shrugged before laying her fork down onto her plate.

After pushing his empty plate away from him, Ben turned to her. "We have some things to talk about, I think, Carrie. Hopefully in the next week sometime, we can find the time to talk for a bit." Marsha removed the plates from the table and then returned with her famous apple dumplings. Ben dug into his with an incredible zeal and after tasting hers, Lynn understood why he did so. Although eating her own considerably slower, she had never tasted one so good.

Carrie showed little interest in hers. She was struggling to decide what to say. Ben's tone had told her more than she wanted to know. She would not lose him! He was the only man she knew who would amount to anything in this town. Well, maybe not the "only" man, but certainly the only man who was also good-looking and had a gentle nature. If she was going to have to get married and tolerate some man occasionally in her bed, she certainly wanted him to be tolerable to look at and gentle. She had heard horror stories of other women and the type of men they had to put up with. None of those for her, no way!

They remained silent through the rest of the meal. When Ben was finished eating, he rose and went to talk to Marsha for a few minutes and pay her for their lunch. During the few minutes he was gone, Carrie spent the time glaring at Lynn, who simply looked out of the windows and watched people walking by on the boardwalk.

Finally, Ben returned and pulled out first Carrie's chair and then Lynn's. Carrie took hold of Ben's arm before Lynn had a chance to do so. Ben, however, turned so that Lynn could take the other arm and then proceeded to walk them across to the door. Lynn relinquished her light grip on his arm so that he could open the door for them. Carrie finally let go and walked through the door with the air of a princess. Ben turned to Lynn for a moment.

"I'm going to walk down and get the wagon. I'll return in a few minutes." He inclined his head toward Carrie. "Plus, I need to have a conversation."

She smiled at the grimace he made. "That's fine. I'll see if I can do something to help Marsha for a few minutes."

Ben watched the gentle sway of her hips as she went in search of the older woman. He turned his attention to Carrie.

"You know, Ben, if she drove a wagon for how many months, she could probably go get her own things from that wagon. That would save you from having to do it for her."

"Lynn can go talk with Marsha while I do it for her. I won't take but a few moments." He walked in the direction of Carrie's wagon and held out his hand for her to grasp while he helped her up into it. He paused for a moment and then decided to talk about the problem now. "No time like the present" was a saying his mom often used.

"You know, Carrie, I've been gone for a year and I thought maybe while I was gone, you would find someone else. Especially since, in reality, who knew if I would make it back. We never really made any promises to each other, you know that?" He lifted his gaze to watch the eyes that suddenly widened in alarm.

"What are you saying, Ben Alenson? That you don't want to marry me anymore? And yes, there were promises. I promised you that I would wait for you. I think that you owe me something for keeping that promise." The lips pouted again, and her eyes filled with tears.

"I know that you told me that. Carrie, I never promised you anything. I don't want to hurt you, but you and I,...we just,... we just wouldn't make a good match. I want very different things from what you want. I had a lot of time to think, and I don't think you and I would do well together." Shaking his head, he felt guilty for the hurt showing in her eyes. He had no desire to hurt anyone. He was trying to be gentle and yet firm at the same time, and that was an extremely difficult thing to do.

"You mean, in that time you were gone, you met her!" The words were spat in fury. "Do you really think she'll be good for you? If she would be, why didn't she stay out there with your family?" Tears glistened as she changed tactics, her voice quieting to a whisper. "I'm the one you wanted before you left here last year. I remember your eyes gazing at me hungrily. I have more to offer you than she does. How can you even think about her over me? How many times did you want me, Ben? How many times did I catch your eyes lingering here?" She pointed to her heaving bosom.

He refused to drop his eyes. "You are an attractive young woman, Carrie. I'm a healthy, normal man. And yes, when I left here, I was inclined to marrying you when I returned. But, I had never told you that, I never asked you to marry me. I never made any promises." He paused for a moment, glancing at his hand that rested on the side of the buckboard. "I won't make you a good husband, Carrie. You are far better suited for someone else, not me. I want to live out of town and I like the roughness of making a living for myself off of the land. You are not suited for that kind of life." His fingers rubbed his chin in deep thought. Then he looked up at her with gentleness in his voice. "I don't really think you love me, anyway. You need to find someone to love, Carrie."

Anger flashed briefly. "Oh, how would you know if I love you or not! You're just a fickle man!" When irritation showed in his face, she immediately regretted her words. She needed to make him feel guilty, not make him mad.

"Oh Ben, how can you say that? I even had house plans drawn out for us." Her voice lowered, and she looked at him through her lashes. "You should see the bedroom I designed for us. It's lovely." No sense in telling him that in actuality, there were two bedrooms that were designed for them.

He saw through her tactics. They wouldn't have worked even before this last confession. Really? She made up house plans without consulting him first? That should have been something they would have done together. As for her coyness, he always had been able to see through her. She flirted when it suited her, and she would press herself against him, but he could see the underlying revulsion beneath it. Funny how he had never really thought much about that until right now. He had the feeling that when it came down to husbandly rights, he would get them only when she wanted to and probably only when he had done something extraordinary to please her. Unless he forced her, and that made the frown deepen even more. He was not the type of man to force himself upon a woman.

His thoughts went to Lynn. He could sense her wariness, yet there was no revulsion there. She had been abused. He had the feeling, that with Lynn, once she was convinced that he would never hurt her and indeed would even show her how wonderful it would be for her, she would have the same passion for lovemaking as she seemed to have for everything else. The more he compared the two women, the more Carrie came up short.

He stared unblinking at the side of the buckboard for a moment, shocked at his lack of insight. How could he not see that about Carrie until now? Actually, in the back of his mind, he knew this. He didn't know how to explain his former thinking that Carrie would make a suitable wife. Not only would she not make a good one, but she also wouldn't even be barely suitable. He pitied the man who finally married her.

Shaking himself mentally, he finally answered Carrie's comment. "I'm sorry, Carrie, I'm sure it is very lovely. Perhaps sometime you can show me." Sighing heavily, he turned away from her and he started to walk down the street towards his wagon. He told her he would probably see her soon, at the dance, if nowhere else. He could see the fury building in her face as she looked first at him and then at the door of the hotel. Slapping the reins on her horse's rump, she sent him one last glare before turning towards home.

Carrie's bosom heaved in agitation. It was all the fault of that other woman. If she had never shown up, then Carrie would be wearing a ring soon and would be supervising the building of their house. But, no, Lynn had ruined everything! Blonde brows knitted together as they contemplated how to remove Lynn from the picture. No great ideas came readily to her head, but she knew that sooner or later, something wonderful would appear to rid her of the problem of that woman.

Chapter 29

"Goodbye kisses"

Marsha showed Lynn to her room and then the other six rooms that she would be responsible to keep clean besides helping Marsha cook three meals a day. The older woman was explaining more when Ben appeared with Lynn's trunk.

"Now you won't have to worry about helping out at lunchtime very much because breakfast and dinner are usually our two big meals. So, unless I say I'll need your help, you can start cleaning any rooms that need it right after breakfast and get those done before dinner." She turned to smile up at Ben as he entered the room. "I think I'm going to owe you, Ben, for bringing me this young woman. You're a fool if you don't keep track of this one." Slapping Ben lightly on the shoulder as she walked out of the door, she flung one more comment over her shoulder before descending the stairs, "I sure hope you leave that Carrie woman alone and start taking Lynn out for dinner instead."

Still grinning at Marsha's outspoken manner, he turned with a chuckle toward Lynn. He shoved his hands into his pockets after setting down the trunk. "Well, I guess you've figured out that what Marsha thinks, she says." He made a face and shrugged.

"I noticed that." Nodding in agreement, Lynn moved towards the trunk. Opening it up, she took the couple of dresses she owned and hung them in the wardrobe standing in the corner. She would get some material from the mercantile first chance she got and start making herself a couple of more dresses. The ones she owned were not in very good condition any longer.

Unaware that Ben had come up behind her, she jumped when he placed his hand on her shoulder. The warmth from his hand radiated through Lynn like a summer day. Gently turning her around to face him, he noticed that she trembled slightly.

"Why do you tremble? Are you still afraid of me, Lynn?" Concern touched his face.

Lynn looked into those dark eyes and nearly drowned with the emotion that swam through them. Her voice was barely a whisper when she finally answered the question.

"No." She wanted to say more, to explain how he made her feel, why his touch made her tremble, but how could she do that? She didn't know where to begin. Glancing first at his mouth, then back into his eyes, she repeated her answer, "No, Ben, I'm not afraid of you. I haven't been for some time."

With sudden understanding, he realized why she had trembled slightly at his touch. He knew why when he saw the single glance that she gave his mouth. He saw it in those expressive dark eyes because he had learned to read and know what she was feeling even when she didn't say a thing.

Slowly Ben lowered his face towards Lynn's. He watched as her head tipped back and her eyes grew large as he bent to kiss her. She placed a hand on his chest and he answered by putting his other arm around her waist, pulling her close. When his lips finally touched her own, she immediately closed her eyes, much to his surprise. He wasn't persistent at first. The feathery touches of his mouth danced against the soft fullness of her own. When she showed no signs of protesting, he increased the pressure of his lips as if trying to taste every tiny part of her sweetness.

Lynn placed her other hand on his chest as the hand that had been on her shoulder dropped to her waist, his long fingers splaying across her side as his thumb pressed against her lower ribs. She had returned his kisses hesitantly and now paused for just a second. She was amazed at the warmth and butterfly wings she felt in the pit of her stomach that his touch brought.

Ben felt a new warmth within his heart when Lynn's arms crept up around his neck. When he heard her make a sound deep in her throat like a combination of a sigh and a cry, he lifted his head to look down into her face. Her head was still tilted back with closed eyes and inviting lips. She opened her eyes to gaze up at him with a new look in her eyes. One that he had never seen before. It was the look of total trust. But there was a new kind of fire there. His breath caught in his throat as the implications of those feelings made a sharp blade of fresh desire course through him. He had won the trust of this woman! The only thing he had ever fought so hard for was the trust and love of this woman. Elation ran like fire through him and he wanted to laugh at the sheer joy of it. Instead, he took possession of that sweet mouth one more time.

Ben finally pulled his mouth away from the softness of Lynn's lips. Pulling her close, he molded her body to his own for just a moment, setting his chin on top of her head and breathing the warm smell of roses from her hair. After a couple of minutes, he trusted himself to talk.

"Lynn, I need to go now." His voice was husky with emotion. "You need to settle in here and I need to go find the judge before going home. Jad and Allen will be expecting some help." Setting her from him was easy enough for a man of his size. At the same time, it was the hardest thing he had ever done. All of the strength had left his arms and he felt weak as he gently set her away from him.

At first, Lynn was surprised, then looking into his face she understood. After glancing at her lips for a second, he raised his eyes to look at Lynn's.

His voice was still husky. "I'm sorry, Lynn. I need to learn better control when I'm around you. You just make me forget that quality." Again, glancing at her mouth, he backed away and started to turn towards the door.

"Ben?" It was a whisper, spoken so softly he almost didn't hear it, but he discerned the loneliness in her voice. "Ben, please tell your family to visit me. I would love to see them all."

"I'm sure they will. I will come fetch you Sunday morning." Stopping near the door, he inclined his head, tipping his hat at the same time. "Until Sunday." The next four days were going to be the longest four days of Ben's life.

"Are you sure fetching me every Sunday isn't going to make it hard on you? I mean you must have other more important things to do than that. It will mean two trips into town that day for you."

"Nothing is more important than you, Lynn." His eyes were so intense with longing as he looked back at her that it sent a shiver down Lynn's back, but it wasn't from being chilled. Instead, it was from anticipation and a feeling of security. "See you Sunday."

"I'll be counting the days."

"As will I." He shut the door quietly behind him.

Chapter 30

"An innocent kiss"

His boots thumping down the stairs was the loneliest sound Lynn had ever heard. She had seen him every single day for months and now she was alone again. Even the days on the trail when they had little interaction with each other he was still there, still close by. There was always the safe feeling knowing that he was only a yell away.

She was used to spending days alone in a hotel room. But this was different than being alone waiting for Jared to return and wondering if he would be angry and want to strike out at her. Or if he would just demand his husbandly rights and humiliate her. That had been a different kind of lonely. That had become the type of lonely of actually hoping and wishing that Jared wouldn't ever come back. She didn't mind being by herself then because it meant, at least for a few hours or a couple of days, that she was not scared.

This time the feeling was not the same. She hadn't felt fear for months, she had friends now, and she was in love with a good man and his family. Being by herself was no longer a reprieve, but instead, she was feeling the true meaning of the word lonely. Having a job would keep her hands and mind busy and she was surely thankful to Marsha. She only hoped that the days would fly by quickly every week because Sundays would be her happiest day.

Quickly putting the rest of her things away, she went downstairs to see what help Marsha hopefully needed. When it was decided that she would return to help in a couple of hours for the supper rush, she went to the mercantile to buy material. Her money was going to be gone, but her clothes were barely wearable anymore. They were old and becoming threadbare, so she decided to spend what little money she had on some material for some new clothes and perhaps some gifts for Ben and his family. That brought a smile to her face as she strode down the boardwalk toward the store she had seen earlier.

After choosing some plain brown wool for two skirts and then a pretty patterned blue muslin for more special days, she waited for Mr. Manning to cut the material into the lengths she wanted. A bolt of pale pink with tiny flowers on it caught her eye. After much debating, she decided to buy enough for one shirtwaist to go with the two skirts. She owned only two other shirtwaists and working almost every day would be hard on them. As it was, it would be hard to find the time to make even these few much-needed items. She contemplated how far the money she made would go and figured that within a month she would be able to buy some more for underclothes. One thing at a time. She could have bought more material now except that she spotted a couple of things she wanted for gifts.

As she lingered at the bolt of pink material, she was surprised by a familiar voice. Turning warily around she met the steady gaze of Jake Emmons. He stood near the door, a mild and friendly look on his handsome face.

"Hello, Lynn. How are you doing?" His voice was carefully neutral as his quick glance appraised her approvingly. "Looks like you're getting rested up a bit. You look good."

Lynn glanced around to see who could be overhearing them. Mr. Manning was helping the only other person in the store with a shovel. Neither one was paying any attention to the two of them.

"Yes, I am finally feeling a little more rested, thank you," she admitted. Shifting the package in her hands, she met his look unflinchingly. "How are you, Jake?"

He leaned forward to catch the softly spoken words. "That was always one of the things that I thought attractive about you." Cocking his head to one side, he studied her slight blush.

"I'm sorry, what do you mean?" Lynn refused to look away from his stare but her throat tightened slightly. The man made her nervous.

Mr. Manning interrupted for a moment, "Is that all Miss, or can I help you with something else?" The older man's question caught Lynn off guard and she turned towards him, her hand still on the pale pink material.

"If I could have a yard and half of this also, please." She patted the material. He cut it quickly and packaged all of her choices along with the buttons and thread she had picked out and laid on the counter earlier. After paying him and gathering her packages she turned around again.

Jake was still standing there waiting patiently for her to finish her business. He now started where their conversation had left off as if there had been no interruptions at all.

"Your voice. Your sweet, soft voice. Some women are too loud and obnoxious. Or they whine too much or nag. Not you. You have that soft, gentle voice. And you just seem to take on life's challenges and make the best of them." His steady gaze searched her face for a moment before finally he stepped forward and held out his hand. "Let me take that to wherever you are going. I've been wanting to talk with you anyway if I ever saw you again. Now's as good a time as any." He took the package in one hand and gestured for her to proceed him to the door. He pulled it open and then followed her out onto the boardwalk.

"Thank you, Jake, I appreciate your kindness, but I'm only going down the street a little ways." She made a low, choked sound deep in her throat when his eyes dropped momentarily to her mouth. The memory was one she wanted to forget.

Seeing her pale face, Jake glanced down at his feet and then back at her wary eyes.

"I've wanted to apologize to you for a long time. I never should have kissed you that time. Or maybe I should have, but not after I had been drinking. I...." He hesitated for a moment gathering his thoughts as he glanced at the street and shuffled his feet. "I was feeling sorry for myself, I guess. Ben seemed to have your attention, but I was the one who was looking for a wife. I was angry and took it out on you when I shouldn't have." His eyes searched hers begging for forgiveness. "Can we start over?"

Lynn's eyes widened with surprise and softened a little bit because of his apology. She had always known that Jake was not a bad man, he was just not the right man for her. He would make someone a fine husband someday. Now, with the apology weighing heavily in her hands, she reached out and placed a hand on his muscular forearm.

"We can't start over, Jake. You're a fine man and you'll make some woman a very good husband someday. But, the truth still holds that I'm not the kind of woman you need." Now it was her turn to hesitate before continuing. "I've been married before, Jake." When he started to interrupt, she held her hand up. Trying to sound encouraging and logical at the same time, she continued, "I think you want a woman who hasn't been married before." She went on hurriedly, "And that's alright to want that. But, I'm not the one. I accept your apology, however, and would love to be friends with you and someday your wife. Remember me telling you that once before?" She smiled encouragingly, not wanting to hurt him but knowing that she probably was anyway.

He gave a slanted smile in return as he answered, "Well, I had to try, you know. You are quite the remarkable woman, Lynn. And, yes, I guess you're right about one thing. I want to be the first. I don't want anybody there before me." His eyes glittered as he studied her face for a moment. "You, I think though, could probably be the exception. Maybe, someday you'll tell me about being married before, huh?"

"Maybe." It was not a promise, it was a compromise to spare any more of his feelings. Suddenly, on impulse, she leaned forward and gave him a kiss on the cheek and a bright smile. "You invite me to your wedding when you find that right one, someday, alright?"

"I will, I promise." Handing her back her package, he gave her one last lingering appraisal, then turned and walked back into the mercantile.

Lynn sighed heavily as she turned toward the hotel. She hated to hurt people. If she could have spared his feelings, she would have, but what could she do? She couldn't very well pretend to love him, now could she? Besides, whenever she thought about a man, no one came to mind except Ben.

Lost in her thoughts, she was paying little attention to others around her but didn't take more than five steps when Carrie stepped in front of her. Lynn flinched back, her eyes widening for a brief second in surprise. Good grief! Didn't the younger woman have anything better to do than show up wherever she was all the time? This was the third time in two days. It was crazy! Carrie's face was contorted with anger, and her eyes were splintered with frost.

"Well, I wonder what Ben will think when he finds out that you are kissing men on the cheek in the afternoon on main street." Hands clenched into fists that rested on her hips and her clipped sarcastic words dripped with venom.

Lynn drew back even more as the maliciousness of Carrie's words hit her. She stared unbelievingly for a moment before gathering her thoughts enough to comment to the little blonde.

"I've known Jake for a long time. I don't really think it's any of your business, anyway." Suddenly, Lynn was angry at the outright accusations the younger woman was making. "You may tell Ben if you want and if you are able to do so before I have the chance." The challenge raised in her calm manner made the other woman seethe with anger.

"I just might have to make a trip out to his house and let him know what a little tart you are! He may not be so infatuated with you once he finds out you're embracing other men!"

Lynn cocked one eyebrow as she smiled grimly and replied, "Me? A little tart? Ha! You don't know anything about me, but believe me, that's the last thing I would be and Ben knows that!" Slanting a sideways look at Carrie's glaring face as she walked by, she made one last comment, "Now if you'll excuse me, I have things to do." With a flurry of skirts, she walked quickly down the street and into the hotel. Once inside she leaned against the door for a moment and let out her breath in one gasp. She couldn't believe it! Carrie was going to try to lie to Ben about what she had seen. She obviously hadn't heard what was said but had decided that what she had seen was all she needed to know. And Carrie had the audacity to call her the tart!

With a couple of shaky breaths, she gathered herself together. Going upstairs, she put her purchases aside and decided to go help Marsha with something, not knowing what the something would be and not caring. Her free time wasn't up yet, but she just wanted to get her mind off of Carrie. Learning her new job would be the best way to do that.

Helping Marsha with supper was a surprisingly rewarding time. The older woman was vivacious and laughing as she and her husband lovingly threw quick retorts back and forth at each other. Ivan was gray-haired, tall and thin but wiry. Marsha, on the other hand, was almost as tall as Lynn herself, but she was plump with an ample bosom and a deep throaty laugh that made her dark eyes dance. They were both full of stories and anecdotes about different people around Oregon City. Even though she wasn't able to put a face to any of the people they were talking about, she knew that sooner or later she would meet most, if not all, of them.

As she served supper to the handful of boarders and a few others who came there for the delicious food, her smile was genuine, and her step had a spring in it. She seemed to be unaware of the spring in her step, although everyone in the room was.

There were several men in the dining room and she received very appreciative glances from most of them. Although they were all friendly, she was relieved that none of them were overly forward. After serving pie to the patrons, Marsha decided that she could wash the dishes and then retire for the night.

"I think that you've done enough for one night, Lynn."

Before going to bed, however, she cut out the material for the new shirtwaist and thought about Ben. The kiss he had given her earlier that day lingered in her mind, and for a long time after she went to bed, she lay awake thinking about the intensity of his gaze just before he had turned to walk out of her room to leave. For as long as she lived she would never forget it.

Chapter 31

"The anger in revenge"

"Prob'ly another two or three weeks at least. Can't be helped." Johansen picked at his nose as he watched with mild interest Jared Malen's reaction to his answer. The younger man cursed the ground they walked on, the rivers they had crossed, and the people who had died delaying their travel even more. The fury in his eyes would have been a fearful thing to most men. Johansen leaned against the wagon wheel and studied Jared with the firm conviction that this man was bent on vengeance of some kind. That was about the only thing that could make a man this angry over something they could do nothing about.

Everyone on the train steered clear of Jared Malen. Of course, everyone steered clear of Johansen Tull, also, but that was beside the point. Even the pretty little widow only stayed with Jared for less than a week. Realizing the real reason behind Jared's offer for the accommodations, another family offered to have her eat with them and help them with daily chores. It was a hardship on them with another mouth to feed, but the Deerson woman had felt sorry for the mistreatment the widow would suffer under Jared's hands if she stayed with him. Jared sought revenge for that, but Johansen stepped in on that little fight. There had been nothing but trouble since this wagon train left Independence without adding that kind also.

Now, as he watched Jared's face contort in anger, he wondered how this man had survived this far without getting killed. Someday, someone was going to lay him low, even if it meant using a gun to do it.

Jared's rage didn't subside for a long time. He couldn't very well take off on his own, even though he wanted to. He had come to realize why Johansen Tull was wagon master. He was a capable man who knew the trail like the back of his hand. Nobody cared that he was so unlikable. As Jared walked back to his wagon, his eyes were murderously cold, and his jaw clenched with a terrifying anger. The seething within him had grown to enormous proportions as he dwelt upon nothing but revenge. The last months of traveling through hell itself was her fault and he couldn't wait to wrap his hands around her pretty white throat as he watched her face go white with fear and her body tremble with the punishment he would mete out upon it! Yes, his fingers fairly itched at the thought of her pleading with him not to punish her! The sweet scene of what he would do to her crossed before his eyes for the hundredth time since they left Independence. He could hardly wait!

Chapter 32

"Sunday"

October 5, 1844

The days passed quickly in some respects for Lynn as she buried herself into the routine of breakfast, cleaning rooms, lunch, and finally supper. She had never been afraid of hard work and since it took her mind off of other things, she welcomed it gladly. There were many regular patrons to the good food and clean rooms of Marsha and Ivan's establishment. Especially the men who came loved the heaping plates of hot, hearty food. Marsha did almost all of the cooking. Ivan kept the cookstove going and firewood heaped outside the back door. Lynn did a little stirring of things now and then, but she was primarily responsible for washing dishes, keeping the kitchen spotless at all times, and waiting on the customers. She was constantly on the go, but she enjoyed the work immensely. Almost all of the customers who came through were friendly and more than once she had been proposed to. When she told Marsha, the large woman just threw back her head and laughed heartily saying, "I knew that was gonna happen so jes' as well get used to it"!

Lynn turned them all down with her soft smile and gentle words. That, of course, just encouraged a couple of them to try even harder. Jess Harper, a homesteader who had arrived in the Oregon country three years before, came in every day that week at supper just to see Lynn. He was a blonde, well-built man of Lynn's height with kind blue eyes and a warm smile. If she hadn't already fallen in love with Ben, she could see herself liking the man well enough to marry him. Marsha had told her nothing but good things about Jess, and she sincerely hoped that someday he would find himself a good wife.

Then there were the old gents who came in almost every day or so telling her that she needed to marry them because a woman needed a man to take care of them. A couple of them were outrageous flirts who made her laugh at their silliness and showy displays of self-worth. Marsha told her some stories about them, too. Mostly funny ones, except for Mason Calhoun. Marsha warned her to steer clear of the man, he was up to no good more often than not. Lynn hadn't seen him anywhere but in there to eat and she was glad. Even before Marsha warned her about him Lynn saw a gleam in his eyes that always made her uncomfortable, like he was watching her biding his time, like a cat watching a bird he couldn't wait to have for dinner. She never stayed very long at his table but served him quickly and then moved on to another table.

With the exception of Mason, she loved the job, even though she was always exhausted when the supper dishes were done and the kitchen was cleaned. She usually ate quickly in the kitchen and then retired to her room as soon as possible.

Sunday morning greeted Lynn with cool, light rain. She didn't know what time Ben would be there to pick her up, but it seemed obvious that it would be rather early. She put on the best of the two dresses she owned. It was a pale blue calico that buttoned down the front. She had a bath the night before and washed her hair. Now she brushed it until it shone. Using a couple of hairpins, she pulled the waves back at the side of her face. Pinching her cheeks for color, she then sat down to wait. She pulled her only chair over to the window so she could watch the street. Hopefully, she would be able to see him coming and be ready.

As she waited, she decided to sew. One skirt was almost done and she had the other one cut out. The shirtwaist was done, but without one of the skirts being finished, she didn't have the pleasure of being able to wear it. She was exhausted at night when everything was finally done so she had sewn for only short periods of time. Although her time was her own after lunch on Saturday, she wasn't able to sew on her skirt as she had wanted to because there was mending to do. She would need to buy material for new underclothes as soon as possible because they wouldn't last through another mending. Marsha had paid her for the four and a half days of work, but she had decided to save most of it except for a small amount she used to finish buying some little gifts to take with her today to Ben's family. She smiled with pleasure at the thought of what they may say to her small tokens of appreciation for all they had done for her.

Ben arrived a little before nine. She saw him down the street where he left the buckboard and her sewing was quickly set aside. Excitement made her heart flutter and she could feel her cheeks stretching from a huge smile. A moment later Ben was pounding rapidly up the stairs.

Ben was taking the stairs two at a time in his hurry to see Lynn. When Lynn answered the door, his eyes glanced appreciatively down her figure. Noticing the hairpins holding her hair in place, he touched one with his finger, then dropped it to her lips. He bent swiftly, gave her a light kiss, and then turned, holding out an arm.

"You ready to go, ma'am?" His voice was like a cold drink on a hot day. Lynn had missed his gentle, deep voice. The smile on his handsome face couldn't have gotten any bigger, nor his eyes any warmer.

"Yes, I am, sir." She answered playfully back. She had been a little surprised at his quick kiss, although she shouldn't have been considering the kiss he gave her when he left here a few days ago. She was more than ready to spend the day in the company of this man and his delightful family. When she grabbed her cloak, he swung it around her shoulders, she took his arm, and they descended the stairs. Ben had just lifted Lynn up into the wagon when he heard Carrie. He groaned and rolled his eyes before turning around to face her. Would this woman never understand that there was nothing between them? His irritation was mounting to the point of anger as the patience he usually had was quickly starting to disappear.

Carrie was decked out in all of her fineries. The pale-yellow dress with lace trim was very flattering against her pale skin. An ivory comb pulled her blonde ringlets to one side so they cascaded over her shoulder. The light touch of color she had given to her lips made her look more pouty than usual. But what caught Ben's attention more than anything else was the pure hatred he saw in her eyes when she glanced for a split second at Lynn. His eyes narrowed slightly in momentary alarm at the depth of feeling in her eyes.

"Before you take her home to your family, Ben, there is something you may be interested in knowing. She may lack some qualities that would make for a good wife, it seems." Carrie cast a knowing smirk in Lynn's direction. She was a little surprised that Lynn didn't look nervous, instead met her gaze directly with eyebrows slightly lifted in anticipation. Carrie's brow creased for an instant before turning back to Ben who waited impatiently with arms crossed in front of his chest. When he refused to respond to her challenge, she tossed her head, making her curls bounce angrily before resolutely continuing.

"Are you aware that she has other men friends, men friends that she will kiss in public?" A satisfied smirk was sent to the other woman when Ben turned to look up at Lynn with a questioning look. The satisfaction was short-lived, however.

"It was Jake. I haven't had an opportunity to explain yet, Ben. I ran into him a couple of days ago at the mercantile. He apologized to me for," she hesitated for a second, inclining her head to one side before continuing, "...for "things" and expressed hope that maybe he could start over. I told him that although I accepted his apology, I desired to be only his friend and someday his wife's friend. I wanted him to know that I harbor no ill will to him and gave him a light kiss on the cheek." She looked challengingly at Carrie. "That's all there is to that."

"Well, if that's all there is to that, I guess we'd better off. Time's a-wastin'." He hid a smile as he climbed up into the wagon beside Lynn.

Carrie's jaw dropped in amazement when Ben turned his back on her, dismissing the entire conversation. She had thought that Ben would be outraged about Lynn's behavior toward Jake.

As he picked up the reins, Carrie sputtered angrily, "You're making a big mistake, Ben. You know that. How could you want her over me?" Suddenly Carrie became aware of the fool she was making of herself and abruptly stopped. A couple of people had stopped on the walk and were listening to the exchange.

"Carrie, we must be going. I'm sorry to upset you and I didn't want to see you hurt. But, you have brought that upon yourself. Mama is expecting us soon at church, which is where your family should be going also and we really must leave now before we're late." Tipping his hat slightly in Carrie's direction, he slapped the reins on the rump of the big bay and they started off down the street.

Ben cast a sideways look down on Lynn as they pulled to the edge of town and started up the hill to the little church. Her eyes were watching the path ahead of them, but he saw the clenching and unclenching of her jaw. This was a first, she was angry and he had never seen her angry before. It was quite enlightening that even in anger, she held her temper and words in check. His big hand covered hers, and then dropping the reins for a moment, he tucked her hand into his arm holding it there for a moment before picking up the reins again.

"You okay?" he asked curiously.

She looked up at him, irritation still present in her eyes. But it surprised him a little that they were also tinged with worry. She dropped her gaze into her lap before answering him.

"Do you trust me, Ben? You don't think I was flirting with Jake, do you?"

Instantly he knew where her thoughts had gone. Jared had accused her of flirting with other men. His jaw clenched at the thought. Anger at Jared's stupidity and arrogance made him frown, but when he looked down at Lynn's pale face, his gaze softened.

"No, I don't believe you were flirting with Jake. I believe what you said by way of explanation and, as you said, "that's all there is to that." I was there when things happened, remember? I know exactly how the story goes. Believe me, sweetheart, Jake is the last man I'm gonna worry about." Giving her a big smile that showed the dimple she loved, he leaned close and kissed the top of her head. Her closeness to him meant he caught the mild scent of rose water. He would have to buy her a gift of some rosewater the next time he went to the mercantile. His mother told him that Lynn had told her that she used to favor it before Jared wouldn't let her wear it anymore. His mother then gifted her a small bottle of her own to enjoy as much as she wanted.

Seated in the church, Lynn was nestled in between Ben and Jad who had given her a big hug when she had come to the pew where he sat waiting. Grace and Allen also gave hugs. Allen had made Shaline stay home one more Sunday to make sure she was healing and wasn't going to be up and about too soon. But she had been persuaded only under extreme protests it seemed, as Jad added to the story with his humorous flourish. Lynn laughed as Jad related the tales of breakfast that morning and the begging and pleading on Shaline's part to be able to come with the family. Grace had to interrupt and point out that Jad, of course, was exaggerating as usual, but that Shaline did want to come but Allen had forbidden it. Cathleen stayed home with mama to help with the baby if needed.

Reverend Statton gave an earth-shaking sermon about forgiveness that Lynn was likely never to forget. Afterward, she met numerous people with names she would have to hear a few more times if she would remember which name went with which face. And then the Alenson family gathered to their two buckboards and headed home. Lynn had been acutely aware of Carrie's glare and whispers to her friends that resulted in Lynn wishing they could have left sooner than they did. Eventually, Ben's big bay was trotting up the hill to the house with Jad, Allen, and Grace following closely behind them.

Cathleen fairly flew down the steps as they came up to the house. "Lynn! Lynn! You came back. I hoped that you would come back! Hurry and see the fish Uncle Jad and Daddy caught!" She was reaching for Lynn's hand before Ben could even help her down from the buckboard. Lynn cast an amused glance at Ben who shrugged laughingly. She laughed gaily as she ran with the little girl to the side of the house where a large washtub held two of the biggest fish she had ever seen.

"See, aren't they pretty? Daddy says we're going to have some for supper. Gramma and Mama make the best salmon. I want to go fishing with Uncle Jad and Daddy next time and they said maybe I can. Do you like to fish, Lynn? Come on, let's go see if there are any eggs, I haven't looked yet because I was helping Mama." She chattered on as she pulled Lynn towards the chicken house. Lynn looked over her shoulder at Ben and smiled as she allowed herself to be drawn with the little girl. A few minutes later they returned to see if the men had started cleaning the fish yet. Cathleen was elated and wanted to watch them for a moment.

Both men looked up as the bubbly little girl and Lynn came around the corner.

"Hey Lynn, you came to help. How kind of you." Jad held out a knife to her with the usual grin on his face.

"Well, I guess I could give it a try, but I'm not sure what it would look like when I was finished, however. I've never cut up fish before." She smiled back at Jad. It was good to see that silly grin again. And good to see Allen. The older man held up a strip of pink flesh for her to inspect.

"Just like this. We're going to slap this in some brine and then the smoker and make some of the best fish you've ever tasted. We won't have any of this tonight, it takes a little longer than that to make. But, next Sunday when you come out we'll have some ready for you. Ben said that you've never tasted smoked salmon, right?"

Her eyes widened in surprise as she turned toward Ben, who had just walked around the corner carrying a knife and cutting board.

"You remember me telling you that?" She had even forgotten about that, and he had remembered? She was amazed.

"I remember everything about you." He kissed the top of her head and was going to put his arm around her waist, but Cathleen was talking again and pulling her in the direction of the back door of the house now. Lynn glanced again over her shoulder at Ben as she followed the bubbly little girl. His eyes were watching the gentle swing of her hips and he looked slightly embarrassed as he looked up to catch her gaze. He tried to smile innocently, but he could tell by the knowing look she gave him, that it must not have been innocent enough. The smile turned into a grin when she gave him a "you just got caught" look. He winked and waved to her as she disappeared around the corner and into the back door of the house.

It was strange how it didn't scare or alarm Lynn when she had looked back and realized where Ben's gaze had dropped to. Not so very long ago it was a terrifying experience connected to Jared. But that was a lifetime ago and this was a different place, a different time, a different man. When Ben simply grinned back at her after being caught, her breath caught for a split second, her pulse jumped, and she felt a warm flush go across her. She hoped that Grace and Shaline wouldn't guess that one of the reasons for her big smile was Ben and his wandering eyes.

"Better be careful where your eyes wander, there brother. I think you got caught that time." Jad had watched the exchange without the other two even being aware that he was.

Ben decided the best way to handle Jad, sometimes anyway, was to just ignore him. He grabbed another knife and helped Allen, who suddenly smiled, fillet out the other fish. Of course, being ignored didn't wipe the grin off the younger man's face. Instead, it served to make Jad throw back his head and laugh loudly.

Cathleen chattered all of the way around the house and through the back door. "Wait 'til you see what Mama and Gramma made you and me. It's so pretty. And I got to help. Mama let me sew on two of the buttons. And Mama says that we can wear them for the dance when we go. If we both wear them, then you and me will match. Isn't that fun? Do you want to match with me? I think,..." The back door slammed as the smell of freshly baked apple pie greeted them. Lynn could also smell baked beans and fresh bread. She had missed the blend of scents in this house and she hesitated for just a moment to soak them all in. Cathleen had gone in search of Mama and Gramma, so Lynn stood perfectly still for a few minutes just looking around, realizing how much she loved this home and the family it belonged to. It still amazed her how much she had come to care for this family in such a short time.

The mention of a gift of some kind reminded her of her own small gifts she had brought but had forgotten in the buckboard. She had been excited about being back here. Then there was Cathleen who could hardly contain herself long enough for Ben to lift her down before whisking her off to see the sights.

Starting for the kitchen and front door to go retrieve her package from the wagon, she was stopped by the sound of Maryanna gurgling and cooing from the bedroom. She hesitated at the door for a moment, looking in at the wiggling bundle on the bed propped between two pillows.

A soft voice beside her made her jump. “Go ahead and get her. I know you want to. She ate just a little while ago and was changed so she should be happy for a while.” Lynn turned to give Shaline a big hug.

“I’m sorry, I didn’t mean to make you jump.”

“That’s okay, I guess I was pretty intent on Maryanna. I’m that obvious, huh?” Lynn smiled wryly.

“Hmmm..." Shaline pretended to think about it for a second. "Yep.” Shaline laughed and pushed Lynn gently into the room.

“Okay, since you’re going to force me.” Lynn laughed in return as she gathered the baby in her arms. They walked into the kitchen together, laughing and talking about the last few days and what little news from town that Lynn had gathered that she thought the two women may be interested in. She didn’t know enough people yet to be able to gather much of the latest gossip for them, but she had tried. The three women laughed and cooked together in the kitchen as they made ham sandwiches for lunch. A few minutes later Cathleen rang the dinner bell for the men to come and eat. It was perfect timing because they had just finished the fish and brought the pieces with them into the kitchen.

Grace took the bowl of fish pieces and set it on the counter as the men went to wash up for lunch.

“Mmmm, I can’t wait for them to get this done.” She turned to look at Lynn. “Ben says you’ve never had smoked salmon before.” Her eyes sparkled as she described it. “The boys have the best recipe! It turns out so moist and tender and melts in your mouth especially with a slice of warm bread and chunk of cheese.” She moistened her lips with her tongue as if licking off some crumbs of the wonderful food she was describing.

“Well with that description, now I can hardly wait to taste it.” Lynn laughed.

“It is very delicious the way Mama says, although I can eat it all by itself, too.” Shaline smiled brightly at the prospect of the delectable fish that they would be able to eat within a few days time, making a deep sigh in her throat.

Lynn burst out laughing at the dreamy looks on the faces of the other two women.

The men walked back into the kitchen to see all three women laughing loudly. They stopped for just a moment and watched since the women hadn’t noticed them yet. Grace made a kissing sound with her fingers to her mouth and then into the air like the Italian family that used to live next to them years ago when they were children. It made Jad and Ben stare in curiosity at what exactly they had missed. Allen just looked amused as his eyes rested on his laughing wife.

"Well, I guess that teaches us a lesson; never leave the womenfolk too long unattended!" Jad rolled his eyes dramatically and shook his head as if a major disaster had just happened.

The three women turned to look at the men behind them. Grace then bent to get the thick slices of cured ham out of the oven as Shaline winked at her husband with mischief in her eyes. Lynn's eyes sparkled as she bit her lip, trying unsuccessfully to stop the big smile on her face.

As Ben walked towards her, he called over his shoulder to his brother, "I agree Jad. They're probably deserving a sound whoopin' or kissin', I'm not sure which." He cringed slightly the moment he realized what he said, wishing he could take back such stupid words. He anxiously searched Lynn's face for any fear or nervousness but was relieved to find none. Instead, one eyebrow rose slightly and her eyes spoke a challenge that he couldn't resist. He reached out for her arm, but she knew his intentions and she swung around the side of the table, quickly placing Cathleen between her and the big man. Ben stopped for a second, surprised at her playfulness and how quickly she had moved out of his grasp while having the baby in one arm. He then grabbed up Cathleen and tucked her under one arm. As she giggled and screamed, he went for Lynn, following her around the side of the table.

"Oh, this is gonna be fun to watch! Big brother has someone else to torment instead of lil' ol' me!" Jad laughed wickedly as he sidestepped quickly to avoid being run over by Ben as he lunged after Lynn into the front room while keeping a firm hold on Cathleen. The little girl was still screaming and laughing in delight.

Shaline's eyes widened with mischief as she laughed at her brother. "Lil' ol' you?! Ha! Since when is that an appropriate description?" She ran to hide behind her husband as Jad made a move to go after her for such a smug comment.

"You got a pretty smart mouth there woman, for being such a little pipsqueak. You can hide behind him now but only for so long!" His eyes squinted devilishly at her as she peeked from around Allen's side at him laughing.

The squeals from the front room intensified as Ben finally caught Lynn by the back door and pinned her between himself and the wall. He turned her around with his free arm as he gave her a firm kiss on her laughing mouth. Her eyes sparkled and danced up at him. If there was a way to stay in that moment forever he would have done it. Instead, he released her arm, and putting his arm around her shoulders, they walked back into the kitchen to watch Shaline still hiding behind her tall, quiet husband. Jad watched from the corner of his eye, daring her to step out from her hiding place.

As they joined the rest of the family Lynn was perplexed, how on earth did a man of Ben's size, with a child under one arm no less, move so fast? She puzzled over that for a moment, thinking that she certainly would never want to be on the man's bad side. She had always thought that Jared, with his boxing skills, moved quickly. But, Ben moved remarkably quick also.

She dismissed her musing as the smell of ham, fresh bread, and coffee filled her nose. She breathed deeply not only for those aromas but also for the woodsy, earthy smell of the man beside her. She felt safe and protected like she never had her whole life. The smile on her face reached deep within her heart and soul, bringing with it a sense of peace that hadn't been there for many years.

The rest of the day passed too quickly for both Lynn and Ben. He had taken her to see the rest of the sawmill. There had never been another opportunity after Carrie interrupted them that day. Lynn's inquisitive questions about it and how it worked made him make a mental comparison between her and Carrie. Lynn had examined closely the different parts of the mill and had honest questions, albeit some of them would have seemed silly to many people. A couple had been similar to Carrie's but not with Carrie's superciliousness and obvious lack of interest. Lynn was truly interested in its operation since she had never been around a mill. Ben found her questions and curiosities heartwarming as he answered with great detail and pride. When they finally walked back to the house, Lynn felt she had some good working knowledge of the operation which made her proud of herself and, she sensed, made Ben proud of her also.

After a wonderful dinner of baked salmon, mashed potatoes, greens, sourdough bread, and apple pie, the women cleaned up the kitchen and then the entire family retired into the front room by the fireplace. They visited for a long time before finally, Cathleen couldn't stand it any longer.

"Mama, can't we please show Lynn what we made? I want to show her the buttons I sewed on. Please, Mama, please Gramma." The pleading in her voice made them all smile as Gramma and Mama both nodded their approval. She jumped up from where she had been playing on the floor with her doll and ran into the bedroom. She emerged a moment later with two aprons. One was a dark blue with deep pockets. Tiny white flowers were embroidered around the edges of the pockets, making it not only practical but pretty as well. The smaller one was also the same shade of dark blue but had little yellow flowers embroidered around its edges.

Lynn clasped her hands together in delight. Aprons had been on her list of things to make after some badly needed clothes, but this was so attractive she would almost be afraid to use it for fear of ruining it. She gave Shaline, Grace, and Cathleen all hugs, and she and the little girl wanted to try them on together so they could match. Cathleen was glowing with pride as Lynn commended her for the nice job she had done sewing on the buttons.

"I also have gifts for you, but I need to go get them out of the buckboard. I forgot them out there earlier." She turned to go get them. Ben jumped to his feet and went with her out the door.

"I'll go with you because I put the buckboard away earlier. It's over by the side of the barn. I had noticed that package then but didn't think to ask you about it. I got sidetracked showing you the mill. I have the tendency to get sidetracked easily when you're around." He grinned down at her.

"Hmmm, well I guess I'll take the blame for that. I think I like your excuse." Her eyes danced up at him as she touched the dimple on his cheek. That was all he needed. By this time, they had reached the buckboard. His arms went around her and he pressed her into the side of the barn. One hand spread across her lower back and the other across her shoulders. When his mouth came down on hers with a ferocity that at first startled her, she hesitated for just a second, but then she kissed him back with her own cautious curiosity. Her arms found themselves holding him tightly around the waist as she pulled him close against her. It was a full minute before his head lifted from hers. His stare was so intense she would have been scared had it been any other man but Ben. But this man held himself different, with a calm fire that she knew would fully consume them both when they became man and wife. She was anxious for that, wanting to become a wife to this man as she had never wanted anything in her life.

When a slight shiver ran up Lynn's back Ben drew back to look down at her. The shiver was not from cold or fear because her eyes were smoldering with a quiet heat. It was an acute awareness of the effect she had on him and the effect he had on her. His heart leaped within his chest, beating his ribs with a breathless headiness at seeing her response to his demanding kiss. He hadn't hurt her but it was the most intense kiss he had so far laid on those soft, pink lips. At first, he thought himself stupid for doing that, but then when it had only taken a second for her to kiss back with feeling of her own, he was elated. His breath drew in sharply and without a word he turned, reached into the buckboard, and handed her the package she needed.

She held his stare when still, without a word, he turned again and drew her to his side to walk back toward the house. She looked up at him with a small knowing smile. The burning warmth in her eyes and the flush on her cheeks must surely tell him all he needed to know; she was starting to feel a fire of her own.

She entered the house before Ben and went to get a refill of her coffee before going into the front room with the rest of the family. She needed an extra moment to compose herself.

Ben hesitated for just a moment at the door and then sat down in his usual chair waiting for her to come in. He crossed his feet at the ankles and leaned back in his chair with his arms behind his head trying to look casual. Jad gave him a knowing look, quirking his eyebrow slightly as Ben narrowed his eyes at him, daring him to say anything. Jad, however, didn't need to; he had gotten a reaction, and that's all he wanted. He grinned happily as he leaned back in his chair with his arms crossed against his broad chest.

He was still grinning a moment later when Lynn walked back into the room with a package in one hand and her cup of coffee in the other. Except for the slight pink to her cheeks, there was no indication of what had happened a few moments before. And since the pink on her cheeks could have been from the cool evening air, no one suspected anything, except Jad, of course. When she glanced in his direction, his eyebrows quirked slightly. Seeing that gesture, coupled with his crazy grin, and she knew instantly that he knew her and Ben hadn't just walked out, got the package, and walked back in. He knew Ben had taken a moment to steal a kiss. Heat flooded her cheeks in earnest and she ducked her head down towards Cathleen.

"Can you guess what I brought you?" She needed an excuse to get Jad's knowing eyes off of her. When she glanced at Ben and found him glaring at his brother, she couldn't help but smile at his protectiveness. Cathleen's excitement made her turn her attention back to the little girl who was excitedly making guesses at what the gift could possibly be.

Lynn finally partially unwrapped the package and drew out two lengths of ribbon. One was blue and the other pink.

"I thought these would look very nice with your pretty braids. What do you think?"

"Oh, I like them!" She ran with them to Shaline. "Mama, can you put them in my hair now, please?" As Shaline tied them onto the ends of her daughter's braids, Lynn turned to Grace.

"The mercantile has some of the prettiest things down there. I thought of you when I saw these." Lynn handed the older woman a small package. Grace examined the silver rose shaped buttons and then gave Lynn a big hug.

"They're beautiful. I cut out a new dress a couple of nights ago and they will look wonderful on it. Thank you, dear, very much." She took them into her bedroom and laid them carefully in a small bowl near her sewing.

Next Lynn turned to Shaline. "You have such beautiful hair and I thought this would look wonderful in it." She handed her a small silver comb. Shaline gasped in delight. After handing Maryanna to Allen, she hugged the taller woman hard in appreciation.

Turning to the men, she handed a red handkerchief to Allen and a blue one to Jad. After both said thank you and stuffed them into their pockets, she looked at Ben.

"I suppose you saved the best for last!" Jad had to make a remark of some kind, thought Lynn as she smiled at him.

"Yes, I did." She handed Ben a beautifully carved pocket knife. He looked at her in surprise. It was the most expensive gift of all of them. Why would she spend all of her money on gifts for them when she needed it herself? He appreciated her sacrifice but wished that she would have kept it for herself. He knew she must need things.

"I don't know what to say, Lynn. You shouldn't have spent this kind of money on me. I know you that you don't have much." He examined the knife again. Then standing, he kissed her on the cheek.

"I needed to say thank you to you and your whole family." She swung her arm around to all of them. "You all have done so much for me. You drew me into your lovely family, a perfect stranger, and yet you welcomed me with a warmth and love I never thought possible." She hesitated for a second as tears came to her eyes. "I needed to do this for you and it doesn't come close to what you have done for me." Her fingers wiped at her eyes as she turned and walked into the kitchen. Everyone sat for just a second before Grace followed her, waving back Ben as she walked by him.

Putting one arm around Lynn's waist, she looked up at the younger woman. "Honey, we're thankful for you, believe me. We all shudder to think about Ben marrying Carrie. You saved us all." She laughed when Lynn blinked at her and then burst out laughing also.

"Amen to that!" Jad, who had ignored his mother's gesture to stay put, was behind them with the rest following. They all sat down at the table and talked about family and Carrie and women or lack thereof in those parts and children and trees until the coffee pot had been emptied for the second time and Lynn looked up at the big grandfather clock that stood just within the front room door so that it was easily visible to both rooms. She gasped at the time. She had to work tomorrow morning early and she knew Ben also had to rise early.

Neither one of them wanted to say that it was time to go. It was way past dark when Ben brought the buckboard around and he lifted her up beside Jad. She would be warm sitting between the two men. Jad arranged a heavy blanket over her legs and around her back as the evening had gotten very cold. The light, gray drizzle of rain had stopped, but the air had a distinct chill in it and Lynn was grateful for Ben and Jad's thoughtfulness.

There was little conversation on the way home except for Ben telling her that he had talked to the judge and found out that it could take several months for a divorce to go through. That was greatly disappointing, but not surprising. Divorce was rare and took a long time. She could tell Ben was frustrated and she felt the same impatient knot within her own stomach.

"How much is it going to cost, Ben? I need to know so I can pay for it." She thought briefly how she would buy from now on only what was absolutely needed. She would waste nothing so she would be able to pay the judge. Maybe if her payments were even ahead a little bit, he would work harder to push it through as quickly as possible.

"I already gave him a down payment. Don't worry about it. I am more than willing to pay for this." When she looked up at him, she saw the hardness in his eyes and knew he wouldn't argue about who was going to pay. She felt bad that it was coming out of his hard-earned money. So she felt even better that she had found that knife for him. It cost her the last of her money, but it was well worth it.

Ben walked her into the dining room of the hotel and gave her a kiss on the cheek since the windows would have allowed anyone outside to see in. As late as it was, there was little chance of that as the town was quiet. But Ben didn't want to take any chances and decided a kiss on the cheek would be enough, although he would have preferred something far more.

It was hard to say goodbye since they both knew they wouldn't see each other for another week. Going into winter, there was much to be done and he couldn't very well leave it all to Allen and Jad. They still didn't have quite enough firewood under cover and they needed to do some hunting also. Their meat supply was running low. Making jerky would take time this week also if they got themselves a big buck or elk. Lynn too would have no time to visit during the week. Her job at the hotel would keep her running for the next few days. Even so, a sadness touched both of them as they turned to go their separate ways.

Chapter 33

"Jad and Carrie"

Two weeks went by with drudging slowness, and yet when each Sunday came, it seemed to blur by with such speed it was like a bird of prey in flight. Ben and Jad stopped by for lunch the second week. They had to deliver lumber to a couple of places in town and Ben grabbed the opportunity to stop by to see Lynn. Unfortunately, they were joined by Carrie who had seen their buckboard close to the hotel after exiting her father's bank. Ben made it obvious that he found the intrusion irritating, but the little blonde refused to be sidetracked from her goal of trying to win back his affections by constantly flirting. She continually made an excuse of some kind to touch his hand or lean in close to talk with him in her low husky voice. Ben knew what she was up to.

Then, to make matters worse, Jad simply sat back with his usual grin, tossing in a few smart remarks now and then. Much to Carrie's irritation, he proceeded to flirt relentlessly with Lynn as she took their orders and then served them. Jad and Carrie's actions caused Ben to frown darkly during the whole meal. He knew Jad wasn't trying to steal Lynn's attention away for himself. He was just up to his usual mischief. Jad loved reactions, whatever they were. Right now, he was doing his utmost to irritate Carrie and he was succeeding magnificently. It was obvious that although she was trying hard to ignore him, she was, in fact, very aware of Jad's outrageous comments and flirting with Lynn. Both men could tell by the occasionally narrowed eyes and the tight pursing of her mouth.

Jad, knowing that he was successful in his mission, kept up the comments and flirtations with a quick wit and perfect timing. Most of the time, Ben would have found them humorous and at times, outright hilarious. Today, however, was not one of those times. Carrie's appearance and insistence of eating lunch with them had turned his mood extremely sour and his patience was running low even with Jad.

Lynn tried, without success, to suppress a smile because she knew what Jad was doing. He was purposely irritating Carrie, but in so doing was also irritating his big brother. She knew he took great pleasure in doing that, too, but she also knew that his primary target was Carrie. It was tempting to play along with Jad's game until she took a look at Ben's face. The heavy scowl marking his brow at the moment almost, not quite, but almost made her feel sorry for Jad when the brothers headed home. If Ben let his little brother have a small piece of his mind on the way home, well, he probably deserved it. But the thought still couldn't keep her from chuckling from the drama that Jad was causing. Jad loved to stir the pot and get reactions out of people even if sometimes anger was the reaction he received. But he would figure it would all be worth it at the end of the day because his antics had stirred up the desired effects: a reaction.

Ben wanted to stop by for lunch to see and have a conversation with Lynn, but Carrie was keeping him sidetracked. When some comment from Jad made Lynn burst out laughing, he turned her way, curiosity and irritation still in his face. Even though the frown was not meant for Lynn, Carrie must have thought it was because she seems to intensify her efforts to keep his attention.

The frown directed at Lynn made Carrie want to jump for joy. Ben being mad at Lynn would be the best accomplishment yet. Jad, however, was driving her crazy and it was time to put him in his place. When Lynn returned to the kitchen it was her turn to stir the pot, or so she thought.

She turned to Jad, "I thought that woman liked Ben, but it looks like she prefers you instead, Jad. I never thought I would meet a woman who could tolerate you that much." She smiled smugly at Ben who looked like he was about to jump out of his chair.

Jad snorted with loud laughter at her remark, almost tipping his chair over backward as he threw himself back in his chair. She really was not a very bright woman. The only positive quality about her was her looks, but they weren't enough to cover over the ugly of the rest of her. Easy on the eyes didn't make a woman attractive if she was stupid, hateful, and vindictive.

"I don't think so, Carrie. Lynn has eyes for Ben only. I'm only the annoying big brother to her. We can laugh and joke together, but Lynn is Ben's woman." His laughter grew louder still at the look of horror and repulsion that made her usually lovely face contort with rage. He decided to make the dig go a little deeper, "Nope, that woman belongs to Ben and I ain't one to challenge that!" He crossed his arms against his chest as he leaned back in his chair, enjoying the looks on his table companion's faces.

At first, Ben sat across the table from him glaring. But in response to Jad's latest remark, he couldn't help but smile. His eyes started dancing at Jad's mischief when he saw the look that passed over Carrie's face. Even though he probably should have felt sorry for the young woman sitting so close beside him, he couldn't. She deserved the smart remarks and everything she got from Jad. He thought about it for just a moment—nope, no feelings of pity welled within him. He almost grinned at Jad. His younger brother noticed his mouth twitching as he tried not to laugh.

"Well we've had enough excitement for one day, I think. C'mon big brother, we got things to do." Standing up, he pushed his chair in and threw his napkin down on the pie plate. Ben did the same and then pulled out Carrie's chair for her. Ben was the gentleman; Jad didn't particularly feel like being one around her. Jad was almost always a gentleman, except with Carrie. She was, hands down, the most obnoxious, spoiled woman he had ever met. He suddenly looked toward the ceiling, blinked twice, and in his head told God thank you for sending Lynn to Ben. To have Carrie as a sister-in-law would have been a hard pill to swallow. He loved his brother dearly, but if Ben had married Carrie, she would have made it almost impossible to be around him. He wouldn't have visited them often, which saddened him for a brief instant because he would have felt the loss deeply. So once again, he said a brief thank you to higher direction.

Chapter 34

"A dangerous flirtation"

October 24, 1844

It's natural for women to notice a good-looking man when they see one. Carrie was no exception, but she looked at them from a different angle. An angle of manipulation and exploitation. Men were a means to an end. What could she get from them that she wanted at the moment, if not necessarily long-term? Most of the time it was the knowledge that almost all men found her very attractive. Consequently, more often than not, just the appraising looks and glances she usually received were enough to appease her. But, at other times, as with Ben, she wanted more than that. She wanted something deeper, with more value. So, when she first laid eyes on one of the newest men in town, she immediately started studying him for her use.

He was a handsome man, lean and wiry in his body. He wasn't what one would consider tall, but he was average height for a man. He exuded a dangerous mix of virility and smoky sexuality that had heads turning all over town, including Carrie's. His sandy blonde hair curled slightly at the edge of his collar as his long strides took him down the boardwalk at a rapid pace. Entering the mercantile, he tipped his hat politely at Suzanne Smith and Leann Seckers, who were just exiting with packages in their hands.

Carrie's eyes narrowed slightly as she watched the two women walk the other direction from her down toward the hotel, where they would probably go talk with Lynn. They usually did every time they visited town. Several of the women on the wagon train regularly stopped by to see that woman whenever they were in town. She had been watching closely for a couple of weeks trying to find something to use against the older woman. Having been unable to come up with anything yet, she felt frustrated, thwarted in her quest for the affections of Ben. Needing a diversion, she decided a new ribbon for her bonnet was in order. She wanted to get a closer look at this new stranger in town. She pushed the door open, overhearing the conversation between him and Mr. Manning.

"Nope, haven't had any of those here for quite a while. I keep hoping a shipment will come through with some, but so far I haven't seen any." Edward Manning, the shop's owner, was talking to him as he pointed to something in the corner just out of Carrie's vision. When Edward heard the bell on the door tinkle, he turned to see who had entered. A slight frown creased his tired face. It made the other man turn to see who it was to cause such a reaction. Carrie could immediately see the appreciation for her good looks in his eyes—hazel she thought as she tried to make out the color without staring.

"Well, aren't you a sight for sore eyes after months on the trail." It was a statement rather than a question. He nodded his head towards her as his eyes darted hungrily to her breasts that heaved slightly above the lace trim on the bodice of her blue walking dress. Then they dropped to her hips, glanced at the pouty full mouth that smiled at him, then back at her breasts. He was almost leering, though not quite, and Carrie found herself drawn to the raw hunger in his eyes. For the first time in her life, her stomach fluttered at something she didn't understand.

Sashaying over to the men, she turned to Mr. Manning. "I forgot to pick up some ribbon yesterday and if I go home without it today, Mama is going to be most unhappy." There, she thought, he would know she's not married. She was single, living at home with her parents. "I need two yards of that blue over there." Lifting her gloved hand, she pointed to a light blue roll on the wall. When Mr. Manning nodded his head towards her, acknowledging her request and reached for the ribbon, she turned her attention back to the handsome man in front of her.

"Oh dear, I hope I'm not interrupting anything important." She widened her eyes in mock horror as if she just now figured out she may have been rude by intruding into the men's conversation.

He shook his head and threw up his hands in defeat. "Never stand between a woman and her ribbon is what I always say." When he smiled his teeth were even and white. No tobacco stains. Whew, that's a relief, thought Carrie. She glanced down at her feet in pretended innocence. When she raised her eyes back at him, he was staring at her breasts.

She blushed prettily as she held out her hand. "My name is Carrie Owen. My father is Jonah Owen. He owns the only bank in town." Tipping her head made her blonde curls bounce on her shoulder. His eyes narrowed slightly as he looked down at her. She felt as if he was looking right through her. It made her suddenly nervous, the fluttering in her stomach disappeared as quickly as it had come. She didn't understand why, but in an instant, she wanted to get the ribbon Mr. Manning was handing to her and escape the shop. When he still didn't offer his name after she hesitated for just a second, she thanked Mr. Manning and turned to leave the shop.

"Well, Carrie Owen, it was a pleasure to meet you. I'm sure I'll see you around." When she glanced back at him with a slight smile, she noticed that this time he was leering. An involuntary shiver ran up her back as his eyes glittered with something she didn't understand. Not something good, but instead something evil. She had no idea how she knew that, she just did. This time instead of her stomach fluttering from something pleasant, it fluttered from a stab of fear. His handsome face suddenly wasn't so handsome.

Just as she shut the door, what she heard made her stop cold for just a moment in shock.

"Well, check again in a week, Mr. Malen. Hopefully, they come in soon. If they do, I'll put one aside for you."

"Thanks, Edward, I appreciate that."

Malen?! That was Lynn's last name. They may not be related. There were several families around the area with the same last names but weren't related. But Malen wasn't really a common name. She had never heard it before Lynn. Although that didn't necessarily mean anything, she was always suspicious of the other woman. She just knew that Lynn had something to hide. This certainly couldn't be her brother unless Lynn was a liar. Carrie had overheard her in conversation with someone the other day saying she was an only child. Besides the fact that they looked absolutely nothing alike that could suggest that maybe they were related. As she walked down the street toward her father's bank, her mind was turning over and over all of the things she knew about Lynn Malen. She had wondered why Ben and Lynn hadn't gotten married yet. Ben had said because they both wanted a little time to settle into knowing each other better before taking such a big step. Now,... now she was wondering if there were other reasons. Well, actually not reasons, but one reason. One really handsome, but unnerving, reason.

Jared walked out of the shop, gathered the reins on the horse that was tied in front, and trotted north out of town. A heavy frown creased his forehead as he pulled the collar up on his heavy coat to keep the light rain from dripping down his neck. He had wanted another revolver, enraged since he had lost his on the last river crossing. His fists served him well, but in renegade country like this, it was a good idea to have a little extra defense with him. He still had his rifle. But he had taken up a habit of wearing the revolver and now felt naked without it.

His thoughts turned to the little blonde beauty who had so blatantly informed him that she was single and had a rich father. She was most definitely his type, if she was in the local whorehouse. He had eyed that full bosom hungrily, and she had loved the attention until his gaze had changed suddenly. He saw that flash of fear in her blue eyes just before she turned to leave the shop. Inside, his guts twisted as he thought of the pleasure she could give him. Her kind usually couldn't handle him more than a couple of times; they didn't like it rough.

He shook his head to clear it, as the real reason he was in this town splintered like angry lightning across his mind. He hadn't found her yet. The wagon train had been here four days and he had been looking nonstop. The thought that she may not even be here but may have moved on to somewhere else made his horse dance sideways as his hands gripped the reins in an angry fist. He had heard about a dance and dinner taking place this Saturday. He figured that would be the best way to see if she was around. Everyone from miles around would come to the dance. It would probably be the last big party before winter got serious and the homesteaders stayed home for most of the rainy season. He had been hearing stories of the upcoming storms. So, he had plans for attending that social in two nights. He was going to find her one way or the other.

Chapter 35

"The dance"

November 2, 1844

Every time she thought about Saturday Lynn smiled with anticipation. Jared had never gone to socials since there was no gambling allowed and he hated dancing. So it had been over three years since she had the pleasure of going to one.

On one hand, the last few weeks seemed to take forever to go by. At the same time, she was so busy every day that the days flew by. It was difficult for it to be both ways at the same time, but somehow it was.

Sundays always brought a smile to her face as well. Her Sundays with Ben's family were wonderful, and that word wasn't strong enough. She never thought it was possible to belong to a family without actually being related. She felt like they were the pieces that had been missing ever since her mother had died and then her father. Her grandparents had raised her well and had loved her deeply but there had always been pieces missing. She only wished she could have known Ben's father. The family told stories about him often, and she knew he must have been a remarkable man. She was anxiously awaiting the time when she would be related to the Alenson family as Ben's wife.

Ben checked with Judge Perkins every time he came to town. Thank goodness, the old Judge said that within three or four months at the most it should be final. It was too slow a process for Ben's liking. His impatience was growing in leaps and bounds every time he talked to Perkins. The judge reminded him that even if it was four months, that it really wasn't that long a wait. Ben had muttered something under his breath about that being a matter of perspective, but the judge chose to ignore the comment. What could they do? The thought was still in the back of his mind that Jared may show up here someday. Not being the type of person to wish something bad to happen to people, he kept the hope to himself that Jared died on the trail. Thousands already had.

The next two days were busy at the hotel. They had all the rooms full, partially because of the newest wagon train that had arrived. But also because there were several single men with a little money who were wanting a hot bath, warm soft bed, and good food. Marsha decided that they would not be serving lunch on Saturday of the social, it would be breakfast only. That way she and Lynn could have the kitchen to make their own dishes to take to the day's gathering.

Lynn rose early Saturday morning, her eyes sparkling as she almost danced into the kitchen. Marsha and Ivan laughed as she came in.

"Starting the dance early, are you?!" Ivan laughed as she twirled around the table where he was rolling out pie dough.

"Why not? It has been so long since I've been to a social, I can hardly wait. I feel like a little girl." She almost giggled as she looked at the two of them.

Marsha threw up her hands in mock frustration, sighing heavily as she looked up at her adoring husband, "Well, I can see how much work we're gonna get outta her today!" Ivan winked at Lynn as she grabbed the sugar off the shelf and started pouring cream into a bowl.

"You will probably get more out of me today because I'm in such a good mood." She playfully smirked at the plump older woman as she grabbed a knife and started peeling potatoes. "What do you think about scalloped potatoes and ham? We have those ham pieces left from yesterday that probably should be used up."

"Oh, that sounds really good. I didn't know you could make scalloped potatoes and ham. If I had known that, we would have had that this week. That's the one thing I have trouble making. Never turns out good."

Lynn looked up, surprised. "You? I have trouble believing that. You're such a wonderful cook. I haven't tasted anything you have made that wasn't good." Her glance caught Ivan's movements. He made a funny face while shaking his head slightly. His wife glanced up in time to see what he was doing. He received an elbow in his ribs that made him grunt, not in pain, but with suppressed laughter.

"You're supposed to be on my side, thank you very much." Marsha's pretended indignation made Lynn laugh as she went back to peeling the pile of potatoes in front of her.

Ivan bent to kiss his wife on the top of her head. Then he went back to the job at hand.

The three of them worked together for the better part of the day baking pies, homemade rolls, blackberry tarts, Lynn's scalloped potatoes with ham, and finally a large pot of baked beans. The Social was to start at about three o'clock and Ben had promised that he would come to get her.

At two she ran upstairs to her room to wash up, fix her hair, and get dressed. She wanted to look special and thought she was pretty successful when the woman looking back at her from the mirror had flushed cheeks from excitement and her hair shone like rich, dark velvet.

Pondering the eyes staring back at her, she thought how much she had changed in such a short period of time. The woman standing before her held herself with poise and confidence that had never been there before. Her lips curved into a large smile as she smoothed down her new skirt and shirtwaist with excited hands. Her hair had grown long enough to pull up and secure in combs and she tied a blue ribbon around her throat. She had embroidered a flower design on it, placing small pearl beads in the center of the flowers. She pinched her cheeks and bit her lips for a bit more color, grabbed her cape, the apron that would match Cathleen's smaller one, and walked downstairs to wait for Ben.

She didn't have long to wait. Ben was on time. He bounded into the hotel dining room and her eyes widened with the pleasure of seeing his large frame in a black suit. She would be the envy of every woman there. Ben was the epitome of masculinity, his handsome face with a huge grin on it that matched hers. His dark hair was slicked back and his boots were polished. She swallowed hard at the sight of him.

"Well, I hope by the look on your face that it means that I look good." He walked over and planted a kiss on her lips.

Blinking with embarrassment, she gazed up at him. "You always look good, Ben. I just didn't think about you wearing a suit is all. And here I am in a simple skirt and shirtwaist. You're dressed to go to a wedding."

"Well, I certainly hope to have one of those soon." The laughter in his eyes eased her embarrassment as he took her arm and they walked to the door. "Besides, your new clothes make you beautiful. I will be the envy of every man there. Right, Ivan?" He turned to the older man as they went out the door. Lynn had not seen them behind her as they left. Now she glanced over her shoulder at Ivan's voice.

"You will be the second man envied, I will be the first." His warm eyes twinkled as he helped his wife into their buckboard. Marsha's smile deepened as she looked at her husband.

"Smart answer, Ivan." Ben laughed as he climbed up beside Lynn and turned towards the other end of town to the Community Hall where the social was being held. Ivan tipped his hat in response as both couples laughed.

They spent the first hour talking and laughing with friends from the wagon train. Ben had seen a few of them a few times, but for many of them, it hadn't been since they first arrived in Oregon City. They all had a lot of catching up to do.

Finally, Ben found Lynn standing by herself for a moment at the punch bowl. He tried to look nonchalant as he sauntered over to her. He hadn't had an opportunity to dance with her yet and he decided it was about time. But he wanted to flirt a little first.

"Hello ma'am, my name is Ben. I've been watching you for quite a while. Would you like to dance?" His eyes danced with mischief as he gazed down at her.

Her eyes crinkled with humor as she decided to play his game. "You were watching me? Why would you do that? Should I be scared?" She tried unsuccessfully to be serious.

"I always watch the beautiful women in a room, especially at a dance. I need to decide which ones I'm gonna ask to dance with me." He leaned against the wall pretending to be bored.

Now it was her turn. "You're watching other beautiful women, too? So, I'm not anything special, just the one you're asking first." Her pretended indignation didn't work well either, because she could no longer hold back her laughter, especially when he suddenly grabbed her into an embrace and started to twirl her around the room to the waltz that was playing.

He laughed out loud at her wide eyes as she clung to him. "Woman, there are only three beautiful women and two beautiful girls in this room and you're top of the list."

She loved this game and wanted to keep it going just a little longer. "Well if you're eyeing three other women at least I'm at the top of the list." Her laughter was light as he twirled her past Jad and his mother. Grace was laughingly protesting some remark from Jad as usual as they went quickly by, so Lynn couldn't make out what the comment was. From the look on Grace's face, it was the usual quirkiness from her younger son.

Several men tried to cut in on Ben, including Jad and Allen. Ben refused them all even though they all protested vehemently that he was not being fair. Ben just laughed at them as he pulled his partner in the other direction. She marveled at Ben's light feet and excellent rhythm. They danced eight in a row until Lynn finally said she really needed a drink of punch. The heat in the room and then dancing was making her very thirsty.

Ben left her sitting near the door as she cooled down from the fresh air that gently filtered through the room. Others stood or sat close doing the same. She sat with her hands in her lap as her gaze moved around the room. Allen and Shaline were talking with friends near the huge tables of food that were displayed across the far wall. When her stomach growled, she realized that she hadn't eaten since breakfast, except for a slice of warm bread at lunch. She had been so caught up with visiting with friends and dancing with Ben that her stomach had been the last thing to think about. Now, however, she decided that when Ben returned she would suggest that they get something to eat. Everything looked delicious and she was anxious to try some of it.

Her gaze wandered again. It slid across some women gathered together laughing and from the slips of conversation she was catching now and then, they were talking about children and quilts. Some of them she knew from meeting them around town. Some of the others she hadn't met yet. They were probably some who came to town maybe once a month and for special events such as this. She suddenly felt a kinship with all of these people. They all had endured a lot in order to come here to the Oregon country. Their lives had been changed in ways that would forever be marked either by tragedy or by good or maybe both. She belonged here. She felt at home and she couldn't wait to start her life with Ben and his family.

Her gaze moved to a group of men, local homesteaders who were working hard to carve out their own destiny, their own lives. Most of them wanted wives and families, but she knew that would come to them eventually because people were moving to the Oregon and Washington country by the thousands.

She shifted her gaze again, this time to across the room. Carrie came into her line of sight. For just a moment Lynn took in the younger woman's dress. It was a beautiful pink taffeta with enough lace and ribbon to put on three dresses. Her hair was pulled up and back to one side with two of the most beautiful combs Lynn had ever seen. Her pale fingers were working a fan as she gazed up at the man by her side. Lynn thought it interesting that she didn't particularly look like she was entranced with the man, nor flirting, which was her usual nature. Rather, she looked wary, almost cornered like a rabbit, but not wanting to run just yet. Lynn shook her head slightly in curiosity as she looked up at the man Carrie was in conversation with.

Lynn would look back at this moment later and wonder how, in this instant of time, all three pairs of eyes locked together.

Space and time seemed to stop. She was suddenly unaware of anything or anyone else around her. The music and the laughter of the couple beside her went silent. All she heard was the roar of silence in her ears as the air was sucked out of her, and in that instant, her vision blurred and went black around the edges. Her hands grabbed the sides of the chair where she sat. For a split second in time, she almost felt like she was going to pass out as every drop of blood left her face. She could feel it painfully drip slowly and yet somehow drain quickly down her cheeks and behind her eyes. It was the strangest and scariest feeling she had ever had. Her knuckles tightened against the hardwood of the seat, and if she could have pulled her eyes away to look down, she would have seen them turn white against the dark wood. All she could see was Carrie suddenly use her fan to point in her direction, her blue eyes piercing into hers with a maliciousness that took the rest of her breath away. But, what made her freeze completely for just a fraction of a second were the hazel eyes that pierced her through to the very center of her soul. Jared had found her!

Chapter 36

"How the silence roars"

Jad and Ben discussed the wonderful smells coming off of the tables and they both decided that it was time to try some of it. They filled three plates and Ben filled up a glass with punch. He decided that he and Lynn could share a glass since he couldn't carry two glasses and two plates. He was barely juggling what he had. As he turned around, looking up as he did so to get his bearings, he noticed Lynn's white face and terrified gaze. He knew immediately what that meant. There would be only one reason for the intense fear he saw on her face.

Jad almost ran into him from behind as Ben jerked to a stop to follow the direction of Lynn's gaze.

Jad looked up first in surprise, then quickly assessing the situation, he turned in Allen's direction. Whispering quietly to the older man, they both set down plates and told Grace and Shaline to stay there. The women were puzzled at the request and started to rise from their chairs. They stopped abruptly at the hard look in Allen's and Jad's faces when Jad pointed to Lynn. Grace started to stand, but Shaline pulled her back.

"No, Mama, let the men handle this." Her voice trembled slightly as both women finally saw Jared.

He had an air about him even at this distance that was mean, cruel, evil. He stood with legs apart and arms crossed loosely on his chest. His gaze hadn't moved from Lynn the whole time they watched, although they had the feeling that he knew he was being watched and was just waiting. He looked like a snake quietly waiting to strike.

Ben's touch on her shoulder made Lynn jump. She hadn't been

aware that he and Jad had even come up beside her. She gulped air when she realized that she had been holding her breath. She hated this feeling, the feeling of desperation, of a morbid paralyzing fear that had taken over her body. Her feet felt like huge chunks of wood that had somehow been nailed to the floor. She couldn't break her gaze away from Jared even though she wanted to. She saw the flicker in his eyes and knew he had glanced in the briefest second at Ben beside her with his hand on her shoulder. Knowing the implications of what that meant made a tremor go through her body.

"Lynn,... Lynn?" The hand on her shoulder shook her slightly. "Lynn!"

Blinking, she finally broke away from Jared's gaze. Looking up, she saw the concern in Ben's eyes. Was concern the right word? Maybe not,... maybe fear was closer to the right word. She was having trouble formulating cohesive thoughts.

"We're right here, sweetheart. Don't worry about anything okay?"

By that time, Carrie had glided over to them. "Your husband is here and wants you back, Mrs. Malen." The words were spat out with such ferocity that Lynn wondered how anyone could be so hateful. Was Carrie stupid enough to think Ben would ever want her when he knew very well the type of person she was? All of her beauty truly was just skin deep. The people near them had stopped talking, sensing that something was happening, although not realizing what yet. With Carrie's comment, the women in the group had gasped in shock and backed away.

"She's getting a divorce from him, so you can tell him that he can't have her back." Ben frowned darkly at Carrie as she swished her skirt from side to side. He had never felt inclined to smack a woman until right now! Carrie had to be the most selfish woman he had ever had the displeasure of meeting.

She pouted prettily, or so she thought. "Well, that's not what I understand from Jared. He came clear across the prairie to get her back and somehow I don't think he will be any too pleased to know that she's trying to get a divorce." She turned around to glance at Jared. He didn't even acknowledge her. His stare hadn't left Lynn the whole time. Carrie shivered slightly at the pure rage in those eyes. She knew whatever was going to happen to Lynn, it wasn't going to be good. But she had decided a while back, that if she couldn't have Ben Alenson, neither could this tall woman who had usurped her place at Ben's side. And maybe someday, although she knew it would take a long time, maybe Ben would forgive her and come to his senses.

She would always be the best wife for him, not this woman with the shoulder-length hair and work-roughened hands.

Jared stared for another moment, then turned and walked out the door nearest to him on the opposite side of Lynn.

Suddenly she stood up, almost knocking Carrie over in the process. "Ben, you need to take me back to the hotel right away." Her voice was higher than usual, her words running together as she put hands on Ben's forearms.

"What?! You're not going back there tonight. That's the first place he'll look. I'm sure Carrie had informed him where you've been staying." His eyes were hard as a rock as they turned to the blonde woman still standing in front of them.

She blinked in surprise at his accusation, "I'm not that heartless, Ben. Although, I'm sure he could find that out rather quickly from about anyone here." Her hand swung around at the roomful of people. "Most people here know where to find her." The sneer on her face was more than Ben could take.

"Carrie, you've done more than enough damage. You are a spoiled brat. A woman who thinks of no one but herself. I don't understand how I ever contemplated marrying you and I feel sorry for the sucker who someday does." Carrie took a step back at the anger in Ben's voice, blinking in surprise. Her cheeks burned with heat as she turned on her heel and escaped out the door at the smirking looks of the few people who had heard the exchange and agreed with Ben. She knew that soon the whole town would know what Ben Alenson had said to humiliate her all because of that woman who didn't belong here.

Jad had even been stopped momentarily at the depth of anger in Ben's voice. Ben remained a gentleman no matter what. So, when he finally let loose his tongue, Jad was shocked. Suddenly, he slapped Ben on the back and threw his head back and laughed.

"Bout time, big brother, bout time!"

Ben didn't like doing that, but now was not the time to be nice and polite. He knew that although Jared had left the building, he wouldn't be content until he had Lynn back in his clutches. The look on Jared's face was unlike any Ben had ever seen before. He had a poker face, from being a gambler. It was devoid of any emotion. But it was his eyes that spoke volumes. Those eyes spoke of an intense need for revenge, and God help anyone who got in the way.

He turned to Jad, "Can you tell Mama that Lynn is staying with us until this is settled." It was a statement rather than a question and Jad just nodded his head in solemn agreement as he headed over to where Shaline and Grace sat patiently waiting. Allen had returned a moment before. Standing quietly behind the Alenson men, he had been a quiet force. Jared had been smart to not challenge them here together. They all knew that he wouldn't rest until he had Lynn again.

"No, Ben. I can't. I don't want to put your family in harm's way. That would be so unfair because Jared is capable of meting out harm to them all. He will come for me, I know it. I can't run forever and I can't hide." She tried keeping her voice down so those standing close wouldn't hear.

Ben could hear the fear and desperation that edged her voice, making it higher pitched than the usual soft, lilting tone she typically had. He pulled her gently over to the other Alenson women and sat her in a chair beside Grace.

After kneeling in front of her, he took both her hands in his. "I will not let him take you away from me, from this family. I will not allow you to go anywhere by yourself. And I will not allow you to think crazy thoughts." His voice was quiet but hard. By his tone, she knew that it would do little good to argue with him. She knew him well enough to know when he meant business.

Jad had stood quietly but now spoke up, "Well, it's highly unlikely that he's going to try anything right now. And since I have heard your stomach growl twice in the five minutes you have been sitting here, I think it's time for you to eat." Ben agreed as he handed her the plate of food he had procured earlier.

She picked at the food, taking a few small bites but not really tasting it. Although agreeing with Jad that her stomach was empty, suddenly she didn't feel hungry. After stirring around the roast beef on her plate for the third time, she put her fork down. Setting her plate aside she watched as Ben, Jad, and Allen talked together quietly a few feet away. Her worried face turned from them toward Grace and Shaline who was holding Maryanna. Cathleen was sitting quietly beside Grace, sensing that something was wrong, although not knowing what. Lynn loved this family to the depth of her very being, and the thought of anything happening to any of them left her cold. Suddenly she was terrified again, but this time it was for them, not herself.

The men were talking with their backs turned away from the women so they could watch the doors, and Grace and Shaline were momentarily distracted by the children. She rose from her chair and moved quickly and quietly behind them until she was hidden from their view because of all the people between them. She sidled along the wall until she was close to the door she had been sitting near earlier. When she saw the men turn to converse with Grace and Shaline, she moved quickly. She knew they would be instantly looking for her. After hearing a cry of alarm from Grace as they realized she was gone, she ran as hard as she could towards the livery. It was the opposite direction from the hotel, which she knew would be the first place they would look for her.

She didn't have to wait long. Ben and Jad both came tearing out of the community hall at top speed and yelling for her. As Ben ran down towards the hotel, Jad ran in her direction much to her surprise. After ducking down behind some barrels sitting in shadows near the west side of the livery, she held her breath until Jad ran by. If she was careful, she could peek out and still see the door of the hall. There were several people outside wondering what the commotion was about. Allen came out and helped the Alenson women and children into their buckboard. He started toward home at a brisk trot promising Jad as he went by that he would return as soon as possible.

An hour passed before Ben and Jad met in front of the Hall. She couldn't hear their conversation but she could tell by their jerky, angry movements that both were agitated. She felt a deep pang in her heart for what they were feeling right now. But, what else could she do? She loved Ben more than she ever thought possible to love someone. What if in this whole mess of things one of them was seriously hurt or even killed? And what if he got killed because of her? What then? What would his family think of her then? How could she go on with that laying heavy on her conscience and heart?

Finally, after another half an hour or so, she saw Ben and Jad jump into the buckboard and take off in the direction of home.

She straightened up painfully and stretched her cramped muscles. As she started slowly towards the hotel a hand grabbed her arm in a cruel grip. She gasped as a wave of fear ripped through her. Jared!

Chapter 37

"The battle"

She drifted slowly in and out of consciousness. The pungent smell of damp earth wafted into her nostrils, and she struggled to open her eyes against the slamming pain in her head. When she tried to move her hands to touch her forehead, she found them held fast by rope. She shook her head slightly, but a piercing light almost blinded her every time she tried to open her eyes. Finally, after several minutes, she succeeded and found herself looking up into the trees with the early morning sun slanting sideways through the mist that weaved itself slowly around and up towards the patches of blue sky. Turning her head up and sideways, she saw the rope that encircled the trunk of a large fir tree. As she laid on the cold ground, she thought wryly how it was only a couple of weeks ago that she and Ben had walked through the woods behind his house. He taught her the names of the different kinds of trees, so different here in the Oregon country than what she was used to.

"Finally awake, huh?" Her attention jerked to the right of her as Jared appeared. He carried a wild turkey in his hand as he sauntered up unhurriedly. Throwing it down in front of the fire he had started earlier, he knelt down in front of her.

"How ya feeling this morn, love? You missed out on the good time we had last night. Been a while since I had my wife to take care of my needs!" He spat the words out with contempt. "And of course, I had lots of needs since my wife left me."

The sneer on his face made Lynn cringe and was suddenly aware of an old familiar discomfort. Even though the vicious blow he had given to her head was now giving her a headache, she was thankful she had never awakened from it. Maybe in the deep recesses of her mind, it was telling her to stay asleep, to not regain consciousness. Bile rose into her throat and it took every bit of self-control to swallow it back. No amount of soap and hot water could cleanse her from his degradation. She squeezed her eyes shut as repulsion washed over her, engulfing her in a feeling of shame and embarrassment. Ben would surely never want her now.

She had envisioned herself belonging to Ben, no other man ever. Just because it wasn't her fault, just because the blame was all on Jared, didn't erase the feelings of helplessness and shame. Thinking that Ben would surely feel the same way if he ever found out made tears come unwanted into her eyes. What was she thinking? He would never find out because she knew that Jared would kill her this time and then leave her remains for the bears or cougars to find. He would then leave this area probably never to return.

"What? Nothing to say? No begging or anything? My goodness, you've changed. You used to beg me to stop." He scratched his chin absently for a moment. "Of course, you're still getting your bearings, I guess. Maybe it's time for some more wifely duties." Taking out a knife, he quickly cut the rope that held her wrists. He stepped back for a moment, giving her time to rub some of the soreness out of them. Then he reached down and jerked her to her feet by her hair and one arm. When she cried out, he laughed derisively.

"There we go. That's more like it, Lynn!" He feigned caring as he gently brushed back the hair that had fallen forward over her eye. Then with one quick sweep of his hand, he finished jerking her bodice open, fully exposing soft, pale flesh. When her hands jerked up to cover herself, he grabbed them, holding them with one hand while he used his body to push hers up against the tree trunk. The rough bark bit angrily into her back as Jared punished her mouth with his own. He ground his mouth against her tender lips, causing her teeth to rip the soft tissue inside. She made a mewling sound against him and struggled in vain, but his grip was strong and the burning anger within him even stronger. Yes, revenge was turning out to be sweet indeed. He would use her for a couple of days before ridding himself of her. She would know the cost of leaving him before she died!

Suddenly, Jared felt himself being jerked back with a force that at once surprised him and made him stumble.

"You filthy pig! What kind of man would do this to a woman?!" Jared blinked twice as he regained his balance. As a skilled boxer, he was quick on his feet, and it only took a moment for him to spin around to size up the man standing in front of him. Ben Alenson was a big man, well-muscled and balanced for a man his size. In Jared's experience, the bigger they were the harder they fell. He had met his match a couple of times, although he had always come out on top in the end. He seriously doubted that this man would be much of a challenge. Ben Alenson may be used to hard physical work, but that didn't count when it came to the skill, speed, and agility of taking a man apart with one well-planned and landed punch after the other.

Jared backed up a couple of steps to let the other man think he had the upper hand. Jared had worked that move to his advantage on more than one occasion. It also brought his rifle back into his line of sight over to his right. Ben noticed his glance and the look on his face dared him to make a move towards it. Jared noticed movement in the trees to his left and the younger Alenson brother appeared. His face was a frozen mask of contempt as he looked first at Lynn and then at Jared. Jared jerked a thumb in his direction as he sneered at Ben. "You thought to bring backup, huh?"

"I don't need backup. I can take care of you all by myself." Ben's face was contorted in barely controlled rage. He and Jad had been up most of the night looking for Lynn. They had wracked their brains trying to figure out where she could have gone. At first Ben had been almost angry with her that she would run instead of trusting that he would protect her. It was his mother that finally convinced him that it wasn't because she didn't trust him to protect her, but that she was trying to protect him. Ben then felt guilty for doubting Lynn's intentions, but he had become scared like he had never been scared before.

Grace had finally said they needed to wait until the morning light. They reluctantly agreed since the dark was giving them no clues. They got about two hours sleep, then pumped up on coffee and adrenalin went back out to look for Lynn. They had no idea where to look. But coming over the hill toward Canemah Bluff, they saw smoke coming from the trees. Not that it would necessarily mean anything —settlers were cropping up all over, and there was a settlement of Indians there as well. But they had been hunting in that area just a couple of weeks ago and there had been no cabin. There was a rather secluded little draw there that Ben had a hunch about.

Ben's stomach twisted in pain and fury when he came upon the scene just a few yards from where he was hidden behind a big fir tree. He had heard someone talking, and when he got close enough to understand the words, he knew without a doubt that it was Jared. He had abused Lynn during the night. Looking at Lynn, he had never felt such a rage in his heart. Her hair was a tangled, dirty mess all over her head. The right side of her face was bruised and bleeding. Both eyes looked black and blue and her neck had red marks where he had choked her. Her skirt had been up around her knees when he first noticed her laying on her side by the tree. And her shirtwaist was torn, although not as badly as now. He had dreamt for a long time of when they would be married and he would finally see her feminine beauty. But not like this, not now. Blood trickled from her lip and dripped down onto the pale skin. Out of the corner of his eye, he saw her try desperately to cover herself up, but the shirtwaist was in shreds. She finally just held her arms across her breasts as she stood dejectedly against the tree. She had glanced up in shock when he had first appeared. Now she refused to look at him. He guessed her embarrassment and shame.

Ben squared off, "Come on over here, you,..." Ben was not one to use cuss words; their mother had never permitted it, and he had his mouth washed out with soap a couple of times before he had learned his lesson. Now, he didn't care because no other words came close to describing the type of man he saw standing in front of him right now.

"You know that this is a mistake, right? I don't have a squabble with you necessarily. It would be better for you and your brother if you both just turned around and left. This isn't gonna end pretty for you, Ben Alenson." Jared's eyes glinted hungrily as the thought of a good fight flashed before his eyes. The hunger for revenge had made him hungry for blood, whatever form that took.

"Not a chance." Ben didn't feel like talking right now. He was ready to take back what had become his. To take back the reason for his happiness, his future.

"Okay, well don't say I didn't warn you." Jared took two long strides toward Ben, squaring off just before landing a blow to the bigger man's ribs. Ben grunted in surprise at the quickness of the attack but didn't waver.

Jared was a little surprised; obviously, he was gonna have to hit harder. Ben Alenson was going to be a little tougher than he had at first thought.

"NO!! Ben just go. Leave me alone. You don't need to do this! I am ruined, Ben. You don't need to do this!" Lynn finally moved. She jerked herself away from the tree when Jared lunged at Ben. Her scream split through the forest with piercing pain as she tried to run toward the two men.

She didn't see Jad coming up behind her and she screamed again as strong arms grabbed her from behind. He jerked off his jacket and swung it around her shoulders as he spoke.

"It's just me Lynn. It's okay. I'm not going to hurt you. Here, put this on." Her breath came in heavy gasps as she fought to calm herself when she realized who it was. She gladly shoved her arms into the sleeves of Jad's jacket and buttoned it up, sobbing quietly as the tears spilled down her cheeks.

Jad turned away to allow her to secure the jacket, but not before seeing more of her than he should have. The sight of soft flesh with blood and bruises on them made his own blood boil. He turned toward the sound of the battle waging in the trees just a few yards from him. Jared was quick on his feet...a veritable panther with light steps as he weaved back and forth to again deliver another blow to his opponent. Jad watched intently, knowing that to step in would earn him nothing at this point. Ben was fighting for the woman he loved against an evilness that was akin to nothing he had ever seen before. Jared's face was twisted with such a raw hunger for blood that he looked like a demon straight from hell itself. Jad suddenly believed in the Devil like he never had before. His keen eyes watched as Ben took blow after blow while throwing plenty himself. He thought he saw a couple of looks of surprise go across Jared's face as Ben threw back almost as many punches as he received.

Jared's eyes narrowed as he jerked his head to the right, narrowly being missed by a right hook. Surprisingly, he didn't miss the left jab that got him in the jaw. The big man was lighter on his feet than he thought. Jared rubbed his jaw as he contemplated the other man for a moment.

Jared stepped back from another swing, but then stepped forward to deliver one, then two, to Ben's ribs again. Ben stumbled sideways. Jared followed, trying to land a couple in his face, but Ben caught his balance and retreated back a few steps.

Both men knew that someone was going to die in this battle; they weighed each other carefully with assessing looks and calculations. Trying to find the other's weaknesses, they parried against each other with the cautious hunger of starving wolves eyeing a bull elk.

As Jad watched the ongoing battle, he realized they were slowly moving towards the bluff that overlooked the falls far below. He didn't know if Ben was fully aware of this fact or not, but certainly hoped so. If one of them fell from there, it would mean certain death.

Ben could hear the faint roar of the falls behind him and moved slowly but steadily in that direction. It was a dangerous direction to go, but it was a chance he was willing to take.

Jared and Ben danced around each other as they took turns throwing hooks and punches. Sometimes they connected, sometimes they didn't. Their faces were swelling, bruising showing purple already from the battering they were each taking. Lesser men would have fallen already.

Jared, much to his dislike, was being forced to acknowledge a worthy opponent. And Ben, although not wanting to admit it, was beginning to feel the effects of the more experienced and proficient fighter. Jared delivered two blows to Ben's one now. Although Ben had more force in his because of the power he used behind each blow, his body was not used to being pounded like this.

Both men were breathing hard. Sweat was dripping off of their foreheads and into their eyes. Twice Jared had to wipe his eyes quickly as the moisture blurred his vision. Ben was used to manual labor and so used to the sweat that ran down his body. He simply ignored it. But he couldn't ignore much longer the ribs that were becoming more and more painful with each landing of Jared's fists. Or the blood dripping off his cheeks from cuts on his face and mouth. Or the left eye that was swelling.

Lynn and Jad followed them as they weaved their way through the underbrush and around fallen trees. Both had been dropped to their knees a couple of times and yet both struggled back to their feet. Jad's fists clenched every time he saw his brother take a fierce blow. And yet, Ben had made his little brother promise to let him take care of Jared. Jad understood because had it been the other way around, he would have wanted the same; he would want the victory over the man who abused his woman. Jad would take care of Lynn. He would also make sure that Jared kept his fighting fair, no guns or sticks or anything else that would tip the scales unfairly.

Jared finally had enough. His body was starting to feel the punishment of Ben's blows. He needed to finish the big man off because he knew he would still have his brother to contend with. He lunged at Ben with fists flying, landing four, five blows into his ribs. With the last blow, he turned slightly and bent low. After he pulled the knife from its hidden sheath from his left boot, he plunged it into Ben's right shoulder.

Ben went down on one knee as Jared's fists pummeled his ribs mercilessly. That drop probably saved his life, because going down on one knee kept Jared's knife from going into his heart or lung. But the pain from the blade was immense as it went deep into already bruised flesh. Ben howled with pain and anger.

Ben lunged forward, and with his left hand grabbed Jared's ankle, jerking his foot out from under him. Jared fell back with a force that knocked the wind out of him for a few seconds.

As he writhed to one side struggling to sit up, he looked up, surprise on his face. Ben pulled the knife out of his shoulder as he grimaced in pain. Blood dripped down his chest and dropped onto the ground at Jared's feet. When he sat up, Ben stepped back to allow enough room for Jared to gain his footing once more. Jared's eyes narrowed slightly; he would not have done the same for the other man. He would have finished the job.

As Jared struggled to his feet, Ben glanced toward Lynn and Jad just a few feet to the left of him. Ben could see the impatience in Jad's stance as he did what Ben had asked him to, but not necessarily liking it. Lynn stood away from Jad, crying softly. Ben tried to make eye contact with her, but she refused. She instead looked at the ground at her feet. The helplessness he felt at her pain and shame gave him an anger so intense that he felt an energy that made him powerful. Jared was fighting with anger and hatred. Although those could be powerful forces, Ben was fighting with and for love. And love would always be the more powerful. Love is what will always come off victorious. It is love that can conquer all.

After throwing the knife over towards Jad, his attention returned to Jared, who finally stood in front of him. He tried vainly to recall if he had ever seen so much hatred on a man's face. He couldn't. There was something bad in this man's blood, something beyond Ben's understanding. How could anyone have this much evil in their soul? How could he love inflicting pain on someone else so much? He didn't understand that kind of evil and didn't want to. He just knew that one of them was going to die today. If by chance it were him, he needed Lynn to know one thing beyond a shadow of a doubt. He held Jared's stare even though his words were for Lynn.

"Lynn? Sweetheart? I need you to know something. I love you. Even after this. And if I survive this, which I have every intention of doing, I'm still going to marry you. You are not ruined in my eyes, sweetheart. What happened was not your fault. I love you. I will always love you. You remember that okay?"

Jared snorted derisively, "You are a sorry man, Ben Alenson! You don't mind something used, huh?! And believe me, I've used her well!" He laughed mirthlessly. Shaking his head, he pointed at Ben, "You are a pitiful excuse for a man. You could have that little piece of fluff in town, what's her name? Carrie something-or-other. But you want this piece of trash instead?" Shaking his head still, he suddenly lunged at Ben, wrapping his arms around the bigger man's waist and taking him by surprise as they went down together on the ground. Jared instantly rolled over onto his knees and punched Ben in the ribs and face four or five times in rapid succession.

Ben crossed his arms in front of his face to ward off the blows, but then Jared directed them to his chest again. He grunted in pain as ribs cracked and his face felt like pudding beneath Jared's knuckles. He rolled up toward Jared, drawing his legs up as he did so. He flung his left arm up and against Jared's arm while swinging his legs against the other man's side. The upward combined force of Ben's remaining strength threw Jared sideways and he rolled down the incline towards the edge of the cliff above the falls.

Jared stopped his fall by grabbing a root. His grip wasn't a good one though, and he struggled to grab hold of something else with his other hand. Ben rolled to one side and shakily got to his feet, standing above him.

Lynn and Jad watched in shock as Ben extended a hand to grab the other man. Jared refused to take the hand offered.

"You can rot in hell, Ben Alenson! I want nothing from you! You are a fool to think she is anything but a little tart, and not a very good one at that. But, I'm going to rot in hell with you before I'm gonna let you have her!" With a final heave of his body, he jerked up and grabbed Ben's ankle, pulling him off balance.

Jad had come quietly up behind Ben unnoticed and at that instant grabbed Ben by the arm. The effort of trying to take Ben with him down the side of the cliff made Jared lose his grip on the root. He fell backward, opening his mouth in a soundless scream as he plunged onto the rocks and then rolled into the water of the falls below.

Ben fell backward, thankfully because of Jad's quick thinking. He lay panting for a moment, trying hard to catch his breath and comprehending the full impact of what has just transpired. Jared was dead. Ben had never been involved in the death of a man and didn't particularly like the feel of it. He laid there with his eyes closed, feeling every painful throbbing heartbeat through his ribs and face. His shoulder ached with a tenacious fire from the knife wound. He knew he needed to get it cleaned soon before it got infected. As he laid there for a moment longer half leaning against his brother who had just saved his life, one more thought came into his head. Lynn was now free!

Lynn had watched the last half hour of rage and fighting with a helplessness that made her feel so weak that it threatened to drop her to the ground. The words of Ben of just moments ago at once gave her hope and yet gave her sadness. Jared's abuse made her close her eyes in grief. Didn't someone like Ben deserve someone better? He was a good man, a very good man. He deserved someone virginal, someone innocent. Ben had made her feel a sense of purity and cleanness, someone cherished and loved. And yet now, how could she even contemplate giving herself to someone who deserved so much better, so much more? She wept into her hands, her heart twisting and shredding itself into a knotted mass of pain. She turned around away from the two brothers who just saved her life. She needed to disappear from their lives.

As she tried to hurry towards the campfire, intending to grab Jared's saddlebag that lay on the ground, she felt strong hands stop her. She knew it was Ben without looking up. She couldn't look up into that handsome face that was now bruised and bleeding and swollen because of her. Her fingers clenched at her side as she fought the desire to gently touch his face and press against him with relief for herself and mostly for him, that he survived Jared's brutal punishment. Yet how could she look him in the face? She kept her eyes at her feet, refusing to reach out to him, refusing to hope. Hanging her head, she just stood quietly as he gently turned her around to face him.

"Lynn? Please look at me. Please, sweetheart." When she still wouldn't meet his eyes, he would have taken her chin in his hand, but Jad caught his eye and shook his head at his older brother, silently stating the obvious.

"We need to get home, Ben. You have wounds that are gonna need attention and quickly, which means after we get back to the house I'll have to go fetch the Doc. Lynn also needs some attention, especially from Mama. We've got a twenty-minute walk back to the house, so you start that direction and I'll grab Jared's things over here by the fire and see if I can find his horse."

Ben nodded in agreement and turned Lynn gently towards the direction of home to start walking. A few minutes later, Jad rode up with Jared's horse.

"Here brother. I'll help Lynn up, and you mount up behind her. I'll walk, it won't take me long. I'm not beat up and bleeding like you are." He laced his fingers and stooped over to give Lynn a boost up and then stepped back. When Ben gasped in pain and struggled to pull himself up behind her, Jad stepped forward and did the same for him.

"I'll be right behind you. Now go!" He watched Ben grimace as he grasped the horn with one hand and turned the horse towards home, kicking him into a slow canter. Jad broke into a run so he wouldn't be very far behind the two of them. Grace and the family would be horrified when they saw the two of them. He knew Lynn wasn't in any shape to offer explanations. Ben was weak and in pain from the beating he had received. He would need to get there as soon as possible to explain everything to the family. What worried him most was the knife wound in Ben's shoulder. It could cost him his life. Worry was also for Lynn since she refused to look at either of them. Jad was concerned that she was blaming herself, feeling embarrassment and shame.

Chapter 38

"Guilt of the innocent"

Allen was the first one to see them ride up and ran toward them as he yelled at the house. Ben was leaning heavily into Lynn who had both hands on the pommel, struggling to support his weight. Allen could see the disarray, the blood, the dirt, and the bruising on both of them.

Grace, Shaline, and Cathleen came running out of the house onto the porch. Grace and Shaline stopped at the top of the steps, their hands covering their mouths with shocked disbelief, and tears coming immediately to their eyes. Grace recovered first and started barking orders.

"Cathleen, run and get me some towels and sheets. Shaline, get some water on right away and from the looks of things better get out the whiskey. If I'm guessing correctly from the looks of the blood on Ben's shoulder, I'm guessing he's gonna be needing the Doc." She whirled around to go help her daughter draw more water when suddenly she swung back around.

"Allen!? Do you see Jad? Where is he?" Her anxious eyes searched through the trees in the direction from where they had ridden.

Allen had reached the two of them by that time. He grabbed the bridle, looking up at the two riders. "Lynn, Ben, where is Jad? Is he alright?" His voice urgent, worried.

"He's fine. He's coming." Lynn whispered the words as she continued to focus on the pommel. How could she look this family in the eye after what had happened to one of their own. This was all her fault.

Ben groaned heavily as Allen practically caught him from the saddle when he tried dismounting. Lynn slid down after him.

Grace, now relieved that Jad was fine, changed her mind about what to do first and hurried down the steps to help Lynn up. "Come, child. Oh, my stars! You poor thing, come let us help you into the house and get you cleaned up."

Lynn stepped back to avoid Grace's hands, tripping over the corner of the step in the process. Allen caught her with one hand as he held Ben with his other arm to help him up to the door.

In that instant, Grace knew something was terribly wrong. Something had happened to Lynn. When her gaze remained toward the ground, continuing to look away from Grace, she guessed what Jared must have done to her. There was no question that this was all Jared's doing. But she was beginning to get an idea of the punishment he had meted out to his wife in revenge. Her heart went out to the young woman who had been through so much pain at the hands of such a terrible man.

At that moment, Jad came out of the trees and yelled towards the house. "Allen!"

Allen turned slightly at the door to acknowledge he heard his name.

Jad was out of breath by the time he reached the house because he had run the last seventy-five yards or so as he panted the words out, "As soon as you get him inside can you go for the doc and then the sheriff? I saw everything, so I'll stay and help Mama and Shaline." He paused for a moment to finish catching his breath before grabbing Lynn by the waist and half carrying her up the steps and into the kitchen. He had seen her reaction to Grace and could tell by her stance that unless she was forced, she wouldn't enter their house on her own. After sitting her in a chair by the fire, he turned to his brother where Allen had sat him at the table. He then turned to his mother.

"They're both gonna need hot baths to soak bruises and wounds." He looked at Shaline and Cathleen as they entered the kitchen at that moment. Their eyes widened at the cuts still oozing blood on Ben and the dried blood on Lynn's face. Jad's coat still covered the worst of everything else and Jad was thankful for that. Cathleen started crying into Shaline's skirt.

"What happened to Uncle Ben, Mama? He doesn't look very good. His face is big and has blood all over it! Mama? Is he gonna be okay? And what 'bout Lynn? Why is she bleeding too? And why does she have Uncle Jad's coat on?" Shaline knelt beside her daughter, reassuring her that they would both be okay but that she and Gramma and Uncle Jad needed some help.

"Can you go get some Epsom salts for their baths, sweetheart?

And grab the salve that's on my shelf in the bedroom, too, okay?" Cathleen sobbed for another moment and then ran to do her mother's bidding.

By the time she came back, Grace and Shaline had put up a blanket to divide the kitchen in half. They wanted the warmth of the stove to warm both Ben and Lynn, but they also needed privacy to be able to work on them at the same time.

After Jad came back with the washtubs, he pumped more water from the cistern that was inside the pantry. He stoked up the fire to heat water quickly while his mother and sister went to work. Shaline tried to strip the bloodied shirt off her brother but finally had to have help.

"Jad! I need you, please. Ben is too heavy for me to get this off of him by myself. He's so weak, he can't help me." Between the two of them, within a matter of minutes, they had Ben out of all his clothes except his long underwear. Shaline gasped at the multiple bruises that covered her brother's big, muscular frame. Because she started to cry quietly, Grace came around the corner of the blanket to see what had upset her daughter so. She, too, inhaled quickly at the sight of her oldest son.

Jad frowned darkly. He wished he could have spared his sister and mother from having to see this. But it couldn't be helped; he couldn't very well take care of Lynn. She needed a woman's touch. He knew that there was no way, short of locking them outside, that he would have been able to keep either woman from helping him right now in Ben's care, especially. He was at least thankful that they hadn't seen how it had transpired.

"Mama and Shaline,... you need to go. Let Jad......take....care of this....." Ben tried to stay upright in the chair, but he was out of breath. Saying just those few words made his swollen, lower lip start to bleed again, and he leaned over onto the table from the effort.

"We're not about to go anywhere, son. Now hush so we can do what we can before Dr. McCormick gets here."

As Ben slumped heavily onto the table in front of him, Jad started cleaning the deep cut in his shoulder. Ben moaned slightly as Jad applied pressure to it to get it to bleed more, thus helping clean it out of dirt. Then pouring just a little at a time, he poured whiskey over it, which made Ben clench his teeth, willing himself to not make a sound and thus upset the women any more than they already were.

"I know, brother, I'm sorry, but until the Doc gets here this is the best I can do to hopefully clean this up."

"Yeah, yeah," Ben muttered through his teeth. When Jad stopped for a moment to closely examine the knife wound more he asked, "Where is Lynn? How is she?"

"Right now, she's sitting on the other side of this blanket in the rocker, trying to get warm. I'm trying to get her cleaned up as well." Grace came back around the corner of the blanket as she heard the conversation between the two brothers. She felt Ben's forehead. "You need to pour more whiskey on that, Jad, we don't him getting a fever." She almost cried herself as she thought of the pain he was feeling right now. He moaned slightly at the pressure of Jad's cleaning and then at the fire the whiskey caused as it bit into the torn flesh.

Grace returned to Lynn who had been listening to the exchange. As Grace started to unbutton Jad's coat Lynn finally looked up at her.

"It's my fault that your son almost got himself killed, you know. I begged him to stop, to just leave. I didn't want him to fight Jared. I'm not worth it, you know. He ruined me. Ben deserves better. He's a good man. He deserves so much better." Her words were barely a whisper and Grace leaned forward to hear them. Lynn lowered her face into her hands as deep racking sobs took over and she wept the bitter tears of shame and loss and regret.

Grace held her close to her for several minutes before saying anything. Then finally, she knelt in front of her. Taking Lynn's hands in her own she quietly answered back.

"First of all, you're not ruined. Whatever Jared did wasn't your fault. The blame lays squarely on him. Second, I know my children very well, Lynn. Ben will love you no matter what happened, no matter what Jared did to you, no matter what you think he deserves. Ben isn't going to stop loving you until the day he dies. And I think I know you, too. I think you aren't going to stop loving him until the day you die. So, when two people love each other that much, don't you think they should be together?"

With swimming eyes, Lynn looked at the gentle woman in front of her.

"After he's had time to think about it, you'll see I'm right. He's such a good man, he deserves a woman who can give him purity and innocence. I can't give him that." Her chin trembled.

"After he's had time to think about it, you'll see that I am the one who is right. Let's not talk about it anymore right now, child. Let's see if this water is hot enough for a bath so you can soak those bruises." Grace dried the corners of her own eyes upon seeing the deep pain and sorrow in Lynn's voice and face. She knew her son, knew that he loved this woman as he would never love again. But she also understood how Lynn felt; if it had been her, she would probably have felt the same way.

On the other side of the blanket, Jad and Shaline exchanged glances. She cringed inside at what Jared must have put Lynn through. When she had turned a questioning gaze at Jad, he just frowned deeply, muttering something about some men are worse than any animal and that Jared deserved the type of death he got, maybe worse. That confirmed one important question—Jared was dead. She was glad he was so that Ben could stop worrying about Lynn and Lynn could stop looking over her shoulder all the time. Every time a new wagon train came into town, she was jumpy and nervous for a week afterward. So now that Jared was dead that worry was gone. But before he went, he caused an enormous amount of pain and suffering. She hoped that Lynn and Ben could work through this and be as happy as she knew they both deserved.

Ben also heard part of the exchange between Lynn and his mother. He made a move as if to try to get up from the chair.

"Where do you think you're going? Sit your butt right back down in that chair!" Jad's voice was stubborn, demanding instant obedience from his older brother. Ben sank back down onto the hard kitchen chair, but not without protest, even though the words were in between heavy gasps.

"I need to be able to talk to Lynn,... it's important that she understands,..." he paused as he tried drawing a deep breath. "I am not going to quit loving,... her just because,... of what Jared did."

It was Shaline's turn to reason with her brother. She was much more gentle in her approach.

"Ben, you can barely breathe right now let alone carry on a conversation. Besides, Mama is getting her undressed and helping her with a bath so you can't go talk with her anyway. There will be plenty of time to talk later." She laid a gentle hand on his shoulder and he acquiesced without any more protest to his brother and sister's reasoning.

He had more pain than he would have admitted to. It had taken every ounce of strength he had left to start walking towards the house when Jad had gone to look for Jared's horse. Then to stay on that horse was possible only because of Lynn, making him feel guilty that he leaned against her so heavily when she was struggling herself.

Now, he felt weak with relief from two things. One, that the issue with Jared was finally finished. And two, that he had made it home with Lynn without collapsing. His big frame had never taken such a pounding. Now, however, he worried about Lynn and the reasoning coming from her lips. The pieces of conversation his ears were picking up from behind the blanket didn't sound good at all, and now he was scared of what Lynn may do. He also knew that he needed to concentrate on his own body being taken care of. If he was sick or died, then all was lost anyway.

Grace finished helping Lynn out of her clothes and into the tub of hot water that waited for her. As she lathered up her hair and began gently pulling the twigs and leaves out of it, she thought again about how this poor girl had been through hell and back more than once.

The scars she could now fully see on Lynn's back added force to the cruelty of one man. Now add to it watching Lynn slowly trying to wash off the blood that had trickled from various cuts and bruises, made Grace's chest feel heavy with pity. She couldn't help but see the dark bruises scattered across Lynn's body. Her wrists were red welts from the rope that had held her hands fast.

When Lynn bent forward to cry softly into the rag she was using, Grace could take no more; she cried with her, holding Lynn's shoulders against her chest as the two women wept together for all the pain and misery that had been heaped upon the younger one.

The blanket may have blocked vision, but it did little for blocking any sounds. After Shaline and Jad exchanged looks again, she peered around one side to find Lynn with head down and sobbing into the rag in her grasp, and her mother with her arm around Lynn's shoulders, her chin on Lynn's head crying with her.

"I'll return in a moment, Jad. I think Mama needs my help in there for a moment." She whispered to her brother who agreed with a brief nod.

Allen chose that moment to come rushing in the door.

"The doc is on his way. I also alerted the sheriff so he is on his way." He gave a quick perusal of the situation in the kitchen, and after giving his wife a quick hug, sent her behind the blanket as he reached for the warm rag that she handed him. He took her place beside Jad.

Within about ten minutes Dr. McCormick showed up. He was a tall, thinly built, but wiry man of maybe fifty-five years. He had a quiet, domineering efficiency with dark piercing eyes that brooked no argument. You stepped out of his path when he showed up or he would throw you out of his path. He had a quick but steady hand that spoke of years of experience. Now, Jad and Allen quickly stepped out of the older man's way as he looked first at Ben's facial bruises and cuts, his ribs, and stomach, and then finally examined the deep cut to the shoulder. Ben winced painfully at the poking and prodding.

"Well, I'd say you've done a pretty good job so far at getting this cleaned out. Now let's see what a little more will accomplish. Allen, give Ben a couple of swigs of that whiskey. He's gonna need it." He turned to pull some tools out of his bag.

"Here Jad, run this through the fire to heat this up a little would ya?" Handing Jad a scalpel, he turned back to his bag again, pulling out some laudanum this time. He handed it to Allen, giving him directions for administering it to Ben, who was already shaking his head in protest.

"I don't want any of that Doc. Just give me some more of that whiskey and I'll be fine." He reached for the bottle to take another swallow of the strong amber liquid.

Dr. McCormick frowned heavily as he contemplated the big man sitting before him. He glanced at Jad with a questioning look on his face, who shrugged and raised his eyebrows, then at Grace who just appeared from the other side of the blanket.

"I doubt he'll need that, Edward, but keep it handy just in case." She had wiped her eyes just before coming around but they were still red and now slightly swollen. Edward frowned again at the usually lovely face of the petite woman standing in front of him. He had been in love with the widowed Grace Alenson from the moment he had laid eyes on her two years ago. He had just never had the courage to act upon those feelings. Grace was a fireball even at her age, and she had never given any sign to him that she would welcome his advances. Everyone knew that she had loved her husband very much. One day, maybe he would finally ask. For now, there were more urgent matters at hand.

"Okay. You know your son. But, I can't have him thrashing about while I work. There is some more debris in this cut that is going to have to be dug out. That's not gonna be fun." He turned his attention to Ben, "You hearin' me, Ben? I'm sorry, but this is gonna be necessary. If you can't be still then you're gonna have to take some of that whether or not you like the idea."

Ben looked up at him nodding his head, "I understand, but I'm not going to want it. Do what you have to do, Doc. Just keep that whiskey bottle handy."

"Okay then. Let's get started." After bending over once more to work on Ben's shoulder, he suddenly straightened, "Allen, didn't you say there were two people injured? I take it that the other person is behind this blanket. Do I need to see them first?" As he reached out for the edge of the blanket, Grace stopped him.

"It's Lynn, Edward. She has multiple bruises and cuts as well, but they are minor in nature. Shaline and I are taking care of her. Please concentrate on Ben." After giving him a warm smile, she turned to her son.

"I know you've been worrying about Lynn, son. So that you can focus on your own injuries right now, I want to let you know that Lynn is soaking in her bath, letting the hot water ease her bruising." She bent down to look her oldest son in the eyes. "It's going to take time, son. It's going to take time."

Ben nodded his head with understanding at the gentleness in his mother's voice. She read the concern, the questions in his eyes, knowing Lynn was once again going through hell. She knew he felt guilty for not finding her soon enough to prevent it, to begin with. He shouldn't feel that way, but he had always taken more onto himself than he probably should. Before straightening to return to Lynn, she kissed his forehead and patted his good shoulder.

Chapter 39

"Love conquers all"

The next hour was not a pleasant one for anyone. Dr. McCormick tried to be as gentle and easy as possible, but it was impossible to not cause discomfort and a couple of times, outright pain. Ben had clenched his jaw so much so as not to make any sound that his jaws now hurt from more than Jared's fists. He felt slightly dizzy from the amount of whiskey he had consumed. By the time the Doc was finished, Ben had thirteen stitches. Nine in his shoulder and four more from a deep cut on his left cheek.

When he was finally able to sink down into the washtub full of hot water, he heaved a sigh of relief. He let his head fall back onto the side of the tub, letting the hot water soak into all the areas that throbbed from pain.

Lynn was sitting in front of the fire, dressed once again with her hair brushed out and sipping a small glass of whiskey herself. She had never been particularly fond of the taste so had to be convinced that it would make her feel better before she decided to try some. She still wouldn't hold anyone's gaze for more than maybe a couple of seconds before looking away. Grace and Shaline worried about her, but for now, there was little they could do other than give her a hug and tell her that they loved her. It was going to take Ben and a lot of convincing on his part to heal the deep pain in her heart.

The house was quiet for a few minutes as Shaline took the baby and Cathleen into the bedroom for a nap. Grace, Allen, and Jad followed Dr. McCormick out onto the porch to talk with him. He had also looked over Lynn's injuries after he was finished with Ben. But he had agreed with Grace; he couldn't do any more than what they had already done. Grace walked him to his horse.

"Thank you, Edward, for getting here so quickly. We all appreciate it very much." She laid a hand on his forearm, "When you come out to check on Ben's stitches in a couple of days, please plan on staying for dinner." Her warm smile reached her eyes as she looked up at the tall man in front of her.

Edward caught himself staring down into her eyes for just a moment before answering. "Of course, Grace. Any time you need me, please send someone. I'll be here quickly." He paused for a moment, glancing at the hand on his arm." I would love to come for dinner. Thank you." After a quick smile, he mounted and tipping his hat, turned towards town.

Ben noticed the quiet solitude of the house as soon as the front porch door shut. Jad had helped him out of the tub and he slowly got his pants on. He had to just sit for a few minutes from the effort. The hot water had helped for sure, but his body ached from the top of his head to his feet. As he leaned forward in the chair, he looked up and grabbed at the blanket still hanging as he did so. Finally, getting a good grasp of it, he pulled it aside. He had been thinking about Lynn almost the entire last hour and now wondered if she was still sitting in front of the fire. When he saw her, his heart went out to her. Her hands were clasping the glass of whiskey in her lap. She stared into the fire as if in an entirely different world.

She was unaware of him watching her until he quietly said her name. Startled, she turned her head towards the kitchen and his voice. Ben's heart almost stopped at the depth of emotional pain and sadness he saw in her eyes. Her face bore no expression as she just stared at him for a moment before finally speaking with a voice so quiet that he had to strain to hear her words.

"Ben, I will be leaving soon. I hear that California is a good place to start over. I think maybe that is the direction I will go. Don't worry Ben, you will find love with someone else someday, I promise. Someone pure and clean." Tears crept slowly down both cheeks as she stared at him for another moment before turning to watch the fire once more.

"No, no. Sweetheart, that's not what you're going to do." Ben lost his grip on the blanket and he cursed briefly as he worked at getting his hands on it again. When he finally did, he gave it one strong jerk and it fell to the floor. At this moment, he didn't care that his chest, back, and ribs had spasms of pain that rippled across them. He didn't care about anything at all except making Lynn understand that for him nothing had changed between them. She was free to marry now and he would give her time to heal physically. As for emotionally, mentally? He would help her through it all. He would be there for her every step of the way. He felt a desperation like he had never experienced before. Look what she had already gone through and for over two years! She could again, and this time she would have the help and support of not only himself, but his family as well. She had become his life, she was in his blood, his heart, the very depths of his soul! He couldn't lose her now, not after everything they had been through.

He looked around toward the door wishing Jad or Allen would come back in. Muttering something about never having what you need when you need it, he turned his attention back to the woman crying quietly in front of the fire.

"What happened to you, sweetheart, wasn't your fault. It doesn't ruin you in any way. You are the love of my life and I want to live it with you. No other woman, Lynn. No other woman, ever, sweetheart." Keeping his voice low and soft, he continued to use words of endearment. She wouldn't look at him again, she just stared into the fire with the tears continuing to run down her cheeks.

Suddenly, he decided that although getting out of his chair was going to be a painful achievement, he'd had enough. He needed to be able to talk with Lynn face to face. He needed to be able to hold her, to convince her that he loved her and nothing was going to change that, ever! He was struggling to stand up when Jad came through the door.

Quickly taking in the scene and his brother attempting to get out of the chair, Jad strode over to him. He put his arms under Ben's, giving him the support he needed to get to his feet.

"You really think now is a good time for you to talk with her, brother? Somehow, I don't think that's a good idea. I think she just may need space for a while." He spoke the words into Ben's ear as he swung the blanket around his shoulders. Ben didn't need to get chilled.

Scowling heavily at Jad, Ben muttered irritably, "All she's doing is staring into the fire. I need to be able to talk with her, to hold her." He earnest gaze asking his brother for help. "She's scaring me right now, Jad. I need to be close to her."

Jad met Ben's gaze with a nod of understanding, then glanced at Lynn. He stepped aside to let Ben limp painfully over to Lynn's side. He squatted, with difficulty, in front of her. Grasping the blanket with one hand to keep it wrapped around him he touched her knee with his other hand. Ben watched as the glaze left her eyes and she focused in on the man in front of her.

"I'm so sorry, Ben." Her hand came up to barely touch the stitches in the shoulder that wasn't covered completely with the blanket. She searched his face, then followed her search with her fingers, gently touching the stitches on his cheek, then the swollen, black eyes and the many bruises on his face. The tears came more quickly. Shaking her head slowly, she sobbed out loud.

"I'm so sorry, Ben. I've caused you so much pain. Look at you! This is all my fault. It's my fault." Her hand dropped back into her lap as she continued to stare at the discoloring on his face.

He caressed her cheek with his free hand. "Sweetheart, this is not your fault. It's mine."

She interrupted. "No! How could you say that?"

"It's mine for not protecting you at the dance. I should have known that you would run, that you would try to protect me and my family. I should have seen that coming and made sure that you didn't. I should have protected you better."

She shook her head, grimacing with memories. The words were muted, strained.

"I could never forgive myself if anything happened to you or your family. These last few weeks I have found what I have always wanted since my mother died. You have given me so much I couldn't let anything happen to any of you."

Her hands grasped the blanket that wrapped around his shoulders. She finally looked into the eyes of this wonderful man who had sacrificed so much for her and had put his life on the line for hers. The eyes that looked back at her, although swollen and turning colors from the beating he had received, were full of love like she had never seen—except once. It was the same love her father had felt for her mother. That deeply rich, enduring love that come what may will never die, never fade, and never be repeated.

Lynn threw her arms around his neck as she slid out of the chair and onto her knees in front of him. Ben almost groaned from the pain as her hands and arms touched bruises and abrasions. Despite what it cost him, he released the blanket and wrapped his arms around her, drawing her close against him as he drew in deep shaky breaths. He hadn't lost her; she was his. At this moment he knew he had convinced her that it didn't matter what had happened to her, his love for her was deep and consuming. He had won!

Chapter 40

"A trust won"

November 30, 1844

They had tried to keep the wedding small. The family and a few friends of the family and, of course, from the wagon train. But, the Alenson family was well-liked, and it seemed to Lynn that the whole town must have shown up. Well, almost the whole town. There was the exception of Carrie and her parents. There was an enormous amount of food. Music was played and Ben swept her into dance after dance while holding her close beside him with a tenderness and love that brought tears to her eyes.

In the last handful of days in preparation for the wedding, Lynn had realized she still trusted him with her heart and the rest of her. Ben was never been too forward in his affections, but he had dropped kisses on her lips at every possible opportunity with a gentleness and self-control that continued to surprise her. There was a warmth that pooled within her, melting away the fears and worries.

When they left the small reception at the big house to finally leave for their own quickly built little house, Ben pulled her close beside him for the short walk. There was no conversation. They were both thinking of what was coming next. One thought with a great deal of anticipation, the other with a great deal of nervousness. When they reached the door, Ben stopped to look down at his beautiful bride. Her cheeks flushed with a shy and somewhat apprehensive smile. When he moved to pick her up, she protested slightly but then clung to him, burying her face in his shoulder.

Ben carried her over the threshold, smiling to himself as he opened the door and found that Jad had done exactly as he had promised. The fire was going in the fireplace and two glasses with blackberry wine were sitting on the table near the rocking chair. The two washtubs were sitting side by side in front of the fireplace also. He had borrowed his mother's as an extra just for tonight. He thought sitting together in front of the fire sounded like something Lynn would enjoy at some point this evening. Now actually seeing everything in place, he was glad he had thought of it. The room looked inviting and cozy.

He set her in the chair and then lit two candles. Ben stood in the middle of the room and looked at his wife sitting in front of the fire with her hands nervously playing with the gloves in her lap. She sat on the edge of the chair, unable to sit back and relax. She couldn't be considered a small woman because of her height and in the last few weeks, she had regained womanly curves after the harshness of being on the trail for so long. But at the moment she reminded him of a small, frightened child waiting to be disciplined, and his heart went out to her.

He slowly removed his jacket and then went over to kneel in front of her, gently pulling her heavy shawl from around her shoulders. Her eyes darted to his face, down to her lap, and then back again to his face.

"You know, Lynn, that I won't hurt you?" Did she still think that he was going to hurt her? Didn't she know by now that his love for her would enable him to keep his own desires in check? That he would never hurt her?

Lynn looked up into his face with wide eyes. "Yes, I know you won't. It's a strange feeling I have." She was quiet for a moment, looking down at her hands before turning again to look at him. "You have unburied something I thought I had lost long ago. I want you to make love to me, but,..." Her cheeks brightened with more color. "I'm still a little nervous, afraid." She gave him a sideways glance as she glanced up from her lap.

Ben's heart again went out to her. He sensed rather than saw the tremor that ran the length of her. "I promise not to rush you. Anytime you say stop, I promise, I will stop."

"Really? You would do that for me?" Lynn stared at him.

"Yes, I love you that much. But, I also have enough confidence in myself and in you, that you won't want me to stop."

Lynn looked at Ben's mischievous grin and couldn't help smiling herself. "You aren't a little overconfident, are you?" She watched Ben's gaze lower to her lips and then back to her eyes. Her breath caught in her throat as she saw the love and adoration in his eyes. He dropped his gaze again.

How her cheeks could get any warmer she didn't know. But she could feel heat enveloping her all of the way from her head to her toes as Ben's gaze dropped lower still to travel the length of her. How could he have this effect on her when he hadn't even touched her yet? She was shocked from her reaction.

"You don't need experience to love someone. Some things just come natural and loving you is one of them." Ben looked back up into her eyes and read the warmth in their depths. His smile broadened as he leaned over to kiss the nape of her neck, resting his hands on the arms of her chair.

"Remember, Lynn, whenever you want me to stop,... you tell me and I'll stop". His warm breath lifted the little curls of dark hair at the nape of her neck as he pressed small kisses there and then down her back to her shoulder blades and back up again. His fingers itched to touch her, but not wanting to scare her, he left his hands where they were to brace himself. A couple of minutes later when she seemed to relax a little, he placed the other hand behind her on the back of the chair as he leaned close to kiss her neck and back. He had waited for so long to love this woman.

Lynn closed her eyes as Ben continued his assault on her senses. Her stomach fluttered wildly as his kisses wandered further and further down her back. How could she feel this way when his touch wasn't even on skin yet? When his mouth moved across her shoulder to the smooth skin of her neck, she held her breath in hushed anticipation of what he would do next. Her fingers clenched lightly in her lap when his lips touched the soft skin at the base of her throat. Then he changed direction completely and after taking her left hand, he started doing the same to her wrist. She was surprised at the pleasure so simple an act brought upon her. Her breath quickened as her head fell back. Her right hand came up to touch Ben's bent head as he continued.

When Ben felt Lynn's fingers threading through his hair, he looked up to see if he had alarmed her. Instead, he saw her eyes closed and head thrown back. With her throat so fully exposed, he took advantage of the opportunity to kiss it. But this time, he nibbled gently at the softness leaving warm moisture on her skin. She gasped with surprise as she looked up at him.

Ben stopped briefly to murmur quietly, "Do you want me to stop, sweet?" He looked into eyes that held no fear, no worry. Instead, they glowed with love and smoldered with something he was slowly awakening within her. He already knew the answer she would give him, but still wanted to hear it from her own lips.

Lynn didn't answer with words. She studied him for a moment before leaning over and kissing him shyly on the mouth. That was all Ben needed. Her arms went around his neck of their own volition as his arms held her tightly around the waist. His kiss this time demanded more and she willingly gave it what he asked for.

He murmured against her lips. "You are beautiful, Lynn. I love you like I never thought to love a woman."

Lynn's breath caught in her throat."Do you mean that, Ben?"

"With all my heart." The smile he gave her was gentle. What a fool Jared had been. But, he was glad because now he had this incredible woman for his own. He wouldn't ever be the fool!

"Then, please love me. Since I know you're doing it with all your heart, please love me." Her cheeks flushed as she spoke from shyness and she pressed them into his neck.

He scooped her up from the chair in strong arms and just stood holding her as he bent his head to kiss her. After a moment he let her feet drop gently to the floor but pulled her up tight against him. His hands splayed across her back and shoulders as he breathed in her sweet fragrance. Her fingers kneaded the muscles in his shoulders and he did the same across her back and down her sides. He smiled against her mouth when he heard a small sigh of pleasure.

"I'm glad I didn't drink any of that wine over near the fire. You make me feel drunk without it." He kissed the corners of her eyes, the tip of her nose, and ducked his head to trace another trail of small, warm kisses down her neck and across one shoulder.

Lynn felt like she was suddenly on fire. Ben's gentle and constant touches on her were awakening longings she was unsure of. All she knew was that within his embrace, she would find love and gentleness.

When Ben decided to unbutton his shirt, he looked down at her, studying her face for just a moment. "I want to love you." It was a statement and question at the same time and he waited patiently for her answer.

There was no hesitation, no nervousness, no fear. "Yes." Ben knew that one simple word meant that she trusted him and loved him with her heart and soul. He almost wept with the knowledge that he had finally won every part of this woman. Because as much as he wanted to make love to her, he wanted, no needed, her trust and faith even more. Now it was complete, because she was finally giving every part of herself to him willingly. He pulled her close to him again, molding her softness against his more muscled physique.

Lynn closed her eyes. She had never in her wildest dreams thought that feeling the warm, muscled length of a man against her would be appealing, but suddenly, she couldn't get close enough. As she snuggled even closer to him wild sensations shot through her. She sighed deeply and reached for his mouth with her own, pressing a small kiss to the side with the dimple. She could feel him smile against her lips and then kiss her back with all the love of his heart.

Chapter 41

"Prairie wind"

He lay in his side with both arms wrapped around her, one hand resting in her hip. Her cheek lay against his chest as she nestled against him. Neither of them had ever felt contentment until now. Or peace, or love.

Ben finally stirred as he whispered against her hair, "I love you with every part of me, my beautiful wife." He cupped her chin and tipped her face up so he could look into her eyes.

"Mmmmm, ..." pink tinged her cheeks, but she held his gaze. "I love you too, way more than you will ever know."

One eyebrow lifted as a big smile spread over his handsome face. She touched his dimple with her forefinger, caressing it before reaching up to kiss it.

"Indeed? Well, I'm willing to spend the rest of my life trying to figure out how much that is. For now, how about a hot bath, together over there in front of the fire in those tubs?"

Her eyes followed where he pointed. "Sounds wonderful. Is there enough hot water for both of us over there?"

"Mmhmm. The tubs have been sitting there all day my dear. So, the water is already warm. All I have to do is pour in some of that hot water. Jad filled those kettles with water. They've been by the fire this entire time. They should all be hot by now." He turned over so that he could sit up on the edge of the bed. She moved up behind him as her arms went around him and she pressed her face into his neck giggling quietly. She had never felt such happiness, such giddiness—actually, she didn't know for sure what to call it.

He grinned over his shoulder at her, then stood and turned around. She ducked her head shyly at his appreciative perusal. When he picked her up, she pressed small kisses on the jagged scar on his shoulder, recent memories flooding her. He had fought for her and it brought tears to her eyes. He walked to the tubs and then set her down beside one. After handing her a glass of the wine, he checked the water to see what it needed. Dumping one bucket of hot water in, he watched as she stepped in and sank down into the comforting warmth.

Then picking up his glass of wine, he stepped into his tub and sat down. He smiled over at her with a heat in his eyes that could rival the fire that was roaring in front of them.

As the hot water steamed around her, she sighed and laid her head back against the edge of the tub, closing her eyes as she did so.

"What was the sigh for, sweet?" Lynn opened her eyes to see Ben smiling warmly over at her.

"I was just thinking about prairies and their wind."

He nodded his head. "Ah yes, the prairie and a woman on a hill trying to catch the wind. I think about that scene often. I think it will always be one of my favorite memories of you." He reached over and took her free hand that rested on the side of the tub, and they were both caught in their own thoughts of that day that seemed so long ago, and yet it had only been a few months.

Her heart was so full of contentment and happiness that she thought she would burst from the sheer exhilarating pressure of it. The prairie winds had indeed been good to her.

Epilogue

August 23rd, 1846

Ben looked around the bedroom sleepily as Matthew's cries became louder and more persistent. He didn't see Lynn anywhere, so he threw his legs over the side of the bed, rubbing his eyes as he reached out to rock the cradle. That didn't last long, however, as Matthew decided that rocking wasn't going to do the trick. He was either hungry or wet or both and wanted attention. After looking out of the window at the sun barely peeking over the horizon, Ben reached in and picked up the baby. Kissing the soft dark hair on the small head he rocked the small bundle in his arms for a moment. Matthew quieted for a moment, although still made little mewling sounds as he decided whether this was going to be the answer to his woes or not.

Ben looked down at his tiny son in his large hands and smiled deeply. He had been completed when Lynn had announced to first him and then the family that she was with child. She had waited until she was probably about three months along in case something happened and she lost it. There had been a glow about her for several weeks and his mother had guessed but had kept it to herself until Lynn chose to tell them. His precious wife had been so afraid to say anything, almost not believing it could be true. They had both believed that she was unable to have children. For her, to be with child was the best gift of all.

Matthew James was becoming more insistent that food had better materialize very soon. Ben laid his son down long enough to change his nappy, pull pants on over his nakedness, and then left the bedroom in search of Lynn. After not finding her anywhere in the house he opened the door to look outside.

He had built their house so that when they walked out of the front door they would be situated on a small rise in the land that overlooked a long meadow and a creek on the far side. Lynn loved the view immensely and he had often seen her standing on the small hill looking out over that scene.

As he looked out now he saw her and smiled. The dawn was breaking with a breeze, warm but light, blowing across the land. Lynn stood on the small rise with her head back and arms open wide as if trying to catch the wind like that time on the prairie. It seemed like a lifetime ago and yet it was only about two and a half years ago. So much had happened in that short time.

As he walked toward his lovely wife, the baby stopped crying and he was able to walk up quietly behind her.

"Are you trying to catch the wind again, sweet?" he asked quietly in her ear.

She had half expected him to find her out here so wasn't surprised to hear him beside her. Her eyes still closed, she wrapped her arms around herself before answering.

"No, not the wind, only catching and keeping what it brings to me." Smiling and turning to face him, she opened her eyes to look up at the big man standing beside her.

"Oh? And what did it bring you, sweet?" Ben caressed her cheek with his thumb before leaning over to kiss her lips.

"It brought me the man I love more than anything else in the world and the little man in your arms you and I created together. It doesn't get better than this does it, Ben?" Happiness flashed through her eyes as she coyly rubbed her palms down his chest and just inside the waist of his pants.

Ben flashed a warning smile, "Watch it woman, or the wind may see you catching something else right out here on top of this hill!" Grabbing her hand, he kissed the palm.

Matthew had decided enough was enough and chose that moment to loudly protest that his needs had not yet been met. Lynn took him from Ben and unbuttoning the flannel gown put him to her breast to suckle. He ate greedily as his tiny fist laid against his mother's soft, white flesh.

Ben groaned out loud with mock self-pity. "Why does he get that whenever he wants and I don't? That doesn't seem fair". His eyes twinkled with teasing.

Lynn looked up at him with another coy smile and raised eyebrows, "Well, when he's done I'm sure I can make you happy, too." She was anxious to return to bed with her husband as soon as this little man was finished. "It's been a month now since his birthing, it's time."

"Really, are you sure? I don't want to rush you sweet if it's not good for you to do so. I don't want to wait any longer, but I can if I have to." Heat was already flaring in his dark eyes and his cheek dimpled with the smile it brought.

"I'm sure." Lynn's smile and the love in her eyes said everything that words didn't need to. He bent to kiss the breast that his son was nursing from and then stood on the small rise wrapping his arms around the waist of the wife of his heart. Looking out at the scene below them, he thought how the wind certainly had brought him good things. He was thankful that he had caught them all.

The End
".....and a beginning"

I Love My Readers

If you enjoyed the story of Ben and Lynn, I would love it if you would take a few moments and review it on Amazon. A review doesn't need much, a few words to say you liked this story and perhaps explain why would be wonderful.

Authors love feedback on their books and it makes our day and maybe even our week to know that we wrote something that you enjoyed. Reviews also help Amazon promote the book to other prospective readers. That especially is important to Indie authors (Independent authors) who do not have the backing and support of a traditional publishing house behind them. For some indies it can help determine whether or not they will be able to continue writing stories for readers to enjoy.

Also, if you enjoyed this book, please tell other people about it.

I always keep an eye on my reviews and I deeply appreciate each and every one. So, thank you ahead of time for a review.

Charli

About The Author

Charli West

Charli West lives in the Pacific Northwest with her husband Jeff. Together they have three grown and married children who are their pride and joy. They are often heard to say that their greatest gifts they ever received are their children.

They currently have no animals because of their very busy life and their love of travel. But through the years there have been many dogs, cats, bunnies, goats, sheep, cows, lizards, pigs, and even ducks and chickens. Her greatest animal love however, have been her horses.

This first book has been about 20 years in the making. Other things were more important at the time so this was set aside. But a good friend and even her husband often mentioned her writing and encouraged her to finish what she had started so long ago. Hence, The NW Wind Series has been created. She hopes that you enjoy the stories and the people in her head vying for attention and a release onto the pages therein. Happy reading!

Books In This Series

NW Wind Series

The NW Wind Series encompasses the settling of the Pacific Northwest, especially the Oregon country. The rich resources and free land drew settlers by the thousands but they also died by the thousands along the way. The dangers were many and varied ranging from disease, exhaustion, river crossings, traversing mountains, bad weather, snake bites, inexperience, almost zero medical knowledge, and wild animals.

Against that background Charli West has a rich cast of characters on the quest for a new life, for land, for love, and for a future. They are a group of people who met challenges head on with determination, fortitude, and hope.

The stories within this series overlap and intertwine with characters and dates. However, each book is a standalone and can be read without cliffhangers.

It is Charli's hope that you pick these books up, sit down to relax, and make some great new friends. They surely want to meet you.

Dance Within The Wind

Book Two

A dying old man. A promise given. An unwanted wife.

Sadie has spent her entire life around logging camps, safely hidden in plain sight and finding a small measure of freedom and solace with her horse, Dancer. She always keeps her distance from the rough loggers until Jad Alenson arrives on the scene. He is different, with a quick sense of humor, friendly nature, and takes pride in being a man who keeps his promises. She knows exactly what kind of woman he wants, and unfortunately, she doesn't fit the criteria.

But with two words Jad seals their lives together, starting a series of events that will either help them build a life together or tear them apart. They will both discover who they really are inside where it counts the most and what's most important to them.

Together they head for home and must traverse the wilds of 1846 Washington and Oregon and all the dangers that involves. But the most dangerous thing of all could be not seeing what is right in front of you until you almost lose it.

Music In The Wind

Coming 2021
Book Three

This is Carries's story. For those of you who love Carrie hopefully you love her even more.
For those of you who hate Carrie hopefully you decide she's lovable after all.

Everyone has a story, a background, what makes us who or what we are. In Music In the Wind we find out why Carrie is who she is.

As for the male main character, you met him briefly in both books One and Two. He has a painful past, too. You will love him.

I can't wait to give you Music In the Wind.

You can follow me on Instagram for the updates at Charliwest_author. Come join me on more adventures in the NW Wind.

Wind Poems

I yield forth a mighty roar
As I whip my fingers through the night
A howl into the darkness
Does my freedom give you fright?
My frenzied hands careen and move
'Round whatever I please
I laugh upon your widened eyes
Your heightened senses tease
Call naught to me
For to stop I will refuse
Until I reach my resting place
New energy to infuse
So welcome me or be afraid
Little do I care which one
My pleasured freedom is my own
Because either way I won

How can I describe the wind
As it blows warm across my face
Its gentle caress upon a cheek
Disappearing without a trace
To catch the wind is possible
Naught
A wasted time for thee
As it howls up through the valley
To make trees bend their knee
It sends the fall leaves dancing
In a wild and frenzied way
I want to dance within the wind
I've oft been heard to say
A spoken word soft yet firm
Its roughened arms reach out
To take a whisper in the wind
And twist it all about
Describe its vanishing act
As the icy blasts gain speed
For some they dread its haughty cold
For me the wind is a need
I envy its free and boundless joy
As I see its path beyond
A blazing kiss within the wind
As it whistles its restless song
A cheery note or sad lament
Laughter or trickling tears
Is just music in the wind
As they're cast into the years
So blow, wind, blow
Caress and writhe and whine
As you pass through our lives
And we meet another time

Made in United States
Orlando, FL
31 October 2023

38409116R00159